Novels by Richard Condon

Emperor of America

Prizzi's Glory

Prizzi's Family

A Trembling Upon Rome

Prizzi's Honor

The Entwining

Death of a Politician

Bandicoot

The Abandoned Woman

The Whisper of the Axe

Money Is Love

The Star-Spangled Crunch

Winter Kills

Arigato

The Vertical Smile

Mile High

The Ecstasy Business

Any God Will Do

An Infinity of Mirrors

A Talent for Loving

Some Angry Angel

The Manchurian Candidate

The Oldest Confession

Other Books

And Then We Moved to Rossenarra

The Mexican Stove/Olé Mole (with Wendy Jackson)

EMPEROR
OF AMERICA
RICHARD CONDON

SIMON AND SCHUSTER

New York   London   Toronto   Sydney   Tokyo

SIMON AND SCHUSTER
Simon & Schuster Building
Rockefeller Center
1230 Avenue of the Americas
New York, New York 10020

SIMON AND SCHUSTER and colophon are registered trademarks
of Simon & Schuster Inc.

Designed by Laurie Jewell
Manufactured in the United States of America

1   3   5   7   9   10   8   6   4   2

Library of Congress Cataloging in Publication Data

Condon, Richard.
Emperor of America/Richard Condon.
p.   cm.
I. Title.
PS3553.0487E47 1990   89-27156
813'.54--dc20   CIP

ISBN 0-671-68643-7

*In fond
Memory of
Hal Matson*

"And were you pleased?" they asked Helen in Hell.
"Pleased?" answered she, "when all Troy's towers fell;
And dead were Priam's sons, and lost his throne?
And such a war was fought as none had known;
And even the gods took part; and all because
Of me alone! Pleased?

I should say I was!"

LORD DUNSANY

EMPEROR
OF AMERICA
RICHARD CONDON

1

IN THE LATE SPRING OF 1988, four months before his thirty-eighth birthday, Colonel Caesare Appleton was having a really *marv*elous lunch in the best hotel in Almôdovar, in southern Portugal, with a ravishing Portuguese woman who wore a red bali-buntal hat and seemed to know all sorts of boring facts about American television shows and performers. In the middle of a racy anecdote about Bill Moyers, Chay's beeper went off and he had to excuse himself to go to the telephone at the front desk. It was his Intelligence officer, Kent Black, who should have known better than to interrupt because he had been told how heavy this lunch with this thriller was for Chay.

"Jesus, Colonel, sorry," Black said. "But I just debriefed eleven refugees out of hundreds who are fleeing north and—"

"What are they fleeing?"

"They keep saying that there is a heavy military concentration on the coast just fifty-two miles south of us."

"What?"

"They say troops are being landed all along the Algarve."

"What *troops?*"

"Colonel, this is the first I heard of it. Troops. Tens of thousands of them. These people are saying that the beach is black with them."

"Call Al Melvin at SACEUR. He can call up an air recce. Besides, he's fused to Israeli intelligence; they'll know."

"He's out to lunch."

"Ah—*shit!* I'll be there as soon as I can find my driver. This better be a full-scale invasion of the soft underbelly of Europe, kid, because you've ruined some really soft underbelly for me." He slammed the phone down.

The Second and Third Battalions of the Seventy-fifth Rangers, out of Fort Stewart, Georgia, were conducting routine field maneuvers in the southern cork forest of Portugal under the command of Colonel Appleton. The exercises were to have been conducted by his lieutenant colonel, but at the last minute the son-of-a-bitch had come down with a burst appendix.

It took twelve minutes for Chay to excuse himself from the unbelievably gorgeous Portuguese woman. When he got back to base, Black had already sent two separate scouting parties south.

Chay called Operation Headquarters at SHAPE in Belgium. He was finally able to reach Al Melvin, Chief of Staff to Chesty Bustonbacher, the Commanding General NATO.

"Al, what the hell is this? I have reports from eleven civilians that there's some kind of an invasion going on along the coast about fifty miles south of me." Chay was in his element. He simply could not believe the luck that an accident of field maneuvers might have put him in command of the defense of Europe. For all of his life he had dreamed of a chance like this. He thought of the nine-year-old top sergeant at the North Slope Military Academy in Edgarton, Alaska, his old school drill sergeant, John DeWitt Kullers, the toughest soldier he had ever known, the man who had made Chay Appleton what he had become—a cool, calm, endowed professional soldier—and he wished, for just a flash, that Kullers could have been watching him today.

"*Whaaaaaat?*" Melvin said with complete disbelief.

"Yeah."

"How can that be? We don't have anything on it. Wait a minute." There was a forty-second silence. "A Saudi AWACS reported some kind of unusual activity on the Moroccan coast this morning but Moroccan HQ said it was a routine exercise."

"Very fishy."

"What? What's fishy?"

"We're being screwed."

"What does your own reconnaissance say?"

"They're not back yet," Chay said, "but if it's the way the civilians say it is, whoever it is will be all over this area in force in less than five hours."

"Call me back when you hear something." Melvin hung up.

Chay called in his commanders and improvised an attack because it would be impossible for two battalions to set up a defense against an army unless they got out as fast as the mechanized units could carry them.

"Good afternoon," he said to the assembled officers. "There is a possibility that a large enemy force has landed on the Portuguese coast directly to the south of us. I have no professional estimate of their strength yet, but I want the battalions broken down into many noisy units and scattered on either side of the main roads through this cork forest. Roll out the MJ-2s. Mine the roads. Plant anti-personnel mines and set up tree falls. Give me massed snipers and a lot of surprise mortar and grenade launcher placements and plenty of SAW crossfire. Lay down smoke and create heavy noise. Make them think a couple of divisions have been waiting for them to land—whoever they are."

"Whoever they are?" Kent Black said. "Who else can they be but those fucking Nicaraguans?"

"Go!" Chay said.

The two scouting parties returned greatly impressed. "We watched the regrouping from the hills, sir," a Ranger lieutenant reported to Chay. "They must have landed two divisions, sir. They have beachmasters yelling at them in Spanish through bullhorns so they gotta be Nicaraguan troops, sir."

Chay got on the phone to Al Melvin again. "Confirmed, Al," he said. "Two divisions of Sandinistas. Full-scale invasion."

"Ah, shit," Melvin said. "This is it, then. They're gonna try to take Europe."

"They fucking well will take Europe and all the Middle East, fahcrissake," Chay shrilled, "if you don't stop moaning and bitching and get to work flying some support in here."

"Roger Over!" Melvin barked.

"Roger? *Over?* Are you hanging up on me?"

"Chay, do your thing, fahcrissake. Put your Ops man on her. I was calling Roger Over, my Exec."

Melvin took the information to General Bustonbacher, commander of NATO forces, who said, "You handle it, Al. I got a golf date with the Prince of Wales."

Melvin went back to his desk and got the Tenth Airborne Command at Fort Bragg, North Carolina, on the satellite phone. Willie Gaffney, operations chief of the Tenth, cleared the request with the Forces Command at Fort McPherson. The Forces Command assigned nine infantry battalions of the Eighty-second Airborne to be flown out of Fort Stewart, Georgia, for a drop into the cork forest. They were to go in seventy-one minutes—after a Pathfinder detachment of 150 men had deployed and set up a landing zone. Operations Control at the Tenth ordered up assistance from two regiments of the Eighty-second based in Vincenza, Italy, to be dropped on the plains just north of the cork forest. Then 16,400 U.S. troops would face about 30,000 Sandinistas.

Chay left the details of the support to his people. He got into a staff car and went out to oversee the diversions.

Five hours and eight minutes later, the Nicaraguans came into the cork forest, in lorries packed with troops, in fast light tanks and eight-man fighting vehicles; SK211 B4 howitzers and ammunition support vehicles rolled up the main highway from the south. They had the pee scared out of them when Chay let loose with the noise from detonations, antitank guns, land mines, and steadily controlled SAW fire. The forward movement to the north and the escape routes to the south were blocked by enormous felled cork trees. The Nicaraguan advance had been deformalized.

The enemy troops had to scramble out of the trucks and scatter while gunfire cut them up. The impact of an explosive bullet destroyed Chay's right hip. He yelled for a medic to shoot him up with a deadener, then he had his people rig up a portable chair litter so he could carry on directing the action. Three separate teams of litter bearers were shot down while they carried him. He remained as calm as a dowager at a garden party but he lost a lot of blood. His troops seemed to double their attack with the confidence he poured into them, but when it was over, only 442 of his 1,600 man complement were alive. Ronald Reagan had been so right when he had pleaded with the Congress for funds and fighting men to wipe out these devils.

The airborne support from Italy, eight combat-sharp battalions, arrived about sixteen minutes after the Sandinistas had entered the forest. The fighting, except for a few tortuous mop-ups, was over by two o'clock the following morning. Cork trees were wrecked. A total of 3,712 Nicaraguan officers and men, together with their state-of-the art fighting matériel, were captured. The validity of the invading force was destroyed.

Chay remained conscious until four minutes after the battle ended, then he keeled over from loss of blood, shock, and exhaustion while the medics ran IVs into his arms and began the transfusions. He was promoted, in the field, to the rank of Brigadier General by a direct order from the President. With only two battalions and without a right hip, he had stopped a major invasion of Europe and the enslavement of millions by the Sandinista horde.

When Chay Appleton was twenty-four years old in 1974, he was sent to Africa as a second lieutenant to base on a 4,900-foot-high plateau in the Shire Highlands with a unit of British commandos. Soldiering had been Chay's life since the age of five, when he had been sent away to military school. He had had a limited experience of life. He wasn't over-bright, but he was as thorough as a soldier is expected to be, and by being fixed in the military mold forever, he had a narrower overall view of life than most civilians.

It would be hard to decide whether he went into the professional Army to escape his parents and his five siblings or whether they had all made fairly sure that there was no other place for him to go. With the excuse that they had to travel a lot, his parents sent him away to pre-primary military school on the North Slope of Alaska and he remained in military schools until he was graduated from West Point when he was twenty-two. Seventeen years of soldiering at the impressionable ages had produced a spit-and-polish soldier who had very little understanding of almost everything all other people took for granted. Because of his long years of soldiering, as a second lieutenant he had the attitudes of a Major General and the solid conviction that he must work until he outranked everyone if he were to put his family behind him. Despite all that, he hardly ever missed an episode of "Guiding Light" or a "Wheel of Fortune" show, but even though he had very nearly memorized "Caesar's Commentaries," he was still helplessly naive. It was a cast of mind which was to remain with him.

When Chay's mother had taken him to the airport in Washington, D.C., for his first flight to Alaska, she had given him the reason for his life. "You'll thank me for this when you are old enough to understand," she said to the sobbing little boy. "You will understand that the only way to go is with a job that pays a fat pension. You are gonna be Army. You are gonna have a pension that makes the post office people look like paupers." Chay never forgot that advice. When he was advanced in rank to heights of command he had never dreamed of achieving, he measured each advance in terms of pension. By force of her will, his mother had enforced a flawed anomaly: she wanted him to succeed in a flashy up-front way. Chay hardly gave his titles any thought; he was more American than that—he went for the money.

Tall people consider short people to be distractingly ambitious, even overbearing, simply because they were born as short people. Chay Appleton was certainly ambitious, and when necessary, he could be overbearing, but this had little to do with his physical stature. His inner qualities had been dictated entirely by the absolutism of the most pronounced caste system in the history of civilization—the military. Chay had begun as a buck private when he was five years old on the North Slope of Alaska and through pre-primary military school, then primary and secondary military schools (and military summer camps); he had risen through noncommissioned ranks until, at the U.S. Military Academy, he made the rank of Captain of the Cadet Corps. Throughout his life he had experienced equality only with women. He practiced military paranoia: he felt either an inferior or a superior, subject to orders from his betters or required to issue orders to the lower ranks. By that dangerous aberration the world had been run for five thousand years.

Chay had no politics. There were friendlies and there were enemies. All friendlies were in the United States, and if they were friendly, they advocated enormous budgets for the Department of Defense and the U.S. Army. He supported all friendlies unless he was ordered to think otherwise. All enemies threatened from outside. They were outsiders.

He had never made a great thing of quoting from Clausewitz or Oliver North, but he knew the finest military tailors and which Washington hostesses were the hooked soldier-buffs, the way other youths might know the names of rock stars. He had memorized the records of generals who had been dedicated politicians the way boys in the 1920s had memorized the batting averages of baseball players. He knew the foibles of Senators and Congressmen who were more than slightly military-simple and not only because they thought there might be a buck in it. He was sound on military tactics: he knew advanced military sciences, and above all else, despite the exquisite, almost *minute*ness of his proportions, he was so instinctively a thrilling leader that it was as natural for him to be elected Captain of the Cadet Corps at West Point as it was for him to remain under constant surveillance by his superiors to get him rapid promotion.

To remember (now) the thrilling television footage from the old tapes in the Smithsonian, the Captain giving the salute with that flashing sword at the head of the Cadet Corps, was to have one's imagination stirred to the opulent glories which had elevated Alexander the Great or to be humbled by the glorious dignity of Robert E. Lee.

From the morning of the first day after battle in the Portuguese cork forests, television cameras followed Chay wherever he was flown by the Military Air Transport Command. Old videotapes showing him in action or being greeted with big, wet kisses in villages from Asia to South America were reedited and rebroadcast.

Two weeks after the broadcast, the Army failed to get a certain letter to him. Although he never saw it, the failure wasn't the Army's fault because it was one of 141,785 other adoring letters, lampshades, brownies, and prayer beads from television viewers all over the world. The letter was from the gorgeous Portuguese woman with whom he had missed out (through no fault of his own) at lunch on the first day of his new life at what seemed like so long before in Almôdovar. Part of the letter said she had never expected to have been so close to and yet so far away from such a thrilling man who was destined to be the savior of her country and a star of international television. The rest of the letter was a close analysis of the American television coverage of Chay, the comparative qualities of the commentators, and the kind of reception she was getting on her television set.

2

CHAY WAS FLOWN from southern Portugal to the U.S. Army base hospital in Landstuhl, West Germany, near Kaiserslautern. A cunning surgeon, flown by the order of the Secretary of Defense from Walter Reed Hospital in Washington, Major General Abe Weiler, an inspired healer with a Perlmutter mustache, fitted him with a stainless-steel hip, then the television coverage began again but in a much more intense way.

The first thing Chay felt as he came out of the anesthetic was a craving for *kalbsbratwurst*. Three years before, in a skirmish with the Nicaraguans on the Hungarian plain, he had lost two toes, and after the wound had been treated, he was sent to Switzerland for Rest and Recreation. At lunch on the second day in Zurich he had discovered *kalbsbratwurst* and he had eaten them every day for as long as his leave allowed him to remain in the perfect city.

He was in the Landstuhl hospital in a semialert state for almost two weeks. Every time he turned on the Armed Forces television, day or night, he was sure that he saw the President and Mrs. Reagan either getting aboard the giant helicopter for the flight to Camp David or getting off it on the return from Camp David, while they nimbly avoided being tripped by their darling little dog and executed a linked series of the most intricate waves and grimaces at the same White House Press corps who were either greeting them or still seeing them off. The ritual made a deep, deep impression upon Chay's drug-hazed mind.

While he was in the hospital, on the day after the hip operation (somewhat too soon the doctors felt) the President called him on open-end television to tell him how proud and grateful the people of America and Europe were that he had turned back an invasion of the subcontinent and how it almost made up for the country not winning any gold at the Olympics again.

Chay felt self-conscious trying to respond from a hospital bed, still fairly dopey from the postoperative sedation, while being surrounded by Juan Francohogar, the White House's own television adviser, and a confusion of television crews. When he had finished his speech, with Chay still pinned mutely to the bed, the President asked if he could do anything for Chay, perhaps to convey messages personally to the folks back home. "Please tell my mother I'm okay, sir," Chay said, "she doesn't look at television."

Francohogar blanched, off-camera, but somehow that charge got past the television censors, perhaps because they knew no one would believe it anyway.

Chay could see his mother brushing off the news of his victory because there was no money in it, then turning away to Dudley or Brill and arguing with them about how much it was costing her to feed them and demanding to know when they were going to get out of the house and support themselves—even though they hadn't lived with Serena for years and had made the journey of over a thousand miles from where they lived just to see if she were all right.

Crews from the international network news shows were all over Chay's hospital room for almost a week after the President called. The BBC, Canadian Broadcasting, Television Diffusion of France, Japanese television, and RTE of Ireland were clamoring for equal time until Francohogar, in his wisdom, worked out a pool coverage arrangement.

Chay was interviewed on segments of weekly and Sunday talk shows. He had an entire segment of the "Wheel of Fortune" to himself and won a considerable amount of money and merchandise. He explained the origin of the word "hot dog" on Australian, Italian, and Portuguese television. Hundreds of feet of the tape were syndicated to hundreds of television stations throughout the world. In the French language he recounted for French television the memories of a friend who had been the friend of a friend of Jerry Lewis about the side-splitting way the Master had eaten a *sandwich de jambon*. Still more mail poured in from all over the world from hysterical people, lonely people, professional patriots, and people who wanted him to intervene with their wives or welfare boards.

After three weeks in the hospital in Germany, where he scored two nurses and a lady psychologist, MAC flew him to Lisbon where he found himself seated in the Presidential palace in a wheelchair, thinking about *kalbsbratwurst*. He was awarded the

Ordem Militar de Torre e Espada do valor, Lealdade e Merito which had been instituted in 1459 by Alphonso V "for heroic acts and outstanding proof of devotion and sacrifice for country and mankind."

The *Ordem* was added to the other decorations he had already earned: the Distinguished Service Medal and the Silver Cross of the United States Army, three Purple Hearts, and the Icelandic Order of the Falcon awarded to him "for services to the country and mankind" when he had ended the Nicaraguan occupation of the country in 1987, having commanded an airborne regiment of Rangers which had taken the Sandinista headquarters in Reykjavik by total surprise.

For his gallantry and courage, his own country could do no less than Portugal. The President sent Air Force One to Lisbon to fly him to Washington. Chay was whisked in a wheelchair from Andrews Air Force Base to the White House where he was awarded the Medal of Honor by the President, who told him that some day his story was going to make "one marvelous movie" as Chay sat at emotionally charged attention on an overcast day in the Rose Garden, facing eleven television crews. As the President hung the Medal around his neck, Chay wondered silently if John DeWitt Kullers was out there somewhere among the tens of millions of television viewers who were watching the ceremony. Did Kullers realize that the lowly plebe who had been a member of his platoon at the pre-primary military school in Edgarton, Alaska, so long before was being decorated with the highest military honor their country could offer because he, John Kullers, four years Chay's senior, had forged a soldier out of common clay, had hammered, drilled, and shaped this man he might now be watching, while all around in the Rose Garden stood the nation's richest investment bankers, the Cabinet and Congressional leaders, dizzyingly high military and naval brass, high-level gofers and Chay's entire family?

Dudley had traveled from Duluth with his wife, Frieda. Dudley was the eldest son who claimed he had been sent home from four schools because his father had failed to meet the costs of tuition and boarding. That was a lie. Dudley had been sent home because he had neither the intelligence nor the concentration to qualify. Dudley played *polo*. He flew *Concorde*. He wore *Lauren*. He had been denied nothing. He had been named after one of the two great loves of Serena's life: Dudley (Vingaro) and Sylvester (Ryan). Deep in her psyche Serena thought of Chay as Sylvester (a bellhop who had taken bets for her father). However, later, whenever she thought of her third son to whom she had given the name Sylvester, she thought of him mainly as a big pain in the ass.

Sylvester had been granted compassionate leave from his monastery in Death Valley. Brilliana, who was Chay's twin, had come up from New York. Jonathan and little Berry were also there to watch the President honor their brother.

All the Appleton siblings were tall, excepting Chay and Brill. They had straw-blond hair, excepting the twins whose hair was golden red. The Appleton sisters were merely ravishing; gruntingly breathtaking. The brothers were handsome, except Chay who hovered between being handsome and pretty because he had a bowed cherry-red mouth and mournful Lillian Gish eyes.

Serena had materialized like the wicked witch of the West. She hadn't been there but when Chay felt someone crowding beside him in the Rose Garden in front of the vast battery of television cameras, it had been his mother. No matter where, she always showed up as the Left in the Left to Right identifications in the captions of news pictures. She looked rather lovely in a new sable coat and a simple little designer frock which the First Lady did not seem to be able to take her eyes off. Serena liked it because it showed off the emeralds.

When the ceremonies were over, the Appletons all returned to the family house in Alexandria. Chay, his mother, and Dudley rode in one of the limousines which had been provided by the White House. Chay sat between his mother and brother. The traffic was horrendous because the streets, like the streets all over the country, were choked with the homeless; not just indigent men, not just the mentally ill, but whole families who had been unable to afford housing since the real estate lobby had come into its own when the Republicans had come into office in '68. Serena would not permit anyone to criticize the Republican Party at any time, so the ride was one continuous *longeur* until they crossed into Virginia.

At last Dudley said, "Jesus, Chay, you're really a celebrity. It was like getting an Academy Award."

"Yeah," Serena said, "Best Supporting Actor."

"Take it easy, Mom," Chay said.

"It's only a piece of tin, baby. It's only worth something if we cash in on it."

"Cash *in?*"

"How do you mean, Mom?" Dudley asked.

"Chay's gotta resign from the Army. He's gotta sign with somebody like the William Morris Office, or some other show biz giant, and make a fortune outta books, movies, endorsements, TV, and personal appearances." She turned to Chay. "You could end up as star of stage, screen, and television. God knows you're pretty enough and short enough and acting could take you straight into politics where we can all make an absolute fortune."

"Forget it, Mom."

"For*get* it?"

"I've been a soldier all my life. That's what I do."

"It's not good enough, Chay. Did it ever occur to you that it just isn't good enough?" Serena's face could have been modeled by Gustave Klimt; high cheekbones (higher than any Eskimo's), a confrontational stare, and an accusatory manner behind teeth which could have flattered a merry-go-round horse. Outside the family she spoke with a slight but unlocatable accent, hauntingly similar to the speech of the late Leopold Stokowski whose phonetic origins could be variously and simultaneously traced to Lodz, Poland; rural Albania; Kilmoganny, Ireland; and an enclave in the northern section of Tokyo. At home, among her children and with her late husband (who had had a light Danish-African accent), Serena spoke in New Yorkese, the Gullah of the north.

Chay enunciated slowly as if, in his mind, he were suffering the past. "You wanted me to make it in the Army, Mom," he said. "It would be a sure income no matter what happened, you said. From the time you sent me away to the first military school—on scholarships—you've been telling me about the pension, and how, no matter what happened, I'd always be able to support you."

"That was nickel-and-dime stuff. We are talking big-time here."

Chay suddenly felt what it had been like to be five years old again, in an Alaskan winter on the North Slope where, after eleven small boys had been marched to their barracks, John Kullers, the nine-year-old Officer of the Day, stood at the foot of a file of cots and shouted the order, "Cadets—go to *bed!*" The small boys had undressed rapidly because of the cold, folded their clothes, placed them in footlockers and climbed into bed. The OD shouted, "Cadets—go to *sleep!*" Each little boy placed his right arm under his head, left arm over the blankets, and closed his eyes. The light stayed on all night long to protect the younger boys from the older ones. No one was ever allowed to be alone. Neither his mother nor his father ever came to visit him, although each of them wrote to him once a month. No one was ever out of uniform. He saw his family for two weeks each year, between military school in Alaska and military summer camp in the Adirondacks.

He had given more than just his life to the Army, he thought. In southeast Africa, after an intensive twenty-week course in rough stuff, he had been raped by a very butch British lesbian, a sergeant major (during a heavy mist/rain at a nudist camp in Nyasaland, when she had mistaken him for a girl). She still sent him a few neckties on each anniversary of the day they met. But that was the Army. His Army. After his field training was completed, he was reassigned to the First Battalion, Seventy-fifth Rangers, in Borneo, to fight with the Seventh U.S. Army Corps to drive the Sandinistas out of Southeast Asia. Ronald Reagan had very nearly broken his heart in trying to warn America that this allegedly "tiny" Central American country was out to conquer the world. In 1980, Nicaragua had had a population of three million people, but by practicing advanced breeding techniques, they had been able to swell to twenty-one million by CIA estimate, almost all of them fierce males who wanted to invade and occupy the United States, rape the flower of American womanhood, desecrate the flag, and ban the Pledge of Allegiance from all American schoolrooms, while making it part of martial law that all women have abortions regardless of race, creed, or color.

When the Indonesian campaign ended victoriously, five months later, Chay was a captain, reassigned to eastern Argentina. In a hard-fought series of battle actions which drove the Nicaraguans as far south as the Patagonian coast where the Navy and Marines finished them off, he had his left elbow shattered at the battle of Bahia Blanca. He was removed to Walter Reed Hospital in Washington, where the crushed elbow was replaced with a stainless-steel joint. He was decorated with the Distinguished Service Medal and a Purple Heart and promoted to Major. That was the upside. The downside was that he would have to go back home so he would have to see his family again.

And now—while the Medal of Honor was still hanging around his neck, still warm from the hands of the President of the United States—his mother wanted him to desert the Army to go into show business. He had had his fill of show business. There was said to be more television tape on Chay Appleton in the field, in hospitals, being decorated, or being greeted in hutches, villages, and cities by more beautiful women of many different colors than any other officer in the United States Army. There had even been talk of making him a White House aide to take attention away from the President's gaffes. He was the photographer's darling because he was exceptionally pretty, as small as a really great film star, and a man who always seemed to be at the center of the most spectacular military actions.

His mother didn't seem to understand (or even care about) the peril which their country faced from Nicaragua. There was no precedent in history for Nicaragua's terrible lust for conquest. Most of all, it was determined to occupy and rule the United States, but that glorious national right which had always been on the side of the United States had stopped the Sandinistas cold in historic battles across the world, which had been photographed by the Central Intelligence Agency. Wherever the Sandinistas struck, American troops were there to meet them, staying on long after the Sandinistas had been driven out. Chay Appleton's life had been dedicated to stopping this evil empire and now his mother wanted him to go into show business.

Serena kept the pressure on Chay to resign from the Army all through the long weekend. Dudley and Sylvester sided with her, Dudley because he resented Chay and Sylvester because he always needed money from his mother for pretty new ecclesiastical frocks. Chay finally had enough, and although they were much larger and heavier than he, he beat them severely and when they went down kicked them in the ribs and head.

Brill supported Chay. She went at her mother, demanding that she stop her brutal demands.

On Sunday morning Brill rolled Chay's wheelchair to the far

end of the porch so she could say, "You've got to get out of here, Chay, or you'll be spending your whole sick leave listening to Mom."

"I was thinking about that."

"I can't get over that you don't actually kill her. We'd all help you hide the body."

"She was after me this morning to start tap dancing lessons."

"She's obsessed. We have to do something."

"What I was thinking was—well, if you could go into Washington and talk to Major General Weiler, the surgeon who put the new hip in, and explain what's going on here, he can have orders cut to send me somewhere else to recuperate."

"You must come and stay with me in New York."

Two days later the Army called Chay to Washington for medical examinations, then they ordered him to take six weeks of R&R in New York after which he was to report to the Forces Command at Fort McPherson near Atlanta.

Serena fought the order. She threatened to go to the President. She sank to her knees and wept and pleaded while Chay packed his baggage. She pressed him hard about how much he would like Beverly Hills and show biz; told him he was breaking her heart, that he was throwing a fortune away. He told her that he was replanning his life so that he could make more money to send her but that he could not leave the Army. He told her he was going to work and scrimp so that, when he was a middle-aged man, he could honestly say that everything he was or ever hoped to be he owed to his angel mother. Cheeks glazed with tears, he promised her that now that his rank had been increased he would be able to increase the amount of money he had been sending to her in order to make up for what he would be costing them by refusing to resign from the Army and sign with the Morris Office.

3

T HE APPLETON FAMILY NAME had originally been Aeble-kobstad. They were an old Danish family which had reached St. John's, in the Virgin Islands, from the town of Thisted, in Jutland, in the second wave of Danish immigration to the Danish West Indies in 1773. The islands were purchased by the United States in 1917, when the name was changed to the Virgin Islands, and given universal suffrage in 1938.

Caesare Appleton was raised on the island of St. John in the Virgins. His birthday was the fifteenth of August 1950, the day of the Feast of the Assumption of the Virgin Mary. The Appleton home in the States was in Alexandria, Virginia. This recurring symbol of untouchability in his life—Virgin (Islands), Virgin (ia), the Virgin Mary—would baffle his biographers the more deeply they probed into his past.

The Virgins are far out in the Caribbean, tiny dots at latitude 17° 45' N and longitude 65° 54' W, in an area believed by medieval Europeans to be Antilla, the ancient mythical land which was known in legend as "the island of the Seven Cities" or "the region away from sunrise."

Although his mother had been born on Featherbed Lane in the Bronx, Serena Appleton never overcame her dislike for Americans, perhaps because her husband, a professional Dane, was a sea-to-shining-sea American. If Serena had a major fault it was avarice, even extreme avarice; a very modern avarice which sought to possess everything yet could hold on to nothing.

When as twenty-three-year-old Sarah Kronstadt she had been an assistant glove buyer at Klein's-on-the-Square, she had planned a tryst on St. John's during her annual summer vacation, with two lovers: one sponsoring (Dudley Vingaro) and one pursuing (Sylvester Ryan). Fate delayed the departure of both men from New York. While she waited with passionate impatience she met the hotel's mixologist, Axel Aeblekobstad, who had seemed to Serena—horny as the waiting had made her—like a Norse god, a sort of super-masculine Viking in soiled tennis shoes unprotected by socks.

Serena was helplessly susceptible to "natural" men. Axel/Adam (she was able to persuade him to change both his names) was almost six feet four inches tall, and although he wasn't quick in any way, he had prodigious dignity which, unknown to her, had been created by a form of dysentery which made him warily stiff in movement, careful and studied, lest a sudden move cause a serious accident; a masked asset which he carried throughout his life.

The young couple was married on St. John's in August 1948. In 1951, after Dudley and the twins had been born, they flew to Washington where Adam joined the Republican Party as a paid worker. By the time of the Nixon election in '68, Adam was well in place as a high-level gofer. He consolidated his position well behind the scenes of Watergate. Three sources identified him as Deep Throat during the Watergate scandals, which greatly enhanced his political prestige, and many thought that because he was so naturally unscrupulous, devious, and self-seeking that he had been President Nixon's role model.

Serena states flatly in her diaries that Chay began his unceasing ragging and nagging of both his father and his mother to be sent away to pre-primary military school in Alaska when he was four years old. Serena recorded that it almost broke her heart. She says, expressing bewilderment, that she does not know how he could even have known about such a school. At any rate, she wrote, it was after months of being awakened in the middle of the night by a small boy standing beside her bed making his harsh demands, having to listen to his cold, rational reasoning as to why he must be sent to that school, that ultimately forced his parents to relent.

She tells, again and again, that that child could not get enough of the severe military life. He insisted on being sent through primary military school then secondary military school until when he was admitted to the United States Military Academy at West Point he knew more about troops, tactics, logistics, and the history of warfare than most colonels in regular Army service. Yet—and this must be seen as a large stumbling point—his own diaries, journals, memoirs, tapes, and self-made videocassettes insist that his mother had banished him from her life when he was five, sending him to Alaska to grow up on the North Slope facing the Arctic Sea, among children who had been similarly outcast. He never failed to say in these accounts how much he loved his mother, but he never relented in his charge that she had abandoned him.

There hardly seems to have been any larger than colossally wealthy male on any of the five continents whom Brill did not inveigle into her bed. Chay resented his sister's sexual ambitions bitterly. His life was bound by total discipline, except where the attractions of women were concerned. To him, Brilliana had contempt for discipline when that interfered with her access to men. Until the Portuguese campaign and the ensuing international television coverage, Brill outranked Chay in sexual achievement.

Her attitude to men to one side, Brill was a delightful woman if one was able to sidestep one's inevitable distaste for her avidity for money and power. Chay was a prisoner of the idea of money and was just as psychologically biased in favor of women as his twin was about men. Both had been bruised by the parent fish as they had all swum in the bowl of early life, colliding with each other's needs. Chay spent his life believing that his mother had abandoned him in frigid north Alaska for some other preference she had. Because he believed his mother had discarded him, he was one of the most sexually susceptible men on the planet because he was frantic about finding a replacement for Serena.

Adam Appleton survived well into the Reagan years as a presidential planner. He was the unnamed architect of the Iran-Contra betrayals of the nation, slyly allowing the President and little Colonel North to take the blame. He had a major hand in the Bitburg shaming, the HUD looting, and the Pentagon procurement crimes. He had made a place for himself as a leading gofer in the Reagan White House, had made a fortune in the stock market from insider information, had interceded for so many defense contractors as a "consultant" and had woven such intimate connections with the Mafia that he had established the foundation of what might have been one of the great American fortunes if it had not been for the profits-profligacy among politicians which had followed Reagan and for his cocaine habit brought on by the high tension of his profession which, in turn, brought on his constant fear of arrest, arraignment, indictment, and conviction like so many of the other aspiring gofers of the Reagan administration. Nonetheless, he had the distinction, for a few short years, of being one of the few among the new 8,112,849 Reagan-made instant-millionaires whose name had originally been Aeblekobstad.

Despite removing his family from the Virgin Islands, Adam Appleton never let his children forget their Danish origins. The Appleton siblings were raised with the knowledge that, by the time the Danes had set sail for the New World in the early seventeenth century, Denmark had been a Christian kingdom for more than six hundred years. Inherently, the Appletons had been Royalists long before Ronald Reagan, so much so that they went all cool and distant if anyone were uncouth enough to remind them that the Bronx had been founded in 1629 by a Dane. Appleton enrolled his children in The Dansk Foundation and Det Danske Brodersamfund, and saw to it that they supported the Danish-American Heritage Association and the Dansk Samvirke, even though the Danish vote was of minor consequence to Reagan. It was like being an American-Israeli in reverse; one's sentimental allegiance was off on some promontory of conversation, allowing ample time for the real business of making money.

Throughout his life in the back rooms of American government, Adam Appleton never stopped hoping that he would be decorated by the Danish king or perhaps have Tivoli Gardens in Copenhagen renamed for him.

On February 24, 1988, Adam Appleton became so desperately ill at Presbyterian Hospital in New York that his son Sylvester, a priest, had to give him the Last Sacrament. Adam cried out for Chay to come and defend him. "Chay! Chay! Fahcrissake, what's happening here?" he moaned piteously. He stared hostilely at Dudley. "You are Prince Nowhere," he said. "Chay is now head of this family. Never forget that." Gripping Chay's hand, he called out, "Long Live Denmark!" and left the world.

At the time of his death Adam Appleton had been indicted twice, charged eleven times, and reassigned four times by the President—about an average score for a middle-to-higher management type in the Administration. He was maintaining three cars and a driver (about $85,000 a year in all for those items alone); a household in two climates with seven servants ($215,000 for a

Swiss chef, a Chinese sous-chef, and an Irish butler). Nonetheless, Appleton entertained the news media at short-order joints such as Taco Loco and Pastrami Ink, not to prove his common touch but because that was the kind of food he liked. He entertained congressmen and other foreign contacts on chartered DC-10s which carried imported belly dancers, serving Iranian caviar as if it were peanut butter. He ran an eighty-seven-foot power boat, wore $897 alligator loafers, thought of his family as people in a Ralph Lauren advertisement, kept a four-room apartment at the Willard in Washington to provide space for congressional quickies, and did twelve lines of cocaine a day.

When Adam died, Dudley was thirty-nine years old; Chay and Brill were thirty-seven; Sylvester, thirty-one; Jonathan, nineteen; and little Berry, seventeen. Dudley had found Frieda, the rich girl of his (and his mother's) dreams. She wasn't a pretty woman. She had a skin condition and a weight problem, but she had a kind disposition and she was going to inherit several million dollars someday. When Dudley had introduced her to his mother, having explained her prospects, Serena immediately took her into her bosom. Frieda's dad was astonished and proud that his little girl had been able to marry a lawyer, or anyone at all, and he gave the young couple $200 as a wedding present.

When Adam died, Chay was a Major in the United States Army, having been graduated from the Academy a few months before the end of the Vietnam War, eighth in his class of 737. Brill had been graduated from Vassar and lived in a lavish apartment in New York which she could not possibly have afforded. Serena spread the word throughout the family that Brill was living on her immoral earnings until Chay demanded that she offer a full apology to Brill in the presence of every Appleton.

Sylvester had entered a monastery of a remote religious order called The Church of the Upwardly Mobile. In the monastic cell where he lived with his vows, accepting bread and water as his due, Sylvester had a 36" color television set, a VCR, ninety-four videocassettes (some of them startlingly raunchy), a $724.95 (wholesale) Korean tape recorder on which he recorded not prayers but what constituted his memoirs of his family. His father's bank records showed a rather large number of monthly bank checks which had been sent to Sylvester and which the young acolyte had spent on gay mail-order robes and vestments, long-skirted soutanes and cassocks, and pretty little zucchettos or chic birettas in the most courageous colors, directly from Partolucci Figli in the Via della Concilazione, Roma. Jonathan had graduated from Andover and little Berry was being educated at home.

After her husband's death, Serena told her children that she was so short of money that she could no longer maintain the house in Alexandria. She removed herself and the two youngest children to the capacious house on St. John's where Chay had been born, and from where she sent out constant appeals to her sons and daughters for financial support.

Serena would have had everyone believe that somehow, from gambling table scraps and other squirrelings by her, the Appleton children had all, somehow, been educated. Adam Appleton's estate hadn't reflected anything like the money he had made and spent in his lifetime. He had been a hooked gambler, in casinos and on Wall Street, and had been forced into a heavy cocaine habit in order to maintain his American point of view, but he had believed with all his heart in the Reagan revolution.

Serena controlled her grief over his death but it must have been there because, seven times a week, when she and Berry were doing their calisthenics together she would say "Day and night" (stretch), "when I wake up in the morning" (stretch), "the first thing I say to myself is" (stretch), "You are going to miss Adam one more day, baby!" (stretch).

Throughout the days, by telephone and by letter, Serena told her children she had had to pawn all the household silver and "most" of her furs and jewels in order to pay for the medical care for her husband's last days. She claimed to have been "too proud" to accept Medicare when, actually, her husband had been too young to qualify for Medicare. Moreover he had held paid-up medical and hospital insurance in the amount of $295,000. His life insurance brought Serena $687,000 and she had wheedled stock shares away from him and had sold them at a time when it had seemed that everything he touched from inside the White House had provided a 256 percent net profit. She had pulled down the occasional heavy chip whenever she could during Adam's winning streaks at casinos. In the earlier days, she and Adam had shared J. Edgar Hoover's racing information which came directly from the Mafia, which didn't even exist then, according to the FBI. She had persuaded him to switch cocaine dealers because the new dealer had offered her 15 percent of the retail price of everything Adam snorted and she had invested these dribs and drabs in a shoe stock which had appreciated by 239 percent. She wasn't a *rich* woman; she had a comfortable nest egg of about four million seven.

The heaviest burden carried by the Appletons was their lust for money. The Appleton family's published, private, and shared memoirs reveal that they thought of little else but money. This obsession is mainly forgiven by the world because it is the dominating American characteristic which was somewhat obscured by the family's adventures, their prodigious sexual couplings, and the dazzling honors which they acquired (or which Chay acquired for them), but their obsession with money overshadowed everything else.

Chay had had to memorize a song, a simple rote repetition which he would shout to himself inside his head whenever he found himself in conversation with his mother:

> *Money, money, always money*
> *Is money a new kind of language of love?*
> *Can you talk about money to an Easter bunny?*
> *Does a dove coo money to another dove?*
> *Money, money, always money.*
> *Can you cuddle up with money in a till?*
> *Is Lincoln's smile sunny as it stares at you from a five dollar*
> *   bill?*
> *Money makes you worry.*
> *Eat it and you choke.*
> *Walk around with shoesfull, load up nine canoesfull.*
> *But the only time it's useful is when you're broke.*

Once he had had to repeat the ditty eleven times loudly inside his head during a conversation with his mother.

W HEN CHAY ARRIVED at Brill's vast apartment in New York, after fleeing from his mother's demands that he sign with the Morris Office, Brill told him a friend of Serena's was waiting for him in the salon.

"A friend of *Mom's?*" Chay repeated with disbelief.

"She has a letter of introduction from Mom."

"I certainly can't see her alone. You'll have to sit in as a witness. Jesus, this is terrible."

A short, wide woman wearing a ridiculous hat stared at his civilian clothes with hostility. Chay had had to leave off wearing his uniform and ribbons in order to be able to appear on New York streets without being mobbed for his autograph.

"Where's your Army suit?" the woman said.

"This is Mrs. Garvisch," Brill said.

"What can I do for you, Mrs. Garvisch?" Chay asked nervously.

"You're gonna be in town for a couple weeks and I'm gonna help you make some easy dollars."

"Thank you," Chay said. "But no thank you."

"First you'll listen. I'm talking a heavy ruble here."

Chay began to back his wheelchair away.

"Look," Mrs. Garvisch said, "a party a night, $7,500 a party. All you do is show up, work the room, say a couple of words to the hostess, then you blow, you don't stay there. Thirty-forty minutes' work for $7,500. But you gotta wear the uniform and the medals, of course."

"How much does my mother get?"

"She gets $2,500 out of a gross of 10 and I take down 20 percent from the gross. I can set you for four appearances a week but that's only the beginning. Maybe three or four store openings at $3,500 a shot, a half a dozen bar mitzvahs and one or two show-ups as an audience-brightener on a couple of opening nights, and in the four weeks you're gonna be here, I can get you maybe $65,000 with about twenty-five big ones going to your Mom, her end tax-free to you."

Chay turned to Brill. "People do this?"

"Do they do it?" Mrs. Garvisch said. "It's my living for three years! How do you think celebrities can afford these rents?"

"I must go now," Chay said, wheeling the chair out of the room.

After three weeks of physiotherapy, Chay was able to walk with his new hip. He took strolls around the city, forthright with his neckties, wearing a gallery of civilian hats: homburgs, bowlers, five-piece tweed caps, all looking large and unexpected on his huge, round head which was said to be, according to his south-of-the-river London hatmaker, S. Patey, larger than the head of the King of Tonga, a man who had weighed over 300 pounds while Chay's weight never exceeded 141 pounds.

He dressed maturely when out of uniform, leaving behind the gay rows of ribbons and the costume jewelry of decorations and medals; four-button suits, waistcoats, suitings often vertically striped to convey an illusion of greater height, and a watch chain, not because he was stodgy but because he wanted to impress with his extreme conservatism. His gaze may have been inward but that's the way he was: a mental sort of chap in a physical sort of way. It wasn't that he was a cold man. Distant would be a fairer description because he was more unilateral than a black hole in galactic space, i.e., he received but gave very little back, which was entirely in the military manner, and if that seems to speak of some unpleasant quality in his personality it was not the case. He was an utterly charming man when the whim was on him—not as continually charming as, say, Ronald Reagan or Hermann Goering, but frequently endearing.

An astronomer-historian likened Chay's presence, in later years, to one of the high-velocity field dwarfs or magnetohydrodynamic solitons. The man was convinced that Chay sent out radiation in the form of photons. He explained the power of Chay's presence by saying that such energy had to go somewhere, and in Chay's case, it had changed human history. Once this "Appleton Theory" had been tinkered with, others began to understand the Chayvian paradox in the context of Euclidean geometry and Newtonian physics, but in attempting to calculate his force, failed to understand what happens to radiation in the framework of expanding curved space, and so they missed the point.

Perhaps one could decry his charm and warmth when one was away from him, but if he smiled, his fierce determination to carry out the basic purpose of smiling which was to please or to take advantage of a fellow being, as the case might be, so strengthed and realigned the muscles which structured his face that gradually, as the years went on, there emerged the most warming and endearing smile that anyone within its presence could remember feeling. The lifting/stretch of his upper lips exposed the teeth—very good teeth—in a manner which men admired and felt constrained to follow as a leader's blazon, while in women it produced a ravening sexual appetite.

Chay never realized he was giving so much comfort with his smile. It is possible that, had he known, he would have smiled less or he would have worked out a method for charging for it because his mother needed the money. As it was, he smiled rarely enough, but when he did, things happened for him. He never understood that he had willed this gift upon himself—all of it generated physically by the arrangement of the superficial surface of the subcutaneous adipose tissue around his malar bone and his masseter and buccinator muscles.

It was Chay—his smile, and above all else the opportunities he created by a lifetime of soldiering—who made the Appletons such figures in the world—all that and the advanced design for the W-54 nuclear bomb, later the SHAM (for Special Hydrogen Atomic Munition). The SHAM could be set off by one person like dynamite. It had been so redesigned and refined that with its radio-controlled detonators, its new M-9 coder/transmitter, and the improved recorder-receiver, the super-conductor power supply, the new shield and lens material, that the entire weapon weighed less than fourteen pounds, smaller than many Thanksgiving turkeys. With all that convenience, it delivered 450 kilotons of destruction when it was exploded in the nation's capital city.

SEEN FROM THE REAR or even when approaching as he walked along Third Avenue on an exhilarating afternoon, moving southward from Eighty-fifth Street on a small shopping excursion during his R&R visit to stay with his sister Brill in New York, Chay did not attract the startled attention he would have drawn had he been in uniform. Some forty million people living in the metropolitan area had seen him recently on television a few dozen times, wearing his ribbons because the shows had insisted on it. However, even though he was incognito anyone observing him would have had to admire his swan-like bearing, high chin, and steady, measured pace, the result of thirty-three years of soldiering out of a total of thirty-eight years of life.

Seen from the front: a waistcoat, a black homburg hat worn in the traditional fore-and-aft style, and fine, sober tailoring. Anyone would have noted the cut and quality of his clothing, of course, but one might also have been shocked by the pallor under the normal ruddiness of his skin. He was still in recovery from long hospitalization and intense exposure to television cameras.

Despite his illness, his ineffable carnality grabbed one's senses even as the distinction of his clothing grabbed the mind. He was wearing a forest green suit with a shell pink shirt under a representation of a Merton College, Oxford soccer team tie in alternate stripes of silver and bright pink. The dark green socks over pink feet the size of pork chops were (almost) imperceptible as he paced out his twenty-three-inch stride (Army regulation for legs of his length). There was no garish nonsense such as a matching green breastpocket handkerchief. It was starkly white, lightly starched. Its sharply pointed edges formed a tiny hedge above the rim of the pocket.

Nonetheless, it was his hat which demanded total attention. It was a black homburg in the Von Papen cut, which his batman had lowered within a rope noose for seven hours in a vat of ice water kept at three degrees above freezing, its brim bound upward.

This process had been followed by enclosure in a drying closet where it had been subjected to nine-mile-an-hour drafts of warm air from all sides until the hat had dried and its brim on either side had achieved a flair which marks the man who cares. One other characteristic of the hat was inescapable. It was very large. It had to be to fit that head, a head greatly (although not grotesquely) out of proportion with the rest of his deceptive smallness.

Historically, it was the hat which came to characterize Chay through the ages. In 1988, a black homburg was a common enough sight throughout the world. There were, perhaps, several million of them being worn. Within relatively few years the hat was identified solely with Caesare Appleton: an essential part of the thousands of busts and statues which adorned public parks. Elsewhere, homburgs were later to be worn by patients in asylums or worn in cartoon strips by cross-eyed men who thought they were Caesare Appleton. Otherwise, homburgs ceased to be worn except by the man who had made them famous.

How this happened is an interesting *bei-spiel* of history. As a general officer Chay, of course, had the privilege of designing his own uniforms. Preoccupied with other things (not the least of which was his first marriage), he often went into battle wearing civilian clothes. In the case of the Battle of Rapallo when he drove the Nicaraguan invader into the sea, he was wearing one of his favorite uniforms, the dress blues of a Colonel of Engineers, but in order to keep the driving rain out of his eyes, he wore the homburg sideways on his head. It was a memorable sight which international television had hosed into the minds and hearts of the free peoples of the world.

The campaign was victorious. His troops cheered him. The sideways homburg became their good luck piece, a rallying symbol. The sideways homburg was Chay's hat; the hat was Chay.

As he walked along Third Avenue he was an impacting sight and an impacted man. This was one of his rare appearances-at-large outside a military unit. He felt as if he were visiting a zoo when he was among civilians. They were beyond his discipline as it were. They wore strange clothing, never saluted, moved at random, and spoke to their superiors before being spoken to.

Despite his artificial hip there was no suggestion of disability in Chay's walk. As with bull fighters he had undergone heinous

wounds which he regarded as the normal profit and loss of his
professional life. Wounds earned in combat suggested heroism
which induced promotions which increased eventual pensions. It
was really no different than in civilian life.

If the 237,491 negative things about the city could have been
removed, New York could have been the most perfect place to be
of anywhere in the world on that flawless day. Chay ached with
good health and when he ached that way he got very horny.

At the hanging sign SCHWALHABER'S, he turned left off the
pavement to enter one of the great landmark delicatessens of any
gastronomic discipline. He was the only customer inside the shop
with its spiced necro-smells. He approached the glassed display
cases which mounted, under subtly colored lighting, twelve kinds
of meat in forms which were smoked, boiled, pickled, broiled,
baked, stuffed, spiced, barbecued, sliced, pie-crusted, packed in
tight skins, and blessed with such dizzying names as *rippchen,
potatiskorv, loukanika, bockwurst, landjager, biroldo Toscano, pinkelwurst, kielbasa Polska, Metz, faggots, andouilles, Gekugellepaste, Gefüllte
Schinkenhorchen, Braunschweiger, Braegenwurst,* and *Andudel.*

Chay's mission to Schwalhaber's was to acquire some *kalbsbratwurst,* which contained mostly veal, some beef, and endowing
flecks of coriander, ginger, mustard seed, and lemon rind, a taste/
texture sensation which had preyed on his palate ever since he
had come out of the anesthetic in Germany. He had vowed that
at the first chance, he was going to buy, have cooked, and eat this
heavenly food. He was going to acquire three perfect sausages,
take them back to Brill's, and have them cooked.

"May I helb you, zir?"

Chay lifted his eyes reluctantly from a whole broiled flanken
which lay in state within the refrigerated case. He stared. He could
not believe what he was looking upon. She stood there encased
in the sort of external beauty which promises an adventurous,
even raunchy, soul beneath. She was wearing an anonymous
white coat, lightly spotted and faintly aromatic, while standing
expectantly, awaiting his orders. She was as delectable as anything
within the display case. He thought wildly, she is Debussy's *Girl
With the Golden Hair!*

He found himself wishing (irrationally) that Captain Preston,
the band master at North Slope, had insisted that he study the

flute instead of making him play the bass drum in the regimental band. He would have rushed out, rented a flute, and played all the Debussy to her across the high barrier of delicatessen which was keeping them apart.

For the first time since it had happened many years before, he had a flash of understanding which related to *kalbsbratwurst*, of his father's agony of incapacity to stop himself from doing what he had tried to do to Brill, and Chay also understood his own relationship to *kalbsbratwurst* as well: its boastful phallic shape, its translucent lack of color, its ring size of 58, and his own unconscious intention to fill himself with many of them so that he would always have more and more of them within himself, never to become impotent.

Staring across the high display case, he had understood everything at the instant he had looked up from the flanken and had seen the woman. Had he been two feet taller he would have vaulted over the counter and taken her in his arms. He felt an instant incarnation of the fleshy dagger within his trousers. The woman behind the display case was the most compellingly lustworthy woman he had ever seen.

"Three *kalbsbratwursts*, please."

"Kalbs? *Kalbsbratwurst?*" She pronounced the "k" as a "g," the "b" as a "p," the "t" as a "d," the "s" as a "z," and the "w" as a "v." Chay shuddered as he nodded in reply.

"It could be a Swiss appellation," he said. "Kalb as in calf— for veal—brat as meaning to fry—in German—and, of course, wurst."

"If it exists we have it, don't worry. I will ask *der Vater.*"

She turned away from him, picked up a wall phone extension and dialed three numbers. There was a hushed exchange in German. "Aaaah!" she said into the phone. She hung up and turned to Chay. "Beim here a *kalbs*bratwurst is a *fein*bratwurst. Three for you?"

"Ja, ja," Chay said. "Yes, please."

She wrapped the sausages. "Someding elze?"

"What time does the store close?"

"Sigs o'glock."

"Do you leave the store from the front entrance?"

"Ja, ja."

"May I wait for you?"

"Why?"

Why? Chay thought. Because I want to screw your little dirndl off, that's why.

"I—I want to talk to you," he said aloud. "I'd like to know you better."

"I leave the store with my brothers. They are very larch men. Three."

"What I have in mind is a really good French restaurant and having them cook these sausages. The French call them *saucisse de veau.*"

"Why not a German restaurant? Oder Alzayzhun?"

"Wherever it will make you happy."

"I like Chinese," she said simply. "What is your name?"

"Chay. Chay Appleton." He was thrown back to the night of his birth. God! Why did he have to think of his parents at an electric moment like this? Why did he have to recall the dopiest, most oft-repeated family story that had ever been told? He forced himself to think sex. He simply would not hold his parents in his mind at a crucial time like this. He thought it was so refreshing that she hadn't recognized him, but on the other hand, he thought, perhaps he should have worn his uniform and ribbons this one time.

"What does Chay stand for?"

It was a ridiculous story which had meaning only for his dead father, and probably none for his mother, but if he said it to her, it would explain his weird name and perhaps somehow establish some kind of a relationship between them. But this was a delicatessen, not a salon. It was simply not the sort of conversation one would ever dream of having with a beautiful girl across a counter in a delicatessen. But he told her.

"My parents had eight children," he said, "six surviving. My father was a sort of shadowy figure in the federal government. He never sought out the elective or appointive offices he could have held but he showed up at least twice a month on one or another of the Sunday talk shows."

"Really?"

"He was photographed frequently emerging from the north door of the White House. He was cosy with power, an insider who was, I think, really a high-grade gofer and now and then a consultant to a few dozen war matériel suppliers."

"That is interesting."

"I was born in the Virgin Islands. I have a twin."

"Twins!"

"A boy and a girl. That night, my father named me—on an official birth certificate—Caesare Appleton."

"What did he name the girl?"

The bell over the shop door tinkled. A customer came in. Chay stepped back from the counter while the woman ordered a half pound of boiled *schinken* and a medium container of coleslaw. When she left, Chay stepped up to the counter again to stare into that beautiful face and to finish his explanation.

"My mother named the girl later. She said she had to find a name which would match the ostentation of the name my father had given me."

"Caesare is a very beautiful name."

"A violent electrical storm had struck the island at the moment of my birth. My father said it was as though God were shaking the skies to tell him that a great man—his son—had come into the world." Chay couldn't believe he was spouting all this. He hardly knew this girl, yet in another way, he felt he had known her through many other lives across the constellations of eternity. "My mother never recognized the name Caesare," he continued desperately. "She said it was a crazy wop name, and she has always called me Chay—short for Chay-zah-ray, the Julian pronounciation."

"My name is Hedda Blitzen," the wonder girl told him.

At three minutes after six she emerged from the shop with three burly silent men who had expressionless blue eyes and *Buerstenhaarschnitt* hair cuts. Chay tensed into karate readiness.

"Ah—Chay," Hedda said gaily. "You are right on time. How nice. Boys, this is my friend, Mr. Appleton. Chay, this is Wolfie and Luddie and here is Gottie."

Chay shook hands with them, then to his astonishment they lumbered away up the avenue.

"But you speak perfect English!" he said, baffled.

"I leave the accent in the store," she said. "Poppa likes us to talk to the customers as if we are right off the boat."

They strolled. "The boys went to college in Florida. They talk like crackers when they are outside."

Animal crackers, Chay thought.

She was even more bewitching out of the shapeless white smock. He loomed over her by almost three inches. She had ash blond hair and was wearing very expensive Italian shoes. Her dress was made of some clinging material, an effect which excited Chay (who had been known to have been excited by a glimpse of a Bedouin woman's ankle as she had faced a firing squad, by a pair of women's gloves in a trash can, in fact by any mention of the word "woman"). She has it all, he thought: great teeth, superb boobs, a terrific little ass, and, he was sure, a fine mind.

As they strolled they discussed where they would have the *kalbsbratwursts* cooked.

"I could say that we could go to my apartment and I could cook them for you," Hedda said tentatively.

"That is a *marvelous* idea!"

"Not on the first date. Never. I am too old-fashioned."

At Das Dinkelspiel, a German restaurant on Eighty-fourth Street, they were told sternly that it would violate the law if the restaurant consented to cook food which had been brought in by strangers. They were laughed out of the Lum Fong Chinese Restaurant on East Sixty-seventh Street when Chay asked them to prepare the sausages in the style of *moo goo gai pan*. He wasn't sure he remembered the designation at all correctly but it was fun to say and it impressed Hedda. But he had the nagging feeling that it had something to do with eggs.

They took a cab to a Greek restaurant on West Fifty-fourth which Hedda said she had enjoyed in the past. Unaccountably, she knew the chef (who looked like a clone of George V) who told them that to please Hedda, he would cook the *kalbsbratwursts* in *pastourna* style, with Greek black-rinded smoked bacon flavored ecstatically with garlic. They would also have some *mezes;* he kissed his fingers, in fact he would join them. Chay responded in a very odd manner. He said flatly that the flavor of the bacon and garlic would be too strong and would completely overwhelm the delicacy of the herbs and veal. He thanked Pappadakis abruptly and escorted Miss Blitzen out of the restaurant.

"But—why?" she asked reasonably. "He was willing to cook them."

"He behaved entirely too familiarly with you," Chay said. "It offended me. After all, he is staff."

Hedda suggested that they try Dea-bholadh, a Gaelic *proinn-teach* in Hell's Kitchen, but Chay wasn't having any more of her suggestions. He took over. They went to La Vieille Poule, an haute French restaurant off Fifth Avenue in the Fifties where they were ejected bodily into the street after they made their simple request.

It was an ugly scene, mitigated only by the earliness of the dining hour which assured the emptiness of the restaurant. Chay had extended the package of sausages to the waiter, explaining his requirement. The waiter had backed away from the package in revulsion. He went off, to return almost immediately with the maître d'hôtel.

"You will repeat to me," the maître d' said, "what you asked this man to do."

"Quite simple, really," Chay replied. "These are three *saucisses de veau*. I wish to have them cooked."

"*Sausages?* You come off the street into a temple of gastronomy and you want us to cook your sausages? Out! Out!" He grasped Chay by his coat collar and pulled him to his feet. He and the waiter began the bum's rush.

Chay struggled. He remonstrated. He swore at them with the scarifying skills of thirty-odd years of soldiering.

Hedda ran along beside them. "No, Chay! Please! Don't!" she pleaded. "It isn't worth it."

Almost instantly they found themselves in the street.

"I am not a vindictive man," Chay said as he helped Hedda to her feet on the pavement outside La Vieille Poule, making a rude gesture to the maître d'hôtel who was shouting hysterically at them in Algerian French from the doorway, "but someday I am going to make these people pay for this indignity."

In the end, before the sausages could spoil, Chay rented a suite in an enormous hotel. He gave the room service waiter ten dollars and explained that he wanted the sausages cooked and served. Gravely, the waiter asked how he would like to have them prepared. Chay deferred to Hedda.

"Chicken breasts stuffed with bratwurst is nice," she said demurely.

"My God!" Chay said.

"Or perhaps you'd enjoy a bratwurst omelet?"

Pale, Chay told the waiter to have the *kalbsbratwursts* parboiled for four minutes at simmer, then to grill them and serve them with smothered fried onions and some Dijon mustard.

They sat, side by side, on the large, long sofa. Chay held her hand. A reproduction of Warhol's *Campbell Soup Cans* hung on the wall behind them.

"I don't suppose you care," Hedda said dreamily, "but Homer mentioned sausages in the *Odyssey*. That was nine centuries before Christ."

"I hadn't known that, actually," Chay said.

"In *The Clouds*, Aristophanes says, 'Let them make sausage of me and serve me to the students.' "

"Sausages mean so much to you."

"I suppose they do."

"I wish I were a sausage that you might care that much for me."

"Oh, Chay!"

"I can't explain it, Hedda. Darling. May I call you darling?"

"Oh. Yes." Her voice had taken on a breathiness which made Chay feel both holy and carnal. "But what can't you explain?"

"That from the moment I saw you this afternoon, standing like Joan of Arc behind those piles of sausages, I have fallen deeply, hopelessly, and helplessly in love with you."

They lost all track of time after that. The room service waiter returned with his rolling hot table but they were no longer in the main room of the suite. He left the *kalbsbratwursts* on warm and let himself out of the room.

Chay and Hedda screwed the night away, and during the rare moments when they were capable of speaking, they took dimensional vows of endless love for each other, and hours later, nibbled on the sausages ravenously. He told her he was just a simple soldier back from the wars. She wept. Having never been allowed a television set, therefore having no idea of the monstrous stature of his celebrity, she had formed the impression (from his hat) that he was a top insurance man or, perhaps, a powerful stockbroker.

All through the early summer, in beds, laying across billiard tables, jammed into telephone booths, or in the backs of hansom cabs clopping around Central Park, they ate *kalbsbratwurst* and made love while Chay pleaded with Hedda to marry him. But he had made the masculine error of appearing for their second date wearing his full uniform with decorations, and she was put off. At nineteen, she was in an antiwar phase. His sudden appearance as a soldier shocked her. His hopes for marriage with her had to be abandoned for the moment, but he moved into her apartment. They had a wonderful seven weeks together, moments which were to stay with them for the rest of their lives. Hedda lived to be ninety-three years old. She wrote four moving and beautiful books about Chay Appleton. The little story of the *kalbsbratwursts*, when the world was young, is among the sweetest and most evocatively tender memories in that timeless record.

6

T WO DAYS BEFORE the orders came through assigning him to the staff of Lieutenant General F. M. "Big Fist" Winikus, commanding general of the Forces Command at Fort McPherson near Atlanta, Brill told Chay that she had become engaged to be married to Wambly Keifetz, longtime adviser to presidents and a patron of the arts.

"He's that rich fat guy, isn't he?" Chay asked.

"He's a large man, yes. At least compared to you he's a large man, and I don't see the sense in marrying someone who is poor."

"I want to meet him."

"What's come over you?"

"I am the head of the family and I want to meet the man you say you intend to marry."

"Don't be an ass, Chay. Just because I got engaged and you weren't able to get engaged because the girl can't stand soldiers."

Chay had redoubled the ardor of his proposals to Hedda, but although she sobbed all through saying it, and through a lot of the copulating which followed, she turned him down. "I could not—cannot—marry a man whose profession is killing," she said.

"My profession is defense!" Chay said indignantly. "What will do you when the Nicaraguans invade if there aren't trained men such as me and Colonel North to shoot them down or to shred them?"

Heartbrokenly, she refused to marry him.

The Forces Command was in charge of all troops in the United States and was in defense of the United States mainland. Its commanding general, F. M. "Big Fist" Winikus, had been a legendary fullback at West Point and had been affectionately regarded by the Army ever since. Everyone was pulling for him to make it to retirement, so that his upgrade in rank to General of the Armies during the Sandinista wars and his improved pension could be secured despite his continuing rough bouts with surgery, arthritis, hypertension, psoriasis, obesity, vertebral crash collapse, an aneurism of the aorta, heavy arterial plaque, incipient cataracts, a trabeculated bladder, a left branch bundle block, liver hardening, and severe asthmatic problems. The Army, which took care of its own, felt that a really glamorous soldier, such as Chay, would tend to take attention away from General Winikus's infirmities. Within two years of his arrival at the post, Chay was promoted to Major General and named as the Big Fist's Chief of Staff.

Winikus had gotten his nickname from a severe anal fistula which had flared up during the final quarter of a 1954 Army-Navy game when Winikus had scored two winning touchdowns before he had fainted from the discomfort.

Chay took over his assignment as Chief of Staff of the Forces Command on March 18, 1990, the day before Winikus left for Washington for an outpatient medical recheck at Walter Reed and for meetings with old buddies at the Pentagon, as well as for a few cautious drinks with protective sports writers at the National Press Club, which had been set up by the Army's Office of Public Affairs.

At 11:04 A.M. on that day, a catastrophic nuclear device was exploded in Washington, wiping out the District of Columbia and evaporating 1,397,200 people. The catastrophe vanished the White House, demolished the Capitol, and caused all but one national government building, the headquarters of the Central Intelligence Agency at Langley, Virginia, to disappear. The total destruction was doubly regrettable because the United States was unable to blame the Soviet Union for it. All nuclear weapons had been abolished on Christmas Day, 1989; NATO had been dissolved; and the U.S. troops on station in Europe had begun to return to the United States. At home, the country had 2,894,600 men and women under arms, all of them under the Forces Command, which was now Chay Appleton's because there was no authority left which could supersede him.

The District of Columbia, despite the fact that the device had been relatively "clean," had produced enough radiation to require that area to be made out-of-bounds for a half-life of ninety-seven years.

While the Big Fist was lifting his first heavily watered bourbon and recalling glorious moments of that historic Army-Navy game of '54, the bomb went off. As far as could be determined it had been detonated inside the White House because satellite photographs showed that the 12¾-mile-wide crater was deepest at the point where the White House had stood.

In the first announcement, the Royalist Party had shared credit for the wipeout of the nation's capital (referred to as "the incident") with the National Rifle Association. When the story broke nationally, the remaining regional headquarters of the NRA hotly and bitterly denied the heinous charge, but the public knew it was still smarting over the last-minute amendment to the Kirk-Mendelson bill, passed the year before, which had banned the sale of new flamethrowers to householders, limiting the legal number to the 311,008 then in circulation.

Immediately after the unjust charges of having collaborated

in the evaporation of Washington, the NRA lost .006 percent of its membership.

Just as the salvo of aerial bombs dropped on Hamburg in World War II killed 42,000 people, the atomic bomb dropped on Hiroshima was twenty times more powerful. With its increased efficiency, despite its smaller size, the SHAM exploded in the White House was perhaps twenty times more powerful than the Hiroshima bomb because all the uranium in the Hiroshima bomb had not been utilized. SHAM stood for Special Hydrogen Atom Munition, an evolution from the SADM which had been designed by combat engineers to cause landslides, to level mountains, and otherwise to disturb the terrain grievously. Busy hands had kept making it more and more powerful.

The measure of which the White House SHAM disturbed the terrain of history is incalculable. It was to bring the Royalist Party to power in the United States. The Royalists had best access to where the American people lived; that vast diamond-bright area of daytime television and prime time soap. In the short time since, the Reagan administration—that shining definition of reigning glamor and romance associated with queens, big money, great dressmakers, great poverty, colorful (moderate) mullahs, glamorous (if shocking) scandals and entertaining South American drug lords—had overtaken the national imagination of a society which had been compartmentalized by money.

Liberty and leadership, so long taken for granted, competed with television, nonparticipatory sex, credit card compulsions, television, relentlessly grinning politicians, and year-round Christmas shopping. The massive feelings toward Royalty had been helped along by the Royalist Party's $35 million annual public relations budget, tax-deductible as a business expense by its collective sponsors. It was to transform unreconstructed political Conservatives, those super-patriots who opposed legalized abortion because abortion could threaten the supply of cheap labor.

Dukedoms, marquisates, earldoms, baronies, and knighthoods were at stake. Stockbrokers' and Cadillac-dealership wives stared at their husbands imploringly over breakfast to bring home an acceptable title. The yuppie virus, which had been fed by the decade of Ron and Nancy, the bull market, and eight unrelenting years of political fantasy, struck as AIDS had struck. It was the possibility of registered aristocracy which assured the success of the American Royalist Party. So, the Evaporation served to spice up the evening news and seemed, to almost everyone, to be a deplorable thing so long as the new team didn't get it into their heads that they could raise taxes.

From the instant the news of the terrible national tragedy was flashed across the country, all Americans went into deep mourning for three days which was as long as the experienced television industry had ever been able to measure their attention span before other "news" events had to be introduced to amuse them. "News" events were daily mass exorcisms which had been innovated by the Reagan Administration (1981–1989): the constant moral bloopers; the Grenada mockery; the Lebanese disasters; the Iran-Contra scandals; the Persian Gulf debacles; the Libya fixation; the Supreme Court appointments messes; Congressional committee exposures; the charges, arraignments, and indictments of high Federal officials beyond any count of corruption in White House history, all of it made subtly glamorous by trivializing it with the word "sleaze"; the almost insurmountable budget deficit which the elderly president kicked higher every day, grinning his Harold Teen grin, so proud of his tailoring; all of it to keep the electorate from catching on that they were being imperiled by their government and the increasingly unregulated marketplace.

The wrap-up of the Evaporation was a token funeral, staged for the television networks in Philadelphia, cradle of democracy, officially burying the government and the Constitution of the United States as the people had thought they had known it.

Liz Wantonberg, idol of millions, star of stage, screen, and prime time, read the moving lines from Matthew Arnold's "Dover Beach" over the token coffin which represented the 1.2 million dead of Washington and its immediate suburbs. Thrillingly, the poem commemorated their mortality, as well as American life since Ronald Reagan:

Ah, love, let us be true
To one another! for the world, which seems

To lie before us like a land of dreams,
So various, so beautiful, so new,
Hath really neither joy, nor love, nor light,
Nor certitude, nor peace, nor help for pain;
And we are here as on a darkling plain
Swept with confused alarms of struggle and
    flight,
Where ignorant armies clash by night.

The bronze coffin which symbolically contained the American government was lowered at the first light of dawn into a steel time capsule at the foot of what would one day be a 1,990-foot-high cenotaph which was to be a translucent shaft of light which reached for the stars. America wept.

A blue heron, a hurtling spear with wings, flew toward the shout of morning. The light was spread evenly, clinging wherever there was no shadow. Honks of geese flew panic somewhere while a northeast wind remembered Norway. The bomb had opened a door to another summer day in eternity. The world, itself so many worlds apart from itself, shook off the gray fog veil. What could be more real to time than obliteration?

God woke himself with his own snoring then heard the rustling of wings in the angel cote. He opened the door to let them float down upon the universe. He could hear Lucifer humming "Onward Christian Soldiers"; always joking. He'd have to check the plumbing before he dyed the night with day. There was a lot to do—forty million houseflies to fashion before he could blow the tons of down upon the necks of newborn showgirls or get out the coat of stars for the looming young evening which was on its way in and was about to ask Dad if it could borrow the car.

7

DURING THE LAST MORNING of Chay's surrogate command of the Forces Command, while General Winikus was conferring in Washington, Chay was in a heavy discussion of ordinance. His beeper went off. It was an urgent call from the Director of the National Security Agency at Fort Meade, Maryland. Chay went to a secure phone. He called the NSA.

"General Appleton?"

"Yes."

"Please wait for voiceprint identification, sir." There was a wait of thirty-eight seconds. "Confirmed, sir. Are you in Building 6 at McPherson?"

"Fahcrissake!"

"A chopper is waiting just outside, sir. It will take you to a fighter-bomber which will fly you to the Director's office."

The plane landed Chay at Fort George Meade, halfway between Washington and Baltimore, twenty-two miles from Washington, site of the headquarters of the U.S. First Army which guarded the star tenant on the property, the National Security Agency, the largest single espionage factory the world had ever known or could imagine. The fort was located where it was because the wise heads in government had reasoned that whereas an enemy might attack Washington, they probably would overlook a li'l ole installation twenty-two miles away. The fact was, if they had moved the complex several hundred miles away from the prime target, all the employees of NSA would have quit to look for other jobs because they would have preferred to stay in Washington.

Chay was met at the second chopper by a Deputy Director NSA who hung a color-coded, computer-punched, plastic-laminated security badge around Chay's neck. They were passed through three hedges of fourteen-foot-high electrified cyclone fences. In the ten-yard-wide areas between the fences, patrols with snarling attack dogs were on the move. On high poles closed-circuit television cameras with telephoto lenses peered downward, rotating to scan all the area. They entered the building through Gatehouse I, the only gate leading to the Pit, as the Director's office was called.

In the gatehouse, they were passed through a checkpoint where two Federal Protective Security guards checked that the faces on the badges corresponded to the faces on the bodies. They were moved into a brilliantly lighted reception area where Chay's sponsor signed for him and reidentified him despite the dizzying heights of Chay's celebrity and security clearance. He was issued a 4" × 2" red and white striped badge which carried a terrible warning against misuse on its back.

Tagged and escorted by the two armed men, Chay passed through the initial check at the Headquarters Building and was taken into the lobby past the Great Seal of the Agency, imbedded into the wall and depicting a threatening eagle clutching a large skeleton key in its talons. Chay entered the high-speed private elevator with the guards, descended fourteen floors into the earth, then was taken along a corridor to a bright blue door decorated with the Agency seal, Room 14B197, the Office of the Director of the National Security Agency.

General Frederic Goldberg, a Brigadier the day before, now a (breveted) Major General in the United States Army, sat behind the Director's desk.

"Freddie!" Chay bleated. "What are you doing here?"

"I'm the new Director of NSA."

"What happened to Admiral Fulton?"

"She went to Washington this morning."

"So?"

"Washington has been evaporated by a nuclear device. And I was Fulton's first deputy, wasn't I?"

"A *nuclear* device?"

"Chay—Washington is gone. The Pentagon is gone. The source of everything—everything—has been wiped out."

"Those fucking Nicaraguans!" Chay yelled.

"Nothing like that."

"Who else could it be?"

"We recorded a telephone signal from a public booth in Reading, Pennsylvania. It was a call to *W* magazine."

"W?"

"Stands for Wealth. It's a trade paper for the great dressmakers."

"I don't get it."

"The Royalist Party is taking credit for the strike. W had to explain that they are a bimonthly, but they said they would pass the item along to the Society Editor of *The New York Times*."

"Aaaaah!" Chay said, suddenly understanding what was going down. "Then you ran a voiceprint check?"

"Bet yer ass. It was a man named Wambly Keifetz, a Wall Street multibillionaire who is into everything, who is always identified terrifyingly by the press as 'a friend of presidents.' "

Chay made a strangled sound.

"Keifetz personally blew up Washington, D.C., and evaporated every installation of the government except the CIA."

"Holy shit!"

"What?"

"My sister is married to Keifetz."

"Tell the chaplain. Keifetz was on the appointments schedule at the White House this morning."

"A whole new ball game."

The Director smiled frostily. "The Royalists stand for one king who sees that his courtiers are taken care of. No Congressional or Constitutional interference, no horseshit about We, the People. It is strictly PR and looting all the way. Ronald Reagan's dream."

"So? I'll arrest the son of a bitch."

"This is bigger than both of us, Chay. We're going to have to improvise. The people who own this country will finally see a chance to become dukes and earls and barons. Their wives are probably foaming right now."

"What are you saying?"

"Chay—the Army is in charge of the country as of this moment. And you are the survivor who is in charge of the Army."

"My God, the Big Fist! He was in Washington this morning!"

"We have that. So you are running the Forces Command with no need to wait for orders because there's no one left to issue them. The Pentagon was flattened with the rest of it."

Chay sank into a large leather chair. "Now he's never going

to get his pension. Jesus, the whole Army was working to hold him together to get him his pension."

"Look at it this way. By now, his essence is floating in the jet stream 112 miles above Yugoslavia. And he'll never have to take another pill."

"But who's going to pay for the Army? The gasoline alone! I gotta get to a phone. Get me an office and send down Colonel Coomber. They have him up in reception. He has to organize fast to take over all civilian communications and have all travel frozen until I get the contingency plans in place."

"I can't even imagine it," General Goldberg said. "No TV commercials for twenty-four hours. It could start a revolution."

"When we have cordoned off the District, organized the media, shot a few looters, and sanitized the contaminated area, I am going into New York to pick up that fat son of a bitch Wambly Keifetz."

8

CHAY GAVE THE DETAILS of cauterizing the District of Columbia wound to the staff people and the First Army. He was ready to go to New York at six A.M. the following morning. He had payrolls to meet and no Treasury Department to meet it. He had called the Chairman of the Federal Reserve Bank in New York and had convened a meeting with its governors at 7:15 A.M. then flew out to Greenwich, Connecticut, aboard a fighter-bomber.

He called Brill from the plane. "Can you set up a meeting with your husband at ten o'clock this morning?"

"What is this all about?"

"Washington was evaporated yesterday."

"I don't understand."

"Tell him the commanding general of the Forces Command of the United States, acting for an American government, wants to talk with him. I'll be there at ten." He disconnected.

The New York bank was one of twelve Reserve Banks in the system, carrying out day-to-day operations: circulating currency and providing fiscal agency functions and payments mechanism services. The seven-member board was seated somberly around the long meeting table when Chay came into the room with a black major, two noncoms who were so brutal-looking that they could have come from Central Casting, and four men armed with automatic rifles.

The Reserve board had assumed that because of their individual and collective incomes, they had been chosen as financial leaders by the military to form a new national government. They appreciated that the meeting had been called for 7:15 A.M., well before the stock market opened, so that they would be able to take measures to make enormous personal profits by selling short when the news of the evaporation of Washington hit Wall Street and to try to control wild trading because of the impossibility of government intervention.

Chay was in the fullest of full uniform with his medals, citations, and ribbons, which extended downward along his left chest for thirteen rows, lighting him up like a Christmas tree. He wasted no time.

He stood at the head of the table. The sergeants stood at either side of the exit. The black major glowered, standing behind the Chairman's seat at the far end of the table. The armed men stood at parade rest along the left wall of the large room.

"I shouldn't be surprised if you people had the terrible news sooner than I did," Chay said.

"We know about Washington," the chairman said.

"The Pentagon, and all of its records, is gone," Chay told them. "The Treasury was evaporated. The policy-making apparatus of your own Federal Reserve System has been vanished. But the United States Army, the Air Force, the Navy, the Marine Corps, and the Coast Guard remain to defend this country in the absence of any other government. So we are here to discuss only two of the consequences of the disaster: one, the protection of the American people and their property; two, how we are going to pay for that protection."

The Chairman spoke. "You don't expect us to pay for them, do you, General?"

"Something like that. But your time is too valuable to waste with chatting. The economy could bust wide open." He nodded to a sergeant at the door. "Take them out," he said.

The sergeant moved into the room. Two of the armed enlisted men stepped forward. They took three bankers out from the left side of the table, moving them through the open door then closing it behind them. There were controlled, gentlemanly sounds of protest but they were gone almost before anyone realized what had happened.

"What are you doing, General?" the Chairman asked with alarm.

"A force of over three million Army, Navy, and Air Force personnel needs to be paid. My suggestion to you is that you arrange things so that we can meet these payments. Otherwise, I am going to have to shoot those people. Then, if necessary, I will shoot you."

"Surely there is an alternative?"

"Yes. If you should decide that you are all expendable, the country will face the problem of 1.2 million combat-sharp troops stationed here being forced to live off the land, as we say. Part of the land we would have to live off would be the banks. To keep operating, we would need to form some sort of government so that we could install some crude system of taxation. I must have an answer by five o'clock today."

9

CHAY ARRIVED at the ninety-eight-acre Keifetz compound in Greenwich in an Army helicopter which held six armed soldiers and a sergeant. They were taken to Flag House, the Keifetz hobby-haunt, in four golf carts. Flag House was a smallish outbuilding which was well-separated from the main house but connected with it by an all-weather underground tunnel. Chay and his seven escorts were admitted by an expressionless houseman who welcomed Chay gravely, told him he was expected, took his hat, then made as if to lead him across the entresol toward the flag room which was in the far corner of the building. Chay stopped him momentarily to say that he wanted a room where the detail could be made comfortable. "I will serve them tea, sir," the houseman said.

It was an extraordinarily palatial interior layout for such an unpretentious one-and-a half-story building. It had its own cross-bow range. It had eighteen-foot-high ceilings. Paintings by masters of the Renaissance were hung on wall after wall. Chay had remembered what he had heard about Keifetz, in particular a marvelously malicious story about a Keifetz apartment in New York where, along one (relatively) narrow corridor, he had hung a War-hol silk screen of heads of Marilyn Monroe between a Titian and a miraculously elegant portrait of St. Agnes in Agony by Zurbarán; how his toilet bowls and toothbrush handles were made of gold; how he piled priceless Persian carpets helter-skelter on top of each other for seven thicknesses of conspicuous consumption; and how he always kept two grades of cocaine for his guests, run-of-the-mill stuff for casual drop-ins and really good blow in the upstairs drawing room for his close friends.

The late President, the Cabinet, the Joint Chiefs, and dozens of senators had been his close friends and where had that gotten them?

Brilliana Appleton-Keifetz was seated at a harp, not playing it because she didn't know how to play it, but she sat as a serene witness to the conversation which was about to start, smiling at her brother.

She thought about her courtship. It had been the most, if not the only, romantic time of Brill's life. She had been seeing Keifetz off and on for two years. He had taken her to concerts, to the opera, to tightly organized picnics with a rigorously selected group of friends whom Brill was later to learn were all paid bodyguards. They had been "good friends," exchanging Christmas and Arbor Day cards but little more. The only times they had ever been alone together were in the vast tonneaus of the various Keifetz limousines where there had always been an armed chauffeur and a footman beyond the separation in the front seat.

Then one afternoon she had a call from David Hanly, the chief Keifetz bodyguard whom she had always imagined to be Keifetz's closest friend, not knowing of the employer-employee relationship at all, asking if she could have her lawyer present at her apartment at four o'clock that afternoon. Brill agreed. She was mystified, but she agreed.

At four o'clock, with A. Edward Masters at her side, Brill received the three senior partners of Mayers, Scanlan and Chapman, a Wall Street law firm having 723 lawyers. Masters automatically calculated silently that, combined, the three men would have to charge their client $2,734.65 an hour. Tea was served, then Bertram A. Mayers, the most senior of the senior partners, cleared his throat like a drum roll at an execution.

"We are here, Miss Appleton—Counselor—on behalf of our client, Wambly Keifetz, to propose marriage to you on his behalf."

Brill gasped. "Marriage? But—"

"Mr. Keifetz is an extremely busy man. It is understood that you will want time to think about this; therefore we have prepared this simple option agreement for your consideration which will cover the engagement period suggested."

"May I have the agreement, Counselor?" A. Edward Masters asked.

"Indeed yes, Counselor." He turned to Scanlan who turned to Chapman who opened a $2,785.25 attaché case and removed three copies of the single document it contained. Mayers extended one copy to Brill who sat, slightly dazed, behind a massive tea cosy placed upon an exquisite Adam serving table which had been a remembrance of the previous Flag Day from Wambly Keifetz. Mayers gave the second copy to A. Edward Masters and held the third copy for himself. All three read the document while the other two partners sipped tea and discussed a possible leveraged buy out merger of India with Scotland.

The document was only five pages long. It said, in part,

This will confirm the agreement between Wambly Keifetz IV (Proposer) and Brilliana Appleton (Fiancée) concerning, among other things, a marriage between the two parties.

1. From this date continuing thereafter for a period of one (1) month, the Proposer has an exclusive, irrevocable option ("Option") to acquire all rights (except for certain filial rights held by her immediate family which are reserved to Fiancée), subject to the right for the Proposer to dine with the Fiancée not more than four times a week, in a public restaurant, and on returning the Fiancée to her residence in the City of New York, State of New York, to give/receive not less than one "goodnight kiss" but not more than two kisses. For the period of this option, the Fiancée shall retain all other rights to her physical person, such rights to be released to the Proposer only by full written agreement of the Fiancée.

2. In consideration of the above, the Proposer shall offer to the Fiancée one (1) diamond engagement ring having a market value of $227,954.85 to be worn for the period of hiatus between the Fiancée's acceptance of the proposal of marriage and the actual marriage itself. In the event that the Fiancée does not fulfill the agreement to marry after she has accepted the proposal of marriage, she hereby agrees to return the ring to the law firm of Mayers, Scanlan and Chapman at 40 Wall Street, City of New York, State of New York, and renounce any further claims thereto.

3. If the Proposer acquires the Fiancée, the Proposer shall have the exclusive, irrevocable right to extend the option to a marriage between the Proposer and the Fiancée and by the payment of one dollar ($1.00) hereby given in hand from the Proposer to the Fiancée who shall renounce any and all claims which may arise out of the conditions of this option agreement and to any and all consequences therefrom.

4. This option agreement if consummated will be replaced
entirely by a marriage agreement which will specify each and
every limitation on any damages whatever which the Fiancée
may presume to have happened to her as a result of the
aforesaid marriage.

Brill and her attorney read the agreement through in silence,
except for the occasional gasp from Brill. Then at last breaking the
silence which followed the reading, Brill said humbly, "I am deeply
moved."

Keifetz was wholly engaged with business matters in Paki-
stan, Manitoba, the Seychelles, and the USSR all during the period
of the option; therefore, he and Brill did not see each other during
that month and therefore none of the contractual kisses were exchanged. However, on the twenty-seventh day, three days before
the option would have expired, A. Edward Masters notified Mayers, Scanlan and Chapman that Miss Appleton had accepted Mr.
Keifetz's proposal of marriage.

The legal marriage ceremony was held in the Oval Office of
the White House, conducted by the Chief Justice of the United
States Supreme Court in the presence of two witnesses: the President and the Vice President of the United States. The First Lady
was matron of honor and Jerry Zipkin was best man. The social
ceremony was consecrated one day later at the Keifetz compound
in Greenwich, Connecticut, in the presence of the editors of
W magazine and the National Review, 38 television cameras, 209
members of the print press, extensive radio coverage, and Oprah
Winfrey. The bride's mother and father attended with 719 other
distinguished guests. Insurance company evaluation of the value
of the wedding presents received was $2,391,572.83. After the
ceremony, the bride and groom went off to a small country in
Central America which the groom had given to his young wife as
a wedding present.

10

WAMBLY KEIFETZ IV was the great-grandson of the founder of the Bahama Beaver Bonnet Company, the world's largest construction, engineering, aerospace, energy, electronics, and communications conglomerate, which employed 169,278 people on megaprojects worth billions of dollars in dozens of countries. It had laid pipelines in Saudi Arabia, Peru, Germany, and Switzerland. It had dug phosphorus, zirconium, iron, nickel, and copper mines in South Africa; designed and built smelters in Chile, Mauritania, and Ireland; nuclear plants in Spain and India; hydroelectric complexes in New Zealand and Newfoundland, and a giant hydroelectic power plant in Quebec which generated 5.25 kilowatts of power and had created a reservoir more than half the size of Lake Ontario. It built reactors, subways, factories, hospitals, ships, airports, a towering city in Brazil, and Jubal, the Saudi Arabian industrial complex which had cost more than the entire U.S. space program. Its oil refinery construction in the Middle East had made OPEC possible. Its constructions throughout Libya had furthered the rise of Mu'ammar Qaddafi and therefore the prosperity of the IRA in Northern Ireland and the *plastique* industry in the United States.

At home, it had been "a strongest influence" on presidents since Chester A. Arthur. At any given time, the Bahama Beaver Bonnet Company, wholly owned by the family's sole survivor, Wambly Keifetz IV, was engaged in building, conspiring, selling, and traducing in never less than twenty countries of the world, averaging 102 megaprojects each year with an average value of $90 million each. When the balance sheet for its current operating year would finally be tallied, the BBBC would report earnings of $17.9 billion.

Bahama Beaver executives were interchangeable with the cabinets of American presidents. The company was closely allied with the CIA, having employed three of its Directors as consultants and having been a business partner of one of them. Shuttling the heads

of the powerful Export-Import Bank which controlled the financing
to the Third World governments as if it were scrip at the BBBC
company store had resulted in huge BBBC construction projects
in the Philippines, Iran, Eygpt, Algeria, and Indonesia, as well as
nuclear projects in Spain, Korea, India, Taiwan, and Brazil, all of
it underwritten by $7 billion of Export-Import Bank financing.

At the urgent suggestion of Bahama Beaver which provided
the evidence that Iran was about to accept a Soviet offer to build
a pipeline the CIA undertook "Operation Ajax" which overthrew
the legal government of Iran and restored Shah Mohammad Reza
Pahlavi to the Peacock Throne. Bahama Beaver built all the oil
installations which Iran required. At BBBC's urging, the CIA had
ousted President Sukarno of Indonesia and replaced him with
President Suharto who proved to be far more amenable to BBBC
interests.

Its fortunes had been enhanced by extremely helpful advice
from amiable and ever-ready presidents of the United States. By
choosing the right sort of employee/friend/consultant, Bahama
Beaver had kept its old markets while opening new ones which
landed billions of dollars in contracts all over the planet. The movement of executives between public and private life was the most
vital part of the Bahama Beaver pattern because megaprojects required public money no matter where they were built.

The company, shaped by four generations of Keifetzes, as
well as being the major player in nuclear power and oil/gas industries, owned the three most prominent investment banking
and brokerage firms on Wall Street. "Had the company existed at
the time of the Pharoahs," the present Keifetz had often said, "we
would have had the contract for the pyramids." Twenty-three
officers of the company had served in the U.S. Senate; sixty-one
in the House of Representatives. Fourteen Bahama Beaver men
and women had been Secretaries of State, Defense, Treasury, and
Interior, or Assistant Secretaries of State, Defense, Treasury, and
Interior. Two BBBC men had served as presidential Chiefs of Staff.

Wambly Keifetz IV was fifty-four years old, four times a wid-
ower, the second-richest man in the world, lacking only that extra
two billion to overtake an octogenarian Bochica Indian in Colombia
who was El Supremo in cocaine production. Keifetz, despite Yale
and the best preparatory schools, had a farting kind of vulgarity

which endeared him to his courtiers, and he had an inexhaustible energy for deviousness. This, with inspired lying and bottomless dissimulation, had shaped his soul until it bulged at all the wrong places. He was surrounded by hustlers, lost women, villains, fixers, and the sort of people whose only possible grounds for sympathy could be if they had recontracted AIDS.

Keifetz stood for Flag, Family, and Country. He was ardently committed to the Flag to which he referred affectionately as "Old Tootsie," and he led the sixty-seven-person staff at Keifetz Hall, Greenwich, each morning in singing the national anthem, controlled by pitch pipe, followed by a massed Pledge of Allegiance in Latin, the original form of the oath as it had been taken daily by the Roman legionaries under Julius Caesar in 40 B.C. with: "I pledge allegiance to the balance of trade and to the Export-Import Bank for which it stands. For tax loopholes indivisible with a kiss-off and a promise for all."

Every word he uttered was patriotic. He *owned* patriotism, much in the manner that the lunatic Right had owned it in the 1980s. It cost nothing and its upkeep was entirely at other people's expense.

The houseman led Chay into a long, wide interior workroom at whose end loitered two burly, not to say lumpy, men outside the library door. The houseman knocked discreetly, waited, then opened the door and passed Chay into the room, lined with floor-to-ceiling shelves of leather-bound books, and occupied by many leather-bound chairs and sofas where Wambly Keifetz was working at a spinning wheel making fine linen thread from 100 percent native flax which he would loom with his own hands into another American flag.

Brill sat reposefully, as alert as a tape recorder. This was the first time she had ever been alone in a room with the two most important men in her life. She had to will herself not to sweat but she remembered the deep past because she could never forget it.

11

BRILLIANA KEIFETZ-APPLETON had fallen in love with her twin brother in the summer of 1965 when they were fifteen years old. That had not changed. "He is so sweet and dumb,"she wrote in her instantly disposable diary, naming no names. She couldn't decide how to handle her emotions. He was her brother, her *twin* brother, but Appletons, she decided, should prefer Appletons. By that definition, Chay was the only possibility if she were ever to be rid of her damned virginity. Dudley was a lump and Sylvester was an aberration. Neither one had any sexual reason for being, as far as she could see, but Chay's energy was so intense that it surely must have a prodigious effect upon his sexuality, she had reasoned.

Brill was a startlingly golden, beautiful child in a languorous body whose eyes were in a desperate hurry. She had accumulated stores of misinformation about life from schoolmates, as other people had. If Chay was military-naive, Brill was street-naive. She had a passionate nose, wide, rubbery lips, and a body like an Amati violin. She would have been a delightful girl if one were able to sidestep the inevitable distaste for her avidity for money and power. Just as his mother was an unattainable object to Chay, for more concrete reasons Serena was Brill's shining example of what not to be, but inexorably she had inherited her mother's money lust and steamroller ego. Even at fifteen she had shown the beginnings of a bosom which would one day be hallowed by collectors of that sort of thing.

Keifetz was wearing L. L. Bean moccasins, gray flannel trousers with emblematic silver fly buttons which carried his prep school insignia, and a navy double-breasted blazer with his old school badge stitched on the outside over his heart. He looked up from the work he was doing as Chay came in. He smiled his lopsided yuppie smile from his purple, beefy face, and said, "I am spinning the thread which will replicate the first Stars and

Stripes which was flown in battle by our land forces, the famous '76 flag flown at Bennington on August 16, 1777."

"No kidding?" Chay said, wholly unimpressed. Chay had deeply Freudian reasons for his distaste of Keifetz, whose origins went back over many years. He was pressingly aware of Brill's presence.

"You will remember its outer stripes were white and the stars had seven points."

"I didn't know that."

"There are some who consider that this was the first Stars and Stripes to have thirteen stars, but the flag historians are unclear on that. I quote the American authority, M. M. Quaife, who wrote, 'Homer, alive, attracted but scant attention; when safely dead and asssured of immortality, numerous Grecian cities eagerly claimed him as their son.' As for the design and commission of the first American flag, Mr. Quaife says that no one bothered at the time to record the name of its creator, or to claim the honor for himself."

"I thought George Washington had commissioned it."

"I'm afraid not."

"But what about Betsy Ross?"

"My dear General—Mr. Quaife says that no one really knows and he is the authority. I mean—it would have to have taken a committee to decide on the design of anything as important as the American flag, wouldn't it? And in Abner Stein's biography of Betsy Ross he proves that she was too nearsighted even to be able to thread a needle at the time of her life when she was said to have made the first flag."

Chay suddenly realized how much he detested this man. Remembering what he was there for, his eyes went opaque. His expression was set at neutral. It had been one thing to speak scornfully about the Royalists with Freddie Goldberg. They had been moiling around Ron and Nancy all during the Reagan days. But it was another thing to shake hands and sit down with the son of a bitch who had set off a nuclear bomb in the White House, an insane little shit who had blown away the entire capital of the United States. Chay was so grossly offended that he was forced to think of his mother to make himself stay icy cool.

This was the publicly invisible leader of the American Yuppie movement; accumulator of the highest 10 percent of American wealth earned within one generation and therefore chieftain of the larger group below him. Combined, the net financial worth of both groups amounted to $2.4 trillion. Keifetz was in the top 2 percent of these, the group who owned 30 percent of all national liquid assets: 50 percent of the corporate stocks owned by individuals, 39 percent of all corporate and government bonds, 71 percent of tax-exempt municipals, and 23 percent of all real estate in the country. The simple faith this brought to Keifetz gave him grandiosity and a singular lack of guilt.

Keifetz did not attempt to get up as Chay came in. Brill made small talk. Chay tried to smile which locked on as a sneer. Chay's expression, despite himself, shifted from neutral to hostile. He refused to take Keifetz's extended hand. Keifetz got the point and struggled to his feet.

Just looking at the man, Chay felt nauseated and murderous at the same time. He had spent all of his time in the U.S. Army fighting little brown Nicaraguans all over the world, tens of thousands of them. Now he was facing an enemy who made the Sandinistas seem as if he had been wasting his time; one man, just one monstrous yuppie, who had obliterated the government of the United States.

Brill curtsied to Keifetz, as was the Royalist custom, and turned to leave the room, moving backward, saying, as she left, "There's plenty of cognac and cigars, and Wambly, would you like some spaghetti tacos?"

"Please, don't leave," Chay said to Brill. "What I have to say won't take long."

She looked at Keifetz. He nodded. She returned to her chair at the harp. She remembered the deep past.

While the two men talked, possibly about flags, Brill stared hungrily at Chay and remembered.

12

DURING THE SPRING VACATION of 1966 Brilliana had walked in on Chay as he was beginning a shower bath. He was naked; a miniature of a muscled, disciplined warrior's body. Brill was glistening with a light sweat. When she complained about the heat, Chay had absentmindedly invited her into the shower with him. It was a normal family thing to do in the Appleton household. Serena had taught her children that the human body was nothing to be ashamed of. In hot weather, parents and children had walked throughout the house as naked as porn stars.

Brill got out of her clothes and into the shower. They took turns under the cold water, then Chay said, "Stand still, you little mouse, and I'll soap your back."

"Look who's calling who little."

It was heavenly. She told herself whenever she needed to bring back the wonderful feeling that she could still feel his hands on her as she stood lusting for him to soap her front as well. The shower had been over in moments, but whenever she called it up again, it still made her mouth dry with desire. By the time she was seventeen she decided she had to do something about her feelings.

It was 1:20 in the morning in the Appleton house in Alexandria. Each Appleton had a separate bedroom. When Brill was sure they were all asleep, she left her room wearing a translucent night dress. She went along the hall to her father's room where he was sitting up in bed in a complete cocaine daze. He really wasn't there at all. The glaze over his opened eyes looked ten feet thick. Brill unzipped his fly and pulled at his white shorts until they showed like foam against his dark trousers. She stepped back from the bed and screamed like a lunch whistle. Her father opened his eyes and seemed to consider the sound.

Her mother burst into the room. She stared at Brill then her eyes moved to the bed and the heinous opening in her husband's trousers.

"What happened? What are you doing in here, Brill?"

"Daddy said he needed me. He called me in here and—and then he tried to—oh, Mama!"

"Whaaaaat?"

Sylvester and Berry came rushing in, yelling "What happened?" in unison. Adam Appleton managed to sit up on the side of the bed as Dudley and Jonathan flung themselves into the space remaining. Serena was staring with horror at Brill.

Brill said to all of them, "Daddy said—he said he was going to stab me with a fleshy dagger."

"Brilliana!" her mother screamed.

They all stared at Adam Appleton with loathing.

"Whassamatta?" he asked, staring from face to face.

Brill put all of her mental power into concentrating on moving her mother to say what she wanted to make her say, but Berry said it.

"We've got to get Chay here," she said. "Chay will know how to handle this."

"Why?" Dudley yelled. Dudley was 100 percent anti-Chay.

"Because he is a trained soldier," Serena snapped, "and soldiers have to make decisions which no one here is able to do."

"In the meantime," Sylvester said, "Father and I will remain locked in this room and pray."

"My poor baby," Serena sobbed, pulling Brill into her chest.

"Mama! Please! Call Chay." Brill was able to burst into tears.

Keifetz resettled himself again. "What's on your mind, General?" he asked.

"I am here to arrest you for the destruction of the District of Columbia with an outlawed nuclear device," Chay said simply.

Brill gasped as if she could empty the room of oxygen with that one shocked intake.

Keifetz extended a silver humidor of forbidden Havana cigars whose aroma alone could have sold for $150 an ounce. Chay selected one, bit off its end, and put the end into an ash tray. Keifetz spat his on the rug at Chay's feet then lighted his own cigar from an enormous lighter which was embossed with the logotype of a Gulf Stream jet airplane. Chay sat with the unlighted cigar in his face until Keifetz took up the lighter again and lighted it. They smoked, staring at each other, but Keifetz couldn't hold a stare the way Chay could. It was a matter of his having been in the military since he was five. No amount of money could stand up to that.

"Where did you get that absurd idea, General?"

"I have a tape and a transcript of the call you made yesterday from a public phone booth in Reading, Pennsylvania, to W magazine in which you take credit for the Royalist Party having detonated the bomb in the White House. Your voiceprints identified you."

"NSA standard procedure, I'll warrant," Keifetz said blandly.

"I have a copy of the Presidential appointments list for yesterday."

"I see." Keifetz puffed on the cigar. The ferocity of his glance at Brill kept her from making a sound. "The new government—temporary, of course—will be called the National Conference for Democracy. Since the District is now out-of-bounds because of radioactivity, they will govern from Dallas—which is approximately equidistant from each coast—until a permanent capital city has been decided upon."

He puffed on the cigar.

"There will have to be a new Constitution. The oath of loyalty by our armed forces will need to be renewed. Alas, when our beloved President was blown away there was no longer a Commander-in-Chief of those armed forces. Therefore, on behalf of the new government, I ask you to accept the job of CINCAFUS."

"As what?"

"As Commander-in-Chief of the United States Army, Air Force, Navy, Marine Corps, and Coast Guard. In exchange for the tapes, voiceprints, and the copy of the President's appointments for that day."

"Oh, Chay!" Brill said huskily. "Isn't it thrilling?"

"And not only as CINCAFUS," Keifetz added smoothly, "but as CINCAFUSCIAFBIANSA."

"Oh, Chay!" Brill said breathily. "Isn't it *wonderful*?"

"What's CINCAFUSCIAFBIANSA?" Chay asked huskily.

This man was telling him about the thousand daydreams he had had since he had been five years old. This man was talking about an ultimate pension greater than all possible pensions.

"Commander-in-Chief of the Armed Forces, the Central Intelligence Agency, the Federal Bureau of Investigation, and the National Security Agency."

"You can do that?" Chay asked hoarsely. No one had ever dreamed of such rank. He could be one of the most powerful men in the world, outranking his mother.

"I can and I will—when I get that tape, those voiceprints, and the copy of the appointments schedule, that is."

"The entire thing is preposterous—"

"No, it isn't, Chay," Brill said all in a rush. "Wamb is leveling. He can do it."

"The instant I get that—uh—evidence from you."

"No," Chay said.

"No?" both Keifetz and Brill exclaimed.

"Even if I were to agree to such a thing, which I do not, you would get nothing until I was sworn in—in front of television cameras—and after the Army, Navy, and Air Force has taken an oath of loyalty to me. *Then*, if I were going to do it, I would give you the evidence."

"Chay," Brill said sweetly, "there has to be an agreement before there can be an agreement."

"Before there can be anything," Chay answered angrily, "I want to know why this loathsome shit blew up the government of the United States."

"Done and done, sir!" Keifetz said, clapping his hands smartly upon his thighs. He beamed on Chay then upon Brill. He got to his feet with difficulty, took a deep breath and began to speak while Brill remembered a glorious night in the distant past.

Brill could almost hear Serena call Chay long-distance collect. Chay knew his mother was very, very tight with money, but he couldn't believe this. "How am I going to pay for this call?" he asked indignantly as his mother told him brokenly of what had happened. "I'll have to put up my side arm as security to get the money. I haven't had a cent from Father in almost three months." Adam Appleton gave his wife large amounts of money to be passed along to the children, but she kept all but 10 percent of it, and in Chay's case, often failed to send any at all because she felt he had deserted the family by going away to school.

"Chay! You aren't listening to me! Your father just tried to rape your sister!"

"It isn't possible."

"On twelve lines a day? It isn't possible?"

"God! Oh, *Jesus!* How is Brill taking it?"

"How do you think she's taking it? She's hysterical! You've got to come home. We need someone to thrash this out."

"Mom! I have no money! I'd have to hitchhike. It could take me twenty-four hours."

"Whenever. Get here as soon as you can."

Chay made it from Culver, Indiana, across one-third of the United States, after having some terrible experiences. Two women had picked him up in their car and had tried to gang-bang him. He had had to use advanced karate to get away from them and they drove off with his suitcase. He was drenched by freezing rain. He was famished because although he had been able to wheedle two sandwiches out of the cook at school before he left, that was all he had to eat in twenty-six hours. When he arrived at the house in Alexandria it was after ten o'clock at night.

They were all there: Serena, Dad, Dudley, Sylvester, Jonathan, and Berry. Brill stood apart from the others as though she had been soiled. They were all staring at Adam Appleton the way people stare at the Big Dipper from an open pasture at night.

"Is this true, Dad?" Chay asked.

"None of this is clear to me, son. I hear what they are saying but I can't make head nor tail of it."

"Is it true or isn't it true?"

"It just doesn't seem possible."

Dudley said, "He should be lynched."

"Shut up!" Chay told him. "Shall I have you committed, Dad?"

"We have to think of the Administration, son. The President has borne an awful burden of guilt because of his Administration. He would only deny that I had done anything wrong and that would set the bloodhounds to yapping."

"He'll have to take his chances with the rest of us," Serena said.

"Besides," Adam Appleton said, "what did I do if I did do

it? The White House will put out the word that it was a natural biological thing I did."

"The President's people would force him to pardon him," Serena said.

"You broke the first law," Chay told his father. "From the beginning it was the law—at the beginning, the only law. How much coke did you do?"

Brill had to get Chay's attention. That was the whole reason for this tiresome business. "He was iced to the top," she said. "His eyes were like diamonds stuck in sand. But he knew what he was doing. It was disgusting."

"Dis*gus*ting?" her father repeated in a shocked way.

"He came at me unzipping his trousers," Brill said brokenly. She was an extravagantly voluptuous girl as she stood weeping, Chay thought. "Daddy reached into his trousers and scooped out"—but she could not go on.

"Daddy said he was going to stab Brill with a fleshy dagger," little Berry shrilled.

Brill directed Chay's eyes to where she wanted him to look. "He wanted to stab me here," she said huskily and touched her crotch with her right hand. She saw that he had made the connection. He was beginning to understand that there were forces in nature that were bigger than both of them. She could see it in his eyes. He was hyperventilating and it looked as though someone had slipped a canoe into his trousers.

"Dagger?" Dudley squeaked. "What dagger?"

"You filthy old man," Serena shouted at her husband.

"I'll kill myself," Adam Appleton said.

"We must pray," Sylvester said.

Chay stared from face to face, hoping that someone would tell him what to do. Only goddamn civilians could get themselves into trouble like this, he thought bitterly. Finally, to have something to do, he ordered everyone but his father out of the room. They all left, except Brill.

Chay spoke to her directly. "I can't tell you how sorry I am. How ashamed for Father."

"Don't be ashamed. Never be ashamed. Please come to my room after you have finished with Father. I have to talk to someone and you are the only one."

As Chay turned back to his father, Adam Appleton was snorting three lines of coke through a shortened Hygeia straw. He lay back on the pillow and said, "Well, son, how are things at school?"

At five to twelve, Chay knocked on Brill's door. Brill was stretched out on her back on a double bed, her lovely head propped up with three pillows. She didn't seem to be wearing anything under the light coverlet. "Lock the door, Chay," she said.

He approached her bed cautiously. She patted it. "Sit here," she said. He sat beside her, close enough so that her arms could go up around his neck. "Oh, Chay," she said, pulling him down to herself.

It wasn't a military problem. It was not even something he had to think about. There was nothing to evaluate. He could smell her and taste her. She was definitely a girl and that wasn't something he could just walk away from.

What happened in the next four hours may have accounted for Chay's attitude toward facts and reality for the rest of his life. Until then, his memory had been as reliable as anyone else's. He recorded things in his mind as they happened and, whenever possible, recalled them accurately. But after that night it wasn't as if he deliberately lied but he evaded the truth, becoming a man who believed what had happened by the proof of what he had wanted to have happened after he had done it. He was never able to accept that he had infrequent sex with his sister. To cover over that ugliness his life became a series of mirages. As with Ronald Reagan, if the truth were disheveled, he refused to see it that way. This quirk applied to everything he pretended to have experienced. Like Reagan, he had a vulgarly oversweet "American" vision of his country which could have been fashioned by L. B. Mayer for Andy Hardy. Like Reagan, he constructed an infinity of mirrors which reflected substitute versions of his life which contrasted vividly from those which other people saw. He told himself that he detested Wambly Keifetz because he was so purple and ugly, not because the man slept with his ineffably lovely sister every night. All of it, every continuing and complex ruse of it, was necessary practice in trying to assure himself that neither he nor anyone else could ever be sure of what had happened between him and his sister until he reached the point that what *may* have happened could not possibly be of any consequence. The guilty consummation was to be repeated again and again throughout their separate marriages, but Chay never acknowledged, even to Brill, that it had happened.

13

"GENERAL—Brilliana—listen to words I have lived by," Wambly Keifetz said earnestly. "Ronald Reagan was the greatest President this country has ever produced. He gave us the FBI race wars, the Qaddafi bombings, the Star Wars flapdoodle, the Grenada farce, the Bitburg shaming, the endless bank failures, the Lebanon disasters, the crumbling national airlines, the rape of HUD, the oligarchy of Big Oil, insured inflation, and the shoring-up of sinister Israeli politicians—all to keep our people diverted and entertained until the Royalty Party could consolidate its position. He fought for an end to legal abortion so that the market for our hard-ticket items would never be jeopardized but always expand beyond the food supply. He taught our people to *get the money*."

"I don't see that I ever got the money," Chay said mildly.

Keifetz ignored Chay's interruption. "I was there, on October 15, 1982, one of the handful of the owners of the country, when Ronald Reagan strode into the Rose Garden to sign the Garn-St Germain Depository Institutions Act, the final step in the process of deregulating the nation's Savings and Loan institutions. With the stroke of a pen he threatened a great nation with bankruptcy and created great fortunes for hundreds of his friends—some of whom, alas, now face prison terms.

"Gad, sir! I can see him now coming down from that copter

and waving all the way at no one at all across a thirty-six-yard course to the White House: beautiful, intricate waves; two-handed waves; behind-the-head circular waves; and lurching forward as if he were daring that darling little dog to trip him. It was Ronald Reagan who taught us that the whole outmoded system was something which stood in the way of getting things done. He ignored Congress and the Constitution. He ignored his own State Department. What he was trying to do, you see, was to reduce the *cost* of government to just himself and one Lieutenant Colonel of the Marines. But it backed up on him when he saw that he, as President, was standing in his own way, and he was handicapped because the news media kept misunderstanding him because he had taught them, along with everyone else, to *get the money*.

"I was forty-five years old," Keifetz continued forthrightly, "when Ronald Reagan began his first term and taught us that money, and only money, was the reason for being an American. In 1983, he ordered the Pentagon to break a fourteen-year moratorium on the production of chemical warfare weapons. And why? Because he could help some of us get the money, that's why. Who brought us the profitable diversions of acid rain and the Pope Plot? Who made possible the redistribution of wealth from the poor to the rich? Think of the generosity of the man! The real income of the top fifth of the pile rose by 11 percent, while that of the bottom fifth declined by 6.1 percent. Reagan was my role model and I wasn't alone. The people who were blessed by just being near him—his Vice President, his Attorney General, his Labor and Interior Secretaries, his Defense Procurement people, his political counselors, his personal press agent, at least two of his National Security advisers—who else but Reagan could have given us that gallant Colonel North?—his CIA Director and all of the understrappers—but why go on? One hundred and twelve of the best and the brightest in his administration came under investigation, were accused of improper conduct, resigned under fire, were indicted, or had their nominations withdrawn or rejected while they did their level best to get the money. Think of it! Eleven hundred and twenty-three lesser officials in his administration were either charged, indicted, fired, convicted, or awaiting trial by 1985 alone! Warren Harding? Richard Nixon? You call those scandals? "*And,*" Keifetz added excitedly, "despite all of the sleaze and all of the gaffes, when Ronald Reagan left office he not only had the approval of 68 percent of the people, based on a three-day telephone poll which got that approval from two-thirds of 1,533 people out of a possible 224.6 million Americans, but the front page of *The New York Times* proclaimed that he had markedly increased trust in government. And I am certain that they wrote trust, not gullibility.

"So, enlightened by his aura, Americans were inspired to *get the money* by any means obtainable and that humbled me. Greed became the meaning of American prayer, and it taught us that those people who couldn't get the money were either weak or stupid and didn't deserve the privileges of democracy. Who else but Ronald Reagan would have the *folie de grandeur* to promise to invite the steel and oil industries to rewrite the Environmental Protection Agency's regulations? Who but Ronald Reagan would have the chutzpah to charge that 80 percent of the nation's air pollution problems are caused by chemicals released from trees? The Reagan ideal had always been to establish royalty in America so that royalty could reward the people who had gone out and got the money without always having to think about how to get around the goddamn voters. That was why I blew up Washington."

"I don't follow you," Chay said. He hated talk about politics. As far as he could see, politics—particularly Reagan politics—had existed only to get the money for the Army.

Brill began to say, "Chay, don't you see—" but Keifetz didn't hear either of them. He was lost in the glories of national destiny.

"I am something of a collector, you know," he said. "You may recall how my collection of beer labels brought $3.1 million at Christie's. Well, I was chairman of the nonpartisan commission which abolished nuclear weapons in late '89, and as luck would have it, I found myself alone with the last existing nuclear device in the world—a small, compact SHAM. So—I collected it. Then, when I saw what I had to do, I packed it into Sir Harry Lauder's golf bag—which was an important part of my golf bag, golf ball, and golf club collection which I had purchased from the James Nolan treasure of golfing objects which brought $4.3 million at Sotheby's, and took the golf bag along to my breakfast appointment with the President. I left the White House at eight-thirty that morning. The golf bag was still in the White House cloak room. I was in Reading, Pennsylvania, when the device exploded."

Chay heard Brill sob. He turned. Her eyes were welling up with tears. "Isn't he beautiful?" she said to Chay. "Oh, Wamb!" she said rushing into Keifetz's pudgy arms, "God just doesn't make them like you anymore."

"What is your answer, General?" Keifetz asked in a courtly way.

"My answer?"

"Are you coming aboard the new government?" Keifetz asked, although to himself he wondered whether he was going to have to have this fellow hit.

Chay replied out of the lifetime of his conditioning. It wasn't a matter of morals or justice. They were talking about military pensions.

"What will my rank be?" he blurted.

"Marshal of the American Union. The first and only Marshal of the American Union in American history. Your insignia will be a shoulder chaplet of six stars surrounding a miniature of the Great Seal of the United States."

Chay's jaw dropped. "*Six* stars?"

"You will command all U.S. military, naval, air force, coast guard, intelligence, and security forces inside and outside the United States. A PX outlet—called PX One—will be established wherever you make your base."

"Uniforms?" Chay asked weakly.

"As Commander-in-Chief you will design your own uniforms, and have the right to salute Marine guards while hatless and in sports clothes when entering or disembarking from helicopters. Your salary will be $225,000 a year plus expenses. You will have the use of a helicopter and a DC-10. Housing commensurate with your rank will be provided."

"Tell him about the pension, Wamb," Brill said.

"Your pension, of course," Keifetz said to Chay, "will be astronomical."

Chay gulped and stared at Keifetz. That clinched it. Ever since he had been a small boy, during the year when she was preparing him to be sent away to military school, Serena had hammered away at him with the importance of choosing a career which would bring in a proper pension. "The Army will take care of us when we are both old and gray, Chay," she had said again and again. The word "pension" was imprinted on his soul. Jesus! he thought. If John DeWitt Kullers were standing here right now, he'd pee in his pants.

14

CHAY WAITED in a suite in a luxury hotel on East Sixty-third Street for orders from the new government. He thought of the day he had arrived at the North Slope Military Academy in Alaska as a five-year-old plebe, the lowest of the low, and he couldn't see how he would ever be able to rise to such ranks as cadet corporal or sergeant. Now he held rank higher than any man who had ever served the armed forces of his country. CINCA-FUSCIAFBIANSA!

For the first time, in a total sense, he realized how much he owed to his mother for having had the courage to send him away and to keep him away for seventeen years, from Alaska through West Point, so that he could learn the art of soldiering so well that they had lifted him to where he was today: Commander-in-Chief of the Armed Forces of the United States plus the Central Intelligence Agency, the Federal Bureau of Investigation, and the National Security Agency.

Holy shit! He remembered how he had wished so hard when he was at West Point that the Vietnam War would last only eight or ten years more so that he might have the possible chance of making the rank of colonel. But the Vietnam War had ended and he had made colonel and anyhow there had been one colonel for every 163 enlisted men in Vietnam because of the "unified" command system. Now he was Commander-in-Chief of all three million of them plus millions of spooks, G-men, and wiretappers!

He walked to a full-length mirror, stood at attention, saluted himself, then as a really gracious gesture on his part, said, "Thanks, Mom."

The new orders arrived by courier at 1710 that evening. Chay was to report to Dallas immediately to his new headquarters in the New Baker Hotel in Dallas, notifying the National Conference for Democracy executive, Beniamiamo Camardi, of his time of arrival at the Carswell Air Force Base. Chay called his aide-de-camp, Colonel Coomber, and told him to lay on air transport to Dallas and to send a car to take him to the East River heliport which would lift him to the military airport.

While Chay was waiting on Sixty-third Street for the orders, Keifetz had boarded his private jet, a renovated Stealth bomber whose interior had been done over into a replica of a Vermont country farmhouse kitchen, complete with a simulated coal stove, rockers, wall-to-wall linoleum, framed wall samplers, and an enormous roll-top desk, and was flying at Mach 3 to Dallas. His deputy, Beniamiamo Camardi, was waiting at the foot of the ramp as Keifetz descended. The two men embraced heartily in the *fratellanza* manner, then got into a government chopper and were flown into town.

"Are you ready for him here?" Keifetz asked as the ship took off.

"Everything is set."

"How does the woman look?"

"Gorgeous."

"I mean how does she *look*? Does she sound as if she knows what she's doing?"

"One hunnert percent solid."

"Well, she has a tough job ahead of her. She has to convince him that he is the phenomenon of the centuries because he has the magic."

"She was Michael Deaver's first assistant for the last six years."

"She has to sell him so that he can't come unsold—which

won't be hard—that his magic came to him in the form of his immeasurable luck. If he believes that, everything has to come out right and he will do anything we tell him because he won't be interested in thinking for himself, he'll let his magical luck come up with the solutions."

"She is a very smart little broad. She knows her business," Camardi said.

"He has to depend on her absolutely to feed his luck, then everything he does, from his point of view, will come out right. And God knows that if they are told about his magic, the people will absolutely believe in him, and we'll stay where we belong, in the driver's seat."

Graciela Winkelreid was waiting for them in the sitting room of a suite at the Mansion on Turtle Creek. She was a beautifully dressed, effectively shapely, inordinately healthy, and bombastically pretty woman with extremely well-cared-for hair, and eyes as large and as blue as the lamps outside British police stations. She shook hands formally with the two men.

It was an unusual situation. Although Graciela Winkelreid was Keifetz's only child (by his second wife), neither father nor daughter had acknowledged each other since Graciela's fourteenth birthday when Keifetz had given her a Mercedes-Benz when he knew well that it was an Aston-Martin which he had promised her. Not only had they not spoken to each other ever since that day, but Graciela had become the leader of a revolutionary/terrorist movement of twenty-nine very wealthy young people who were dedicated to destroying the Department of Defense, all banks, and in the chaos that followed, their parents.

Graciela had studied terrorist techniques all over the world, with the IRA in Northern Ireland, with the Japanese Red Army, with the Tupamaros, and with three of the Middle Eastern terrorist groups out of Libya and Iran, including Hiz b'Allah, but time had mellowed her, and she had switched her political allegiances to the Republican Party where she had joined the Reagan Revolution and had won renown as one of the President's manipulator-handlers. Michael Deaver had praised her as having "one of the most completely dishonest and duplicitous minds ever to bring credit to an Administration."

"I apologize for the need to rush," Keifetz said, "but I had to meet you and have one little talk, as I am sure you understand."

"Oh, yes," she said.

"The fee arrangement is satisfactory?"

"Oh, yes."

"For the first six weeks of your work with Marshal Appleton, I shall want you to submit to deep hypnosis twice a day to convince you that, in effect, you *are* Caesare Appleton because, through me, you are going to be the source of most of his ideas over the next few years. Every morning, from the moment you are awake, you must think as he thinks and ask yourself what he should do and where he should go that day to meet his destiny—a destiny which I will have programmed for you. Then, using your formidable experience and skills as a public relations executive, we must convince the American people that he is their darling and their savior. He must begin by becoming the most irrationally popular man in history, then go on from there."

"That is a breeze for Graciela," Camardi said. "Look what her team did for Reagan."

"I look forward to the day when Chay will run for reelection— if we will still have elections—by campaigning against government," Keifetz said happily. "Just as if he had not been the government he was campaigning against. That will be the proof that you won the day, Graciela, because that was how we ran Reagan for a second term as governor of California."

"I know the exercise," Miss Winkelreid said.

"If mistakes are made, he must be trained to automatically put the blame on someone else. He must convey the illusion of always staying in tune with the people when, actually, they will be straining to stay in tune with him."

Miss Winkelreid sipped delicately at her tea.

"Television, of course, is everything. Pictures, and their seldom-relating commentary, crowd out thought. With television paving his way, Napoleon could have taken Moscow. Hitler could have had a Hollywood contract. With television, the French revolution need never have happened. Marie Antoinette would have chatted glamorously on the ten highest-rated talk shows. Cake would be in. Bread would be out. After all, we have only to look at Reagan."

"Graciela knows everybody who is anybody in television," Camardi said.

"If you are ever in the slightest doubt," Keifetz told her reassuringly, "refer to how you did it as a White House handler and you cannot miss. Marshal Appleton is famous now, but you must make him famous for being famous. Then, when he seems to have reached the apex of all American glory, I will perform the apotheosis, and he will rise to magnificences of which you could scarcely dream."

"I am sure not," Miss Winkelreid said.

"You may have wondered why I chose you, a woman, to pave the road to this rendezvous with destiny. That you are a superbly qualified public relations technician has only to do with results. But your success with the raw material which I am placing at your disposal will depend greatly on your being a woman, because our Marshal of the American Union was sent away from his mother by his mother when he was five years old which brought him an irradicable sense of unworthiness and made him lust for the approval of all women. Indeed, because his father was scorned by his mother, because his father was a ruined cocaine addict, the Marshal was forced to feel that everyone found him unworthy. By leading him to the altar of television, you will be consecrating his loss and promising him redemption from his unworthiness."

While he waited for his orders at the hotel in New York, Chay called Hedda Blitzen at Schwalhaber's delicatessen.

"Chay! Oh, thank God!" she said. "I just heard the news. I dreaded that you might have been in Washington. Oh, Chay— the President and all those people are dead. Those beautiful buildings are gone."

"I know." She was making him very horny. "I had to tell you I am thinking of you."

"Of *me*? Where are you?"

"New York. There was a meeting."

"Am I going to see you?"

"There's just no time, sweetheart. I've been ordered to Dallas."

"Dallas? Why Dallas?"

"It's—it's the new capital. After things settle down—will you come to Dallas?"

"I can't just leave the store. Mayn't I see you tonight?"

"People are waiting for me. Keep thinking how you can get to Dallas. I have to go now. I love you."

"I love you, Chay."

He replaced the telephone softly.

"CINCAFUSCIAFBIANSA! Man! That is *rank!*" He thought of John DeWitt Kullers. He looked up into the hotel mirror. "You've come a long way, baby!" he said.

He telephoned General Goldberg at Fort Meade. "Did you pick up the signal yet, Freddie?" he asked.

"Yeah. Terrific. Congratulations. Even if it does sort of shorten my tour here."

"No, no!" Chay said. "You'll carry on as before. I'm in command but you still run the NSA show."

"Thanks, Chay. What can I do for you?"

"My temporary headquarters will be in the New Baker Hotel in Dallas. I want you to bring me the tapes, the transcript, and the voiceprints of the Reading call in a burn bag. And the White House appointments schedule. Give me two copies and be sure there are no others."

"Jesus, Chay, is that how you swung it?"

"Later. Get down here."

When he had hung up on Goldberg, Chay called Eddie Grogan, Director of Central Intelligence.

"What can I do for you, Marshal?" Grogan asked with his loathsome confidentiality.

"I want you to find a man. About forty-five, large nose, loud voice, mottled complexion, name of John DeWitt Kullers—that's Kullers—k-u-l-l-e-r-s—who attended the North Slope Military Academy in Edgarton, Alaska, in 1955, thirty-five years ago. He is an extreme example of the military type. You could start with our own Army records, but if he were still in the Army, he would be such a senior officer that I wouldn't need you to look for him, so try the French Foreign Legion, the Chinese Red Guard, et cetera. I want to know what happened to him and if he is still alive."

· · ·

The fighter-bomber got him to the Carswell base outside Dallas at 2240.

Beniamiamo Camardi was waiting for him at the bottom of the ramp. It was an easy move for Camardi because he had just seen Wambly Keifetz off to New York.

"Marshal Appleton! Marvelous!"

Chay was startled. He would have to get used to the new rank (and the pension).

"Have you talked to Keifetz?" Chay asked, just to be sure.

"Six hours ago—at least. Everything is strictly set."

"When will my new commission go through?"

"It's through! It's all been done except for the media to make it official."

"When's the swearing-in?"

"Tomorrow morning, eleven o'clock, at Convention Hall. We thought maybe we'd do it at the Alamo but we got trouble in San Antonio."

"What kind of trouble?"

"General Black has notified us that if we establish a government without elections or a Constitution that he will arrest and execute all of us," Camardi said.

"I'll handle it."

"This has gone beyond talking, Marshal. He gave us an ultimatum. They had two of our people shot today." Camardi shrugged. "We need heavy protection."

"When your session opens tomorrow morning, the hall will be surrounded by my troops. I will wipe Black out."

They rode into town together. "What do you do in government, Mr. Camardi?" Chay asked.

"I am the Mafia representative to the National Conference. And Mr. Keifetz's deputy."

"Has the signal of my appointment gone out to the Forces Command, the fleet, and the bases overseas?"

"Throughout the world, Marshal. They are cheering. You should see the signals that come back to us. And let me tell you something. I would hate to be a Nicaraguan today. Not that I wouldn't hate to be a Nicaraguan any day," Camardi added hastily, "but today, in spades."

"Give me the name and number of your Public Affairs Officer

and I'll have my people work out the news media arrangements
with him."

"It's a her. And wait until you see her. Gorgeous. Absolutely
gorgeous—if you like gorgeous women."

"Give me the number."

"The name is Graciela Winkelreid. You want the private home
number?"

"I have to talk to her. Wherever."

Camardi wrote Miss Winkelreid's name and home number on
a slip of paper. "So when am I gonna see you?" he asked as they
pulled up at the New Baker Hotel.

"I'll call you."

15

A S KEIFETZ FLEW from Dallas to New York, he telephoned
Serena Appleton in Alexandria, Virginia.

"Mother?" he said softly into the telephone.

"Who is this?" Serena said.

"Wambly. Wamb Keifetz."

"What is this mother shit?"

"Just staking my claim to be a part of your family."

"Whatta you want?"

"I stumbled on a business proposition you might be interested
in."

"Ah. Yeah? What kind?"

"Money for you."

"I'm innarested."

"A car will pick you up and take you to a chopper to fly you to New York."

"If it's business it would be better if Brill didn't know about it."

"I agree. One hundred percent. We'll meet at my office. The car will bring you there."

"What time?"

"Be ready to go in thirty-five minutes. We'll meet in two hours' time."

Keifetz kept a hideaway, backup office, overlooking Central Park, high up over West Fifty-seventh Street, which he used exclusively for his commerce in agricultural products derived from the coca leaf in a complex system whose distribution blanketed all of North America and Europe. Keifetz kept his work with cocaine utterly separate from his activities with the Bahama Beaver Bonnet Company.

The office was totally a state-of-the-art installation which was operated by two computer scientists (and an armed office boy/bodyguard) who controlled all information, from the growth and labor conditions on Keifetz coca farms inside the Peruvian, Bolivian, Ecuadorean, and Colombian jungles to the instant cash transfers of hundreds of millions of dollars daily from account to account in banks across the world until the money came out the other side as an entirely clean and legal, if tax-free, entity.

Serena was led into Keifetz's office by Phil Vitamizzare, the armed office boy/bodyguard who left them immediately. Keifetz had slipped into a maroon velvet smoking jacket with mauve velvet lapels and was wearing monogrammed carpet slippers made of unborn vicuna skins. It was a glorious room, a classically masculine study in burnished walnut and fine book bindings, *sans livres*, which towered on three sides from floor to ceiling; an authentic room whose thicknesses of oriental rugs and an utter authenticity of English Georgian furniture set off the single, but huge, Constable which was hung on the one book-free wall of the room.

"Very nice, Wamb," Serena said. "Terrific view."

"Please sit down, Mother," Wambly said. "Would you like an Orange Whistle or perhaps a refreshing full-bodied pot of Assam tea?"

"I'm more of a coffee person, Wamb."

He hit the intercom. "Coffee!" he murmured.

"It's been a long time between coffees," Serena said. "Actually, although you are married to my daughter, I don't think we ever met before."

Keifetz sighed. "That's the way of the world. I am such a slave to my business that it's a wonder I know who I am."

Vitamizzare brought in the coffee, put the tray down, and left the room.

Keifetz poured the coffee.

Serena said, "What's on your mind?"

"It won't be revealing family secrets to tell you that Brill has mentioned to me that you might enjoy augmenting your income," Keifetz said, passing her the coffee. "Therefore, I have been doing my best to custom-tailor a spot which would fit your talents to a T, and yet not take away too much time from your work in the arts and with the philanthropies."

"No kidding?"

"Would that interest you?"

"Would that interest me? Are you kidding? How much does it pay?"

"Oh, well—as for the pay, I thought—how about a nice steady three thousand dollars a week?"

"Three thousand? A week? What is this?"

"Tomorrow morning, in Dallas, your son, Chay, is going to be named as Commander-in-Chief of the Armed Forces of the United States."

"That's nice. He'll be very good at that. But what about my job?"

"That's your job, in a way. We plan that Chay shall go on to greater things and we wouldn't want him to lose sight of where his responsibilities lie."

"I don't follow you, Wamb."

"I want to pay you to tell him to do the right thing."

"Aaaaah."

"You have a mother's influence. He adores you. You'll do what you always did, all of his life, try to guide him along the right paths. He'll be grateful—in the end. It can all lead to great things for him."

"This is absolutely up my alley!"

"I had hoped you'd think so."

"You're gonna pay me three thousand a week—"

"And expenses."

"—and expenses—just to do what I do for him all the time as his mother—just advise him and guide him?"

Keifetz nodded endearingly. "A courier will bring you Chay's programming for each day on the evening before that day. It will be necessary for him to live in Dallas so I am sure you will want to go to Dallas almost immediately so you can set up a home for him and put some comfort into his life."

"Give me a couple of weeks to close the house in Alexandria then I'll go. I'll even cook for him." Keifetz shuddered. Brilliana's descriptions of her mother's cooking had been vivid and revolting.

"Just one thing, Wamb. Like what will the programming be?"

"Mainly, although there will be heaps of other things that will crop up, you will want to convince him of his almost magical luck— the kind of rare luck which solves all of the problems for a very, very lucky man without his having to wear himself out thinking up solutions to the problems. Just so he gets it firmly fixed in his mind that his luck will carry him through no matter what happens, and that anyone who tries to go against that luck will find themselves in deep doo-doo."

16

MOLLY TOMPKINS, Chay's batman, was waiting for him in the gigantic suite at the New Baker Hotel. Tompkins was a tall, blindingly gay man who gave the impression that he could not have been anything other than a soldier, and as a soldier, he could not have been other than Marshal Appleton's batman. Tompkins had already had the news of Chay's ascension and had been sewing the new rank insignia on Chay's tunics.

"Six stars!" he said. "Did you ever?"

Chay ordered dinner. "From now on, only you will prepare my food, Sergeant. At least until we can nail down a thoroughly reliable cook."

"Sah! I have just the man."

"Who is that?"

"My fiancé, Private First Class Chester Haselgrove."

"Bring him in at 1600 hours tomorrow for interrogation."

"Sah!"

Reading from the slip of paper Camardi had handed him, Chay dialed the Public Affairs Officer's number.

"Miss Winkelreid, please. Ah. Yes. Miss Winkelreid. This is Marshal Appleton."

There were murmurings through the telephone system.

"We'll need to coordinate plans for the announcement tomorrow morning. I am at the New Baker Hotel. Suite 3420–21–22–23–24–25–26–27–28–29. I'll be ready to meet with you in fifty-three minutes." As he hung up, Sergeant Tompkins came into the room with a platterful of sandwiches and a half bottle of claret.

"Sah!" Tompkins said.

"We'll need a magnum of Krug '61 with some sterlet caviar and blinis in here in forty minutes."

"Sah!"

"After you have opened the wine, you will go off duty until 0600 tomorrow morning. After these sandwiches, I'll want my dress blues with fullest decorations. And my whangee stick."

"Sah!" Tompkins wheeled and left the room. Chay hoped that Camardi actually knew what gorgeous was.

17

THE DALLAS CONVENTION CENTER had been transformed by 912 workmen in 7,394 man-hours into a bicameral chamber. The larger chamber, where the delegates to the National Conference for Democracy were to sit, would be constituted after the leadership had outlined the proportions of the new government to (temporarily) appointed representatives of the fifty states of the union. The smaller chamber was to hold the Body of Elders, which would be the senior half of the legislative body, having fifty members.

The investiture of General Appleton as Commander-in-Chief of the Armed Forces and as Director of the CIA, FBI, and NSA took place at 7:00 A.M., broadcast simultaneously by satellite along with the command cadre and total forces personnel of the Army, Navy, Air Force, Marine Corps, and Coast Guard together with all employees of the CIA, FBI, and NSA swearing their Oath of Allegiance to him on posts and in offices and laboratories all over the world. The time was chosen to lock into the eight and nine o'clock news time slots on the East Coast morning talk shows.

The ceremony took place in a large circus tent which had been set up in the parking lot outside the Convention Hall so that the enormous media coverage could be accommodated.

There were nineteen television camera platforms within the large air-conditioned tent. There was comfortable seating for 1,700 of the working press. National and international radio was accommodated by a thicket of 174 microphones, with 18 parabolic mikes for shortwave coverage and for commercial audiocassettes. The news photographers worked on a moving, turning, circular platform which rotated around the circumference of the tent. The platform had a diameter of 203 feet and gave each photographer the equal opportunity to photograph Marshal of the American Union Appleton, placed at the center of the ring, in close-up or at any angle during the swearing-in ceremonies. The platform moved at a constant speed of 4.6 miles per hour.

The swearing-in was done by an established leader of American back-channel politics and government, the philanthropist/ park-bench philosopher, Wambly Keifetz; awesomely, ponderously heavy with authority and body weight, wearing, for reasons of continuity, the black robes of a Chief Justice of the Supreme Court. Marshal Appleton's twin sister held a Bible and the new Marshal swore his solemn oath to uphold, protect, and defend the future Constitution of the United States which would separate the powers of government into four equal divisions: the Executive, the Legislative, the Judicial, and National Security.

Caesare Appleton would be the nation's first Chief Magistrate of National Security and, historically, was the first head of the quadripartite government to be so sworn in.

The oath-taking was followed by a speech of acceptance by the new CINCAFUSCIAFBIANSA which Miss Winkelreid had crafted, and which was followed by a forty-minute photo opportunity.

The Marshal was as close to being dazed by events as he could ever be. Exhausted from an exacting if exhilarating night with Miss Winkelreid, who had, in a mysteriously adhesive way through every startling move of her body which had moved under him, around him and over him, hammered into him arcane findings of astrology and numerology plus a considerable amount of loins-reading, he felt that he had just stumbled through a time frame into an area of his life which by the total and dimensional luck which now surrounded him would make any mistakes he would have made at any other time of his life prior to this utterly impossible. He was protected by an aura of luck. He had the overwhelming feeling that no matter how he might seem to be losing his way in the years to come, his luck would always carry the day and boost him over the heads and shoulders of all others. It was very heady stuff. The statistics, factoids, palm print readings, and horoscopes she had produced in between their various couplings were the most convincing things he had ever read. He felt thirty feet tall as he took the Oath of Office.

Immediately after the acceptance speech, before the photo

opportunity began, while he seemed to be congratulating the new Marshal of the American Union, Keifetz, *sotto voce*, said, "When will you deliver those items?"

Marshal Appleton nodded. "By tomorrow, I think," he said as an NBC floor man took him by the elbow to turn him to face the cameras for a series of solemn-gay-pensive-defiant-smiling head shots.

Three-minute-twenty-second-excerpts from Marshal Appleton's speech which Graciela Winkelreid had written for him—or at least said she had written for him after she had received it by courier from Wambly Keifetz—were broadcast on the national and local news that evening while simultaneously being broadcast to the television stations of the world via satellite. The broadcast syndication rights to the full speech subsequently brought in $815,762.27.

The Marshal said (in part): "It is not enough that the Sandinistas have destroyed our nation's capital and murdered our beloved leaders with an internationally-outlawed, heinous nuclear device, but—as a further abomination—they have somehow, perhaps through the use of brain-contaminating drugs, infected units of our own armed forces. With deep sadness, I tell you that the Fifth Army of the United States, whose headquarters are in Fort Sam Houston at San Antonio, Texas, have entered into armed rebellion. As I speak to you, my old outfit, the Seventy-fifth Regiment of Rangers, is taking the headquarters of the Fifth and arresting their ringleaders."

To the dismay of the nation, General Black and the key rebellious elements of the Fifth Army escaped capture by being absent when the surprise attack happened.

18

GENERAL GOLDBERG was waiting in the suite at the New Baker Hotel when Chay returned from the swearing-in ceremonies. Chay sat him in a comfortable leather chair, gave him a jar of thirty-year-old Scotch and a shockingly expensive *Romeo y Julieta* cigar, and said, as he smiled down at the tape, transcript, voiceprints, and appointments schedule laying on a large polished table, "You done good, Freddie."

"You, too."

"When are you up for retirement?"

"Nine years."

"This is what I have in mind. I can retire you now with four stars, full pension. I can get you the title to a nice little $700,000 house in Palm Springs—or Florida—plus maybe you'd enjoy a cosy holiday apartment in San Francisco or Paris—plus, say, a ten-year contract as a consultant to one of the big defense contractors at $270,000 a year, with expenses and a lifetime supply of these cigars. Whatta you say?"

Goldberg grinned. "Effective when?"

"Effective as soon as you tell me you have found a strong replacement."

Goldberg got to his feet. "Man, you certainly are a visionary."

"Wait'll you see what I have lined up for you tonight—talking about vision."

"Yeah, Chay?"

"Graciela Winkelreid. Absolutely gorgeous."

After Goldberg had gone, Chay called Keifetz at his Dallas palace.

"The shipment you were asking about just came in," he said.

From the middle of Highland Park, Keifetz was at Chay's suite in the New Baker in twelve minutes, driving behind a wailing police escort. He stared at the evidence on the large polished table. "That appointments schedule is a copy."

"Of course it's a copy. The original was evaporated with the White House. This is the surviving copy."

"Where did you get it?"

"It doesn't make any difference."

"But you got it from someone."

"Sure."

"I can't take that risk. You'll have to give me the provider as well as the rest of it."

"No."

"Why not? Surely you understand that I can't have someone walking around who heard that tape—who made those voice-prints."

"He's Army. The Army is mine. I take care of the Army."

"What are you talking about?"

"I mean I want you to set him up with a house in Palm Springs and an apartment in Paris—or wherever he says—and I am depending on you to get him a job as a consultant for $270,000 a year plus a lifetime supply of *Romeo y Julieta* cigars."

"To do all that, I'll have to know who he is."

"Of course. But I am holding out a copy of the tape and the prints and the schedule. If anything happens to him, I give the tapes to the networks."

Keifetz walked to the window and stared at downtown Dallas. He turned. "Well, it's not as bad as it could be," he said, "because I've got a lock on you. I taped the meeting when we made a deal on these tapes and prints in the first place. If you ruin me, I'll ruin you."

"Fair enough," Chay said. "Just take care of my man."

19

BLACK'S MUTINEERS of the Fifth Army hit Dallas at 0907 hours the following morning, blowing away the roof of the Convention Center with low-level bombing and strafing members of the National Conference for Democracy caught in the parking lot, killing two.

Chay was ready. He had brought in tanks and troops from Fort Hood at Killeen, about eighty miles south of Dallas. When Black's tanks crossed the Trinity River to invade the downtown area, Chay's tanks rolled them back and his artillery blew them out of action. His antiaircraft fire knocked down all eighteen of Black's air attack. The heaviest street fighting was around the Kennedy Memorial on Houston Street which drove Black and his remaining troops into the courthouse where they were pinned down under siege.

Chay sat in an open staff car in front of the Memorial with an M-16 on the floor at his feet, facing a full view of the entrance to the courthouse on Commerce Street, surrounded by mobile gun emplacements which were trained on the courthouse, but with his concealed troops well out of sight. As he lolled on the leather upholstery, his feet extended along the length of the seat, he delivered an ultimatum to Black over a heavy-duty PA system, ineffably aware that network and cable cameras were covering the entire scene from the roofs and high floors of the surrounding buildings.

Suddenly, large rebel tanks rolled around the corner of Commerce Street, protecting two companies of infantry behind them. Apart from the men trapped inside the courthouse, they were all that was left of General Black's troops. The tanks made straight for Chay's staff car.

In full view of 55 million viewers in the United States and perhaps an equal number reached by satellite across the world (in Europe it was middle to late afternoon and across the Soviet Union and Asia it was going into prime time), while his heavy guns crippled the oncoming tanks, Chay leaped out of the staff car, snatching up the rifle, and ran out into the street delivering rapid fire. The hand-to-hand fighting was intense as the troops loyal to the Conference leapt out of trucks and, by force of numbers, over-powered the Nicaraguan partisans of the U.S. Fifth Army.

At no time did the cameras and the emotionally charged com-mentators lose sight of Chay. They, along with 100 million people, watched him mow down eight of the enemy just as General Black, yelling an incoherent challenge, appeared at the top of the steps at the entrance to the courthouse. Chay's attention was diverted for that one moment and he went down with a bayonet through the thigh, a thrust which missed the femoral artery by a fraction of an inch. The entire world cried out with horror. Laying on the ground, bleeding profusely, pointing directly at Black who was now twenty-odd yards away, Chay raised his bamboo whangee and, pointing it directly at the mutinous commander, yelled, "Nail that son of a bitch!" and every syllable of that command was picked up clearly by parabolic microphones and relayed round the world.

General Black was overpowered by Chay's troops and taken captive. Bodies littered the street. The terrible noise of battle was stilled. Simultaneously, hundreds of millions of people in bars, kitchens, beds, and living rooms sprang to their feet and cheered, as obedient as Pavlov's dogs. They were "the visual generation" which television had conditioned away from thinking into reflexive watching, the generation which had only seen Ronald Reagan—his fine figure, his juvenile's face, his flawless tailoring—but had never heard what he was saying and had been saying, trained by the incessant persuasion of televison to adore him.

The short battle was the most thrilling moment of entertain-ment in American history as, clinging to the shoulders of two large, weeping soldiers, with his sergeant (cast by Graciela Winkelreid) playing out a mournful "When Johnny Comes Marching Home" on a harmonica, every note broadcast to the viewers, Marshal Appleton looked directly into the hand-held video cameras which had materialized before him, smiled a gallant smile, gracious in victory, and said, "Now justice and our indivisible nation have been served and I thank God," sinking backward onto a stretcher which the paramedics had brought up.

. . .

Five billion people in a huge living room had been sitting there for decades, watching light and shade. As some left for the john, more entered the gloom, all sipping six-packs as the heroine got laid. 'Twas monstrous concubinage, *droit de voyeur* extended now five billion times. But who had who and who got paid was known only to the Frères Warner and the NBA members who had paid their dues.

Does it not seem passing strange? The mayhem there, the palmistry of lewdness produced at such low cost? A pod of wattage for a chair, to enjoy, in congress, busts of stellar consequence? Villains into shining heroes, tailored changelings by the magic wands of light? But wait! Keyholes for pain are not all it reaches. It proves that the possession of money, reason for such Eden, is why we're here. That leeches may try to get it—lay-abouts, black queens in pink Cadillacs—therefore the murder season is all year round. As is the lying, cheating, arson, beating, duping, treason, dishonor, rape—prayers by mockers, tears from bawds, jeers by parsons. I beg, don't jape. There we are, massing gaily, seeking new thrills, waiting to march into video tubes, finding our wills, as once those dancing children did, under the Koppelberg Hill.

20

T HE TWENTY-THIRD and twenty-fourth floors of the New Baker Hotel were commandeered as a headquarters and hospital for the Marshal of the American Union. When the wound had been treated, the Marshal ordered that he be rolled on a gurney

to a chaise longue in his office, and had General Black brought to
him.

He was stretched out, white as surgical cotton, when Black
was brought in by MPs and Chay's Chief of Staff, General Melvin,
Black's hands manacled behind his back. Black's face was battered
and swollen. There was blood on his tunic. Chay ordered the MPs
to remove the handcuffs and told them all to leave the room.
Melvin protested harshly against Chay taking such a risk.

"Risk? Kent was a classmate, Al. You know that."

When they were alone he offered Black a drink and a cigar.
Black refused. "Bad for the teeth," he said.

"You must have put up quite a fight, kid," Chay said.

"Not really. This happened after they had me in the stockade.
Somebody wanted a confession. I thought it was you."

"I may want a confession, but that's no way to get it."

"Hombre! You really made it, Chay. Marshal of the American
Union! Six stars! Holy shit!"

"How did you get mixed up with such people?"

"What people?"

"The Sandinistas."

"I don't know any Sandinistas."

"Then why did you mutiny?"

"I didn't mutiny. I was supporting my oath to the Constitution. Your side revolted against it."

"There is no Constitution and the oath was transferred to
me."

"And to who and what were you transferred, Chay?"

"The continuing government of the United States."

"Well, I don't accept the new, continuing government. I don't
recognize it. What's happened to you, Chay, selling out to this
bunch of assassins? They destroyed not only the entire command
but the government of the United States!"

"Kent—lissena me." He took a deep breath and put his faith
in the magical luck which Winkelreid had proved he had, which
he had to have had to have come through that street battle where
the odds were thirty to one. "Nothing is either as bad or as good
as it seems. All you have to do is to sign a statement giving reasons
why you attempted the coup today and confess to the past attacks,
and we can work out an acceptable solution."

"Acceptable to who?"

"Acceptable to you, first and foremost. I can have you disappear into the system and come out on the other side at some comfortable place without a worry in the world."

"I was afraid of that. Jesus, Chay, are you ever going to realize that there is life outside the Army? I used to watch you soldier while you slept, for Christ's sake."

"I have to have a confession to save you, kid. Important people were murdered. Part of an Army was subverted. I may have to have what is left of them shot to bring the rest to their senses."

"Jesus, I hope so. But I can't do that, Chay."

"You may know that whatever confession you will make will not be true—maybe I will know it—but no one else will."

"No."

"The alternative is bad."

"A firing squad?"

"No, no! Please try to understand. We have to have a confession for the news media—no matter how you feel about it—which will admit you were acting for the Sandinistas."

Chay thought of what the interrogators were going to do. Kent Black was one of his oldest friends. The man could speak Danish, for Christ's sake. Chay had given him this girl when they had been on leave in New York when they were upperclassmen and it had turned into such a big thing that the girl had taught Kent Danish. The other guys thought they had invented some kind of a code when Chay and Black had talked to each other. His father had nearly blown his mind when he took the two of them to dinner at that great spaghetti joint on Fifty-sixth Street and, on signal, Black had begun to chat with him in Danish. Kent was a terrific officer. Chay started to tell himself that maybe he should just get Black out of this mess but then he thought of the company sergeant on the North Slope in Alaska, a red-headed guy, nine years old, named John Kullers. That was a soldier. Man, he thought, that was the toughest son of a bitch I ever faced before or since. There was no other way. This was war. Black had gone over to the other side and he had to be made to serve as an example for every soldier under the flag, or else what was the meaning of discipline?

"But I wasn't acting for the Sandinistas," Black said.

.   .   .

The head of the DDI interrogation team called him at 5:17 the
next morning to report General Black's confession and death.
"Send it over here," Chay ordered.

When the confession arrived, Chay read it as he sat in the
bathtub with Black's statement held up by Molly Tompkins. He
was outraged. It read as if it had been copied straight out of
McGuffey's Reader of Political Confessions. He was disappointed
in the DDI team. In the future, he would have to put Grogan's
people on these things, not only to give it some style but to make
it sound true. This goddamn thing had blood all over it. What
kind of people were running interrogations? How could this be
shown to the media? He was going to have to talk to Al Melvin
about it, in some indirect way, but Al would look at him as if he
had peed in the soup. In the future, Eddie Grogan would definitely
have to take over the confession detail.

He told Molly to have an orderly serve his breakfast at his
desk in twelve minutes' time. His thigh was very tender and he
had to favor it greatly. Molly dried him and dressed him as he lay
on the chaise longue in his office and thought about the rumors
of mutiny by the Pacific Fleet. Zendt probably had it all under
control, if it had happened, but it was a television opportunity
that he probably shouldn't pass up. He wondered if he gave the
networks a tremendous show of battle with dummy shells whether
that would solve the problem, but he had to make sure that none
of his people would be hurt. Some elements of the Second Army
had rampaged around Fort Gillem. They had helped themselves
to a lot of other people's women, some banks had been robbed,
and mostly they had tied up a lot of massage parlors without
paying a dime. It was just high spirits. He'd rip a few asses off
and everything would settle down.

Topology, the study of the properties of geometric figures as
they are distorted or deformed in various dimensions had, long
before, been applied by Chay to his own deviousness which was
usually so successful because it sprang from his enormous en-
dowment of great and good luck.

"Among the many varied things extant, there are properties
that change when you break them, but not when you bend them,"
he had explained to Brill. He had taken deviousness further. He

had applied the String Theory to it, a theory which depends on whether six other dimensions exist in the universe. Chay took deviousness seriously, as a matter of tactics rather than of character.

Molly told him his mother was calling on line one. Eight-fifteen in the morning! He nodded. Molly hit the button which released the call into the amplifier.

"Hello, Mom," he said dully.

"See what I mean?" Serena's voice rasped at him. "If you had grabbed that Paramount contract when my people offered it, you wouldn't have a hole in your leg today. Lissena me, Chay. The international coverage you got after that kid ran you through is like pure gold. Fox and Columbia are in line behind Paramount at the Morris Office. I am talking big percentage points here, Chay. They are gonna offer a gorrontee like you never heard such numbers and on top they wanna pile 11.3 of the gross. I am talking the kinda money that makes your pension look like bupkis. Whatta you say? You want the world onna silver platter plus a shot at any broad in pictures?"

"Mom, for once and for all," Chay replied wearily, "I am not going to leave my work."

"Okay. All right. On your head then, butchkie. If you don't care that your mother could end up a wreck worrying about how she's gonna support six children." Serena broke into tears. "I can't take the worry, Chay. I can't take it. I'm too old."

"Mom—please listen. Things are working out. I'm going to be able to add 4 percent to your weekly check."

"Well. That's very nice. You are a very sweet boy, Chay. Now the big news. I am moving to Dallas with Jonnie and Berry so I can take care of you. I am gonna sew for you and cook for you and we'll be one big wonderful family together."

"Mom! No!" he cried out into the telephone. But she had hung up.

As if they had deferred to Serena, the Appleton siblings called in rapid succession. Dudley was on the line the longest and said the least. Sylvester told Chay to refuse any medical treatment because he had mustered an entire religious community and their powerful prayers behind Chay. It all took twelve minutes out of an important day but Chay was warmed that they had all taken the trouble to call him.

Hedda Blitzen was nibbling on a *pinkelwurst* and watching the "Today" show when she saw Chay leap from an open car brandishing a rifle and facing down a gang of soldiers who were spilling across the street toward him. She screamed when she saw him take the bayonet in his thigh.

She finished the *pinkelwurst* then called American Airlines and was on the 9:17 flight to Dallas after trying frantically and unsuccessfully to get a call through to Chay. She called her brother Wolfie just before she left the apartment.

"Wolfie? Hedda. I'm leaving for Dallas right away."

"Dallas?"

"My friend, Chay Appleton, has been hurt."

"Chay Appleton?"

"You met him outside the store once."

"Chay *Apple*ton? Marshal of the American Union Appleton? The television star? You *know* him?"

"Please explain to Poppa and call Gretel to cover me at the store. I'll be back as soon as I can." She hung up, packed a bag, and ran.

At the New Baker Hotel in Dallas she had a lot of trouble even to find out the number of Chay's room. The reception people just went stony on her. She demanded to see the manager which appeared to be even more difficult so she reached across the reception desk and held the clerk tightly by the front of his cutaway jacket. "I am the Marshal of the American Union's fiancée," she said fiercely, "and if you don't tell him I am here—all the way from New York—he is going to tear this lobby down."

"Your name, please," the clerk said, still in her grip.

"Miss Hedda Blitzen."

He extricated himself from her small fist, picked up a tele phone and dialed. "This is the reception desk," he said into the phone. "Miss Hedda Blitzen is here." He listened. "She says she is Marshal Appleton's fiancée. I'll hold." There was a two-minute wait. "You are to go to Suite 3420," he said to Hedda. "Front!"

Chay had been arranged on the chaise longue when Hedda came into the room, his face flushed with excitement as he tried to figure out how he was going to bang her with the handicap of a game leg. She was a small woman but perhaps she would be able to straddle the chaise longue.

"Miss Blitzen. Sah!" Tompkins said.

"Oh, Chay! I saw it all! It is terrible!"

"Good heavens, you sweet thing. An occupational hazard. Missed the artery. No infection, no fuss. I'll be up and walking in three days."

"Three days," she said with disappointment. "The 'Today' show said—"

"Come here." She sat close to him. He reached up and pulled her down to him. "God, how I missed you," Chay said hoarsely then devoured her face, while he fumbled under her skirt.

"Chay! Oh, Chay. Ooooooh, *Chaaaaay!*"

As it developed, she *was* able to straddle the chaise and still be able to lean forward to allow him to chew manically on her breasts as if they were bunches of grapes. It all turned out to be better physical therapy than anything the Army doctors could have recommended. It stimulated his circulation, toned his thigh muscles, and in a most positive way, accelerated his recovery. So much for the conservatives who teach that the missionary position is the only way.

It was decided that, for the time being anyway, until he was up and about, at least, she would stay with him in the suite.

"Sergeant Tompkins will show you where you will be," the Marshal said. "And no saluting. This isn't the Reagan White House."

21

GENERAL BLACK'S FIFTH ARMY had not responded to the evaporation of Washington the way the Second Army, and possibly the Pacific Fleet, was responding. It had not robbed banks, sequestered gorgeous young women, raided saloons, or commandeered massage parlors. Nonetheless, subversive elements of the Fifth Army had made war on the National Conference for Democracy and, in sudden prime time appearances on Texas television, had charged that the NCD was an illegal government. Worse, there were civilians who agreed with them.

Therefore, whenever a really hard Sandinista line surfaced after Black's capture, the public seemed to anticipate that Black was going to be sacrificed because on the national morning shows broadcast just a few hours after his death, a top country singer and a headline cowboy trio were on the cameras of two different networks wailing out a fully arranged C&W threnody called "Kint Blagg Dahd Fer Yew." It was a raging hit. Government polls showed that 22 percent of the public believed that Black had been murdered by the government because they knew there was no other way to control his protest. The same poll showed that 31 percent believed that the NCD was merely a cover-up for turning the government into some kind of dictatorship—up 9 percent from ten days before.

With increasing boldness, a part of the media (which was immediately marked by the government as being in the pay of the Sandinistas) extolled Black's memory. But the single thing that was driving Wambly Keifetz into near hysteria was that country song, repeated at random on radio and television throughout all hours of the day and night. It was as if the Nicaraguans were jamming the airwaves.

"Dead, for Christ's sake," Keifetz exploded at Chay, "he's bigger than Elvis and Marilyn combined. You've got to do something about it. Did you ever hear such crap as that goddamn song?"

With a choked voice, he recited the lyric which was sweeping the country.

> He stood on the courthouse steps
> Takin' bullets like the rain,
> He answered them with quips
> And said, "Are you insane?"
> We're fightin' fer ahr flag here,
> Ahr peepul, right an trew,
> an' if you sully Uncle Sam
> It's a-gunna go right baaaaaad fer
>   yew.

Chay took up the refrain, laying back on the chaise, a cushion under his bandaged thigh, singing in a nasal, mocking, high-pitched burlesque of the Grand Old Opry, squeezing the dipthongs into sausage links:

> Blagg is baag, Blagg is baag,
> 'Cause he nivver went away.
> He'll find us ahr salvation
> Long a-fore the Judgement Day.

"Don't joke!" Keifetz snapped. "This one little thing could undo all American hopes for decades to come."

"Then we'll make him a national hero."

"What?"

"We'll give him a hero's funeral."

"Whaaaaaat?"

"I'll deliver the eulogy myself. We'll tell them that because he was a patriot, he volunteered to join the enemy camp so he could expose them for what they are, Sandinista rats. We'll produce medically certified photographs to prove that he was shot in the back as he stood on those courthouse steps calling out to me for help. We'll prove he was cut down by a Nicaraguan death squad planted among his own troops to silence him."

"Jesus, Chay, that could do it. But how will you get the pictures?"

"Oh, we'll pick up some Nicaraguan sympathizer and have Grogan's people do the job on him, then we'll lay him on his face and make the shots."

"Splendid. Capital! Oh, bully! Now—the Second Army and the Pacific Fleet."

"I am scheduled for that in twenty minutes."

22

CHAY SAT ON THE CHAISE behind his desk in Dallas, facing the Combined Chiefs and snarling into the satellite telephone at Admiral Zendt at Pearl Harbor. "I want you here in Dallas by no later than tonight," he said.

"I've got a pretty bad tooth, Marshal," the Admiral said. "The dentist will be here in twenty minutes."

"A bad *tooth?*" Chay yelled. "You're lucky you don't have a bad neck from hanging on a yardarm. Compare that to a bad tooth, you son of a bitch!" He disconnected heavily. He spoke to the Signals Officer who was standing by wearing a backpack and a headset. "Get me the Second Army Commander at Fort Gillem."

"General Quest? Shut up! I'll do the talking. Be at my headquarters in Dallas in five hours."

"No way, Chay," General Quest said.

"Get here. I may even be able to save your neck." He disconnected.

He addressed the Joint Chiefs at random. "They let their people tear up the countryside, then they're surprised when I come down on them. Zendt is one thing. You could say it was just high spirits, but Quest's troops robbed banks. They harassed beautiful women. They appropriated the contents of liquor stores and bars, and Quest tells me he won't come in to talk about it."

The Signals Officer told him Fort Gillem was calling.

"Quest has come to his senses," Chay said to the Joint Chiefs.

"General Quest is unavailable, sir," the Signals Officer said.

"Unavailable?"

"A Command Sergeant Major is standing by for your orders, sir."

"A Sergeant *Major?*"

"Command Sergeant Major Kullers, sir. He is in command at Fort Gillem pending further orders, sir."

"Kullers?"

"Yes, sir."

"K-u-l-l-e-r-s?"

The Signals Officer repeated the spelling into his headset. "Yes, sir."

"What are his first and middle names?"

The Signals Officer put the question to the telephone. "John. DeWitt," he said to the Marshal of the American Union.

"Tell him to stand by." He spoke to Al Melvin, the Chairman. "Ask the computer for a transcript of Sergeant Major Kullers's record."

Somehow, Chay managed to maintain a semblance of composure but within himself he was dazed. He had been hurled back over the decades to the North Slope of Alaska. He was five years and two months old again, not particularly sure of himself, and facing the drill sergeant of the Cadet Corps who was reaming him out because he had found the suggestion of oil on Chay's rifle. He had lived in awe of John DeWitt Kullers all through pre-primary maneuvers and all the way into the third grade when Kullers had disappeared after four years of inspired and inspiring soldiering. He had been sent away somewhere to a military junior high school for tenth-graders, but he had left behind a legacy of discipline and command which had never been equaled in Chay's subsequent Army experience.

Here was more proof of his new-found magical luck. At the moment when he most needed a totally trustworthy and accomplished soldier by his side, John DeWitt Kullers, the soldier's soldier, had materialized.

Fighting himself for calm, he ordered the Signals Officer to put Kullers on the satellite phone.

"Sah!" the response came through the amplifier loud and clear.

"Why has General Quest been unable to come to the phone, Sergeant?"

"General Quest has been confined to quarters. Sah!"

"By whom?"

"He was in flagrant violation of U.S. Army regulations. Sah!"

"But who ordered his confinement?"

"I did. Sah!"

"What of the other officers on the post?"

"Five have been confined, sir. Those remaining have been paralyzed into inaction. There were severe riots, robberies, and other violations, sir. Regulations indicated that something had to be done so I took the necessary action. Sah!"

"Do you require orders for transport, Sergeant Major?"

"No. Sah!"

"Be at my headquarters in Dallas as soon as you can get here this evening." Chay disconnected.

The meeting with CINCPAC, Fleet Admiral Harvey Zendt, took place in the office of the CINCAFUSCIAFBIANSA, nerve center of the American defenses for the Free (Anti-Nicaraguan) World. It was not an understated room. Marshal Appleton was stretched out on a Louis XV chaise longue which had been set on a pedestal behind a $71,000 Florentine desk large enough, were it not impractical, for a helicopter to land upon. The desk was highly polished and cleared of everything: no distracting papers, in-baskets, or telephones.

Chay faced Admiral Zendt and the Joint Chiefs: Melvin, CJCS; Krolik, Naval Operations; Bennett, Army; and the head Air Force honcho, Bessie Lear.

Bessie was such a motherly-looking woman that a military constructionist could have said that she was miscast, but she was the only DOD executive in almost twenty years who had been able to bring the price of Air Force toilet seats down to a reasonable level. She knitted throughout the meeting. She was unfailingly sympathetic, but she was known in every air unit as the most monomaniacal despot-disciplinarian-martinet in all the six services including the Space Command. But with her soft, white, wavy hair, her pink cheeks, and her prosthetic smile which seemed to admit shyly to having invented apple pie, she had been the invaluable spokesperson for all the Armed Forces until Chay had come on the scene.

"Mutiny in wartime. How does that sound?" Chay asked Admiral Zendt.

Chay looked out of the hotel window across the clear sky to Las Colinas and the airport. At last he spoke again. "The networks—that is to say the American people—must be served. Strikes must be staged. Tremendous noise must be made. We want an operation which will save the taxpayers tens of millions of dollars and thousands of lives."

"I don't follow you, Marshal," Admiral Zendt said.

"I am saving your neck, for Christ's sake."

"You want me to shell my ships with dummy shells, bomb them with dud bombs, and shoot them with blank ammunition?"

"Precisely."

"How will you fool the men? How are you going to keep the crews of the Pacific Fleet quiet for the rest of their lives?"

"When the battle is over, Admiral, and democracy is respected once again, your men—whose food necessarily will have been drugged to take them out of consciousness all during our mock-assaults—will be shipped out to other installations around the world—scattered as it were—and the men from the other installations will replace them."

"What if the stuff doesn't work?" Al Melvin said. "What do we do if they all start remembering and blab about a staged operation?"

"Al, lissena me. Six or eight units of the Pacific Fleet are going to be locked in their area for about six hours of the most exciting television this country has ever seen. Are you going to tell me that some crappy sailor who yammers that the whole thing is a fake is really going to convince any decent American who has been pinned to his set thoughout the battle? They've been brainwashed by television since 1947, Al. Are they going to believe some asshole gob or do they believe in television?"

23

CHAY READ Kullers's personnel file for the third time while he had the man wait outside the room. Kullers had made sergeant in the first year of his enlistment in the Army, and twenty-three years later, he had soared to the rank of Command Sergeant Major at Army Corps level. He had been offered, six times over the years, and had refused to accept, battlefield commissions and opportunities to receive officer training, and had had his services requested by two foreign governments and three emerging Third World nations, but by paper-shuffling techniques known only to master sergeants, he had eluded all of it. He had been decorated three times and wore battle ribbons commemorating eighteen combat engagements with the Vietnamese and the Nicaraguans. He had never been absent on sick call.

It was certainly, beyond any doubt, the same man who had formed his life thirty-five years before in Alaska. He thanked God for Army discipline which had been driven into Kullers for all of his life because even if Kullers did find out somehow that Chay had been the five-year-old cadet at North Slope, Chay's rank, and the Army's deification of it, would prevent Kullers from taking over his life once again and pouring scorn upon it.

He pressed the buzzer to have Kullers sent in.

The door opened. A flawless Sergeant Major, the very model of a noncommissioned officer, entered the room. He had the instinctive grace and training to project awe at being admitted to the presence of the Commander-in-Chief of the Armed Forces, yet he was also able to provide a sense of equality-through-utility as if rank were co-equal with function, that Chay might *be* the Army, but he and other noncoms made the Army possible.

Kullers was of average height, a long-waisted man who would appear as a giant when seated, and who, in the sense of dense muscularity and the promise of protection to all who came into his care, suggested a large and indestructible tree. He was gnarled.

Such hair as he had left was as red as autumn Canadian creeper. His deeply lined, character-stained face had the immutability of sculpture, and the high shine of his boots was blinding. Three consecutive French legionnaires could have shaved with the crease in his trousers. A faint smell of gun oil packed the air within two feet of him. His eyes were still very blue, very clear, and very hard. Chay shuddered.

"Sah!" Kullers shouted on coming to a halt directly in front of the CINCAFUSCIAFBIANSA's desk. There was a beautifully executed salute, regulation to a micro-angle in every nuance of its stance; incomparably perfect, Chay thought, remembering the thousands of times he had practiced trying to achieve such a salute from North Slope to West Point.

"Sah! Command Sergeant Kullers reporting for court-martial."

"There will be no court-martial."

"United States Army regulation number—"

"Sit down."

"Sah!" Kullers found a chair.

"There was a mutiny and an insurrection at Fort Gillem. How many troops were involved?"

"Less than a hundred, sir. They were led into the marauding by the officers, sir. General Quest announced that he intended to take over the State of Georgia as—well—as a sort of kingdom, sir."

"Was he drunk? His troops robbed banks. They abducted women. Massage parlor workers are in a state of exhaustion without a cent to show for it."

"I am told the general takes peculiar powders, sir."

"I want an open and frank answer to the next question, Sergeant Major. Do you have any information which could lead one to believe that General Quest had any contact with the government of Nicaragua?"

Chay asked the question for the tape machine which was whirling inside a drawer of his desk. He knew that the only possible answer to the question would have to implicate General Quest as the betrayer of his country because no other possible explanation would satisfy the pundits who did the thinking for the country on Sunday morning television. Quest was a traitor who had sold out to Managua, and he was going to have to be shot so that, for once and for all, an example could be made.

"I couldn't say, sir," Kullers answered. "But the general does speak Spanish."

"What would such a crazed plan do to the morale of American troops around the world? It would be a triumph for the Sandinistas. A modern Trojan horse."

"I concur, sir. That is why I sealed off Fort Gillem."

"The Army will never forget you for what you've done. Dismissed, Sergeant Major. Return to Fort Gillem and keep General Quest under close arrest."

Kullers stood, saluted, executed a perfect right-about-face, and started to the door. Chay called out to him. He halted and turned just as smartly.

"I am going to award you with the Distinguished Service Cross, and I should be very much surprised if the State of Georgia doesn't decorate you as well.'

"*Sah!*"

"When this mess has been settled you will be transferred to my headquarters staff as Command Sergeant Major of the U.S. Army."

"Sah!" Kullers wheeled and left the room.

As Chay watched the door close behind his hero, he felt both profound gratitude and deep resentment; gratitude because Kullers had remained in the image in which Chay had cast him so long before; resentful because the man had not relaxed his superhuman quality, preventing Chay from successfully patronizing him.

He dictated a short directive to General Melvin into the thin air for the tape machine in his desk, ordering a court-martial for General Quest on charges of plotting with the enemy for the overthrow of the government of the United States and that he be found guilty and shot forthwith. He transferred John DeWitt Kullers to Army headquarters in Dallas, and promoted him to Sergeant Major of the Army. In the future, from the distance, the red and white markings on Kullers's sleeves with their wreaths, chevrons, arcs, and stars would make him seem like a tattooed

Maori warrior. He was now officially the ultimate sergeant in the ultimate army of the world.

24

T HE MATINEE and evening exercises with Hedda Blitzen had worked wonders with Chay's wounded thigh. The doctors allowed him to walk with the help of a rubber-tipped cane, although for mobility he still spent most of his time in a wheelchair. Late in the evening of the day of the terrible news that General Quest had sold out to the Sandinistas, a telephone call came through for Hedda from Luddie, her brother in New York, to tell her that their father had been taken to St. Luke's Hospital for a carotid thromborendarterectomy.

"Hey, that sounds serious," Chay said.

"Poppa will never be able to pronounce it. God knows how it sounds in German."

The decision to part again was agonizing and the pain of it kept them busy upon the bed for most of the night. Chay was convinced that he could not function without her, at a time when his faculties had to be at their keenest. Weeping piteously, ensnarled in the sheets, Hedda promised to return as soon as she knew that her father was safe. "That little delicatessen throws off more money than you might realize," she explained with anxiety. Chay promised her that by the time she returned, even if she were, please God, to be back by the following afternoon, that he would have found a sweet little house for them.

Hedda left at seven the next morning for the airport, refusing Chay's offer of a fighter-bomber to speed her to New York on the preposterous grounds that "it wouldn't be fair to the tax-payers."

After she left the New Baker Hotel on that enchanted morning, Chay tried to think about his magical luck and the mutiny at Fort Gillem. Having been surrounded by people for every hour of the day for all of his life from pre-primary school onward, he believed he could not think if he were left alone. The theory was totally untested because for all of his life he had never been alone—going as far as always leaving the bathroom door open, barking orders in place, and always sleeping with a staff sergeant on duty inside the bedroom door. Not that he had ever believed that his ecstasy in knowing Hedda came from loneliness. She was his woman. That was the simple fact, and there would never be another woman who could ever take her place.

Wambly Keifetz, a man who lived in the future to serve the present, had had Chay and Hedda under constant (close) sur-veillance by teams of Eddie Grogan's people since the afternoon they had met outside Schwalhaber's in New York. Keifetz had no intention of allowing Chay to become involved, or possibly think of marrying, a woman as far beyond government control as Hedda Blitzen. He was sickened to see that they seemed genuinely to love each other. In his experience people in that state were difficult to manipulate.

Keifetz had seen that Hedda's father being stricken by a fash-ionable disease presented a clear opportunity, and working with Grogan's staff psychiatrists, he conceived a plan to intercept Chay at the crossroads, as it were, by playing on Chay's innate male susceptibilities which Keifetz knew could divert him away from the young delicatessen heiress.

He began with a congratulatory meeting which showered Chay with praise for the way he had handled the incidents within the Pacific Fleet and the treachery at Fort Gillem.

"Your intuition concerning General Quest's sellout to the San-dinistas was absolutely brilliant, Chay," he told the young Mar-shal.

"There was no other explanation," Chay said. "Quest speaks Spanish. He certainly allowed the mutiny—God knows the reparations the government is going to have to pay out to those massage parlors—and the whole thing was a sublime opportunity for Nicaragua. Quest had to be a traitor."

"Will you order a court-martial?"

"I am going to have him shot out of hand at dawn tomorrow."

"You are a leader, Chay. I cannot tell you the comfort that brings to the country."

"There was nothing else I could do."

"We must have a little celebration. A very dear friend of mine, the widow of Admiral Effing, is having a little buffet supper to-night. Her house is right in Highland Park. I'll give the address to your batman and we'll meet there at 10:15, shall we?"

Chay had wanted to wallow in his loss of Hedda, and his leg was giving him more trouble than usual. "Very kind of you, Wamb, but I just don't think I'm up to it tonight."

"Nonsense. Won't hear of it. See you there at 10:15." Keifetz patted him on the shoulder and left.

Chay had Tompkins dress him in the blues with full decorations. He slipped his black homburg on sideways and hobbled across the pavement at his private entrance to the New Baker, leaning on his rubber-tipped cane, and entered the armored personnel carrier in which his personal military staff sat waiting to take the seven-minute ride with him to Mrs. Effing's.

He entered Mrs. Effing's house on Laurel Street through tall doors which had been copied from the Hotel Santabucci in Paris, once the palace of a goombah of Napoleon I, into a cortile which ran along the axis of the house. The hall was about thirty feet wide by about eighty feet long with opulently painted ceilings showing angels and goddesses done in the style of Boucher. Two urns at either side of the great doors were of Egyptian granite, made during the craze for Egyptian art that had followed Napoleon's African campaign. The wood walls were in the style of Sansovino, whose buildings skirted two sides of the Piazza San Marco in Venice. The chandeliers were said to be from a Spanish cathedral. The long rug of the hall was one of the finest surviving Spanish floor-coverings of the fifteenth century. It had been made for the next-door neighbor of Christopher Columbus in Genoa, although the legend persisted that the two had never met. A dolphin table

from the Sciarra palace in Rome and a large blue-and-white por-
celain bowl of seventeenth-century China dominated the center
of the hall. Everything in the room, indeed in the house, was a
copy that had been commissioned by Eddie Grogan as stage dressing, an important part of the surveillance of the Royalist community.

A lively bit of either Mozart or a Chet Baker record could be
heard faintly above the sounds of many hyperactive people talking. A solemnly stoned butler took Chay's cloak and hat. As his
hostess came toward him the world's most susceptible man teetered forward toward the pit of love.

"Marshal! O, Marshal Appleton!" she cried out, curtsying
prettily. "I cannot *believe* that you cared to come to my little buffet
supper!"

She was utterly elegant and so scandalously beautiful that
there was an instant starting within his trousers despite the heavy
metal cup his hot blood had forced him to wear wherever he knew
there would be women. The pain of suppressing all that swelling
tissue into such a confinement was intense, but he had borne pain
before in a gallant cause.

"Madam," he said, having no idea who she could be.

"Ah, Marshal Appleton," Keifetz's sugary voice murmured
at his elbow. "Excellent! Excellent! May I present to you our hostess, Madame Ulyssa Effing—brave widow of the late Admiral
Forest Effing—Ulyssa, this is Marshal of the American Union Caesare Appleton."

"Welcome to my little home," Ulyssa said. "Now you simply
must come in and allow me to show you off to the others."

"Mrs. Effing offers a very fine grade of cocaine," Keifetz said.

"Thank you," Chay said, "but a glass of celery tonic and Mrs.
Effing's company will do me as well."

She swept him into the main salon to be stared at by the
crowd which the new government had attracted to Dallas, most
of them iced-out on blow from a large punch bowl which was set
out on a glorious copy of a Georgian table at the center of the
room. There were so many nationally known gofers, layabouts,
and pundits in the enormous room that, for a moment, he thought
he had wandered into a party at Brill's or a double-page spread
in *W*. Then he recognized who they were. These were the key

American Royalists. Keifetz was their leader and this entrancing woman was one of his hostesses.

There wasn't another uniformed person in the room other than his own staff of six: a lieutenant general and his aide; a fleet admiral and his aide; an ecstatically-famous lieutenant colonel of Marines, and a SWAAF captain whose iron-gray hair had just come out of rollers.

Madame Effing guided him swiftly through introductions to those guests standing nearest the door. The other guests were too stoned to bother to turn toward him. Chay overcame the urge to order his staff to draw their swords and go around the room striking everyone smartly across the buttocks to enforce a sense of respect for rank. Mrs. Effing led him off, chatting, toward the somewhat inaccessible conservatory.

"Some of these people are under the influence of controlled substances," Chay exclaimed to his hostess.

"Controlled? Substances?" A tiny woman, she stared up at him through pinpoint pupils. He lost his heart for (relatively) ever. He held her hand after they had entered the conservatory, staring deeply into her eyes and giving his powerful male smells a chance to work their claims upon her. He had signaled to his aide-de-camp to leave them alone.

Mrs. Effing sank to her knees before him.

"No, no, my dear," he said in a kindly way, drawing her to her feet again. "That is really not necessary. I am only a simple soldier."

"Oh, Marshal!" she moaned. "The power of your masculinity leaves me faint. I am as excited as a young girl. You must allow me to fellate you, sir. Please—you must!"

She fell into another deep curtsy, or so he thought. He had noticed how punctiliously the Royalist women held to correct verb forms, not deigning to sink into the vernacular. He had to admit, then as well as later when he daydreamed upon the moment, that he had to admire the woman's degree of cultivation.

Earlier that day, Mrs. Effing had debated what the effect of a suden offer of fellatio would have upon the Marshal. "How do you expect me to hold the regard of the man," she said to Keifetz who had been coaching her, "if I go down on him five minutes after we meet?"

"My dear woman," Keifetz had said to her, "do you really think I just jumped into this thing? I have been over the tactic again and again with Grogan's psychiatrists in whose computers exist the densest personality profile of Chay Appleton ever assembled. That data shows him to be one of the most susceptible men on this planet, a man who, by the force of his mountainous ego and his forever unrequited attraction to his mother, will be overcome by the idolatrousness of your offer to fellate him. He will be helpless, Grogan's people assured me. The prize we seek will be won."

"Will I be allowed to see that psychiatric profile?" Ulyssa asked.

"Just as I will have to control him, so will you, on your own turf. You will need to know that he will only acknowledge what has happened if it matches what he wants to have happen. A massive factor in the profile is that absolutely nothing anyone could say or do would shake his total faith in events as he saw them happening, whether that was realistic or wholly illusory. He will be our anchorman, sitting there with his hair neatly combed and his tie straight, his tailoring absolutely breathtaking, reporting to media and public alike what we tell him to say. And God knows the press will cooperate. They are making so much money now that they will drown the first man who tries to rock the boat."

"But—actually—" Ulyssa said, "I will have quite different assessments to make."

"You will be part of the team which will insulate him from the raspings and difficulties of life. You will be one of the stage-managers in a production in which every moment will be scheduled, every word scripted, every camera position chalked with toe-marks. He is a soldier, Ulyssa. He will have little to do with the invention and implementation of policies. And even though he will not have given us direct orders, we will all know what he wants us to do. There is positively enormous precedent for that."

As she moaned and whimpered over Chay, her hands undid the front of his sturdy military trousers. When she found the metal cup she gasped, but she had known fastidious men before, and she understood at once how to zip it away and simultaneously to stand aside. The great hawser of flesh uncoiled itself as if driven by a giant steam catapult and leapt out into the room like a bonsai-ed sequoia. She gasped her admiration and immediately revised her plans. She sank back upon the floor, pulling her rouged and dimpled little knees up beside each of her tiny, pink ears. The Marshal of the American Union fell upon her with a hoarse cry, entered her, upped her and downed her, inned her and outed her, building their shared sensations to the apex of a giant emotional pyramid. Then, during a long silence, Chay lay inert upon her, racked by Cheyne-Stokes breathing. Cupid's candy arrow had pierced his heart.

25

COVERED BY LIVE and taping cameras of eleven national and international networks, Chay leaned on his cane at General Black's graveside. All of the print media and the television news shows of the previous two days had been filled with authenticating proof that Black had been shot in the back by Sandinista traitors who had been planted in his own ranks.

Chay conferred the Distinguished Service Cross upon the memory of the dead man for "patriotism above and beyond the call of duty" and paraphrased, with moving and beautiful elocution, the heartbreaking "Cowboy's Prayer" because three consecutive national polls (of 1,200 people at each polling) showed that the cowboy ranked 9.2 percent higher in the admiration of the American people than their runners-up, the Teamsters, or *their* runners-up, the Hairdressers.

"Help us, Lord," Chay said in part, working the tremolo, "to live our lives as my old pard and classmate, Kent Black, did, as he makes his last ride to the country Up There, where the grass grows lush, green, and stirrup-high, and the water runs cool, clear, and deep, that You as our last judge will tell us that our entry fees are paid."

America wept unashamedly. They knew Kent Black had ridden home, and the promise that there would be one last use for their money grabbed their imaginations and their hearts.

With the convening of the National Conference for Democracy, Dallas became a city abounding with secret agents of every major power, with lobbyists and pressure groups from western Europe, Asia, and the Third World, and with a diplomatic corps which had been accredited to the Conference in Dallas until such time as a permanent American capital city could be chosen, a matter which would take up the next six and a half years. It was estimated that there were more than seventy-eight press agents for the film actors who aspired to politics. Dallas had become a rallying point for the television clergy with their big bucks and their fancy women. The restaurants were littered with rock singers, Mafia executives, and Right-to-Life advocates who had poured in to exploit the national merchandising opportunity.

It was also a deeply religious crossroads, beginning with prayer breakfasts every morning which led into pious opening ceremonies for each session of the National Conference for Democracy. Some years before, corporate ecumenism, which had been so long in the process of finding itself, had conjoined with the Anglican Church of England, Scotland, and Wales, the Lutheran Church of northern Europe, and the Episcopal and Presbyterian Churches of America (and 426 other Protestant sects) with the Holy Mother Church of Rome.

This ecumenical union of world religions surged out into the Middle East and into Asia as the Keifetz Plan proved to their Elders that there were huge savings to be made if the streamlining of world religions were done. Islam and Hinduism, the multiple religions of India, the Buddhists and Shintoists of China and Japan, joined into one working union with the religions of the west: Catholic, Protestant, Mormon, and Jewish under one Central Committee chaired by a CEO called the Ecumenical Pope whose world headquarters were at the Ecumenical Vatican in Rome.

Operating savings were enormous. Tables of organization were reorganized to productive efficiency. Profit and loss statements took on a healthy glow while yields multiplied, permitting, within two years, a consolidated stock offering which opened on world exchanges at $23\frac{3}{8}$ but which, ninety-six hours later, had surged to $38\frac{1}{2}$. Fortunes were made. By the end of the first seventy-eight days the stock had leveled off at 71.9. As a result of the profit-taking, the entire subcontinent of India was air-conditioned: houses, offices, factories, within eleven years of the original issue following a three-for-one split.

The gypsy parsons who rained show biz fire and brimstone and raunchy sex upon their electronic congregations from television pulpits and motel units were tolerated because they had replaced vaudeville among the senior citizens. From its television tabernacles it provided electronic novelty strip acts and soft porn sermons, amusement parks and big ticket lotteries, lewd but good-natured sex, and merchandise giveaways accompanied by rousing prayers and gospel rhythm hymns.

The Church of the Upwardly Mobile, the Royalist sect, the serious religion which was destined to become the official faith of the United States, had been founded within the new, combined sepulchre of the Holy Spirit, Ecumenism. Although the Holy Father in Rome was still a (devout) Catholic, the College of Cardinals was now entirely mixed in its religious affiliations and the Curia was wholly the product of the Harvard School of Business. The Papal Nuncio was on hand in Dallas to bless the opening and closing meeting of the Conference and was altogether very helpful in assuring the effectiveness of the government's contacts with God.

However, as well as becoming a nest for religious leaders and foreign spies, Dallas had become the most crowded national rendezvous for hookers of every price, gamblers, soldiers of fortune, astrologers, and freelance miniseries directors. Fast food chains added honky-tonks to their premises. The natives made more money, more quickly, than they had anywhere in the state since the last great Meadowland oil strike on Northwest Highway by John Jackson in 1989.

Dallas became a souk of sin and conspiracy, all of it covered with a vast cloak of respectability and do-rightism which was so

American, woven by the National Conference for Democracy whose inspired members, seen on television during each session, were sitting to re-frame and re-create the American federal system.

It was said that every other tree in Highland Park, safe haven for every legislator, was bugged. Houses were being rented for $7000 a month, a full $1500 more than the going market rate. Hotels were packed.

The Sandinistas were active. Although every attempt at formal meetings for the Conference was made, there were so many violent diversions, assaults, bombings, snipings, riots, and mass attacks made by "Nicaraguan-inspired mercenaries" (as Marshal of the American Union Appleton referred to them in his weekly television talk to the nation) that the real government decisions were being made in the smoke-filled hotel suites, on scrambler phones, and in the backs of stretch limousines whose engines were kept running and whose radios were turned on to impede bugging.

A temporary lull in the street fighting in the fifth week of the Conference permitted a decision to be made concerning the location of the future capital city of the United States, in that the former national capital (Washington, D.C.) was overradiated. The new capital was to be placed equally between Europe and Asia at Gardena, a suburb of Los Angeles, California. The place-name was to be changed to Washington West.

Chay thanked his stars that Eddie Grogan, the long-faced, lugubrious, rubber-lipped Director of Central Intelligence, had secretly made sure that his headquarters at Langley, Virginia, had been architecturally secured against blast and radiation at a cost of $70 million in unaccountable funds earned from the CIA's cocaine-import earnings. The structural protection would not have worked, perhaps, but by some freak of meteorological timing (or by God's will), the prevailing winds had carried the fallout and the great fire storms caused by the evaporation away from Langley. This meant that all the secret records on almost 300 million people still alive across the world were still available. Agents who were protected against radiation could enter the building and bring the records out to be copied under radiation-free conditions.

Eddie Grogan had escaped from the Evaporation by helicopter to a safe house in Trenton, New Jersey. Never believing for one minute that all nuclear weapons had been abolished, he was on guard against the Sandinistas and the Soviet Union. He had prepared his escape to Canada when he learned from a hotel television screen that not only had no other city in the country been attacked, but that the people whom he respected and feared most in the world, the Royalists, had taken responsibility for the bombing. When the American government was being reconstituted in Dallas, Grogan was at the side of his mentor, Wambly Keifetz, who told him to stay close to Marshal of the American Union Appleton, to accompany him south to Dallas, and to report on his thoughts and movements.

Grogan was to be Chay's "eyes and ears" for many years to come until, unfortunately, he became old and relatively useless, and Chay had to give the signal to have him eliminated—or so one version of the story goes.

26

UNTIL HE WAS FORTY YEARS OLD, Marshal of the American Union Appleton was shockingly thin and could very nearly have been described as "tiny." He was decidedly not tiny, of course. At five feet six inches, including the four-centimeter lifts which added 1.5748 inches to his viewpoint, had he had more meat on his frame he could have been considered a quite substantial man—at least when seen on television towering over his aides (who, among themselves, called him "Big Chay"). In the fashion of the day, he wore his hair on the longish side, falling to his shoulders to create a comradeship, Graciela Winkelreid told the news media, with the youth of the country. However, there was nothing absurd about his riveting green eyes. Liz Wantonberg on "Good Morning, America" said Chay had "absolutely boiling green eyes." This was no affected biographer speaking. She had seen those eyes really close up. The eyes and the man had charmed her, she said, but they could also be "somewhat terrifying."

Twice during that crowded first two weeks after assuming command in Dallas, Chay had had to order his troops to fire on assembled pro-Nicaraguan rioters in eleven American cities. That the riots had been organized by a despotic Central American ambition was proven by the direct action taken by armed mobs, as a result of the way the subversive section of the news media referred to Chay's efforts to bring peace in Philadelphia and Baltimore as "massacres." To bring further proof of conspiracy, the Sandinista sympathizers struck at Chay's most cherished possession, his family. In a kangaroo court retaliation against his measures to calm the national community, an unauthorized band of brigands calling themselves the "Congress for America," who were beyond a shadow of a doubt Nicaraguan mercenaries, proclaimed by pamphlet and pirate radio that the country was being taken over by the most reactionary force in its history. They ordered that Chay be captured and brought to trial "dead or alive." This subversive group carried out the incursions against his family in the Virgin Islands.

Chay, in New York for meetings with Keifetz and Camardi, was attacked as he emerged from WhataBurger, an elite dining place on West Fifty-second Street, but with his magical luck (now to be even more greatly marked by Graciela Winkelreid, Serena, and Wambly Keifetz), he slipped out of the grasp of the two men who had seized him and, running toward his staff car shouting, caught the .45 caliber automatic pistol thrown to him by his driver, John DeWitt Kullers, who was himself unable to shoot because Chay was in the direct line of fire. Chay turned and shot his pursuers down—shooting carefully and with extremely precise marksmanship—shattering their ankles to stop them but not to kill them so they could be questioned.

They were questioned. They did confess to being in the pay of Managua. They died from their wounds two days later.

The affair was a national sensation which unified the country against a common enemy. It was such a news event that it required a massive press conference which involved *sixty-one* television camera set-ups of all five U.S. networks, the Canadian Broadcasting Company, the BBC, French Radio-Television Diffusion, Japanese television, the Sino-Soviet all-Asia network and, in fact, total coverage of the world, to be repeated, in full or in excerpt, every hour on the hour. Because over two thousand print reporters and photographers had clamored to attend the press meeting, the massive interview was held from the stage of the old Broadway Theatre at Fifty-third Street and Seventh Avenue. Immediately after the long meeting, Chay was summoned to Dallas where a seventy-minute television opportunity had to be staged at the airport while the National Conference for Democracy was voting him a citation for his courage in action and for his valiance in exposing the Sandinista plot. The decoration brought the start of one more row of ribbons to the left side of his tunics which now had to be counterweighted on the right side to offset the weight of fourteen rows of fruit salad on the left side which sang of his gallantry. Regulations forbade the wearing of these colorful boasts except on ceremonial occasions, but for Chay, as it had for Colonel North long after he had left the Marine Corps, life had become one long ceremonial occasion. The rows of campaign ribbons glowed as if they were powered by some inert gas, but because he was a somewhat short man, they gave the effect that he was wearing one-half of a sandwich board which advertised a paint shop.

Almost immediately on Chay's return to Dallas, the family house on St. John's was bombed. Serena took Jonathan and Berry into the open fields to hide until dawn. The house was sacked and burned to the ground.

Within two hours, Chay was able to send a B-1 bomber for them which flew them to New York where they stayed with Brill. Dudley and Frieda, then Sylvester, joined them in an ecstatic family reunion. Chay put a military bodyguard on all of them for two weeks until the apparent danger had receded.

Chay became an American hero. His picture appeared twice a month on the cover of the *National Enquirer*, the newspaper of national record; on T-shirts and breakfast food packages; and he seemed to live on television news programs and talk shows. The name Caesare, always shortened affectionately to Chay, became the second most popular male christening name in the country, after Ronald, which was sometimes shortened to Ronnie or Ron.

Chay brought his mother, Jonathan, and Berry to Dallas to live in a sweet little house at 3525 Potomac (now a national shrine). However, as soon as he possibly could, he moved into a mansion within a small park-like estate of twenty-two acres in University Park, in a statuesquely fashionable area slightly north of the cathedral-high Presbyterian Church which confirmed the spiritual substance of the area.

Unfortunately, almost two dozen properties had to be condemned to make way for the estate, but undoubtedly the owners had gotten a fair price for them if they could prove they were loyal American citizens and not Nicaraguan agents. As Wambly Keifetz pointed out, it wasn't as though there were no precedent for that sort of thing. Ronald Reagan had had the FBI conduct extensive surveillance on thousands of Americans who, he believed in his heart, had dangerous sympathies with Sandinista plotters. Confiscation was just a natural step after that.

By effecting to protest the move to such a mansion, Chay demonstrated his essential humility and escaped from his mother's cooking in one deft stroke. At last, he gave in to the public's will and moved into the new residence, which carried an evaluation of $13,378,062.27, made possible by the sincere generosity of a few close friends; a freely given gift from General Dynamics, Big Oil, the Teamsters, Lockheed, the American Medical Association, Martin-Marietta, the Used Car Dealers of America, and the schoolchildren of Dixon, Illinois; all entirely anonymously, calling themselves "The Friends of a Simple Soldier," a nonprofit organization which had been incorporated in the Cayman Islands.

They wanted Chay to have a "snug harbor" in his later years. The gift of the deed to the house to Chay, presented by a group of darling Illinois schoolchildren, as shown on national television, was an entirely open-and-aboveboard matter. The nation choked up when tears filled Marshal Appleton's eyes as he accepted title to the property. The show got a rating of 67 even though it was broadcast at 3 P.M. Central Time.

The house was called Rossenarra, an ancient Scandinavian word which had evolved out of the Danish occupation of Ireland in the sixteenth century. The name meant: "Shimmering on the Hill Where Is a Fortress/Holy Place/Warm Cow Barn (or place of community singing)," depending on the translations from the old Norse-Erse. Rossenarra was a Georgian presence, sober and majestic. It had 67 chimneys, 180 windows to be cleaned, 140 clocks to be wound. It required a household staff of 120, including a flower girl who filled the house with Chay's favorite honeysuckle, sweet pea, and roses. Its footmen wore red waistcoats with brass buttons. It had 7 guest suites and 16 single bedrooms with bath.

Chay was awakened each morning by the sound of bagpipes played by his batman, Molly Tompkins, who had been sent to the Juilliard School to study the instrument. The guards were "Chay's Own," the Seventy-fifth Rangers, and no matter where the guests might roam on the manicured grounds, a group of serving women, dressed as nursery rhyme milkmaids, followed them at a discreet distance, ready to offer hot picnic lunches.

It became commonplace for a hundred, sometimes as many as three hundred, guests to gather at Rossenarra for tea and cocaine. Chay did not snort cocaine nor smoke it nor shoot it. He carried the tragedy of his father in his mind, and he could not forget how his father's enslavement to cocaine had brought about the incredible experience with his sister, if that had really happened. Princes, statesmen, Liz Wantonberg, Party Secretaries, Prime Ministers, great junk painters and heavy metal rockers, lords of the Mafia, and the great national news anchormen would sleep there in the gilded suites.

The Pope of the Holy Mother (Ecumenical) Church blessed the house, its outbuildings and garages by satellite on the first day the Marshal of the American Union moved in, an event commemorated by a small engraved plaque attached to the top rail of the back of a chair in the west loggia, the "tea" room which gave onto the bowling green garden. A President of France looked across this vista and was reminded of Versailles, perhaps with a certain rue.

The American architectural historian, James T. Maher, in his monumental *Twilight of Splendor*, wrote: "The chimneys are cold now, the fireplaces empty, and the lead dolphins that once spouted silver arcs of water into the summer air have been torn from their supports in the dried-up pool, almost ninety feet in diameter, at the lower end of the *tapis vert*, a four-hundred-foot carpet of turf now clotted with weeds. In the moonlight, a statue of Ulyssa

Appleton, draped in the baroque folds of a magisterial robe, stands near the temple portico of the palace entrance, but it watches not. Its head has been severed from its shoulders. At the upper end of the garden *allée*, Serena Appleton, carved in limestone, lies face down in the Texas mud, toppled by the alien reflex of madness from her high stone base."

Even after Washington West would have been completed, down to paved streets and street lights, Chay would have continued to maintain his residence at Rossenarra, he told *Ultra*, the Texas magazine, not as "the southwestern White House" but as his full-time official residence. He had become as Texan as George Bush. The government came to him when need be.

He promoted his brother, Jonathan, to the rank of full Colonel of the U.S. Army Engineers. Young Jon had made tens of millions of dollars for Chay and himself through shrewd real estate investing in the Greater Gardena area, particularly in Lawndale and, at his mother's urging, had set aside 8 percent of the windfall to be shared among his other siblings. Dudley immediately invested his share in a harebrained scheme to bring outdoor ice skating rinks to Southeast Asia.

Chay took good care of his mother and the family. He created a Commission for the Evaluation of Soil-Sampling Procedures and made Serena its consultant at a salary of $135,000 a year and expenses. He was able to put Brill in on the ground floor of the burgeoning sixth television network, with substantial stock options. He secured for Berry, then an undergraduate at Barnard College in New York, 20 percent of the stock in the proposed newspaper *The Washington Post West* which he would permit to be published in the District of Columbia West when the government had been reestablished there. He presented Sylvester with a gorgeous set of chasubles in dotted swiss and splashed scarlet, with the most madly-cute collection of varicolored birettas and pastel zucchetos which Sylvester simply adored.

On November 17, 1990, Chay wrote to Dudley at Djakarta, "I have just received $1.5 million for you from the family's share of the CIA income from the cocaine industry. It will be paid into your account here. Do not protest that this is too much or that you do not deserve it. Money does not have the worth it once had. A simple example: a ticket to the coronation of Henry I in 1068 cost one crocard; that of Henry II's went up to a pollard. At any of King John's frequent coronations the price soared to a suskin and, in Henry IV's time, it cost a whole dodkin. The lesson to all of us is that inflation is the enemy.

"Let me have news of you and specific dates as to when you will quit that steamy sink to return to your wife. Were not your wife pregnant I would try to persuade you to spend some time in Dallas but you are needed in Duluth." (Dudley had been disbarred in Texas but held a job as legal recorder to a savings and loan association in Duluth which he had severely jeopardized by going off to Southeast Asia.)

Despite his prominence in the American government, Chay did not have full access to its financial resources. He had to rely on "the kindness of lobbyists," who seemed more than willing to wager on his expectations of more total influence than he had at present. For a man of his temperament, raised by his mother, this made him feel financially insecure.

He decided to solve the short-term problem by marrying a rich woman. Dudley had introduced him to a Mrs. Mabel Chappas, who might have been on the overmature side, but she had between twenty and thirty million dollars from a large piece of the north-eastern wholesale loan-sharking business which her late husband had left her. Chay invited her to meet Serena but there was a negative chemical interchange between the two women so nothing came of it. He shifted his attentions to a Mrs. Alma Wisden, under the impression that she had inherited an enormous fortune from her late husband, but Mrs. Wisden was sixty-three years old, and Brill talked him out of the idea which later turned out to have been the soundest of advice because a subsequent examination of her IRS records showed her to be penniless.

27

AT BREAKFAST on the very first morning in Dallas, while Chay waited for the construction at Rossenarra to be finished which required that he stay with his family, Serena pressed him about what he was going to do to help the career of his brother Jonathan, whom Chay had been able to place with the Drug Enforcement Administration in the Virgin Islands. "He's only a boy, Chay," Serena said. "He belongs at your side. It could happen that some of your charmed life, your magical luck, could rub off on him. You hear what I'm saying?"

Chay smiled tolerantly as if he believed such a thing could happen, but Graciela Winkelreid had discovered some wonderful little "luck" pills (she called them) which Chay had found out through Wambly Keifetz were really just vitamin pills but nonetheless they had seemed to increase his natural luck, and since that was something one didn't fool with, he continued to take the pills regularly, and as hard as it was for even he himself to believe, his luck had become an almost tangible thing for him.

Chay gave Jon a spot commission as a Major, U.S. Army, although he was very young, and put him on his staff as an aide.

Dudley and Frieda moved to Dallas and found a house nearby on Asbury Avenue. Capitalizing on Chay's influence, which had had Dudley's license to practice law in Texas reinstituted, Dudley opened a law office. Serena was harsh in her insistence that Chay speak to the Papal Nuncio about having Sylvester transferred from the Death Valley monastery so he could be near his family. Sylvester was made Chay's chaplain. At first, Brill refused to leave New York because Keifetz spent as much of his time there as he did in Dallas, but Serena kept after her, citing the endless opportunities for making money in the nation's capital, and she took the credit for changing Brill's mind. Within two months, Brill was established in an elaborate mansion on Lakeside Drive in Highland Park which had been commandeered, fully furnished, from a family which was suspected of being Nicaraguan sympathizers.

Things were so touchy in terms of public unrest that every morning a Bradley full-tracked fighting vehicle would call for Chay at the Potomac house and drive him to his headquarters in the former Dallas Public Library building. Chay would stand in the open cockpit, corncob pipe between his teeth, a pearl-handled revolver hanging at each hip, wearing his black homburg hat sideways and waving at the dense crowds lining the street to watch him pass. Jonathan rode in the tonneau of a staff car in front of the Bradley, as a precaution against land mines.

The Appleton family became American television favorites—Brill entertaining the meaningful world of fashion, Royalists, and international funsters; Sylvester in his gay magenta chasuble at the General's side, mumbling Latin pieties; Dudley and Frieda doing whatever it was they did their level best to do but usually failing at it; Jonathan as smart as paint in a freshly pressed uniform and decisive swagger stick; Berry scoring at Barnard spelling bees, and Serena impressing the television viewers of America with her proprietary interest in the arts, her work of rolling miles of white gauze bandages for the Red Cross, and her natural modesty, so admirable in the mother of the country's most famous soldier.

Acting as the nation's chief executive until the NCD could regroup to deliberate on the form the new government would take, and at Wambly Keifetz's suggestion, Chay sent his brother Jonathan to Gardena, California, to eradicate the around-the-clock commercial poker layouts which were the principal industry of the town, and to begin arrangements to move its population (and that of the towns of Hawthorne, Lawndale, Willowbrook, Torrance, Compton, and Carson) from an area of 63.7 square miles, having more than 450,000 people, to Rancho Cucamonga and San Bernardino.

To prepare the area for "the buildings of pompous marble" for the new capital city which would transform the Gardena area into the seat of government, the Conference retained 1,631 architects and employed 417,834 people at the (then) average rate of $19 an hour.

A significance of this earliest expenditure was that it necessitated an immediate return to a Federal income tax program. The national treasury was at low ebb. As Federal government and projects widened, Federal expenses grew.

It had been estimated by the committee of engineers and architects assembled by Jonathan Appleton that it would take four years and two months and would cost $128.54 billion and some change to plan and build the new capital. However, this estimate did not include housing, schools, universities, entertainment, slums, hospitals, embassies, restaurants, nor other construction which is required to give character to a modern capital city. The replicas of principal edifices such as the White House, Blair House, the Capitol, the Supreme Court, the Pentagon, the Occidental Restaurant, and the great presidential memorials were to be copied faithfully.

Within the guarded, even frightened, councils of the NCD, in suites at the Crescent Hotel and the Mansion on Turtle Creek, the new legislature exchanged views on what were to be the meanings of modern America.

28

THERE ARE MEN who collect women only to use them. Caesare Appleton may have used women, as the complex and revealing record shows, but only with their wholehearted collaboration. His richly contrasting biographies and four autobiographies tell that, in his lifetime, he loved only five women, beginning with Hedda Blitzen whom he described in a principal autobiography as "an astrally-glamorous international fashion model and a member of an ancient, aristocratic Hanoverian family." None of these meetings had ever happened as Chay recorded them. They were recalled as they had not occurred to cover up what had actually happened—which was entirely honorable but, since the experience with his sister, Chay could not be sure.

The fact that Hedda had never been a model or that her family was from Alsace-Lorraine was quite beside the point. And that she had been a delicatessen clerk when he met her was not something he evaded for reasons of caste. It was just that, since the night he had entered his sister's bed, Chay had not wanted anyone to know the true facts about anything in his past to the point where, working with such distinguished biographers as Abner Stein and Charles McCarry, or rearranging the facts of his life for the ghost writers who assisted him with his autobiographies, Chay always needed to change the truth to something else for fear that the truth might lead to his exposure.

It is also characteristic of the man, undoubtedly going back to that night in the sheets with his twin sister, the night he had been summoned home to adjudicate the matter of his father having "tampered" with Brill, that the accounts which he gave to his biographers were totally at variance with what had happened in his life with the women who had been the most important to his life. It was as though he were not sure that the circumstances of his meeting and his courtships of these women (as these had actually happened) would be "safe" to reveal to a biographer who would then tell the world; as though he had no balanced moral view of sexual relationships whatever. Therefore, although they made for stirring biography, each one of them was purposefully wrong in the accounting by its subject.

In the autobiography which was written while he occupied his first really high office so that the book would be ready for publication immediately after he left office, or moved on to higher office, when the public was ready to buy it, and publishers would be ready to bid up the advance for it, Marshal Appleton tells of the romance-drenched night when he met Hedda Blitzen for the first time.

Chay, the account states, in his early thirties, had just won his star as a Brigadier General. He was temporarily stationed on Governor's Island, in New York's harbor (although it was a Coast Guard station, not an Army post, at the time). All the officers of the post, Chay recounts, had received an invitation to attend a charity ball aboard the new luxury cruise ship, *Santa Paula*, which was anchored in the upper bay.

In the course of the fete, seven of the most beautiful (and utterly unreachable) fashion models showed the clothes of the great fashion designers. "My heart almost leapt out of my chest," Chay wrote in the memoir, "when I beheld the fourth mannequin to walk out. She was exquisitely formed—everything in perfect miniature—her coloring hauntingly like that of my own mother. I looked—and I was lost. I had fallen in love for the first time in my life."

Chay records that he was overcome with panic that perhaps no way could be devised by his aide to be introduced to this exquisite creature. When the fashion show was finished he went to the bar and—a most unusual occurrence for him—downed a straight spritzer. He was detained there by fellow officers who tried to persuade him to go with them to some raucous affair in Greenwich Village, but Chay broke away and went off to find his destiny.

The model he sought so feverishly had left her dressing room to return to Manhattan. He wasted precious time trying to find out her name and agency affiliation, then, the autobiography says, "I rushed up the companionway to find her. I was directed to an afterdeck where a helicopter was turning its rotors. I saw her in the distance—too close to the ship's rail in that jostling crowd. I rushed toward her. The crowd of models and their entourages pushed abruptly backward away from the noises which suddenly came from the chopper and—my God!—pushed my darling over the ship's railing and sent her toppling into the sea. I did not hesitate. I dove over the ship's side, a distance of perhaps 112 feet, straight down, not even thinking whether or not I could swim—which, of course, I could—or that I had one stainless-steel hip and a stainless-steel elbow to sustain her as well as myself. She was in my arms in seconds. I held her head high over the water and told her she was going to be all right. 'Who are you to take this risk for me, a total stranger?' she asked with an exciting, breathy voice.

" 'I am General Caesare Appleton,' I said to her, 'and I am in love with you.' "

.   .   .

The second great love of his life, albeit it a secret one until the Abner Stein biography was published, was Graciela Winkelreid, who became his Secretary of Interfacing, a cabinet rank, and who met with him, alone, more often than any other member of his Cabinet. Winkelreid was surely Chay's closest government adviser. Close to the (moderate) Iranians and to the leaders of the "Contras" (the 116 Latino officers and men which the CIA kept stationed in Honduras), it was utterly unknown that she had also been the CINCAFUSCIAFBIANSA's lover from the day he had arrived to take over all government forces in Dallas. Appleton is reserved about his relationship with Miss Winkelreid, saying "but that is for a later volume of these memories when I will be freer to express my soul. Just allow me to say now that perhaps were it not for Graciela Winkelreid, I might not have discovered my almost magical luck which made it possible for me to surmount everything which would try to block my path."

Third among these few women in the great man's lifetime was the melting beauty Ulyssa Effing, whom he married. In the Appleton autobiography, *The Meaning of Caesare Appleton* (Harvard University Press, 6 vols., 3993 pp., $221.75), Appleton writes: "I was a fatalist. But I believed in my almost magical luck which was confirmed again and again by astrology, numerology, sand readings, and the other sciences by which our government is steered. I had unassailable luck, as my angel mother reminded me daily, she (and it) always seeming to sit on my right shoulder. Because of that luck I was convinced that my fate was tied to my friendships with rich woman friends, perhaps most particularly to Ulyssa, the wealthy young Creole charmer whom I met by chance in Dallas while she was doing field work for her doctorate in retail display at the Neiman-Marcus department store. Ulyssa, I was to learn, was the daughter of an extremely wealthy New Orleans family having the most distinguished Mafia connections."

There had been the usual amount of talk by the envious, Appleton wrote, who would rather gossip than seek out the truth, that Mrs. Effing's maternal grandmother had been a banana-skinned Afro-American woman. Connoisseurs of grace and beauty, could they have seen this noble flower of the Old South, would have applauded such an ancestry had it been so, because surely something blessedly exotic had produced this hothouse passion flower of Dixie.

"Ulyssa loved me beyond the call of a heart's cry," Appleton wrote. "She served me devotedly. If she had influence over me it was on the side of humanity. Her gentleness overruled the excesses of passion which I was liable to commit upon this saintly woman."

Chay's memoir of their meeting is a moving and gallant thing. Ulyssa had been named Miss Cajun Country Cooking by the rice growers of neighboring Louisiana, and through the cooperation of the Dallas Junior League who were persuaded to transfer a substantial cash gift to Chay's mother quite unbeknownst to Chay, it was arranged by the rice industry that the CINCAFUSCIAF-BIANSA would eat the first bowl of old-time Cajun Country jambalaya. (There is a footnote in the text of the memoir which gives the ingredients of the dish. It is made with pork, chicken, and shellfish, with red and green peppers, tomatoes, and celery gently sauteed in oil with garlic, then simmered gently with raw, down-home rice for 30 to 40 minutes in four cups of down-home water flown in from the bayou country.)

Chay's memoir reports that, in full uniform, on camera, rolling his eyes and singing a deep mmm-*MMM* as if he were an end man in a postbellum minstrel show, he took a deep whiff of the glorious aroma of the famous regional dish. At that moment, when he looked up at the extraordinary beauty of the young woman, Ulyssa Effing, who had just served him, the then-available NBC TV archive television tape was theatrically comical.

He started violently as he saw her, knocked over a glass of Texas champagne as he tried to stand up, then eased back down as she put a gentling hand on his shoulder, saying, "Howdy, Marshall, I'm Ulyssa Effing, Miss Cajun Country Cookin', here to serve you." Just then, if the band had played the national anthem he could not have stood up without adjusting his clothing. She sat beside him. He called for another bowl of jambalaya and they ate hungrily together. At that moment Chay began his headlong pursuit of Ulyssa Effing, a young widow with a fourteen-year-old son.

There is another reference in the various autobiographies by Chay Appleton as to how he met Ulyssa. The *National Enquirer*, the establishment newspaper, carried a notice in 1990 that the government had overruled the National Rifle Association and had announced that all unauthorized flamethrowers were to be surrendered to the authorities. Flamethrowers were popular with sportsmen, particularly in the inner cities. The National Rifle Association defended their use with the popular slogan, "Flamethrowers don't incinerate people; people incinerate people," and stoutly maintained that it was every citizen's Constitutional right to own and use one. But 11,603 schoolchildren had been unnecessarily burned to death by them so Chay's government had reluctantly called them in.

When the security team appeared at the Effing household to enforce the ruling, Ulyssa's son, Elvis, home from school, protested having to turn over his late Dad's own weapon. He was told (sarcastically) to take the matter up with the CINCAFUS-CIAFBIANSA.

Elvis wrote a schoolboy's letter to the Marshal of the American Union. A gracious audience was granted by Chay to the boy, which was covered by network cameras. It was one of those scenes which had warmed the history books from Abraham Lincoln to Ronald Reagan. The solemn-faced adolescent asked to be allowed to keep his father's flamethrower as "a matter of honor." Moved by the boy and the television cameras, Chay agreed. The story was on the evening news all over the world. The country became ecstatic over an endearing moment from real life so straightforwardly and honestly told.

Two days later, an elegant lady telephoned to thank the Marshal for his sympathy for her son's dreams. It was a sweetly dignified, arm's-length talk, not recorded for national radio. The Marshal, utterly charmed by the lady's voice, asked to visit her, and permission was granted. What followed became part of the history of the great marriages of American history.

Sheila Plantenbower, wife of an Australian foot soldier with whom Chay became wildly infatuated during the Nicaraguan invasion of northeastern Australia, was one of the few strikeouts of

Marshal Appleton's life, something which he admits with chagrin in his popular book which brought a record-breaking $20 million advance.

Chay was the most famous man in the world even then, but that did not matter to her. Plantenbower, despite the stark, starker, starkest fact that Chay offered her the world on a curb-service basis, could not stand short men, and she (seriously!) preferred the husband she already had. "I was too circumspect, too proud, or too sentimental to have her husband executed," he wrote in the autobiography, "so I had to face heartbreak and one of the few failures of my career."

He loved Elizabeth Danworthy, his brother Jonathan's fiancée, even though he tells us he had good reason to suspect that she had other reasons for her involvement with him. "She was an enormously wealthy name fucker," Chay (or his associate author) writes, and in that Chay was the biggest name ever to rise above the horizon of history (with the exception of one or two religious figures), she took him to her bosom almost as a conceptual duty. They went through all the motions and there can be no doubt that Chay was entirely sincere in his obsessive devotion to the woman, but nothing he wrote about her had the immortal ring which had knelled for the Blitzen, Effing, and Wantonberg love affairs.

Throughout all that yearning congress of loving, from the beginning, Chay had loved, worshipped, and lusted for—on and off—Liz Wantonberg, the greatest star that electronic entertainment (excluding the people's church) ever produced. The two wandering, wonderingly wistful lovers were always unfaithful to each other in their fashion, but whenever Chay was blue (or really horny), he writes, he "would have Wantonberg smuggled into the palace, or a tent, or the back of a limousine, or into the occasional telephone booth, and we would rediscover happiness together."

There were several hundred other "incidental" women but that wasn't love as literature knows it.

29

B Y THE END of the tenth month of the establishment of the
National Conference for Democracy in Dallas, political terror was
at its height. The delegates had passed laws which were necessary,
but through a national misunderstanding, because there did not
seem to be a Federal government as they had known it, the American people, severely conditioned by the Republican Party in the
past, had happily assumed that they did not have to pay Federal
taxes.

The Marshal of the American Union was charged with enforcing the tax laws, and what followed has, alas, been referred
to by unsympathetic historians as a Reign of Terror. Actually, as
Marshal Appleton's autobiography shows, it was no more than
martial law. Forty to sixty thousand people died unexpectedly,
hundreds of thousands more lived in paralyzed fear, but as Appleton wrote, "Within no time at all, most of them saw their
responsibility to the new government and paid up, ending the
difficulty and closing the incident."

Although Chay, as CINCAFUSCIAFBIANSA, had been forced
to order his troops and his secret agents to undertake what was
so loosely called "the terror," he never let a day go by without
making a public announcement by personal appearance on national television. As he projected the anguish which was so imbedded in his sincerity, his boyish appeal, levering the hearts out of
the mothers of men and causing the men themselves to want to
do something—anything—to hide, to flee to Canada, or to find a
way to change their Social Security numbers, Chay used his ex-
pressive eyes for television—hurt, shamed-by-others, ready-to-cry
Peter Pan eyes, or betrayed Oliver North eyes. With the right
television makeup, they seemed to leak out of his face like pieces
of canned fruit. *But only when the occasion demanded it.*

Combined with his (prematurely) graying hair and the (now)
seventeen rows of campaign ribbons lighting up the left side of
his torso, this supreme expression of deep commitment told his

countrymen that he was willing (a) to take the spears, (b) the fall, (c) the hill, (d) the scars, and after all of that, to (somehow) give the salute. He would look the No. 3 camera right in the lens and tell the American people that, even though he was CINCAFUS-CIAFBIANSA, he de*plored* what the troops and the undercover people were doing out there to white, Protestant American citizens in the median-income bracket; the killing of tens of thousands of them; the burning of homes; the deportations to labor camps; *all of this must stop!* He pleaded with the people to remain in their cellars and attics until the ravaging troops could be brought under control.

Whenever the Marshal made one of his national television appeals after one of his absolutely-necessary massacres, it was rated as drawing an 87 percent viewing audience, or in any one of his many press conferences where he took questions from news media proxies who had been assigned by the Army for security reasons, subsequent national polls (of the requisite 1,200 people out of 287,849,301 Americans) showed that the country solidly supported what he was doing.

He made examples of several commanding officers under field grade, denying them PX privileges and far worse. All in all, the American people, through the power of television, knew that Chay Appleton was not only one of them, but as he writes in an autobiography, "a patriot who had proved his dedication to the cause of freedom over and over again in the victorious Nicaraguan wars in defense of the American way of life."

Even as the appalling numbers of the dead were buried, no guilt or shame or blame had clung to the Marshal of the American Union, for, as he tells us, "If the American people ever had a friend, I was that friend."

The American people had neither forgotten nor forgiven the "Reign of Terror," as the tax harvest time of the immediate past was so unfortunately named. The massacre of 108,397 of their friends, neighbors, and countrymen had not gone down well at all. Giant rallies of three and four hundred thousand people at single meetings were held simultaneously in forty-one American cities. State governors, who did not dare to call out the National Guard, demanded with the harsh-voiced voters of their states that the government by the National Conference for Democracy be dissolved.

The government fell. It dissolved itself. On July 23, 1990, a month before Chay's fortieth birthday, in order to get the public's mind off negative aspects of the massacres, a coup d'état was organized by a man of the people who seemed to rise up out of nowhere: Citizen Keifetz.

He was a little-known Wall Street philanthropist who had been the moving force behind the great work of the television evangelists of the country; the man behind the nomination of J. Danforth Quayle; the selfless planner who had invented junk bonds.

Keifetz took charge, telling cable, network, and local television cameras alike that he would remain at the head of government only long enough to return civil order to the country. "I am not a politician," he said with the odd sincerity of the overweight. "I am a citizen who is committed to his duty. When this crisis has passed I will go back to my own life. Until then, with the rest of America, I will have to make sacrifices."

A poll of 247 people from coast to coast, from all walks of life, taken after Keifetz had assumed power showed that 47.1 percent endorsed him, 22.3 percent were opposed for religious, moral, political, or dietary reasons, and 30.6 percent had no opinion, with a 35 percent margin for error. There was a certain amount of rioting in the inner and outer cities, and in the towns and villages, as well as in the countryside, but police, the National Guard, and tested combat troops soon enough persuaded the dissenters that they had made a mistake.

Instantly, for reasons best known to themselves, the entire Conference lived in fear of *their* lives. Marshal of the American Union Appleton was seized and jailed by executive order. His IDs were taken from him and there was the possibility of a capital charge.

When this shocking news thundered out of the talking heads of the six national anchormen on the nightly television news, the nation recoiled and shouted out its horror. Never in their wildest highs had they dreamed that the revolution could go that far. They were being told to believe a ludicrous impossibility: that the Mar-

shal of the American Union, a national icon who had worked day
and night for American freedom and who had shown so many
times, on shows which had outrated Michael Jackson and Barbara
Walters, how gladly he would have given his life in the defense
of America against the Sandinista tyranny, had been seized and
imprisoned.

Marshal Appleton was seized at noontime on a Friday as he
sat at his lunch cooked by his mother. He smiled gratefully (it
seemed to television viewers) and put up no resistance, but in
front of the TV cameras, he was manhandled. He was confined
to a cell in the Highland Park City Hall building, less than a mile
from his little house on Potomac Avenue. The news went out on
the main wire within seconds and was flashed across television
screens from Edgarton, Alaska, to the Florida Keys. Americans
could not believe their eyes as they watched the highest-ranking
military/security officer in history being led, handcuffed, from a
police car into the Highland Park City Hall building, wearing his
famous battle hat, the sideways black homburg.

Network and cable television cameras taped heart-wrenching
shots of his mother, the capital's social leader, Mrs. Serena Appleton, clacking hurriedly across the pavement and up the rotunda
steps into the building to bring her son hot soup and nachos,
followed by the Marshal's popular brother, Lieutenant Colonel
Jonathan Appleton, and his pretty little sister, Berry. On camera,
his younger brother Monsignor Sylvester blessed the building and
the Louise Childress Public Library which it contained, as well as
the fire and police stations, and the guards who enforced his brother's imprisonment; an endless ritual.

The Marshal's twin sister, Mrs. Wambly Keifetz, consented
to speak to the television cameras. She was a beautiful woman—
even, it could be said, an *exceedingly* beautiful woman—wearing
a scarlet topcoat trimmed with black fox and an insouciant black
fox shako over her golden red hair. The television reporters taste-
lessly reminded her that her brother had been jailed on orders
from her husband.

"You may be sure that is an utter lie!" Mrs. Keifetz replied
into the cameras. "My husband has no knowledge of this arrest
of a man who is probably the most authentic hero in our history.
America knows! An American hero has been clapped into this vile

prison by a Nicaraguan hope of—at last—evening up the score with its most deadly foe—my brother—this country's champion. That is all I have to say." Her eyes flashed with pride then over-brimmed with tears. Her smile was dazzling. As she strode into City Hall, the reporters and technicians, every one of them an impartial newscaster, broke into sustained cheering and applause.

That evening in the mansion on Lakeside Drive, Brill told her husband that, this time, she thought he had gone too far.

"He is a headstrong young man who got too much power too quickly," her husband said. "Not that he has abused that power, but he must be reminded that evil things can happen if he does. I had him arrested to remind him of just how vulnerable he can become. We don't want him acting on his own, do we, my dear?"

"It seems to me you are going to hobble him enough by loading that hooker of Eddie Grogan's on him."

"Chay is an extremely healthy young man. He needs what a young man can get from Ulyssa Effing. We couldn't have men like that go on thinking that they run the country, could we? Any more than we could allow the people to think they ran it."

"I want to help him!"

"And so you shall, dearest. You are the one who must take him false hope then leave him scrambling on the ice. It's all for his own good after all."

Brill stalked out of the room and got her hat and coat, to get over to the jail. Keifetz stared after her sadly. His surveillance tapes in deepest files had revealed, in starkest totality, the precise relationship that his wife and her brother had enjoyed at every possible opportunity over the years and the knowledge made him determined to make Chay pay for the shame and heartbreak he had caused an innocent husband.

When he heard the front door slam, Keifetz dialled Eddie Grogan at the New Baker. "Everything's on schedule," he said into the telephone. "When Mrs. Keifetz leaves City Hall, I want you to send a police car to take me there."

30

A DENSE PACK of print reporters, photographers, video cameramen, radio backpacks, and media patch workers from newspapers, newsmagazines, networks, cable operations, foreign outlets, wire services, and syndicates had swarmed outside the Highland Park City Hall building overflowing the pavement into the street as far as intersections to right and left, halting any possibility of normal traffic.

In his cell, the Marshal of the American Union had insisted that he not be treated any differently than any other prisoner, but because there had not been any other prisoners for many years in the daintily arranged community, there were no rules to be broken. Chay's cell was an ample three-room arrangement with a barber chair, a Jacuzzi, a bath, and three telephones. One telephone was a hot line, installed ten minutes after he had arrived, which connected with the switchboard at his headquarters, a precaution taken in case of invasion by Nicaraguan forces. The other two lines, connected with an emergency switchboard which had been installed in the Louise Childress Library (a facility closed for the duration of the emergency), were for normal outside calls.

Although the turnkey was sure he must be there, Chay could not be seen from outside his cell whose bars had been covered by medieval arras hung from ceiling to floor along every surface. Chay kept the key to the cell to prevent the entry of unwelcome visitors and to preserve his sense of personal dignity. He read a great deal as well as watched videocassettes of "Guiding Light" and "Wheel of Fortune" which his family brought him daily. He had the occasional young lady visitor. In fact, by the end of the evening that Brill made her visit, he had actually felt overtired from visitors.

The intrusions had begun at 7:10 A.M. with a call from Hedda Blitzen in New York who had just learned from the "CBS Morning Show" of Chay's arrest. When the call came in he thought it was on the direct, emergency line. He leapt out of bed, snatched it up, instantly making plans to defend his country.

"Oh, Chay, how could they do this to you?"

"Who is this?"

"Who? You ask me who?"

"Jesus!" He had suddenly recognized the voice and realized that, what with Ulyssa and this and that, he had forgotten to call her for five months.

"Chay! Are you all right?"

"How did you get this number?" he wailed.

"I still have friends at your headquarters even if you don't know I'm alive."

He realized then that he wasn't talking on the hot line. "But—how did you get through?"

"The way I always got through. I used the password."

How could his people have permitted the same password for all of this time? Did he have an organization or did he have to do everything himself? he thought bitterly. In his first week in Dallas he had given the password "Anytime" to a few dozen women and nobody in the entire security forces of the United States Army had done anything to change it.

"Oh, yes," he said. "The password."

A really rotten thought hit him. He had been in this dungeon since two o'clock yesterday afternoon. Why hadn't Ulyssa called him? She not only had the password, but she could have gotten the hot-line number from Eddie Grogan. He began to wonder who his real friends were.

"Hedda, darling," he said into the telephone, "I can't talk to you now. There are guards all around me. But as soon as they give me pen and paper I am going to write you a letter."

As he hung up, his breakfast was delivered from room service at the Mansion on Turtle Creek. It was lovely; hot oatmeal with a touch of whiskey, a really heavenly *pipérade*, mounds of hot raisin toast, and a pot of Blue Mountain coffee. He tucked it in then he called Ulyssa again and let the connection ring sixteen times. I can't stand this much longer, he thought. Something terrible must have happened to her. He went to his desk and wrote her a short note:

Dearest, Someone has cut your telephone line to prevent me
from gaining the surcease, the wonderment, the comfort of
hearing your darling voice, giving me back the reality of my
life. Surely you haven't lost the secret number here? It is 528-
0607. Call me the instant you receive this so that we may find
a way to bring us into each other's arms before this day's sun
has set. How I miss you! Hurry! Go now! Call me!

He took the automatic pistol, a 9-mm Beretta, out of the top
drawer of the desk, went to the cell door, drew back the tapestry,
and banged against the steel bars with the butt of the weapon.
Delbert Farkas, the turnkey, appeared at once, clutching a copy
of *Gourmet* magazine. He was a vague, underwater kind of man
who still had eleven years to go before he would qualify for his
pension.

"Sir?"

"See that this letter is delivered by police messenger at once,
Delbert." Chay handed over the sealed envelope.

"Yes, sir!" Farkas took the envelope and disappeared on the
double.

At 11 A.M., three hours after Ulyssa had surely gotten the
letter, Graciela Winkelreid, the government spokesperson, was
admitted to the cell by authorization of Beniamiamo Camardi. She
had concealed herself from the hundreds of news media people
outside the hall by laying on the floor of a fire truck under an
arrangement of hoses and was driven directly into the fire house
whose doors were immediately shut, then she was smuggled
through the contiguous municipal building to the prison area.

Inside, the City Hall was as uninhabited and silent as a nec-
ropolis. Delbert Farkas studied Miss Winkelreid's pass carefully.
When he was sure it was authentic, he led the way to Marshal
Appleton's quarters.

Chay was delighted to see her. "Miss Winkelreid!" he said,
drawing her in, dropping the arras, and locking the cell door.
"How very nice."

"The government had an unusual request this morning, Marshal," she said. "Director Camardi, as you may know, has strong
ties to the film industry and—"

"I have made myself absolutely clear on that," Chay said

sternly. "I will not appear in films no matter how much pressure my mother brings."

"I don't understand."

"That's what you're here for, isn't it? To secure my signature on movie contracts?"

"No, no, Marshal. Liz Wantonberg came to Dallas last night. She is starring in the anti-Sandinista rally at the Texas Stadium tonight and she wants to be able to tell them that she had come to the rally straight from you. It would mean so much for the cause, Marshal, and it will attract a gigantic amount of TV."

Chay was dazed. The woman who had been his goddess since he had been a little boy wanted to come to him, to be with him? It certainly takes the sting out of not hearing from Ulyssa, he thought. "Liz Wantonberg?" he asked pathetically. "The star of stage, screen, television, radio, and videocassettes?"

"I am almost certain it is the same Liz Wantonberg."

Chay got a grip on himself. "Oh, all right," he said. "I'll see her at four o'clock. Tell the turnkey on the way out, will you?"

"Yes, sir." Miss Winkelreid turned to go.

"Miss Winkelreid! Where are you going?"

"Back to the office, sir."

"Is this all we have to say to each other after that wonderful night at the New Baker Hotel?"

"I did want to talk to you about an extraordinary television appearance, sir. Right from this cell. I have prepared a statement for you which will have the nation marching on this prison if the government doesn't release you at once. It can't miss, sir. We'll get ratings such as we never saw before, sir."

Chay stood beside his simple soldier's cot and beckoned her to come to him. She moved in, taking a sheaf of typewritten pages out of her handbag. His hands went behind her dress and unzipped it. He pulled away the Velcro strap holding her brassiere. He pulled her down upon the cot.

"You are the most exciting woman in government," he said huskily.

When Miss Winkelreid left, Chay took a long, hot bath. He ordered three dozen oysters for lunch, all thoughts of Ulyssa gone from his mind. After lunch, he hung a DO NOT DISTURB sign on the cell door, wrapped himself warmly in a goose down quilt, and slept soundly for two hours. He was awakened at 1515 hours by his batman, a qualified masseur. In no time Chay was entirely restored and refreshed.

From the moment he awoke, Liz Wantonberg was never out of his thoughts, yet in no part of his imagination did he anticipate any intimacy beyond (perhaps) shaking her hand. But unexpected things had happened to him throughout his life because of his magical luck, and he always had to be sure to be ready. She was, after all, an older woman (in a manner of speaking), perhaps forty, even fifty years older than he was. But daring to dream in spite of himself, he wondered wistfully if he might get lucky—luckier, that is.

He got into the tropical dress whites of a Fleet Admiral but eschewed underwear which, for anyone but the CINCAFUS-CIAFBIANSA, would have been decidedly *infra dignitatem*.

His guest was only one hour and forty-seven minutes late. She arrived just before six o'clock. As a showperson she had naturally approached the Highland Park City Hall by its main entrance. She had no intention of being smuggled into the jail. For one thing it would have been an impossibility because she traveled with a media entourage of eleven people who had been assigned to her by the great exposé magazines and the afternoon TV talk shows. They had followed her day and night wherever she went for the past fifty-eight years, through blizzard and zephyr as it were.

The Wantonberg arrival added wildly to the bustle of the hundreds of working newsmen outside the Hall. They were desperate because there had been no news of the Marshal for three hours. The television people were able to surmount the problem by constantly photographing City Hall from different angles while changing the running commentaries, but the print people were stuck.

When the mystical star-courtesan stepped out of her limousine, flashing her wonderful smile and saying, "Hello, boys and girls!" they became so feral with excitement that the Highland Park Fire Department had to threaten them with power hoses unless Miss Wantonberg was at last allowed to pass into the building. She was taken directly to Marshal Appleton's quarters in the jail.

Chay could not believe she was such a tiny woman. He towered over her! Because of the size of the giant theater screens of his boyhood, and the height of her leading men, he had imagined her as a tall woman, twenty-three feet high. But her beauty, even after decades of his staring at it in still, video, moving, black-and-white and color photographs, dressed and entirely nude, almost made him lose his balance and fall. Her thick, lustrous, raven-black hair (which so short a time before had grown on the head of a young farm girl on the banks of the Hsi Chi River in the Chin Chiang region of Fukien) hung all the way down her back to her sweet hips which had so often cradled men.

Her teeth had been sculpted in downtown Beverly Hills by the Master craftsman, Dr. Jack Ramen. They gave radiance to her perfect smile, a warm, endearing smile while it lasted. Her skin was the flawless skin of a girl who had grown up on a Devon farm in western England long before the onslaughts of air pollution or makeup. Her eyes were as deep as space and the color of the twilight of all history. Inappropriately for the hour, Chay thought, she was dressed in a close-fitting lilac evening gown, then he remembered that she was going on to deliver the keynote speech at the giant Anti-Sandinista Rally later that night.

Her long dress had a bare midriff which exposed an enormous amethyst imbedded in her navel. The color of the dress complemented the gem and they both matched the contact lenses through which she watched him with incomparable lewdness.

It had been said that her physical beauty and sensuousness had only been surpassed in all human history (according to scholars who had been retained by the distributors of her films) by a Sumerian woman named Ehc who had lived in the court of Sargon of Akkad, at Ashur in the Upper Tigris valley, in 2340 B.C. These anthropoarcheologists and the publicity department at the studio had established the provenance of this claim beyond all doubt. Even though at the time of Sargon the archaic cuneiforms were still very crude instruments of communication, they had left a trail of royal inscriptions, treaties, administrative accounts, and word lists compiled by scribes and scholars. Contemporary documents, together with other archeological findings, had served to correct, expand, and make sense of the record of Ehc's sublime beauty as being nonpareil in all human history. Liz Wantonberg's perfection was second only to that.

Marshal of the American Union Appleton stood stock-still when she entered the cell. Delbert dropped the arras behind her. Nailing Chay to eternity with her beautiful eyes, she walked with grave dignity to a place directly in front of him. Without speaking, she unzipped the fly of his dress whites and sank her hand into the opening in its trousers, its wonders to perform.

Fifty-six minutes later she rose from the floor, leaving Chay in a pool of spent energy, his eyes rolled back in his head, his body inert. She slipped into her lilac sheath, patted her hair here and there, and left the cell. They had not spoken, instinctively saving the pillow talk for when there would be pillows.

Brilliana Appleton-Keifetz arrived at 8:10 P.M. The cell door had no bell so Delbert scratched on the ninety-five-knots-per-square-inch which made up the back of the multiple prayer rugs which shielded the entrance.

"Marshal Appleton, sir? Your sister, Mrs. Appleton-Keifetz, is here."

"Ah," Chay said foggily. "How nice." He lifted the *saph* to one side and opened the door. "Ah, Brill," he said dreamily. "Thank you, Delbert. That is all." He closed the door, turned the key, and dropped the prayer rug back into place.

"Chay, are you all right?"

"All right?"

"You seem catatonic. As if you'd been deeply drugged or hypnotized."

"No, no. Just a busy day. Much of a media mob outside?"

"No, actually. I was surprised. They all seem to have left. I suppose they can't be expected to stand out there all night."

"They might have gone to that Anti-Sandinista Rally."

"Do you think this place is wired?" Brill asked.

Chay shrugged helplessly. "By whom, for heaven's sake? Wambly?"

"Chay!"

"Why not?"

"Wamb has finally figured out that he may have painted himself into a corner by having you arrested."

"So?"

"He's going to call a press conference and tell them the whole thing was a Sandinista plot."

"Never mind that nonsense. Come here, you gorgeous little devil." He took her by the hand and led her to the simple soldier's cot.

31

A S BRILL LEFT the Highland Park City Hall at 9:57 P.M., the police car parked in front of the Keifetz mansion was notified by radio-telephone. It flicked its headlights which beamed into a main room of the house, on and off. Within five minutes Wambly Keifetz, head of the American government, came out with two bodyguards and got into the police car. The two men in the front seat were Grogan's men, not police.

The car drove directly to the Highland Park City Hall, an elegant Spanish-Colonial style hacienda in a park-like setting on the west bank of Turtle Creek. Keifetz and two of the men with him left the car immediately outside police headquarters and entered the building. They were taken to Marshal Appleton's cell. One of the men cleared Delbert Farkas out of the area then joined Keifetz and the interrogations specialist, Larry Minyon, inside Chay's cell. The three men looked down at the naked, utterly spent body of the Marshal which was sprawled half on the bed and half on the cell floor.

"Give him a jolt," Keifetz said.

Minyon removed a hypodermic needle from a medical case and loaded it from a vial. He swabbed the Marshal's inner thigh then injected the full load into his venous system. The Marshal twitched.

"Keep him warm," Keifetz said.

Hank Franks wrapped the Marshal in a maroon wool robe. The Marshal's eyes flickered open as Franks lifted him from the floor and propped him up on the bed.

"Thank you, boys. Now take down those rugs from the cell bars and wait for me in the car."

The two men stripped the rugs off so that Keifetz could chat without wondering if anyone were eavesdropping outside. By the time they had gone, the Marshal of the American Union was wide-awake.

"Jesus, Wambly, what did you hit me with?"

"Just a vitamin shot."

"What happened to me?"

"You had a delayed reaction to Liz Wantonberg. That's all."

Chay remembered. He shook his head like a punch-drunk fighter. "There has never been anything like it," he said thickly. "Lemme tell you she is a piece that surpasses all understanding."

"I sent her."

"How come?"

"I had to move that army of media people out of there. When she went in, they lost all perspective and when she came out they followed her to find out what happened in here."

"You can tell Liz Wantonberg what to do?"

"I made her some money in the market a few times. Then, yesterday, I finally agreed to sell her a piece in my diamond collection if she would come here and do the job on you."

"But why get rid of the media? I thought everything we do depends on the media."

"So I could have a private talk with you."

"About what?"

"About making you Chairman and CEO of the United States of America."

"How long have you had that idea?"

"Since you saved Europe from the invader. Since you got the Medal of Honor in the Rose Garden. The combined national surveys show that you are the most constantly televised American since Ronald Reagan which means that the public has been conditioned to adore you. You are ready to take his place. Offshore oil! Giant arms sales manipulations! Influence peddling! Reinventing and sustaining the Nicaraguan threat! Exhorting the nation to fight a tiny, poor Central American country instead of the crippling American use of drugs! We'll provide the scripts for you. We'll do your thinking through Graciela Winkelreid. As far as you're concerned it will all be make-believe, just as it was for Ron. You'll be at peace inside a world of fun, myth, and fantasy. You'll wave and grin and enjoy Camp David II and while you're waving and grinning, and wearing all that beautiful tailoring, Graciela will be thinking up things to keep the people's attention away from the dense hedges of men around you—men who are inspired to get the money. Things like the Qaddafi bombings, the Star Wars flapdoodle, the failures of banks, the crumbling of airlines, and the shoring up of savings and loans will be seen as absolutely nothing compared to how you are going to keep the American people entertained while we *get the money!*"

"Wamb—what are you really telling me? If you want to make me Chairman why did you have me arrested and thrown into this place?"

"You had to be martyred!"

"Martyred?"

"Anyway, what's wrong with this place? I saved you for a while from your mother's cooking. And do you realize, Chay, that Liz Wantonberg—and this is a proven archeological fact—is the most beautiful and sexually magnetic woman in 4,280 years of human history and that in *all* human history since the dawn of time only one other woman was ever considered to have been more exciting?"

"Jesus, who was that?"

Keifetz waved the question away impatiently. "Some Sumerian called Ehc. The point is: by having you arrested I gave you the vitally necessary flavor of a martyr. The people know that you tried to save them from themselves by enforcing their duty to pay taxes—they've been conditioned to paying taxes for centuries and they feel deep guilt when they don't—so that when you, the hero who became their conscience, were seized and jailed for doing what they knew to be the right thing, they suffered for you and with you and loved you all the more for it."

"But I had over a hundred thousand of them shot."

Keifetz shrugged helplessly. "So take away television and try to explain Ronald Reagan. Anyway, if you have to have an explanation, you were their father. You were punishing them."

Chay exhaled sharply. "It sure is tricky stuff, fooling the people."

"All right. The time has come to get you married so that they may simultaneously see you as one of themselves—the owner of a First Lady."

"Married? Who?" Chay knew in his heart that he would never survive marriage to Liz Wantonberg.

"For Christ's sake, Chay, what's the difference? Ulyssa Effing. She's photogenic. She wears clothes well. We'll set her up with a couple of causes, and we'll rehearse her in adoring you for the cameras."

"What happened to her? I've been in this jail for almost three days and I haven't heard one word from her."

"Blame me. Ulyssa is a useful item, Chay. If you screwed up—if you refused to listen to reason—why should we waste her? I told her to dummy up with you. I sent her to New York with some of Grogan's people for a shopping holiday."

"Wamb, please," Chay said wearily, "what do you want from me?"

"We are going to give the people a taste of the good old days."

"How?"

"Tomorrow I am going to renounce as custodial head of the American government and set the period for campaigning and national elections."

"But doesn't that smack of democracy?"

"We are going to give them the mind-bending boredom of what the media calls the 'race' for the presidency just one more time so they'll know when they are well off. We will field ten or twelve candidates and watch them move in a pack across the country, stultifying and confusing all thought or possible interest for months as they swell the advertising revenues of the television industry, while helping the telephone companies and the printing business."

"But why start that waste all over again?"

"So that the entire agonizing process can end in a complete

deadlock in two brokered nominating conventions, until the leaders of both parties choose you as the only possible compromise candidate."

"That will cost a fortune!"

"Altogether it will cost $213 million and some change."

"Who has that kind of money?"

"While we take it from the taxpayers, we will give them an entertainment, a diversion, in return. Your forces will invade the Atlantic island of Nantucket. Then we will pave the entire island from edge to edge to establish the largest single military airfield in the world, but even so, it will just about be large enough to accommodate the transport planes flying in cocaine from South America then out again to all of North America."

"Try that, Keifetz, and Americans will just say no."

"So we'll have to take our chances. Cocaine is our answer to the terrible deficit, to our $3 trillion debt, the hundreds of billions that the failing savings and loans are going to cost the taxpayer, the gigantic trade imbalance, the vital but billions of dollars worth of costly clean-up of our toxic wastes, the modernization of our nuclear fuel plants, our endless space programs which literally go nowhere, and our hopelessly inadequate education and social services. We have a heaven-sent opportunity here. Cocaine is a vegetable product which does not require costly manufacturing plants, designers, and R&D costs. It is an industry with the lowest overhead intensity—a few thousand South American Indians, planes provided by the CIA, a few sturdy coca gins to make the powder. It only costs 6 percent of its retail price to bring it to market and— *presto!*—a 2,683.41 percent profit. It can solve all of this country's problems."

"You are a brilliant man. Really, Wamb."

"You will leave this place tomorrow after your statement to the nation via television and go to a quiet, very private wedding ceremony."

"Ulyssa?"

"Yes."

"Does she know?"

"I think so. On the day after the wedding, I shall announce that I am stepping down in the very near future. There will be the usual fanfare about the unexpected national elections, and we will have various people announce their candidacies. The campaigns will torture the people to their breaking point—but we can't extend them to fourteen months as we did in the past because that would certainly lead to a revolution. Four months of bone-breaking boredom, then into the deadlocks and the smoke-filled rooms, then the dramatic announcement that you will be the candidate of both parties."

"But—"

"But what?" Keifetz asked with irritation.

"Won't the voters be suspicious if both parties endorse the same candidate?"

"My dear fellow! Do you really think the American people, raised from childhood on television, see politics as anything more than wholesome entertainment? Our politics have become undistinguishable from television programming. Think of politics as American opera. What is there for them to be suspicious about? It is only their government—which has been screwing them from time immemorial."

Following Chay's moving international television broadcast from his cell, over 1.5 million telegrams, 691,862 pieces of mail, 2,700 lampshades, 236 leather bookmarks, and 8,256 neatly framed wall mottoes in 37 languages poured into the executive offices of the government in Dallas. The overload was so great that the Dallas communications facilities couldn't handle it. Telegrams and letters had to be baled and shipped in from points as far north as Memphis and as far east as Jackson, Mississippi, then rushed to Citizen Keifetz's office by air freight.

Chay was the key to the hearts of the American people. Even Liz Wantonberg, who had never spoken to him and had met him only once, flew to his cell again from Hollywood to give him a quick boff as an act of homage.

The retiring head of government, Citizen Keifetz, persuaded the investigating commission that the country could not afford to lose so able a soldier. Appleton was declared innocent and freed. But he was relieved of his command. His name was removed from the active list, and he was put on half-pay. Humbled by the will of the people, he was still as ready to serve them as he had been on the day he had graduated from West Point.

He appeared on television and the People Meters which photographed all viewers as they watched reported that there was not a dry eye in the country.

Chay returned to the little house on Potomac. He disdained gloves as a luxury he could no longer afford. He rarely dined out and the word was spread that he was flat broke, a charge which, if it could be proved, could go severely against him in government.

For the sake of his country, he managed to convince Wambly Keifetz that Jonathan Appleton must be kept on in charge of the preparation of Washington West, and this was done. Chay wrote to the lad (*The Appleton Papers*, People Magazine Press, 17 vols., $259.85): "Whatever may happen to you, remember that you cannot possibly have a warmer friend than I, one to whom you are more dear or who is more sincerely anxious for your happiness. Life is a dream that fades away.

"Please send me a recent videocassette of Miss Liz Wantonberg (in the nude if possible), and if your work should take you within speaking distance of her, please tell her how I would cherish her autograph."

Chay's position in his society, to be as precise as possible, had fallen to that of a washerman in the Tamil regions of India, a level which is two ranks lower than the pariah caste. His "untouchable" period was to last for six days.

32

A T 1600 HOURS on January 26, 1991, Mrs. Ulyssa Effing, in the presence of the head of government, Citizen Keifetz, and the CIA administrator, Eddie Grogan, was married to Marshal of the American Union Caesare Appleton by the Mayor of Dallas, Claude Albritton III, in a simple ceremony which took place in the main vault of the Texas Commerce Bank, Hillcrest branch, in an attempt to keep the news of the marriage from the groom's mother, as well as from the American people who, it was felt, were not yet ready for such news. Owing to a difficulty in obtaining necessary documents, sworn statements were accepted which allowed the bride to understate her real age, forty-two, by four years. On the record the bride was now thirty-eight years old, the groom, forty. Each of the wedding party slipped out of the bank separately to reconvene at a wedding reception in the wine cellar of the Crescent Hotel.

The reception was attended by members of the immediate family excepting the groom's younger brother Jonathan who had agreed to take their mother and Berry out of the city.

Chay had not dared to tell his mother of his marriage because of Ulyssa's reputation for extravagance, so it had been arranged that Serena should visit her son Jonathan's real estate in the projected District of Columbia West while the wedding took place. Chay told her the news over the telephone from the wedding reception so Serena had to accept what was done, but not before she had yelled at Chay that Ulyssa was "an old woman with a grown child" about whom she had heard "many messy stories." But on the positive side, she had also heard that Ulyssa was a rich woman, so once again Chay's fabulous luck came through for him.

One letter reached Chay which he would have given anything never to have received. It was from Hedda Blitzen. It said:

My life is a torment to me because I have learned that I cannot devote it to you. You are married! (I shall never accustom myself to this thought. It is destroying me and I cannot survive.) I will let you see that I am more faithful than you to our pledges, and even though you have broken the ties which bound us, I shall never marry another. I wish you happiness. I wish that the wife whom you have chosen will make you as happy as I had intended that you be. In the midst of your happiness, do not forget Hedda, and weep over her lot.

Following the reception the newlyweds retired for two days. On the morning of the third day they left together for their first joint photo opportunity on Nantucket Island where the groom would lead the forces of freedom against an invasion, already launched from Lebanese ports, by the Iranian army and naval forces.

After the photo session, covered by 1,347 newsmen and the television cameras of the world, it was impossible to keep the marriage a secret from Serena. Worse, the bride's personal maid, Rosie Currie, sold intimate information concerning the marriage to the *National Enquirer* which broke the story on Page 1 with a picture taken with a garter camera by a chambermaid at the honeymoon hotel. A statement was issued in Chay's name which hotly protested the story. From there it caromed around the nation until it landed in the little house on Potomac Avenue in Dallas.

"I can't believe Chay has married that Effing woman!" Serena screamed.

"It's just a rumor, Mom," Jonathan said. "It doesn't mean anything."

"It means there goes a sixty-million-dollar movie contract! Everything was set! The Morris Office was twenty minutes away from a deal! He could have picked his own stories, had the director of his cherce—I would have gotten him final cut! We all woulda been on Easy Street. I could have segued Berry into feature parts while I groomed her for stardom. You, yourself, coulda been a top agent."

"Chay didn't want that, Mom. It could never happen."

"We've got to get him out of this."

"He's *married* now, Mom."

"She's a slut! Get Dudley and Sylvester and Brill over here!"

A family conference was called at the Potomac house. Her children were seated on the two deep, soft burnt-orange sofas which had been arranged in an L-shape while Serena stood in the middle of the room and implored them to save their brother. "It's no use, Mom," Brill said, "I have never seen two people so in love. You don't have a prayer of breaking it up."

"Wherever they are," Serena said grimly, thinking of the money she had lost, "they gotta come back. And when they come back, they are gonna find me waiting on the front steps of her house and we are gonna see about this thing."

Ulyssa wrote to her mother-in-law. Serena replied by return of Federal Express. "Your charming letter, of course, could not have added to the delightful impression I had already formed of you. My son has told me of his happiness which is enough to ensure not only my consent but my approval. My own happiness lacks nothing but the pleasure of meeting you." Chay had dictated the text of the letter to Jonathan and Jonathan had had to sign over to his mother ownership in two city lots in downtown Compton, California, in exchange for her agreement to write and sign the letter.

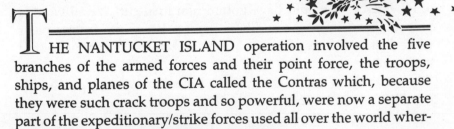

33

THE NANTUCKET ISLAND operation involved the five branches of the armed forces and their point force, the troops, ships, and planes of the CIA called the Contras which, because they were such crack troops and so powerful, were now a separate part of the expeditionary/strike forces used all over the world wherever the Sandinistas would strike at freedom.

The immediate diplomatic excuse for the landings of the first task forces on Nantucket Island was to rescue an excursion party of twelve Winsted, Connecticut, Sunday school pupils who had gone to the island on a flat-rate American Express holiday among the sand dunes but who, the CIA had learned, were now threatened by a Nicaraguan massacre. The salvation of that little band of Americans was the popular reason for the invasion by American troops, an angle which would satisfy the *National Enquirer* and provide entertainment for the taxpayers. The secondary reason was the presence of a disguised labor unit of Nicaraguans who were building an airport to receive the planes, troops, and logistical support for an impending attempt by an Iranian military and naval force which was rumored to be en route to Nantucket to bring total offshore support to the Sandinista war plans for the invasion of North America.

The invasion by U.S. forces was supported by the donations of schoolchildren in all fifty states through a contest sponsored by a breakfast food company which was introducing its eighty-seventh identical product, this one based on dried oats and nasturtium seeds, and through the nominated collections by various television pulpits of the evangelical church which were controlled by the CIA, each contribution reducing defense costs—for the United States ran the thriftiest defense effort in the world.

The media warned sternly that the Iranians, cause of so much trouble in the past by their accepting arms in trade for hostages, were even at that moment sending men, arms, and matériel to the government of Nicaragua. Democracy teetered on the edge of extermination. The world watched with anxiety.

Marshal Appleton landed his armies on the sixteen-mile-long, three-mile-wide Nantucket Island, a combined force of 70,000 troops which increased the population of 5,107 on the island by more than fourteen times. Although it was twenty-five miles south of Cape Cod and fifteen miles east of Martha's Vineyard, its Indian name, Nantucket, meant "far-away land." It was a "far-away land" to the Sandinistas and Iranians who sought to desecrate its soil.

On landing, Chay discovered that although he was the CIN-CAFUSCIAFBIANSA, he was not in command of the operation. Due to the American "unified command system," anything which happened on Nantucket Island was "owned" by the U.S. Navy because the objective was surrounded by water, even though the occupation and defense of the island was entirely a land operation. The invasion was under the orders of the Atlantic Command in Norfolk, Virginia, whose chief, Fleet Admiral Mark Singer, served as "front" commander while Vice Admiral Carleton E. Simpson, on a carrier off Rio de Janeiro, served as his "operational" commander.

In between, the chain of command was effectively tortuous. Singer's headquarters transmitted their orders to CINCUSNA-VEUR, the United States European Command in London, England, who, as soon as they could (considering the long lunch hours), sent the signal to COMSIXTHFLT in Gaeta, Italy. This naval command channel whisked the order to Vice Admiral Simpson in Rio de Janeiro who, as the immediate battle stations commander but one, flashed the orders to the CINCAFUSCIAFBIANSA on the ground at Madaket on the western part of Nantucket Island. This chain of command made possible the employment of 132 admirals, 46 commodores, 603 shore-based captains, and a vast census of junior officers.

It was not until a team of 22 SEALS, the Navy's own elite troops, was sent ashore in pre-dawn darkness to rescue the Mayor of Nantucket and the entire team found themselves trapped inside this house by three barricading Nicaraguan-manned BTR-60 armored cars that Chay began to grow restive. BTR-60s are very poorly protected vehicles which can be penetrated and destroyed by the lightest hand-held antitank weapons, but the Navy had felt that the nautical way to put a SEAL team ashore was to have them swim, so there had been no room for weapons. The SEALS were pinned down and trapped with the Mayor and his family. All but one of the SEALS were wounded.

Not until then did Chay blow his top and wipe out the entire "unified" command system which had done so much to lose the war in Vietnam and Lebanon.

From that moment forward the assault was to be under a "specified" command: i.e., the CINCAFUSCIAFBIANSA. However, in the course of the changeover, there were a great many deplorable "accidents" because the addled "unified" naval commanders didn't know anything about land warfare—operations which would be based on airborne assaults and commando rescues. By tradition, however, because the operation was "owned" by the Navy, the representation of "specialists" from any of the other services was small and of low rank. There was no single command for the ground forces under Navy "ownership" because the Army, Navy, Air Force, Marine Corps, and Coast Guard had been unable to agree on which services should be included.

The American system was unique in the world because of its

"unified" structure which displaced strategy to make corporate harmony possible. The Joint Chiefs of Staff was only a gentlemen's committee which protected the "equal rights" of all of the armed services. The United States had no unified general staff. Each of the services was allowed to perform to its own whims and needs for that services' individual glory. Below the Joint Chiefs the six "unified" commands utterly controlled each of their separate forces. Until Chay blew the whole thing into the sky, there were separate unified headquarters for Europe, the Pacific, the Atlantic, and Latin America, in addition to two overlapping commands in charge of home-based forces.

Chay did not like to be the one to upset military tradition even if the reforms had been pleaded for over the past fifty years, but on the other hand, his 70,000 troops were charged with displacing the 679 Sandinistas who had been landed on the island, of which 636 were construction workers with no more than draftee military training and not more than 43 were professional soldiers, including 22 officers. Nor was the island protected by any kind of an air defense system. Although the Nicaraguans had been described as being "heavily armed," they did not have any tanks or artillery. Their job was to build an emergency airfield for joint Nicaraguan-Iranian operations under the guise of building a parking lot for a projected large shopping mall.

While Chay's exasperated orders went out, traveling some-times twice around the world to reach a field commander who was four miles away, his own troops were ordered to dig in around the shorelines and wait to spring the big surprise on the invading enemy. Aircraft carriers, light cruisers, destroyers, and submarines surrounded the island. The barge of the CINCAFUSCIAFBIANSA plied from flag ship to shore to bring Chay to the battle wagons for photo opportunities, or the Navy brass into Supreme Head-quarters for war councils or tennis. The five combined armed forces and their incalculably sophisticated and expensive equipment were lined up in concentric rows around and around the island.

U.S. Air Force sorties of reconnaissance, fighter, bomber, gun-ship, and radar-bearing aircraft darkened the skies and shattered the historic New England quiet. However, for the first ten days or so, until the "new" system of specified command could be put into place effectively, any sorties had to be called up from Nantucket to Rio to Gaeta to London to Norfolk, Virginia, then the confirmation or denial had to go back through the same chain of command, resulting in a number of mistakes which caused fatalities.

There were foul-ups at first, as there are in any invasion. There were some Intelligence failures by all five services. The Army, because its logistical people had thought the whole thing was going to be a Navy operation, had had to use Exxon road maps of the tiny island with improvised grid coordination systems. No terrain contours were shown. The Marines went into battle using British maps which had been printed in 1756. The Navy had no maps at all, and the Air Force had made its own maps the night before the invasion. Worse, they used yet another set of grids for locating targets on the ground. One result, and heaven knows that many results were identical to it, was that the air attack on the proposed Nicaraguan landing strip destroyed a Nantucket hospital because no hospital was shown on the homemade Air Force maps.

An air strike ordered through those circuitous international channels, called by an admiral in Norfolk, hit a U.S. Army command post because the grid coordinates of the two services didn't match. Twelve Navy air strikes were delivered against U.S. Army positions. A Delta Force team was dumped into the open sea by mistake and all were lost.

The U.S. Forces had no notion of where the Sunday school students were. A battalion of Navy SEALS, lost in the sand dunes, stumbled over them and almost killed all of them until the students were rescued by their own desperate hymn singing. Army ground units and Marine units were unable to talk to each other because their radio frequencies were different, so the carnage was bad. Nor could any Army units talk directly to Marine and Navy aircraft delivering air strikes in support of ground operations. During the initial days of the Nantucket Island landings, the Army was forced to send calls for air strikes back to their headquarters in Fort Bragg, North Carolina, further complicating the command chain. The message then had to be relayed via satellite to the Navy commander, who passed the requests to the air controllers aboard the aircraft carriers. None of the special operations missions had any military value. As it was, all but one of them failed.

Nonetheless, the 70,000-man combined U.S. Task Force easily overcame the 679-man Nicaraguan labor battalion. Although 18 U.S. Troops were killed in the invasion and 116 wounded (the official DOD count which may have been off by 327 and 3,821, respectively), the remainder of the force carried on so gallantly that 19,600 Armed Forces Expeditionary Medals were awarded to a large percentage of those involved in the invasion (97.9 percent), including 127 cooks.

However, as the DOD explained in papers published sometime after the action, the prime reason for the invasion was to defeat the threatened attempt by an Iranian armada which was speeding across two oceans to provide total support to the Sandinista war machine.

During the first weeks of the U.S. occupation of the island, the Iranian high command must have gotten wind of the forces waiting for them and halted their naval advance several hundred, or several thousand, miles off Nantucket, well within international waters, doing nothing which could be construed as a hostile action. What the U.S. news media at home reported, through Department of Defense news teams, was "one of the great military standoffs" in history.

That the Iranians had sailed was never in doubt because it had been observed by Israeli intelligence, and any information which cost that much had to be accurate. Aerial scouting missions sent out by Supreme Headquarters kept reporting that the enemy must be retreating faster than they could be overtaken because no Iranian fleet had been sighted. Marshal Appleton, after sifting through all the evidence, made an appearance on camera before the American people and proved to everyone that the Iranian threat was not only imminent but had to be smashed.

The occupation and the defenses made possible by the Marshal's bivouac on Nantucket Island cost $2.1 billion, which made the tiny island the ranking financial center of the North Atlantic. As American taxpayer money poured into the tiny island to insure its defense, a replica of Wall Street sprang up in Siasconset town with satellite links to New York, London, Tokyo, and Hong Kong—all based on money, which created credit, which created money, which extended credit, which made money. That was the by-product.

The main product of the occupation of Nantucket was the total paving of the entire island, from east to west, from shore to shore, to make it the largest airport in the world for the intensely heavy air traffic which would carry cocaine from the jungles of South America into the supermarkets of North America.

34

WHILE THE AMERICAN FORCES were digging in to be ready for the Iranian advance, the CINCAFUSCIAFBIANSA and his bride basked in the joys of an idyllic honeymoon. The setting was perfect: powdered sugar beaches, good tennis, fine golf, and really crackerjack yachting in crisp, early autumn New England weather. There were wonderful parties, exciting picnics with some really good-looking young officers for Ulyssa while her husband planned the defense of the island against Iran and began his mission to pave Nantucket over. At last, the Navy vindicated itself by providing the smartest sort of receptions aboard flagships and submarines.

Ulyssa, even though she was a professional party-goer, was thrillingly exhausted by the gay life at the forefront of freedom, deeply in love as she was with the CINCAFUSCIAFBIANSA. The formerly young couple was truly happy until the early afternoon of the middle day of the second month when Ulyssa returned to the house on the rise which overlooked the harbor of Nantucket town and found a letter addressed to her on the entrance hall table.

She knew she recognized the handwriting even though it was

impossible because she had never seen it before, and her heart leaped. Her husband was inspecting the construction of the gigantic cement strip which would within the year cover the entire island, but nonetheless she jammed the letter guiltily into her reticule, certainly intending to conceal it. She hurried up the broad staircase. When the door to her boudoir was locked behind her and all the shades had been drawn on the second-story windows, she sat inside her lighted closet surrounded by its ninety little frocks and party dresses which she had "borrowed" from designers, and opened the letter.

She had instinctively recognized the sender of the letter. She realized that it was not the handwriting which quickened her pulse and shortened her breath, but the heavy, heady animal scent, so like the smell of a summer zoo, which had set off wild and erotic alarm systems inside her being.

The letter was from François Max Felix, the most exciting man she had ever known. Felix was the sort of shabby shambles of a man whom no one ever notices, excepting women. He had dirty fingernails and a nose like a boxing glove, made love in white linen knickers, and ate pastrami sandwiches during the act when he wasn't sipping odorous rye whiskey, but those quirks, as thrillingly dirty as they could make a girl feel, were surface things when compared to what he brought to a woman. They became meaningless, forgotten annoyances when he lifted his arms and let the gusts of his natural odors envelope the woman he (currently) loved. Felix had made his life with, by, and—to a minimal extent —for women. In the eyes of other men he was the promoter of impossible schemes: antigravity brassieres, electrically illuminated T-shirts with imprinted animated pictograms and advertising messages, AIDS-resistant aphrodisiacs, and other illusory propositions which brought him about 6 percent of his income. The remainder, the 94 percent—and a substantial income it was—came from the kindness and generosity of women.

Felix was the sweet man of all time who inevitably attracted women either because they each believed she would be the one to reform him or because she wanted to keep other women from having him.

Ulyssa had not stopped seeing Felix, in secret, since she had married Chay. Felix had been moved into her little house on Laurel Street which she had kept after she left to become the chatelaine of Rossenarra.

Felix had a complexion the color of mayonnaise: soft and translucently pale and aromatic. He had heavy, dark, "interesting" bags under his eyes. He dressed to impress women, wearing multicolored caftans around the house or suit jackets which were extremely tailored and skirted in the prewar British fashion. Ulyssa had told close friends that "no other man I have ever known really understood how much a woman is interested in a man's underwear." Felix bought colorful, used women's evening gowns from a Salvation Army outlet then, at his design, the patterned material was fragmented into large squares and reassembled by an elderly seamstress who was in love with him into brilliantly stated if motley sets of boxer shorts and sleeveless undershirts.

In her secret code-written records, Ulyssa ranked him as a lover (almost) nonpareil; high among (number eight actually) the greatest lovers she had ever known. She was also, like all other women who had possessed him, hypnotized by possessing him where other women had failed. He rated so compellingly high on her list of needs that, as she read his letter, she had both vertigo and nausea from the sudden lack of blood supply to the balancing centers in her inner ears. She experienced the terror of possibly falling out of the chaise longue. She read the letter eagerly:

Dearest Woofie:
    I have roamed the world trying to forget the power of your thighs (I can feel them crushing my temples now). I try to stifle the hot memory of the enduring arch of your back, and your unmatchable vocabulary as you reach climax; vocal, vibrant, deliciously vicious as you loose the abandonment of a woman who has been promised ecstasy but who has never found enough of it, etc. etc. I cannot forget one drop of your sweat as it drenched me or the explosions of orgasm which almost tore you apart, etc. etc. I will be waiting on our bed in Dallas. I will end my life unless you bring your incredible body to me, etc. etc. I have five days before I must be gone again. There is a misunderstanding with the SEC, the Fraud Squad, and some crazed husbands who don't know what they

are saying, but I have a terrific opportunity in artificial opals coming up and (I think) I can get you a piece of the action for an amazingly small investment.

Hurry! My God! I think I'm going to come!

> Your own,
> Bimptie

Ulyssa packed a bag, forged a military travel pass on a sheet of blank printed passes in her husband's desk, then wrote a careful note to explain to Chay why she had to leave the island.

> Dear, darling Chay
> [she wrote hastily]:
>
> I am wracked with the pain of what is best to refer to as a "woman's complaint." This has happened before so, thank God, I know what to do. I must put myself in the hands of the only gynecologist who has ever been able to find relief for me. I will call you in (about) five days, after I get out of the hospital. This is not something which we could allow Army doctors to handle. I know you cannot put yourself in my place but I also know that, of all men, you will come closest to understanding. It is possible that it could be that I have eaten too much codfish.
>
> All my love (and more),
> Ulyssa
>
> P.S. I should be back in your arms in less than a week.

Five hours later, thanks to the speed of fighter-bombers, Ulyssa got out of a taxi in front of the Laurel Street house in Dallas, paid the fare with a fifty-dollar bill but didn't wait for change, and hurried up the elaborate crazy-paving to her front door. A harsh voice stopped her in her tracks.

"Just a minute, hooker," she thought she imagined hearing the voice say. She turned toward it, hot with outrage. She faced a tall, brass-blond woman of a certain age whose chilling pale blue eyes drilled into her.

"How dare you?" Ulyssa said. "Who the hell are you?"

"I am Marshal of the American Union Appleton's mother," the woman said. "I am head of the family which you have shamed."

"*Shamed?*"

"Your gross and greasy lover is waiting for you inside, stripped to the waist, wearing white linen knickers."

Ulyssa shivered. "My lover? You are insane, madam. He is my father."

"I described him to Mr. Grogan not an hour ago. He is your lover."

"What do you want from me? This is all a terrible misunderstanding. My husband will not countenance such harassment."

"I want your marriage annulled."

"*Annulled?*" Panicking, Ulyssa ran up the path to the front door. "You are undoubtedly a common blackmailer and I shall report you to the police. And—no matter who or what—you could not be my husband's mother!" She slammed the front door behind her. There was a series of loud clicks as she locked and bolted Serena out.

Serena stared after her. A long, black limousine pulled up at curbside directly in front of the house. The door opened. A soft ingratiating voice called out from the car. "Mother?"

Serena turned. She recognized the kindly face of her son-in-law, Wambly Keifetz, head of government. She walked to the car. Wambly drew her into the tonneau and shut the door.

"How rarely do we ever have a chance to visit," he said. "But it takes a heap o' livin' to run the government. How are you? How have you been? You are looking even more beautiful than usual."

"Wambly, do you realize what is going on inside that house?"

"A girl and her dad, Mother. According to our information, a family crisis had come up and your daughter-in-law was forced to rush back to Dallas to help her father."

"A girl and her dad, my ass," Serena said. "Right now they are going at it hot and heavy in there, costing my son his faith in the future."

"Let's drive through the lovely Turtle Creek area," Keifetz suggested. "A wonderful opportunity has come up and I want to share it with you." He tapped on the glass separation and the car rolled slowly toward Lakeside.

"Just one minute, here!" Serena shrilled.

"You are aware that our nation's capital is going to be established in and around Gardena, California?"

"I heard that."

"I have been lucky enough to secure title to a square block of property which is smack in the center of what will be the most vital area of the new city."

"Yeah?"

"And because I am a member of your family, I want you to have the protection of owning that property. It is only right."

"Own it? What's it worth?"

"Today sixty thousand dollars. Tomorrow perhaps six million."

"Well! You are a generous boy."

"I want to protect Chay from the heartbreak of having his own mother tell the world that his bride had had a secret tryst with a lover when the fellow who was supposed to be her lover was actually her father."

"Then I would say you had hit on the ideal solution."

"I knew you would agree with me," he said, patting her hand.

Ulyssa was entangled with F. M. Felix on the floor beside the king-sized bed. She was soaring like a rocket in the self-destruct mode, just reaching the explosion of climax when the bedroom door burst open admitting Eddie Grogan, two extremely burly men, and two photographers, one of whom was using a hand-held television camera. Grogan commanded her to continue what she was doing until both photographers had completed their intercut setups.

The photography team left. The two burly men led Felix out of the room and out of the house. Grogan sat facing the outraged, weeping, extraordinarily frustrated Ulyssa, still on the floor.

"Eddie! Fahcrissake! Are you crazy? I am Mrs. Caesare Appleton!"

"How long do you think you'll be his wife after what you just did?"

"Did? *Did?* Whatever you think I did, it didn't get done. Where are your goons taking François?"

"Get dressed."

"You're not going to tell him?"

"Do as you're told and it's our little secret."

"You swear it on your Agency scapular?"

"Sure."

"His mother—"

"That's being taken care of. You are the inside track on what Appleton thinks. Graciela Winkelreid can't be expected to carry the whole load. That's why you got this job. The alley cat days are over, kid. One more little adventure like today and we turn you in."

Chay was away from base for two days, inspecting defenses, playing poker and tennis, and delivering advance bulletins to the Signal Corps TV cameras which would be covering the Iranian invasion in lieu of letting the American networks having to face the dangers of such coverage in the victories of the forces of freedom over the Iranian violators of the Monroe Doctrine.

In rapid succession, wherever he went on his tour, he received the news of Ulyssa's assignation from Dudley and Sylvester. After he had read each message, when Chay was sure that all of his staff—batmen, officers, and bodyguards—could not see or hear him, he got into the large refresher tank of ice water which had been installed to invigorate him on tropical Nantucket mornings. He lowered his body under the water and, with his mouth clamped shut, screamed inside his skull until, at last, he had gotten accustomed to the Ulyssa-Felix idea.

He wrote to Dudley.

I am suffering great unhappiness but a veil has fallen from my eyes. I blame myself for allowing one person to so occupy my thoughts as to exclude all other meanings. God! I cannot tell you how I regret that I allowed Hedda Blitzen to get away! I swear this to you: when I return home after this war is done, Ulyssa and her miserable lover will pay.

In despair, for this was Caesare Appleton's Valley Forge, he telephoned Eddie Grogan on the scrambler and ordered him to Nantucket Island. What follows was taken, word for word, from

Grogan's notes on the meeting which were recently uncovered behind the altar of the St. Agnes In Agony World Ecumenical Church on Gun Hill Road in the Bronx, City of New York, while the church was being razed to make room for a much-needed telephone exchange.

Grogan was taken directly to Chay who locked them in the room, turned up the music on the automatic organ, and said, "I have no doubt that you know what this is all about."

"Your wife," Grogan said.

Chay winced. His eyes fell. He looked sick.

"Have a drink, Eddie," he said, pouring them both Dr. Peppers from a giant economy-size bottle. "We'll split the work," he said. "I'll handle my wife. You handle this fellow Felix."

"Whatever you say, Boss."

"He is a loose-living, self-indulgent man, Eddie. He needs discipline, and I mean hard, relentless discipline."

"I agree with you 100 percent, Chay. What do you want me to set up for him?"

"I think he should be enlisted in our Marine Corps and a personal drill sergeant assigned to him. Unless you can think of something better."

"We do have better solutions but I don't think I should burden you with details."

"All right. Just do it."

"Can I help you with your end on this?" Grogan asked.

"Help?" Chay said distractedly. "How?"

"Well, I can find work for her in a joint in the rice fields of southern India."

"I'll handle Ulyssa."

"When will you be going back?"

"I thought I'd sneak into town and surprise her."

"When?"

"The sooner the better. This has to be handled now."

Within forty-eight hours, Chay had turned over the command of the anti-Iranian forces on Nantucket Island to Lieutenant General Benito Juarez Bennett and had set off in Air Force One with a twelve-plane fighter escort for Dallas. Inevitably, the word of his arrival leaked to the press. A crowd of 31,000 (police estimate);

the 16 television network and cable outlets; 697 of the print press and photographers; local, national, and worldwide radio; plus his brothers Dudley and Jonathan, were waiting at Love Field when Chay landed. The crowd had been hyped so much and so ceaselessly about how Chay had once again saved his country from pillage, rape, and sordid disgrace that they were transformed with gratitude and admiration. Their only desire was to touch him.

The Marshal was trapped aboard his plane because the police could not hold back the idolatrous crowd which had exploded out of every exit of the airport buildings to be beatified by a simple soldier's presence. It took a battalion of Chay's own Seventy-fifth Rangers to bring order. Heartbreakingly, 8 people were killed in the crush and 116 were badly injured. Tragically, among the dead were 2 of the very Sunday school children whose imperiled picnic on Nantucket Island Chay's forces had gone to liberate in the first place. They had been flown in from Winsted, Connecticut, to present a bouquet of flowers to the Marshal with the affecting message (gold letters printed on red satin) of "Thank you, sir." The nation mourned them but with the help of the TV news anchormen appreciated the irony.

Within ninety-five minutes calm was restored, allowing the Marshal to come down the ramp before the lenses of most of the television equipment then available in the western hemisphere. The viewer audience as far out as Papua and Beverly Hills was rated by all surveys at 92 percent, meaning that approximately 600 million people had shared a few wonderful, wonderful moments with Chay.

At last the troops got the Marshal off the tarmac and into the light tank which sped him to the helicopter which took him behind the walls of Rossenarra.

Ulyssa was not there. Tipped off that Chay was about to land, she had driven to the airport to meet him, but needing to get her make-up right, she had arrived too late, then had been swallowed up by the crowd.

However, the other women of Chay's family were waiting on his doorstep when he arrived home. Serena called Ulyssa "that little whore" before Chay had come down the ramp from the chopper. Serena urged him to come back with her to the house on Potomac Avenue.

"I'll stay here, thank you," he said. "Others can seek other accommodations."

He kissed his mother, his sister Berry, and Dudley's wife, Frieda, on their cheeks and went into the house, slamming the door behind him. It was evening before Ulyssa was able to get back to Rossenarra, greatly disheveled. She found that she had been locked out. She did not lose her nerve. She collapsed on the floor of the porch outside the locked main door then sent her son Elvis, who had also showed up, through the laundry chute to plead for her. Elvis was totally convincing because Chay liked him. With a tear-streaked face he pleaded with Chay not to abandon his mother because he was afraid she would kill herself if she had to face the rest of her life without him. Chay broke down, gave in, unlocked the front door and Ulyssa rushed into his arms.

It was a tender, sweet, and moving moment. From far above with golden voices the angels sang to them: "Weave costly songs. Tell us things so majestical in their love, so pressed into time that they lose their wings for flight to unblessed empty hours which sit lamenting around us, nodding blindly, counterfeiting the coin of our memory. Weave lights with your voices. Carve deep your marks into the trunk of the tree of our lives. Freeze leaves falling from it. Make a sweet park around it. Invoke a carousel of hours—reprieves revolving and repeating—not ending 'till the music stops."

When Dudley arrived at Rossenarra the following morning he was disgusted to find the lovers in bed, smiling shyly as they ate breakfast. It was a flawless reconciliation.

François Max Felix, chemically installed in a permanent daze by CIA scientists, had long since been packed into the hold of a tramp steamer which was one of the CIA's proprietary interests, and was on his way to work for the rest of his life in the refractory chromite mines on the island of Masinloc in the Philippines. As the ship crossed the South Pacific he thought of a woman just once; the fleeting image was that of a Miss Tintle who had taught him spelling at P.S. 169 in Manhattan so many years before. He had never liked her.

35

TWO WEEKS AFTER Chay had returned to Dallas, Dudley, who was more unstable than ever when it came to politics, arranged a secret meeting for Chay to listen to Beniamiamo Camardi, the Mafia's representative in the government, who said that the leadership wanted a coup d'état which would install a firmer administration. Since Chay was the only government official who had been sworn in, that meant that he was being asked to handle it.

Camardi said, "We must formalize the installation of an executive, legislative, and judicial branch of government."

"You mean we haven't been having anything like that in the government?"

"Not exactly."

"But what about the National Conference for Democracy?"

"That was more like a—well, like a presidential commission. It didn't mean anything because it didn't have any power to do anything."

"My God, then, Ben, my rank—my pension—is illegal!"

"Not exactly illegal. Wambly Keifetz endorsed it. But now he wants a new Constitution and positive programs like taxes. What we want from you is the assurance that the Army—in fact all the armed forces—won't make a big fuss when we install the new government."

"The *new* government?"

"You know what I mean. Everybody is gonna go along."

"Well, it's all right with me."

"You'll support us on television?"

"Why not?" Chay said.

"Keifetz has this terrific idea," Camardi said. "He's figured out a way to wipe out the deficit and the terrible Reagan debt and—"

"I know—with packaged, advertised supermarket cocaine."

"Is that terrific or is that terrific?"

"Ask Keifetz. I'm a soldier, not a grocer."

36

THE ASCENSION of Wambly Keifetz and the Directory to the leadership of the American government brought a rather trashy crowd to Dallas. The Nouveau Old Guard would have nothing to do with them, but the business of the country had changed. American business had once been directed toward making things and selling them. Now the manufacturing process (except for weapons and armaments, still our prime export industry) was done in Japan, Singapore, Germany, Britain, Taiwan, and Korea, causing 22.7 percent unemployment but saving the brand-name owners a considerable amount in overhead and taxes. The hard-core American industry now was the proliferation of money through blips on computer screens or as impulses on magnetic tapes, with hairdressing, sports, and organized crime as the primary industries. The national discipline was dedicated to developing the ability to generate a profit. Capital, in the form of billions of tons of paper profits, was moved with the efficiency (not counting the number of bank failures) which had once been shown in the distribution of goods. Ethics had to suffer, beginning with the White House and the Congress before the Evaporation. The accumulation of money is not the natural goal of the human spirit.

The newcomers to Dallas, as the new center of action in the nation, were a crassitude of politicians, feverish bankers, reckless speculators, investment touts, money-shocked brokers, and the newly respectable Mafiosi with their inexhaustible supply of capital.

As Wambly Keifetz had insisted for all of his life, as indeed the old outlaw President of the 1980s had demanded, money is everything and you must keep spending it whether you have it or not. It may have been, and undeniably was, cheerful, but on the other hand, it was also wholeheartedly vicious. By definition and according to Hollywood, people who live by their wits have to be amusing people (and Keifetz typified his times as much as the Great Waver had typified his), so, in its own way, Dallas was a fun city.

The shabbily sinister side, as opposed to the glitzily sinister side, of the Keifetz government was Eddie Grogan. He was a pale, gangling, slack-faced, liver-lipped man who had a dreadful glassy stare and a shambling gait. Grogan relished other people's deaths by violence. He looked like a cartoon of an Irish-American bouncer on his day off. Terror was his hobby. Within the first ten minutes of being introduced to him at Fort Meade immediately after the great Evaporation, Chay had said to Grogan, in a totally unveiled threat, "If you ever cross me, Eddie, I'm going to have you shot where you stand."

Grogan, totally convinced, had answered. "Hey, Chief! What kind of kidding around is that?"

Chay was the only man Grogan respected because Chay had the real power, not that this restrained him from trying to betray Chay. Foul-mouthed from childhood, a Dickensian-style villain, this man who had failed to pass the Civil Service examination for sanitation worker was perhaps the most effective secret police chief in history.

Grogan conspired internationally. That was his job. But he also had people he had larded throughout Dallas life from the salons to the saloons. One of these people was Ulyssa Effing, whose husband, Admiral Forest Effing, had been executed.

Effing had been a member of the National Conference for Democracy. He was one of a tiny radical group who sought to prevent American schoolchildren from owning automatic and semiautomatic assault weapons. The NRA/NCD had accordingly enacted the Law of Suspects who were defined as "those who by their conduct, their connections, their remarks, or their writing show themselves to be partisans of tyranny." Effing, for his views which were against the Constitutional right to possess arms, was denounced and arrested. He was confined to the dreaded prison on Preston Road in Dallas which had once been a branch of the YMCA. He was tried before the Revolutionary Tribunal with a group of forty-nine offenders of whom forty-six were found guilty, the Admiral among them. He was shot the same day. Ulyssa Effing was a widow.

Although she had not seen nor spoken to her husband for six years, Ulyssa felt the blow sorely, because through the past association with him she was immediately brought under suspicion. Fortunately, she found an unemployed actor named Nicky Jackelson who, for a small fee, went to the archives of the Committee for Public Safety and ate her entire file.

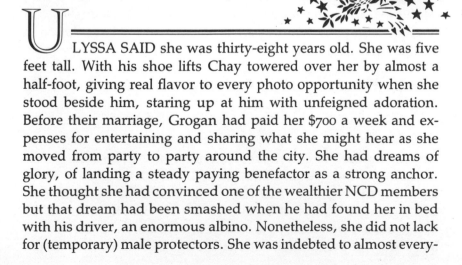

37

U LYSSA SAID she was thirty-eight years old. She was five feet tall. With his shoe lifts Chay towered over her by almost a half-foot, giving real flavor to every photo opportunity when she stood beside him, staring up at him with unfeigned adoration. Before their marriage, Grogan had paid her $700 a week and expenses for entertaining and sharing what she might hear as she moved from party to party around the city. She had dreams of glory, of landing a steady paying benefactor as a strong anchor. She thought she had convinced one of the wealthier NCD members but that dream had been smashed when he had found her in bed with his driver, an enormous albino. Nonetheless, she did not lack for (temporary) male protectors. She was indebted to almost everyone but had somehow managed to hold on to her jewels and those, together with her credit standing with a ruthlessly powerful dress- maker who was one of the great forces of W magazine, plus a speaking voice more sensual and musical than Orpheus's flute, as well as the steady rumor that she had come from an enormously wealthy New Orleans bookmaking family, had contrived to create the illusion that she was a woman of standing.

She had a pretty house on Laurel Drive where she gave al- luring dinner parties. Keifetz who was (inevitably) one of her lov- ers, dined there several times a month. To run the house she needed a chauffeur, a cook, a houseman, a chambermaid and a personal maid, all of whom she had so convinced of her future that they worked for quarter-pay at 22 percent monthly interest excepting her personal maid, Rosie Currie, who deferred all of her wages for 50 percent weekly interest and frequently loaned Ulyssa money as well.

Ulyssa knew that Chay thought she was a rich woman. She talked it over with Keifetz. "Am I right or am I right in not letting him know that I don't have a dime? He's an important man. Why would he need my money if I had any money? He thinks I'm going to inherit New Orleans. Let's not straighten him out of this, Wamb. Okay?"

Keifetz was amused that Chay had taken the time to fall in love and that Chay might be dismayed because Ulyssa didn't have any money, but he explained to her that only Chay's mother would be shocked when the news came out. In his own appallingly secret heart he wondered wistfully what his own wife Brill could see in such a total schmuck.

All during the period of Chay's courtship, Ulyssa had been deeply involved with F. M. Felix. It was an open secret among the fast crowd.

The surviving members of the NCD completed a new Con- stitution for the United States of America. It streamlined the former Constitution and decreed that there be a chief executive to be known as the Chairman and CEO of the United States of America; two legislative bodies to be elected by the people, made of an upper and a lower house; a judiciary; and a National Security arm. In the interim period until national elections could be held for the

Executive and Legislative branches, three Directors to be appointed by the National Conference for Democracy would administer the government.

Of the three Directors chosen, two were of the people, unknown to government: Wambly Keifetz and Beniamiamo Camardi. The third was the well-known Director of the Central Intelligence Agency, Edward Mulhaus Grogan.

"We are the temporary custodians of democracy," Wambly Keifetz said to the television cameras, "and we will serve until the voice of the people has been heard to return the rightful government of, for, and by the people to this green and happy land."

It was a solemn and thrilling day for the American people. They were told—and the resultant groan could be heard from coast to coast—that although there would not be any dangerous election reforms such as a national primary, nine candidates from each Party would enter the race for the highest office in the land and that these eighteen inexorably, relentlessly uninteresting men would campaign throughout the land for four months. People wept openly thinking of the mental cruelties to come; endless speeches without syntax, hopeless declarations which had been punishing clichés in 1803.

The slates for both Parties included a mendacious gypsy parson who talked to God, a Marshal of the American Union, two state governors, three senators, a black civil rights activist, and the candidate of Big Oil without which no American election would have been genuine. It was a roster of time-servers, gofers, and lobbygows; an irascible farm state senator; a billionaire; a sex enthusiast; a confused man who resembled Uriah Heep; and two John Kennedy look-alikes.

Gordon Godber Manning, who had been Secretary of State at the time of the Evaporation and who, therefore, would have been in line to assume the Presidency, was permitted to emerge from retirement to head the Democratic field. Venerable Franklin Marx Heller, seventy-seven, grand old man of Rockrimmon, whose age alone made him the certain Republican candidate, was front-runner for the Grand Old Party. Each candidate's appeal was to a separate constituency.

Immediately after something called "caucuses" in the State of Iowa, the whole thing became a blur.

The "race" inched forward month by month. Charges and countercharges were flung. Campaign advertising became so scurrilous that mothers turned their children's heads away from television sets when candidates appeared on the screen. All fifty states felt the agony of the effort. In all $391,763,017 was squandered, mostly in Federal funds, most of it going to television networks and stations.

Chay, to a certain extent, and under the constant advice of Graciela Winkelreid, stayed above the fray. He emphasized his experience in foreign affairs by accepting an honorary degree in Russian studies from Exeter University in England, by conferring the prize to the winner of the Tour de France, the great bicycle race, and by opening the Hall of Knowledge at Disneyland outside Tokyo. He took long, solitary walks through the grounds of Rossenarra, grounds which had been enlarged considerably when eleven neighbors on all sides of the estate had been discovered to be Sandinista sympathizers. As he walked, he pondered on his choice of running mate in the upcoming campaign. In the end of the agony of decision to choose the man who would live "a heart beat away" from the Chairmanship, he chose his batman, Mallard "Molly" Tompkins, for the key post. Although not an international figure, Tompkins was a longtime associate of the Marshal's, and he had Chay's total confidence and regard. "He is a man who knows what it is to serve," Chay said as he gave America his choice.

To save the wear of travel and the exhaustion of old-fashioned campaigning, the two men appeared, together and separately (if necessary which it never was), through the miracle of special effects which were produced from a studio on the Rossenarra grounds at prime time on alternate days of the week. Each campaign speech was given against a different, startlingly realistic, dimensional photomural background using back-screen and front-screen projection of a different American city or locality, starting with Iowa farm-and-tractor backgrounds then proceeding to snowy New Hampshire settings and true, truer, truest representations of the other states. In this way, it was possible for the candidates to seem to visit Hawaii and Alaska, and because the vice presidential nominee was always within call, Chay's suits were neatly pressed, his shoes immaculately shined, and the flair of his "lucky" homburg rolled high as it crossed his forehead. "Mallard Tompkins will be more meaningfully engaged than any other vice president in our history," Chay told the American people proudly.

Dressed in a variety of uniforms, appearing against the backgrounds of every state of the Union, Chay made speeches on toxic waste, the greenhouse effect, acid rain, school prayers, and "the cocaine solution" which would free the nation from the deficit; the terrible national debt, the savings and loan burden, the nuclear reactor cleanups, and perhaps most important of all, the drug problem, as the sociologists called it, inasmuch as people would not be required just to say no to narcotics any longer. Chay, personally against cocaine because of his firsthand experience with his father, knowing that it made its users steal, lie, cheat, steal and sell anything and everything including themselves, while they risked imprisonment, nonetheless was persuaded by Miss Winkelreid that it was a surefire political move because the public had been so deeply brainwashed by the news media to fear the deficit and the terrible, terrible national debt which Reagan had accumulated. The foreign debt alone was just short of reaching $397.5 billion or 32 percent of the gross national product. The Reagan spending requirements had reached such heights of national thrift as to become so complex that it now took fourteen pages to instruct a Defense Department procurement officer how to purchase a fruitcake, including the requirement that the presence of vanilla "be organoleptically detected but not to a pronounced degree" so that "when the cooled product is bisected vertically and horizontally with a sharp knife, it shall not crumble nor show any compression streaks, gummy centers, or soggy areas, or be excessively dry or overprocessed." That ruling alone, although requiring a staff of seven to develop it, would save hundreds of dollars, but there was still a long way to go.

Immediately following Super Tuesday, the subsequent Super Friday, and the wrap-up Super Monday primary elections, the pundits told the anchormen and the talk show hosts who did the political thinking for the American people that both conventions were going to be hopelessly deadlocked.

Conjecture as to which candidate would emerge from the inevitably brokered conventions immediately assumed that there was only one man who would be acceptable to both parties and, therefore, to the American voters, inasmuch as one followed the other as day the night. Television, the bellwether of the national mind, spoke no other name than that of Marshal of the American Union, Caesare "Chay" Appleton.

Finally, the Democratic Party, through the voice of Gordon Godber Manning, made the historic announcement that the leaders of the Party had met in caucus all through the night and had chosen Caesare Appleton as standard bearer for the Party. This was accepted unanimously by vote of the Convention. The Republicans threw the decision to the open convention, recording the vote in full view of the television cameras. Chay Appleton was the unanimous Party choice.

The country overflowed into the streets to express their relief and happiness.

Standing in an open gazebo in the lovely garden at Rossenarra, Chay accepted the nominations of both Parties in humble spirit. He said, "I am simply unable to comprehend that you have chosen me to serve as the Chairman and CEO of our great country. All of heaven has fallen upon me, but between now and election day, I will campaign with might and main, heart and soul, mind and spirit, and hope that, by the grace of God, you will elect me as your Chairman."

That night after Chay's simple supper of cold meat and celery tonic, Hedda Blitzen called him from New York. It nearly broke the candidate's heart.

"Chay?" her tremulous voice said. "I had to tell you how proud and moved I am by the wonderful news."

"Hedda!"

"No tears, my darling. And no heartbreak. That's life—*c'est la vie*—or, as Poppa would say, *das ist die Lebensbeschreibung.*"

"I must see you!" Chay cried out into the phone. "All this is as nothing without you by my side."

"Someday, my dearest. Perhaps over the rainbow." She hung up.

38

CHAY OPENED the campaign on Labor Day against the thrilling front-screen projection of Detroit. He came out for organized labor. Computer surveys of the four past election TV tapes turned up any number of authentic backgrounds for his subsequent campaign speeches: the exteriors of big city factories where it was always 5:45 A.M.; senior citizen compounds in St. Petersburg, Florida (shuffleboard in the foreground, palm trees in the background); big city shopping plazas. He was seen driving huge farm tractors; wearing feathered headdresses on Indian reservations; in the driver's seat of enormous eighteen wheelers; or helmeted and grotesque on a General Sherman tank. Indefatigably, Chay covered all fifty states, yet he was able to sleep in his own bed every night. It was a long, hard-driving, and costly campaign which won an Oscar for Special Effects in that year's awards by the Motion Picture Academy of Arts and Sciences.

The cocaine issue, on balance—as the Sunday morning TV pundits and syndicated print columnists explained to the American people—had more positives than negatives. One, it would eliminate the deficit and the terrible national debt within two months, bail out the savings and loan associations, and provide the money to clean up the reactor plants. It would permit large-scale government research and development to mature and fructify the myriad of undiscovered gadgets which the public would want to buy when they saw them, and not only digital, fiber-optic cable, high-resolution television. It would banish forever the possibility of increased taxes and insure prosperity well into the twenty-first century. There were drawbacks, of course. Every plan had its drawbacks: national physical debilitation, overcrowded mental hospitals, a startlingly high budget for prison construction, parentless families, and tripled homelessness, but by and large, it was a sound policy, soundly arrived at. Congress endorsed it with wild enthusiasm. A national poll on voter attitudes to the cocaine issue showed 28 percent for, 22 against, 13 percent don't know, and a 37 percent wait-and-see factor. The packaging, credit card, and advertising industries gave the issue full marks, and as the polls reechoed voter enthusiasm, all of the clergy climbed aboard the cocaine wagon.

The Marshal and his running mate were swept into office by 13 percent of the registered voters, a light turnout for an election year, but by a unanimous expression of acceptance by both parties. As Democrats, they carried 73 percent of the total vote cast. As Republicans they carried the Sun Belt and American Samoa.

The turnout of 13 percent, the pundits immediately pointed out, should not be seen as some abruptly negative phenomenon. It represented 3.67 percent more than the national turnout in the previous national election, and even though voting was said to be the common denominator of democracy, voting had declined from a peak in 1960 when 62.831 percent of the voting-age population had turned out. Caesare Appleton's tallies showed that he was on the way to restoring faith in democracy, particularly by his choices for cabinet posts.

A newcomer, John DeWitt Kullers, was named Secretary of Defense and a DOD consultant at $755,000 a year. Edward Mulhaus Grogan became Director, Central Intelligence, and Attorney General. Beniamiamo Camardi took over the leadership of the Recreational Stimulant Agency which would administer the new cocaine program as well as the portfolio of Health, Education and Welfare. Wambly Keifetz protested directly on national television that it was his intention to retire to private life, but as the pundits reminded the public, he was a man who had met his duty more than halfway for all of his life. He accepted control over the State Department and Treasury.

Appointees to the Supreme Court were divided among seven former Keifetz employees who had served as legal counsel to one or another of his many successful companies, and two neo-liberals.

For the swearing-in ceremony at the portico of the new "Pink House" in Dallas, as Rossenarra was called affectionately, the Marshal, as close friends still called him, wore a simple $495 lapis-colored polo shirt and a pair of $867.25 French-blue camel's hair slacks from Ralph Lauren, a pair of $878.95 alligator loafers from Gucci, and a $1,804.29 blue, black, and gray sports jacket from Aquascutum because Graciela Winkelreid's public relations people wanted the public to have the maximum thrill the first time they saw him out of military uniform. Mrs. Appleton held the Bible in an $11,735 outfit by Bill Blass, a representation of stunning all-American good taste.

On the day of Chay's inauguration, 7,634 people were killed by Grogan's people—grumblers in the big cities and people here and there who refused to understand the benefits of change. The country now appeared to be a military dictatorship, at least that is what it was called by the press and television of Europe, but it certainly was not, as the new Chairman/CEO quickly proved on television in a warmly sincere talk to the nation. He told America that it was clear what the people wanted in their hearts: a return to the one, true ecumenical faith for formal occasions such as school prayers, with the readily available entertainment of electronic charismatic televised religion so that folks didn't have to get out of bed on a Sunday morning—for Americans were a religious people.

They wanted the appearance of a balanced budget, he pointed out, but not the reality of one because that would be impossible; one so that all private interest groups, and the great State of Texas, could share in the government's generosity. Chay gave them those things, and his brother Sylvester, Cardinal Appleton, was the nation's consultant on God.

Chay spoke to the people every Sunday noon through cameras with voice-activated teleprompters. He repeated again and again, "No Royalists or revolutionaries; only Americans."

Terrorism was put down without mercy. Chay put a chicken in every pot and a Japanese car in every garage. The people adored him—or were arrested or left the country. They had good reason to adore him. His ascension to the Chairmanship marked the first time since 1981 that the nation had not been at war with Nicaragua.

Chay studied the Manual of Republican Presidents day and night during the transition period before he was sworn into office. He developed a knack of public speaking until, without saying anything at all, people would be convinced that he knew something. Chay got so good at it that even he seemed to believe what he told the people, therefore they believed it. Professional politicians and news media people couldn't get it through their heads that the people could believe it, but they did.

The great force behind every decision Graciela Winkelreid and her staff made in the Pink House was the pollster, Egbert Willy, who cost the Republican National Committee, year in, year out, an estimated $4.1 million a year. Willy had the talent for making his principal clients, Wambly Keifetz and Caesare Appleton, feel good. They took great comfort in his consistently upbeat reports. Willy met Graciela Winkelreid every day, the Chairman once a week. He said of the Chairman and the First Lady, "They are sophisticated users of public attitudes." Working with Miss Winkelreid's speeches, Willy developed a system for "pretesting" or "marketing" every phrase the Chairman would use in every speech. The speech would be read to an assembly of seventy-five people brought in from the streets. Their pulse-responses, breathing, and blood-chemistry changes would be calibrated by computer to each phrase in the speech. The processed findings would be printed out with the number-ratings of phrase-approval figures printed in the right-hand column in red. Egbert Willy and Miss Winkelreid developed "power phrases," also called "resonators"; phrases such as "Evil Empire" and "Contras, who are the equivalent of our Founding Fathers," and "Oliver North is an American hero," which were the lines which had been measured to be the most effective in altering public feeling. Willy's "pretesting" gained Chay worldwide admiration as the Great Interfacer.

Once he had mastered the Manual for Republican Presidents, Chay rarely made decisions, particularly political decisions. Staff people would pass the word. "He wants this" or "He wants that" but no one really ever saw him say so. He would be shown the decisions the gofers had made and he would nod absentmindedly and go into an anecdote about his days as a young Army captain. As he was moved from one event to the next, Graciela Winkelreid or her staff gave him a tight briefing on every move he would make. People were beside themselves with admiration over the way he could hit his toe marks for best television camera focus.

Sylvester had told him that God had a plan for him, just hotdogging his own religious bent, but Chay believed him, which, with the deep faith in his magical luck which everyone around him had instilled in him, accounted for his lack of self-doubt or of ever being needlessly concerned with controlling any of the duties of his office. He wasn't just passive; he was entirely disengaged as the Republican Party's Manual of Presidents had insisted that he must be, or as the news media put it, his was a "hands-off presidency," a more obscure definition. He gave his subordinates no direction. He preferred them to infer what he wanted. He made no demands and gave no instructions. He filled his time with an unusually large number of ceremonial functions, photo opportunities, and blank chats with visiting heads of state in the Hexagonal Office. As his wife, Ulyssa, said, "He makes things up and believes them. He has this great ability to build these little worlds out of fantasy then live in them."

Truth became a problem to be solved.

The Pink House staff photographers shot eight or ten thousand pictures of Chay every month and between nine and eleven thousand feet of television tape, the best of which was released to the news media. This took up a great deal of Chay's time. Graciela Winkelreid and Ulyssa decided which images the public would see: Ulyssa when the shots included her, Miss Winkelreid all others.

To the world at large, perhaps, it could have been—it might have been—that Chay's staff was able to give the impression that he was a well-informed chief executive, but he had insulated himself for so long from the more mundane realities of life, perhaps ever since the night Brill had taken him into her bed, that as the Pink House aides built ever more complex structures of deception he found it difficult to keep clear which things he was or was not supposed to reveal. He was a ruler at the mercy of events and his own subordinates. He developed the knack, even beyond the demands of the Manual, of forgetting to whom he was talking in the middle of a telephone conversation.

39

GRADUALLY, the Chairman introduced the trappings and the etiquette of royalty. The nineteen rows of medals and battle ribbons were retired to the new Smithsonian Institution which was being planned for Washington West. Chay's new uniform was a rich maroon velvet suit made by H. Huntsman and Sons of London. People began to walk backward when leaving his presence. He received members of the diplomatic corps twice monthly as well as having fixed ceremonial meetings with high officials of his secret police. Every ten days, precisely at noon, there would be a review of troops in the courtyard of the campus of Southern Methodist University. Every ten days there was a formal dinner in the great gallery at Rossenarra for two hundred guests. Very little of what the Chairman did, beyond his morning shower, was not covered by television. The adventurers who had made up the first wave of political opportunists were shunned.

According to the Vice Chairman, Mallard Tompkins, when the guests had been ushered into the receptions at Rossenarra Mrs. Appleton would be announced and would enter on the arm of the Secretary of State/Treasury, Wambly Keifetz, who would present the members of the diplomatic corps to her, not speaking their names but identifying the countries they represented. During these rites, the Chairman/CEO would enter unassumingly, unannounced, surrounded by his bodyguard. Usually, he wore a simple kilt of Reagan plaid and carried a slender, bamboo whangee to stroll among the spectacular hairdos of the senators, the showy jewelry of the military, and the explosions of color and design in the servants' costumes, particularly Cardinal Appleton's. The contrast was emphatic. Chay's presence was so electrical that all eyes instantly swung to him when he entered a room and not only because he always entered with twelve armed bodyguards.

Graciela Winkelreid and her PR people felt that if the old commoner ways were erased steadily at the rate of eight or ten a day, that in a relatively short time only the word for what Chay stood for would need to be changed.

Ulyssa forbore wearing low-cut dresses. She appeared in public wearing Queen Mary hats, executing Queen Mary waves. Ulyssa misunderstood the entire exercise. She thought Chay wanted the country to return to Republicanism, that he was playing the temporary role of constable while preparing a presidency for Gordon Godber Manning who had been Secretary of State at the time of the Evaporation and was the surviving successor to the last President under the old Constitution. By correspondence and other means Ulyssa gave Manning every reason to believe that Chay was preparing the way for Manning. Chay to correct this had to write to Manning in smoldering fury, saying:

> You must no longer look forward to your return to
> government. Your path would assuredly lie over 100,000
> corpses. Sacrifice your personal ambitions for peace and the
> well-being of our country. I will gladly do what I can for your
> peace and repose in retirement.

The Appleton family despised Ulyssa. They feared that if things went her way, such as the reestablishment of practiced democracy, it would cost them much rank and money. They leaned hard on Chay until he took the time to straighten her out. The Appletons must have considered this of first importance because they had to interrupt the building of substantial fortunes in real estate, works of art, insider knowledge, and diamonds to do it.

Serena had had to beat on Chay until he understood his duty to distribute the benefits of his office to his brothers and sister. Dudley was made a Senator. Sylvester, a Cardinal, affected a sacerdotal lorgnette, in cruciform, through which he peered under the crossbars of a miniature rood to which had been nailed a miniature image of the naked body of Barabbas, the thief. Jonathan was given a Brigadier's star to enhance his position as the leading land developer of Washington West.

Ulyssa spent two-thirds of her time protecting herself from the Appleton family. Although Chay was fonder than ever of his little dukke, he did not trust her with other men. Eddie Grogan kept round-the-clock surveillance on her, while Chay was in and out of his velvet trousers with Liz Wantonberg, whom he flew to Dallas almost weekly. In helpless retaliation Ulyssa ran up enormous debts. She ordered 1,095 dresses in the first year of marriage, three for each day; 643 pairs of gloves; 149 hats. When Chay attempted to settle with the suppliers at half-price they said they had already paid Ulyssa a third of the gross amount as commission, so Chay had to have all of them shot.

Jonathan met a Miss Elizabeth Danworthy in California, heiress to a fortune. She was a stunningly beautiful young woman with startlingly thrilling legs. Jonathan brought her to Dallas and Chay fell head-over-heels in love with her, creating a complex emotional situation because he was already deeply in love with Hedda Blitzen, Ulyssa, and Liz Wantonberg. Chay had a great amount on his plate, as it were. He just couldn't find the time, so eventually he had to send Miss Danworthy back to his brother in Washington West.

40

AS THE COUNTRY was settling back into its self-congratulatory torpor, on May 9, 1993, a task force of 450,000 Sandinistas loomed out of the South Pacific in enormous troop-carrying submarines and attacked the eastern and northeastern coast of Australia, digging in from Townsville to Cooktown, to establish staging areas to conquer and control the countries of Southeast Asia, then intending to reach northward to wrap its tentacles around China, India, Taiwan, Korea, and Japan, threatening the

American lifeline supply of automobiles, video recorders, capital, noodles, television sets, telephone-answering machines, and 117 other items vital to the American people.

Panic struck the unprepared and lightly defended cities of Djakarta, Singapore, Beijing, Seoul, and Tokyo. The vastly interconnected industrial region braced itself for the inevitable assault by a superbly trained and equipped barbarian force whose ruthlessness was legend. As with one voice, Asia cried out to the United States to come to its aid.

Chairman Appleton was in the mid-mounting of his lovely wife when his brother Dudley, a Pink House aide, burst into their master bedroom shouting, "The Sandinistas have landed in Australia!"

The Chairman wheeled off Ulyssa who shrilled, "Oh, *shit*, Dudley!" and shied a perfume bottle at him.

"Aus*tra*lia?" Chay said, visibly shaken either by the news or by coitus interruptus. "By God, Ronald Reagan was right. They *do* seek world domination." He swung out of bed, disproportionately ithyphallic, causing the First Lady to stare at him even more adoringly than for the television cameras at the swearing-in ceremony. Chay picked up the red telephone at bedside, and standing like a naked, pink Ares, he defied the traditions of the Republican Manual for Presidents and barked commands. "Get Secretary Kullers in here on the double and send in the Vice President. I have to get dressed."

While Mallard Tompkins togged him out in Delta Force Commando battle dress and blackened his cheekbones and forehead for television from a can of shoe polish, Chay tested his commando knife and with one quick slice took off the top of the bedpost then slid the knife back into his boot to take hotline calls from the Premiers of Australia and Japan, calling their battle chieftains into Dallas for an urgent war council. Ulyssa wandered off to try to calm down her jangled nerves in a hot tub, wondering where François Max Felix could have gotten to. Chay stayed on the red phone, ordering the Joint Chiefs and the National Security Council to convene in the War Room immediately.

When the Australian, Asian, and American battle chiefs were assembled at seven minutes after five o'clock Central Standard

Time, each threatened country voted to mobilize their troops and to amass them as a solid and hopefully unbreakable force along the northeastern perimeter of Australia within the next seventy-two hours. Chay, as the most experienced Commander against the wily Sandinistas, was elected Commander-in-Chief of the Combined Forces in Australia and Asia (CICCFIAAA), expanding his title to CINCAFUSCIAFBIANSACICCFIAAA, and voted unlimited powers.

Helmeted and in battle dress, scarred with shoe polish, Chay went on international television via satellite to issue a ringing warning to Nicaragua to withdraw or accept the consequences.

The Congress of the United States immediately placed restrictions on the Chairman's movements. He must site his headquarters "not less than 500 miles from any battle zone." It was established by law that he could not spend more than two weeks in any given month on foreign soil, fearing that he would lose touch with his elected duties in the direction of the war.

Chay flew to Darwin, Australia, and established a giant pincer—an enormous military nutcracker of 937,000 men of twelve nations, a stupendous feat of organization and coordination—at the northern Sandinista flank at Cooktown and at the southern flank below Mackay. The Nicaraguans occupied the northeast coast, 1,600 miles from the nerve center of the Allied campaign at Darwin. The opposing commands were separated by Arnhem land, a vast aboriginal reserve; the Bay of Carpentaria with its twenty-two-foot-long crocodiles; and the width of the rugged, tropical Cape York Peninsula.

Within sixty-seven days of some of the hardest fighting Chay had ever not personally undertaken, he had crushed the invasion of Asia by the Sandinista horde. Only 26 prisoners were taken. All told, 449,974 Nicaraguans were wiped out to a man, and their equipment was sold at auction to countries in the Middle East who would then resell them to Nicaragua for the next campaign.

The victory was not only a redoubtable feat of arms but a triumph of diplomacy. Chay had to juggle the egos and ambitions of the military and political leaders of eleven disparate nations while shuttling back and forth between Dallas and Darwin to administer the government of the United States.

$\mathbf{A}$LTHOUGH exultantly victorious over life (on the face of it and if his mother were excluded from the quotient) and a world hero such as human history had never seen before, Caesare Appleton found heartbreak in Australia.

When he had the time to think about women—perhaps in the twilight moments before he fell into sleep, all during the day, and when he awoke each morning—he may have thought broodingly about how he had exchanged Hedda Blitzen and a little cottage by a waterfall for the mockery of power. Or thought hotly about the thunderbolt moments in the sheets with Ulyssa, Liz Wantonberg, Brill, Graciela Winkelreid, or even the conjectural Portuguese woman whom he had never had the chance to know carnally. Hedda would always represent love beyond love, a fruit of unattainable perfection. In those twilight moments he could tell himself that he had never really found love; not *real* love.

He thought he had found it in Darwin; before setting boot upon Australian soil, before he had even seen his specified command headquarters for the Allied defense of Australia and Asia.

Darwin is the capital of the Northern Territory of Australia. It is in a sparsely populated, largely undeveloped region which sits like an Anzac campaign hat with sweat showing through the felt at the top of Australia.

In 1888, when the Minister for the Northern Territory, a Mr. J. C. F. Johnson, saw it for the first time, he immediately proposed to his government that the entire area be returned to the British. Darwin is very, very hot. One gets thirsty. The thirst of the troops in Mr. Johnson's time had to be slaked, so a pipeline was laid by the Bahama Beaver Bonnet Company to bring water across the desert. When Chay arrived the water was still simmering under the tropical sun so that all Darwin faucets, no matter whether labeled H or C, gave out warm water.

Air Force One, carrying Chay and his staff and the regulation cases of Spanish champagne for barter with the natives, landed at Darwin International Airport at seven minutes before noon in the tropical Australian midsummer. The official welcoming party on hand to receive the Allied high commander had decided wisely to remain well within the air-conditioning of the single corrugated aluminum shed which was the airport building proper. Peering down through his bedroom cabin porthole, Chay watched the heat rise in flanneled layers.

The airport's mobile ramp rumbled directly toward the halting plane, a long passenger disembarkation tunnel, driving slowly, impervious to the heat. The linkage of plane and tunnel was achieved. Four quarantine officers came aboard the Chairman's plane, three men in long white socks, dark blue shorts, and short-sleeved white shirts with epaulettes, led by a Junoesque figure of a uniformed woman with blue-black hair, a large passionate nose, and a jaw like a hammock filled with fat people.

She stood at the head of the aisle and shouted, "Every passenger will remain seated to be sprayed!"

The chief of the Chairman's Secret Service detail yelled, "Hold it, lady!"

Al Melvin, Chairman of the Joint Chiefs of the combined Allied Chiefs of Staff said, "Who the hell are you?"

"I am your Quarantine Task Force commander," the woman replied. "There will be no talking. You are about to be sprayed against fruit fly."

"This is Air Force One, fahcrissake."

"All right, men," the Quarantine commander said. "Do your duty."

One of the men went directly to the pilots' cabin; the other two advanced down the center aisle of the airplane spraying thick mists of disinfectant and DDT throughout the central area; the fourth man headed toward the private quarters of the Chairman and CEO of the United States further aft.

"Just a goddamn minute here," General Melvin roared. He turned to his aides. "Arrest these people," he said while two Secret Service men were grabbing the two Aussies who were spraying the aisle.

"Arrest? Did you say arrest?" the woman shrilled at him. She stared at the Chairman's aides on all sides of her, drenching them with her scorn. She yelled in a great and frightening voice, "What the farkin' 'ell is garn arn 'ere?" just as the Chairman emerged from his stateroom. He was wearing the fatigues of a staff sergeant of Bravo Company, ¼ Infantry USA, a gesture of humility which brought moisture to the eyes of the journalists who were present.

"Who are these people?" the Chairman snarled. "Get them out of here."

Every man on the plane moved forward.

"Halt!" the woman yelled. "If you are concealing fruit or vegetables I warn you *for the last time* to surrender them and undergo a thorough spraying or face individual fines of $50,000."

The Quarantine officers who had been spraying the cockpit emerged and went to the Quarantine officer in charge. "The little sergeant who just came in is the Chairman and CEO of the United States of America," one of them whispered to her. "This is the Headquarters plane of the Supreme Commander of the Allied Forces."

She looked at him as if he had gone mad. "What difference does that make?" she demanded to know. "Don't you realize that they may plan to smuggle fruits or vegetables into Australia?"

Chay approached her as a zookeeper might approach a white rhino. "My name is Appleton," he said. "We are here to defend your country against the Nicaraguan invader."

"As we are here to defend it against the fruit fly," she said. "There can be no talking during the spraying. Return to your seat." She stared at him so fiercely that Chay forgot who or where he was because he was staring into her piercing lamps of eyes and was so shaken and shattered by the great pink cushions of her mouth that during the spraying he thought of them as wildly exciting primary sexual characteristics. He forgot his high office. He forgot his holy mission to destroy the barbarian threat to oriental civilization (as he knew it). But he was unable to bring himself to take command of her or to devise the strategy which would bring her into the large double bed in the aft-section of the plane, so, meekly, he took a seat on the aisle in a richly upholstered wing chair. He did not take his eyes off her while the spraying of the plane and all of its passengers was being completed.

Suddenly, as if God had just finished forming them from native clay, the Premier of Australia and the Chief of Staff of the

Australian Armed Forces, the Premier of the Northern Territory, the Premier of Queensland, a Minicam operator from the Australian Broadcasting Company, and the Mayor of Darwin came pouring into the plane through the passenger tunnel. The Premier of Australia, a usually serene man named Dick Richards, took in the scene of the intensive spraying enveloping the Chairman/CEO of the United States and yelled, "Stop that bloody sprying at once!"

"Stop the *sprying*?" The woman glared at him, shocked to her nipples. "This plane could be loaded with fruit flies! Or don't you care what happens to Australian fruit and vegetables?" She turned to the other quarantine officers. "You will continue to do your duty, men," she said with a quiet but terrible voice.

"Throw'er out on 'er pointed 'ead!" Richards shouted. "Out! Out!" It took three burly Secret Service men to manhandle the woman off the plane. As she struggled to free herself from them, she shouted, "I go under protest!" The other quarantine officers left quietly, their eyeballs rolling upward in their heads.

Chay sat in a dazed heap, looking as Dorothy may have looked when the tornado dropped her in Oz. He signaled for Eddie Grogan's man to come to him. "Find out everything about that woman," he ordered. Then he got up to greet the Australian politicians. "Gentlemen, gentlemen," he crooned, "how very kind of you to come out in all this heat to greet me."

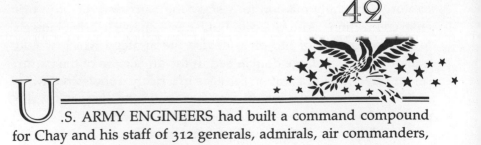

42

U.S. ARMY ENGINEERS had built a command compound for Chay and his staff of 312 generals, admirals, air commanders,

Marine honchos, and Coast Guard people, as well as colonels, majors, captains, lieutenants, and a Headquarters cadre of 1,900 noncommissioned officers and men together with the Chairman's own Secret Service detail, his Household Guard of the Third Battalion of the Seventy-fifth Rangers and the 346 clerical civilians who kept the Army staff in operation. The Headquarters complement also included the Supreme High Commands of the Armies, Navies, Air Forces, Marine Corps, and Coast Guards of the eleven South Pacific and Asian allies, their personal staffs, their NCOs, enlisted men, and clerical help, together with cooks capable of preparing the myriad native dishes of each country. Graciously, Chay dined at a different national mess every night, suffering continuing indigestion.

The compound contained forty-one brick buildings comprising offices, barracks, officers' and enlisted men's clubs, PX installations, a television studio, eleven tennis courts on which any players would have dropped from heat exhaustion had they ever been used, a gymnasium building with a hot water swimming pool, two movie theaters, and a vastly sophisticated, rigidly guarded building within three high barbed wire fences which would transfer the High Command's signals from base to the fighting units in the line, to Dallas, and to anywhere else in the world if necessary, via satellite. The compound, which had cost the American taxpayer $17,839,426.16, was a small town of 7,219 people which would be named Appleton, N.T., after its gallant commander had departed victorious. It was situated about eight miles east of Darwin on the Stuart Highway on the way to the Kakadu National Park in Arnhemland, out toward the East Alligator River.

For the first forty-two minutes of his arrival, the Chairman was engaged with a collect telephone call from his mother. She filled him in on the weather in north Texas; told several vicious untruths about Ulyssa; marveled over his almost magical good luck, as though two shining angels always hovered above him to protect him and to guide his unerring choices; went on and on about some new cassocks which Sylvester had had made by a little woman in Constantinople; and how the Morris Office had actually been able to improve Paramount's offer by 2 percent. Chay was able to get off the phone only by pretending that the Premier of

Japan was choking on a chicken bone and that he had to help him.
Serena let him go because, in her mind, everything that was worth
having came from Japan.

Chay switched phones to talk heavy government business
with the Pink House Chief of Staff and the majority Leader of the
Senate in Dallas. The Congressional Pay Raise Bill was under the
same heated debate which had tied up all Congressional legislation
since 1988. His Chief of Staff, a choleric compulsive shouter, ruled
that if the Pay Raise Bill finally looked as though it were going to
reach the floor again that Chay would have to fly back to Dallas.

"I just got here, for Christ's sake," Chay said. "Tell the
Speaker to sit on it. What's a couple of weeks more to those guys?"
He hung up heavily.

It was half-past six, Darwin time (half-past three the previous
day, Dallas time) before he could reach Eddie Grogan.

"Is Ulyssa behaving?" he asked.

"So far, so good," Grogan said.

"Did your man here contact you?"

"We have that well in hand, sir. He'll bring you a sealed report
on the subject by breakfast tomorrow, your time."

"Anything on the Nicaraguans?"

"They're locked into their northeastern Australian enclave.
The Navy has closed off the entire coast. They may try to break
out towards Sydney."

"I'll be meeting on that after dinner."

At breakfast the next morning Chay ripped open the plain
manila envelope which Grogan's man had delivered. It had been
resting on his plate as he strode into the room. He removed two
8" × 10" black-and-white photographs and immediately began to
wonder how they could have possibly been taken.

They were stunning pictures. The first showed the woman as
she stepped out of a shower stall. She had a long, elegant body,
a deep chest with foaming boobs, an athlete's waist, and long,
exquisitely formed legs. She was toweling her crotch. The head
was turned to one side as if it were looking at something out-of-
frame. He imagined that he had never seen such a flawless profile.
He sat, totally absorbed by the profile (and the boobs), looking as
if he never wanted to see the woman in full face; wonder-struck,
bemooned; marveling at the cutting edge of her nose and trying

to measure the height of her cheekbones which were higher than any Eskimo's; shuddering over the turnip-like sensuality of her chin. Then, with aching reluctance, he shuffled the second photograph on top of the stack and gasped as if a thick cord had been jammed into his throat.

In the photograph she was studying her flawless teeth in a mirror; her impossibly white and perfectly formed teeth behind lips of pink, tropical sponge. Her eyes were as clear as if they had been painted in against alabaster, fringed with lashes which were as thick as the cowcatchers which had been at the front of locomotives before the airlines had had the politicians make railroads unlawful. Abruptly, he turned the pictures face down upon the table and picked up the report.

Subject: Sheila Plantenbower, 29, a "Northie," born and bred in the Northern Territory, Australia. Married 11 years to Lionel Plantenbower, 34, computer salesman now serving in 09th Australian Fusiliers on Cape York Peninsula; 4 children: Wanda, 10; Tigris, 9; Walter, 8; and Tennyson, 6. Ecumenical Methodist. Commander, 1st shift, Northern Territorial Agricultural Quarantine Service at Darwin International Airport; dedicated officer. 1753 High Higham Road; Tel: 347. Member: Book-of-the-Month Club; Australian Botanical Society. Has no social life. Spends free time cooking for children and writing letters to husband.

Query: Do you want letters intercepted?

Propping the more revealing photograph of Mrs. Plantenbower against a ketchup bottle, Chay ate a simple soldier's breakfast of mango juice, oatmeal, kippers, scrambled eggs and bangers, toast, and plain tea, formulating his plan to get her into his bed that night. I'll show her what a social life can really be, he thought greedily. One hour and five minutes later, as he was being dressed by the Vice Chairman's fiancé, Corporal Chester Haselgrove, his temporary batman while the Vice Chairman's duties kept him in the capital, he was urgently summoned back to Dallas by the Speaker of the House to try to bring some measure of agreement to the salary increase controversy which was boiling over; the leadership badly needed heavy Pink House help. The issue was overwhelmed by its sheer size. Subterfuge had been succeeded by congressional ruse which had called for altered stratagems to be gerrymandered by other contrivances, dodges, and illusory tactics until the bill as it was drafted and redrafted had become the largest, longest, and most confusing bill ever to be considered by Congress, covering more than 3,600 pages, weighing 11.8 pounds and covering everything, by way of smoke screen, from bar hostess training programs to marijuana substitutes and including a bitterly controversial rider which would make it law to have to give all workers who had been continuously employed by the same company for more than twelve years one week's notice before firing them. The entire bodies of the two Houses had been heavily involved in considerations for the bill for many years. Congressmen and senators had died or otherwise had not been returned to their seats. Entire congressional staffs and its leadership had changed. Over 974 legislators had sat on committees which had explored the Congressional Wage Increase Bill and inevitably the entire process had become deadlocked once again.

The time had come for the seventeen committees and commissions involved to blend all of their compromises. Chay had to return to Dallas to begin intensive lobbying from the Pink House; twisting arms, soft-soaping, making deals, and promising anything.

Sheila Plantenbower seemed to fade further and further away, but actually, deep within his heart and trousers, Chay never let her compelling essence leave him.

43

IN THE SIXTY-SEVEN DAYS it took Chairman Appleton's command to drive the Sandinista forces out of Australia, the sort of a war which even Ronald Reagan's publicity people had never thought of, Chay had to make three return trips to his nation's capital to lobby for the Congressional Pay Raise Enabling Act in person, on television, in heated meetings, and by telephone. In between all of this intense persuasion he bounced from Dallas to Darwin to meet with the combat commanders of the Allied American, Anzac, and Asian nations to plot the strategies for military victories. A team of eighty-three press agents worldwide coordinated by Graciela Winkelreid emphasized again and again to the American people and, by satellite, to the polyglot viewers of the world, that never before in history had an American Chairman maintained the steady, sure, if tumultuous, government of his nation at home while he personally commanded the troops, fleets, and air forces of twelve nations in a conflict on which the freedom of more people than ever before depended.

Through it all, and without any help from the horde of public ralations people, he pinpointed his fiercest concentration upon Sheila Plantenbower, using every trick of his implacable determination to get her into bed.

It was at the height of his worldwide triumphs that heartbreak set in. There was nothing he could do, no blandishment he could bring, which would change her resolve not only to remain true to her husband but to reject, utterly and completely, the Chairman and CEO of the United States, Marshal of the American Union, and CICCFIAAA, and any and all plans he most certainly had had for abandoned sex with her.

He did all the little things: put a car and driver at her disposal; interceded with the Premiers of Australia and the Northern Territory to have her reinstated in her old job in the Australian Department of Agriculture—with a 16.8 percent raise in salary. He sent bowers of flowers to her house directly from a Bahama Beaver

Bonnet Company flower farm in West Palm Beach, Florida, to which he had been given access, as well as autographed photographs of Liz Wantonberg for her children. He pleaded with her to understand "fully and completely" that he was not, repeat NOT, pro-fruit fly. He wooed her unceasingly which meant the grossest kind of flattery and promises of untold wealth and power at his side, as he told her he would discard his wife and make her, Sheila Plantenbower, First Lady of the United States.

Nothing he could do or say had any effect upon her indifference to him. She used him. Through him, she got orders placed to the credit of her husband for extensive computer purchases by the Allied forces, every one of them to the benefit of the company which had employed Lionel Plantenbower as a junior salesman when he had been a civilian. She flickered slightly in a measure of coming to life when Chay mentioned Liz Wantonberg because the timeless actress was her husband's idol, as she was the idol of every fighting man on both sides of the war.

Chay discovered that Sheila Plantenbower was a shoe freak and had dozens of pairs of shockingly expensive shoes sent to her from Paris, Milan, and Endicott, New York, but no matter what he conceived to do for her or her family, she would not permit him to touch her. The more helplessly abject he grew in his courtship, the colder and more distant she became. When the commissions from the computer sales exceeded $211,000, after each of her four children had been assured of a lifetime civil service job in the Australian postal system, when he had been able to put through a wartime ruling that tourists could be flogged publicly if they attempted to bring anything vegetable into Australia, because she was an entirely fair woman she stood well across the room from him, slipped the shoulder strap from the left side of her dress and flashed her bare left breast at him for six full seconds, then, as he stared hungrily, she slipped the strap back into place and said, "Now we are even."

A crucial thing happened after Victory Day in Australia. The defeat of the Sandinistas had been total, and as a tribute to the memory of Ronald Reagan's dreams, the handful of surviving prisoners of war were to be caged and exhibited throughout Southeast Asia and the United States. Because of the unending television coverage of Chay Appleton on the bridges of battleships, or making hard decisions in War Rooms, or climbing into the cockpits of airplanes, or interrogating enemy commanders, he had become a hero such as had never been recorded before in the (taped) annals of the history of the world.

By almost universal demand (the word "almost" is used only because television reception was not what it might have been among the Eskimo peoples of northern Greenland or among the Indians of the Patagonian desert), it was petitioned by the people of the world that Chay lead a victory march across Asia, through unprecedented scenes of hysteria and worship, from Australia to Indonesia, through India, Thailand, and Vietnam, into China, Korea, into Japan then forward into the most uncontrolled, tele- vision-whipped hysteria of all, through representative cities of the United States. He was swept away from Sheila Plantenbower. It was as though his reason for living had been taken away. He had convinced himself that the voluntary exposure of her naked left breast—the repository of her heart—was the revelation of her true intent, and he knew that given time, despite the fact that the war was over (because he could delay her husband's demobilization for decades if necessary), that it was only a matter of time until he would possess her utterly. Victory had ruined everything. He was to be vanished from her as if a great tidal wave had swept across Darwin to drag him out into a sea of despair. He would be toured and exhibited as if he were a caged Sandinista invader, like a circus animal, while the woman he loved stayed far behind, untasted, never to be experienced because unless he could get that pay raise for Congress they would never grant her an entry visa. His heart was broken.

Every American old enough to comprehend television stayed staring fixedly at his set watching Chay's thrilling procession through the great cities of Asia. In India the government gave him the title which had not been in use since the Great Mogul in 1617, *Jahangir*, which means "Conqueror of the World." The televised sight of The Rain of the Ten Thousand Caresses in Bangkok— which involved eight tons of flower petals, a rite of homage which had not been allowed for 673 years, withheld from the human spirit since the reign of Baghut II who had saved Siam from six consecutive invasions—drove an alarming percentage of viewers into convulsions of ecstasy. The sales of six-packs soared, and as Chay was swept through the cities and the ancient civilizations now mainly engaged in making digital players and wristwatch television sets for export, he was decorated by country after country until, by the time he landed in California, the rows of campaign ribbons on the left side of his military tunic had grown to thirty-one, making him seem as though he were wearing one-half of Joseph's coat of many colors. The effect was so moving, so shatteringly loaded with explosive television emotion, that tens of millions refused to leave their couches around the clock, forgetting to eat anything but Ritz crackers and beer, unmindful of the workplace, uncaring that the schools had been closed by government order.

When the Victory march reached Japan, as Chay stood at the epicenter of Disneyland and accepted the ancient sword of Baron Asahina, the first samurai to enter martial history, the great dam which had been shoring up the admiration of the world broke, and from central Kenya to suburban Connecticut, from the iced television aerials of inner Siberia to the warm hearts and hearths of Beverly Hills, the people of the world sprang to their feet and cheered Chay Appleton as if he were in the room with them, marked indelibly by the simple gallantry and unrelenting courage of the man.

The Omnibus Enabling Act which made the Congressional pay raises a law was passed on the day Chairman Appleton left Asia for the mainland of the United States. At the moment he was being adored, even deified, by the people of San Francisco, the legislative discovery was made of the rider in the Omnibus Continuing Resolution which was the pay raise bill: Item No. 2,156 on Page 3,442, as drawn up by Wambly Keifetz's people, stated that the American Republic had been transformed into an Imperial government over which Caesare Appleton, then Chairman/CEO/World Hero, had been named as the nation's first monarch, Emperor Caesare I, absolute ruler of the American people.

It was a thrilling legislative discovery. The nation was overwhelmed by the novelty of the new law amid the triumphant homecoming of the hero himself. Applications from people of every walk of life poured into the Pink House in Dallas for individual letters-of-patent which would create knights, barons, earls, viscounts, marquises, dukes, and princes. The rank and file of the public which had no hope or expectation of titles were swept off their feet by the glamor of the television industry's awe at what Congress had wrought to multiply the sale of commercial time. The country was to have not only an emperor, but a peerage, a nobility, a House of Lords, and a House of Commons.

Chay, on his part, knew that not only had he never attained Sheila Plantenbower, he had lost her forever.

On the day after the ruckus over the spraying of Air Force One on his arrival at Darwin, Chay had had Grogan's people find Plantenbower and bring her to him. She struggled in the tight grasp of two burly secret agents, wild with indignation, as she was dragged into Chairman Appleton's presence. He ordered the men to release her and leave the room. "She is not armed, sir," the fatter of the two understrappers said, "but we feel she should be sedated. She bit both of us, sir."

"Armed, you farkin' bullies? Sedate me?"

The two men left the room.

"Why did you resist?" Chairman Appleton asked earnestly. "Was it out of guilt?"

"*Guilt?*"

"You defied the head of your government yesterday. You attempted to assault the Chairman of the Board and CEO of the United States of America with insecticide. You were sacked. I presume, if I have any knowledge of how these things should be done, that you have been thoroughly and publicly humiliated."

"What has any of that got to do with you?"

"I want to help you. You were only trying to do your job in the best way you knew how. I admire you and I want to see justice done."

"If you're interested in justice, do something for our boys who are out there fighting the barbarian foe in Queensland. Get Liz Wantonberg out there to entertain them. That's what you can do."

"First, I think we'd better concentrate on getting you out of the fix you're in."

"My husband hasn't as much as seen a film since this war started. Do you think that's fair? Do you think that's good for morale?"

"What is his rank?"

"He's a common soldier and proud of it."

"Do you think he should have rank?"

"Of course he should have rank! He's a brilliant man!"

"Then we'll make him a sergeant."

"If you can do that then you can get him off that dangerous duty, but if you ever tell him I said that I'll never speak to you again."

"I'll see that he's put in charge of all beer distribution throughout the Allied forces."

"Would that be behind the lines?"

"Oh, yes. Because I admire you—exceedingly—" He reached out a hand to touch her but she backed away.

"You mean you want to get into my drawers."

"Mrs. Plantenbower!"

"You do. I can sense it."

He got up from his chair and approached her slowly and carefully. "Would it be so wrong," he said softly, "for a man to want—with every fiber of his being—to possess a woman as fiery and as transformingly sensual as you?"

"Yes. Quite and entirely wrong. I am a married woman and a mother."

"My destiny—guided by my almost magical luck—is to lead the people of the world," he said simply. "It breaks my heart to say this, but what we could have together would not be of long duration. I am the leader of the free world and my life is at the world's beck and call. Your husband is off at the war. We would have one brief moment in an eternity which we would never, ever forget. Our secret paradise." He put his hand gently on her bare upper arm.

"Watch yourself, Mr. Chairman!" She pulled her arm away from him.

"Do you believe in your heart that your husband has never looked at another woman?"

"In all of his life, my husband has been attracted to only one other woman besides me—Liz Wantonberg, star of stage, screen, video, radio, television, cable, and satellite. But—as that is a harmless, unattainable, adolescent sort of yearning—I tolerate it. It has nothing to do with me. And please mark well that I do not go in for outside cuddling."

"How can you be so sure, my dear? How can you believe that you would not find me as fulfilling as I find you?"

"Because I can't stand short men. Short men turn me off. My husband is six feet four. All muscle and sinew, all man. You could fit in his back pocket. I want you to understand this backwards and forwards, Mr. Chairman, so that you won't continue to waste your time." She stared him down. He returned to his chair.

"May I go now?" she asked.

He nodded hopelessly.

Chay had Plantenbower's husband made a sergeant and had him put in charge of the three Kray super-computers which kept track of all the beer drunk by the Allied armies. He passed the word that the USO was to deliver Liz Wantonberg to Australian Army Headquarters within twenty-four hours. When Wantonberg landed on the Cape York Peninsula, one of Grogan's men handed her an envelope which was sealed with the Great Seal of the Chairman of the United States. It was a letter for her eyes only from the Chairman/CEO/CINCAFUSCIAFBIANSA. The letter asked for a favor.

When a certain Australian supply sergeant was sent to her tent that night, would she entertain him in a way that the young man would never forget? Miss Wantonberg read the note, smiled softly, then spoke to Grogan's man.

"Please convey to the Chairman," she said, "that I will be happy to do as he asks."

Sergeant Plantenbower was sent to Miss Wantonberg's tent at 2240 hours that night. He emerged, dazed and disoriented, at 8:47 A.M. the next day. In the meantime Grogan's people, using infrared cameras, had made a video—with sound—of what had transpired on Miss Wantonberg's bed, on the tent floor, against the tent pole, and in a large tropical hammock. A copy of the videocassette was delivered to Sheila Plantenbower at her home in Darwin that morning while her children were at school. She played the cassette.

Chay waited eight days for a response from her. He heard

nothing. When he had Grogan's people bring her to his office she made no reference to her husband's conduct.

"I wanted to tell you," he said, "that I arranged for our USO to provide entertainment for the troops in your husband's sector."

"Oh, yes. Very good of you. Lionel was so pleased to have actually seen her in person."

But as almost everyone in the world knows, excepting those who are directly involved, plans involving other people are not as simple as, say, playing checkers with a five-year-old. They have a way of going awry. The results of the Wantonberg encounter with Sergeant Plantenbower, instead of hurtling Sheila Plantenbower into the Chairman's arms, created a labyrinth of irresolution which became more complex than a human psyche could fathom. Sheila Plantenbower was in love with her husband. Sergeant Plantenbower fell in love with Liz Wantonberg. The Chairman/CEO of the United States was in love with Mrs. Plantenbower, and Liz Wantonberg, since that encounter in the Highland Park jail, was in love, in her fashion, with Chay Appleton.

Every inch of the way from Darwin, as his triumph and Graciela Winkelreid's press agents created the hundreds upon hundreds of photo opportunities to entertain and impress the people of the world, Chay remained heartbrokenly aware of his loss. Protected by his Life Guards, the Seventy-fifth Rangers, he was never able to line up any of the gorgeous stuff which reached out to him, adoring him, crying out to be able to touch him, to give him what he had never been able to get from Sheila Plantenbower. Every honor, medal, and high order which he received on that glorious journey through the steams and shrines of Asia only underscored that he had lost the precious essence of the woman he loved.

Things began to improve in Chicago where he met a really attractive young WAC NCO named Evelyn Rose who was on recruitment poster duty and who had been assigned to him for a joint photograph to be used to stimulate enlistments. What had been penciled in as a fifteen-minute photo opportunity at 9:15 A.M. turned into Chay's commissioning her as a Major so she could take a place on his staff in Dallas because she cheered him enormously. She was such an artist at what she did that she helped to drive the torture of Plantenbower out of his mind. By the time he reached New York, and the Clerk of the Senate had discovered that within the Omnibus Continuing Resolution was the Congressional Pay Raise Bill, Chay learned that he had been proclaimed as Emperor of the American Republic and all wistful thoughts of Sheila Plantenbower left him forever.

44

WAMBLY KEIFETZ flew up from Dallas to meet Chay in New York. They were alone in the sixty-seventh-floor triplex which Keifetz had arranged, between Fifth and Madison, built with exterior layers of twenty-two-carat beaten gold into which one-foot-wide rhinestones had been set.

"Have you seen the morning news or read the newspapers?" Keifetz asked.

"When would I have the time?"

"You have been made Emperor of the American Republic by an Act of Congress."

"That's an oxymoron." Then Chay stared with awe-struck surprise and wonder. "You did it! You delivered for the Royalists!"

"Let's give credit where it is due. Whatever we have achieved as Royalists we owe to Ronald Reagan."

"No, Wamb. If I am Emperor, you did it. You blew up Washington. You kept the war going with the Sandinistas. You let Congress think it could get its raise without any trouble."

"Well, I did do my part. Now you'll have to do your part."

"Whatever you say, Wamb."

"I have four of Eddie Grogan's psychiatrists standing by. With hypnosis, biofeedback, and one or two psychotropic drugs, they are going to make you believe in your own infallibility. The fiction of government of the people, by the people, and for the people is over. Ronald Reagan returned us to the fiction of the divine right of kings."

"I don't follow you, Wamb."

"Just let Reagan be your role model. Or England's Charles I, whose chief of staff, Sir Robert Philips, defined the condition precisely: 'If anything fall out unhappily,' he said, 'it is not King Charles that advised himself, but King Charles misadvised by others and misled by disordered counsel.' "

Keifetz stared into Chay's eyes and spoke earnestly: "When presented with evidence that Ronald Reagan had acted against established law, the people, the Congress, and the media either refused to believe it or they placed all the blame on those who had carried out his orders—such as his man Deaver, or the flabby Meese, or little Colonel North."

"Well, he got away with whatever it was."

"The law of the divine right of kings got away with it. Reagan's command which was contrary to law was void. The doer or the adviser was guilty. And if there were a Reagan command which turned out to be in error, it was because of misinformation fed to him. Study the media of the period, Chay. It's all there."

"The people may have believed it then, but the people today will never believe it," Chay said.

"Chay, you have been made our Emperor. As we speak, television has begun to repeat the Reagan Doctrine to the people over and over and over again, that all men were created unequal and that they owe their obedience to their monarch because their Creator has endowed him with a divine right to sacred authority."

"We'll never get away with it, Wamb."

"Television and only television elected Ronald Reagan, did it not? His lovely tailoring, his Harold Teen manner, his acknowledged genius as a waver—why else would the owners of the country have chosen a failed movie actor to fill the presidency? Television! The key to all minds and all hearts because it permits the people to be entertained by their government without ever having to participate in it. It is no accident or great feat on your part, Chay, that you seem to be the one man in modern times who is cut in the mold of Charlemagne. You were created, bit by bit and piece by piece, by television, plus all the thought and planning which brought you this far and this high. If Ronald Reagan had not invented the Sandinista threat and had not created both the historic deficit and the terrible national debt, all this could not have happened. You are a great leader because of television. A hero because of television. The husband of one of the great beauties of all time. Believe me, Chay, because of all the care I have put into this, the people already believe you have strong ties with divinity."

"But—what about Congress—the Constitution—the Supreme Court?"

"Chay—hear me," Keifetz said patiently. "Representation is fiction. It was an idea invented by the Founding Fathers to impose a government on the subjects of a new nation. But now we have television, and Congress has never been any more interested in government than the people are, but interested only in being re-elected. Essentially, all that representation stuff was clumsy and wasteful. Direct rule, the economical way, can only happen through absolute monarchy which can only work by invoking the law of the divine right of kings. Hence the CIA psychiatrists."

"You are asking me to let three quacks make me insane."

"It's not as if you won't be getting anything in return, is it, Chay?"

"No thanks, Wamb." Chay yawned. "If I have to be Emperor, I'll do it with the mind I have."

"There are compensations for being divine."

"No thanks, Wamb." He yawned mightily again.

"I'm afraid it's too late to back away."

"Really?" Chay said languidly. "Why is that?"

"It was the breakfast you ate, you see. It was heavily medicated. The reconditioning has already started, old dear."

45

THE SHORT PARAGRAPH in the Pay Raise Enabling Act had, as well as designating Chay as Emperor, created a Royal Family for the United States. Dudley was designated as Chay's heir, after which the crown would go to Jonathan because Dudley and Frieda had no children. Both brothers were created "Princes of Empire" with an annual allowance of $1,375,000 from the Privy Purse which, to Dudley, was an enormous fortune but to Jonathan was only a drop in the bucket. Both brothers were given palaces on Turtle Creek with another $513,867.85 a year for maintenance and $704,863.22 for entertainment and expenses. Sylvester became the Emperor's Grand Almoner with a $73,482 a year credit at Partolucci Figli to order as many pretty chasubles and divine little hats as might be required. In the first year he exceeded the allowance by $41,932.67. Brill and Berry were made Royal Princesses. Serena was addressed as "Madame Majesty, mother of His Imperial Majesty, the Emperor," although, at court, this was to be shortened to "Madame Mother." Serena felt so left out of the titles and the clothing allowances that she refused to attend the coronation. She had wanted to be called Empress Mum and to be dressed by whichever couturiers whose clothes had the highest resale value.

Until the last moment, the Appleton family tried to prevent Ulyssa from being crowned. They worked the Congressional Committee in charge of Coronation Arrangements. They organized letter writing campaigns and rent-a-mob demonstrations outside the Pink House. Serena harangued Chay whenever she was able to slip past the guards into his presence. Their case against Ulyssa was that she didn't have enough "class" to be crowned as Empress.

The coronation itself created a great deal of family bitterness. Dudley and Jonathan were told that their roles in the proceedings would be to appear as "Grand Dignitaries of Empire" and not as Royal Princes. It was a subtle distinction, but their mother and sisters were able to prove that it had been done by Ulyssa for maximum humiliation. If they were expected to serve as Grand Dignitaries, they said, then their wives could not be expected to carry Ulyssa's train. There were three days of deadlock. Chay ended the impasse by ruling that Dudley and Jonathan could participate as Princes. Their wives and sisters could appear as Princesses who would "hold up the robe" not "carry the train." There was still no Imperial title for Serena so she blew off the coronation entirely by going to Las Vegas.

Nonetheless, whether Serena was absent or present, James Richard Blake, in his epic canvas depicting the coronation, painted her in a proud and central position.

Since her marriage to the Emperor was childless, and she was fearful because her marriage had only been a civil ceremony performed in a bank vault which could threaten dissolution of the marriage should Chay find it convenient, Ulyssa visited the Pope secretly at the Mansion on Turtle Creek—a grand hotel—when he arrived from Rome for the high coronation Mass. She told him her "secret."

The Pope notified Chay that, as a condition for his taking part in the holy investiture/sacrament, there must be a prior religious marriage ceremony. Chay was forced to agree, and on the afternoon of December 1, 1994, a private religious ceremony took place in a chapel at Sparkman-Hillcrest, the most elegant funeral home in America in that its cemetery was on a slope facing Neiman-Marcus at North Park.

Cardinal Appleton administered the sacrament. Wambly Keifetz and Eddie Grogan were witnesses. Ulyssa asked for and received a certificate of Holy Matrimony from the Cardinal.

Chay wrote in bitterness to Beniamiamo Camardi, his Mafia adviser:

> My family is jealous of my wife and of Elvis, her son—in fact
> of everyone near me. All I can say is that my wife has nothing
> but diamonds and debts; not one envious, hostile, or
> rancorous thought in her head. She is a sweet-natured woman
> who does my family no harm. She only wants to play
> Empress for a while, to have more diamonds and more
> dresses. Elvis doesn't have $50,000 to his name but I am fond

of him. You can be certain that Ulyssa is going to wear the
crown. She will be Empress if it costs me 200,000 men.

Caesare Appleton was crowned and anointed as Emperor of
the American Republic at the Presbyterian Cathedral in University
Park in Dallas on New Year's Day, 1995. He was forty-four years
old.

To assemble all elements for the ceremony, the schedule began
at 6 A.M. when the military contingents began the march to their
assigned positions. At 7 A.M. the first guests were admitted to the
cathedral. At this same hour, the great dignitaries set out from
their assembly point in the parking lot of the Hilton Inn on Mock-
ingbird, moving with ponderousness through the streets in their
ceremonial robes which had been rented from the Western Costume Company of Hollywood to reach the places in the church at
8:15 A.M.

All along the line of the march, buildings were decorated with
red, white, and blue bunting, artificial flowers, and banners which
urged the citizenry to try any branch of the House of Pancakes.
At nine o'clock the diplomatic corps set out in large automobiles.
Simultaneously leaving from the Keifetz mansion, the President
of the Republic of Ireland and the Sultan of Brunei, following a
State Department breakfast, set out with their host Wambly Keifetz
in his capacity as Foreign Secretary and with 101 other representatives of the governments representing the United Nations.

At the same hour, Pope Francis Albert II, clad in a white alb,
descended the steps at the Mansion on Turtle Creek followed by
a retinue and took his place in a stretched, state landaulet Phantom
VI Rolls-Royce which had an open, roofless tonneau. Fixed to the
roof over the driver was a large replica of the triple crown of the
Papacy. By custom, it was necessary that the car be preceded
through the streets by a papal chamberlain riding astride a humble
mule and carrying a large wooden cross. Progress was slow. But
the enormous crowds which lined the way, 92 percent Ecumenical
Baptist, were awestruck.

The Pope's entrance into the magnificent Presbyterian church
was spectacular; first to enter was the bearer of the apostolic cross,

escorted by seven acolytes carrying golden candlesticks, followed by one hundred ecumenical bishops and archbishops; then the Pope was carried in on his throne, wearing the triple crown and escorted by seven cardinals.

As Francis Albert proceeded to the stationary papal throne near the high altar, he was acclaimed by a massed choir of 212 voices singing *Tu es Petrus*. Enthroned, he had to wait eighty-nine minutes for the arrival of the Imperial couple. The delay was caused by, among other things, Ulyssa's hair.

At last, in the three-block procession, in the deliberately formal slow march from Rossenarra to the cathedral, the Emperor wore half boots of white velvet with gold embroidery and golden buckles, white silk stockings, white velvet breeches, a jacket of crimson velvet under a short velvet cloak lined with white satin and fastened on one shoulder with a diamond clasp, and his ever-identifying black homburg worn sideways.

Ulyssa wore a hyacinth-colored dress with long sleeves and a train which weighed twenty-three pounds, eleven ounces, made of silver brocade covered with golden bees. Her bracelets, clasps, hairpins, and necklace were all of gold, set with jewels or with the antique cameos of which she was so fond. Her diadem holding four rows of pearls interlaced with diamond leaves rested upon a mass of tiny curls.

The Imperial slow march departed from Rossenarra at 10:30 A.M. to the sound of cannon. The royal couple moved out preceded by the U.S. Marine Corps Band, augmented by the Dallas Philharmonic, each playing different selections, making a thrilling parade of 412 instruments accompanying twenty squadrons of cavalry and armored personnel carriers. Hovercraft held fixed positions at hundred-foot intervals above the heads of hundreds of thousands of citizens, tourists, and vendors who were choking the streets below for twelve blocks in all compass directions requiring the attentions of the police of Dallas, Fort Worth, Denton, and Waxahatchie. Not that the crowds were in any way disorderly. They were hushed and respectful as befitted a citizenry upon whom the gift of an Imperial presence had been bestowed.

When the Imperial procession reached the cathedral, Caesare I and his Empress were accoutred with coronation robes in the changing vestibule just off the lobby. What with the delays, the slow march, the photo opportunity necessities, and Ulyssa's hair, it was now ten minutes after noon. It was at the entrance to the cathedral that the difficulty arose. The Imperial Princesses refused to carry the train of the Empress. A hasty meeting was called by the Emperor in the vestibule where he made terrible threats to his sisters, his face so pale and his voice so shaking that they moved at once to take up their appointed tasks.

Following the Princes and Princesses Royal in the Imperial pageant came the network cameramen with their hand-held equipment, then a procession of those Peers of the Realm who had already received their Letters of Patent: two Dukes, Gordon Godber Manning, now Duke of Westport, and a Hollywood superagent who was a close ally of the Emperor's mother; a Marquis, who was the leader of the Teamsters Union; three Earls, two Viscounts, a Baron who had been Ulyssa's dentist; and four Knights.

Dudley wore a white silk tunic over his stooped and rounded shoulders and trailed an ermine-lined mantle of flame-colored velvet which was powdered with golden bees. He wore a floppy velvet beret with ostrich plumes and many diamonds—so many in fact that the television people complained bitterly about the many reflected bursts of light until, in another delay, the stones were dusted with talcum powder, infuriating Dudley.

The repeated bee motif caused one television commentator to report erroneously that the Emperor was preparing the country for Mormonism, but the bee was the Emperor's symbol for industry and through its appearance he hoped to inspire the American people to become a kinder and busier nation.

A simple wreath of gold laurel leaves encircled the Emperor's head. He slow-marched up the aisle at the speed at which a daisy grows upward. As he passed the rear of the great church the bearers of the regalia fell in behind him as the Imperial Princes and the Peerage peeled off into pews. Wambly Keifetz, in green as Grand Huntsman, bore the orb; Elvis Effing, also in green but with a scarlet dolman sleeve, as Colonel General of Chasseurs, bore the ring; Lieutenant General Benito Juarez Bennett, as Marshal of Empire, carried the chain. Edward Mulhaus Grogan, as protector of the Faith, held the crown and scepter, and someone whose identity was completely confused by television commentators but who was Jonathan Appleton bore the case for the mantle.

All of the regalia had been made in South Korea excepting the crown and scepter which had been made in Taiwan because of a continuing jeweler's strike in Seoul, which had, too late, been overcome by mass riots.

The ecumenical Mass began. Ron and Nancy, could they have seen this spectacle, would have wept with joy to see the dreams they had dreamed come true before their eyes. As Pope Francis Albert II anointed the Emperor's head, neck, and hands, Chay, not wanting the conservative wing of his government to witness the Pope conferring majesty upon him, took the crown from the altar and placed it on his own head. He then crowned the Empress who burst into tears. At her moment of greatest glory she was wondering what had happened to François Max Felix.

To the accompaniment of a superbly rendered *Vivat Imperator in Aeternum* by the massed choir, Chay swore on the Gospels to maintain the territory of his empire.

As the Imperial pair left the altar and proceeded together slowly to the western end of the nave where they were to ascend twenty-four steps to the great thrones, their solemn dignity was marred by an argument among the Imperial princesses as to the "proper method" of carrying the Empress's train. The Emperor snarled viciously at his sisters, again saying something threatening to them: short, succinct, frightening sentences which were inaudible to the cameras but which gravely shocked the Pope. Immediately, the sisters picked up the train and the Empress was able to move to her place on the throne.

Mounting a dais, the Pope raised his hands aloft in blessing and intoned, in a quavering voice, *"In hoc olio confirmare vis Deus, et in regno aeterno secum regnare faciat Christus."*

The talking heads of the network anchormen appeared directly upon the 143 million television screens in use around the world, saying, "The most glorious and august Emperor Caesare I has been consecrated and enthroned."

The nation careened off into a wild three-day, three-night celebration.

$\mathbb{A}$S IF FROM THE STRAIN of travel, the Emperor's language during the coronation, and Tex-Mex food, Pope Francis Albert II passed away in a state of grace in the second week of the reign of the first Emperor of the American Republic. The College of Cardinals was bricked into solemn conclave at the Burgenstock, an empyrean of hotels and restaurants in (ecumenically) neutral Switzerland. Each hour as they deliberated over the choice of Francis Albert's successor, the Emperor's mother, in Dallas, increased the pressure on her son to get the papacy for her boy, Sylvester.

"You had him made a Cardinal. So you'll have him made a Pope," she said.

"Mom, what can I do? This is strictly a church matter. It is something I have to stay away from."

"This is a very important thing to me, Chay. I am a highly religious woman."

"Mom—please. Try to understand. I simply cannot—"

"You think they can come up with somebody who'll look better in those robes and skullcaps than Sylvester? Do you know anyone alive who can wear a zucchetto like him? He's made it his life! What? Maybe you're afraid he'll take the play away from you on television."

She hounded him, ringing every possible change on every illogical argument. She was seated at his bedside when he awoke in the mornings. She followed him through corridors talking steadily. On the third day he cracked.

"All right, Mom," he said. "I'll try. I suppose he deserves a shot at it, I guess."

He lobbied the entire ecumenical spectrum; wheedling, threatening, coaxing as he telephoned the Archbishop of Canterbury and the Dalai Lama. He cajoled Jimmy Swaggart. He talked to chief rabbis, to ayatollahs, and to imams. He reached the members of the Southern Baptist Conference in mid-convention. He lobbied, by telephone, through the State Department and by courier, in

India, in Stockholm, and in Salt Lake City. He made deals. He exercised all the privileges of ecumenical democracy, making some pretty rough deals. But to make sure that everything would absolutely turn out right he had Eddie Grogan put some people inside the conclave at the Burgenstock as ecclesiastical janitors. While they cleaned and made beds, they electioneered, persuaded, passed along information from individual spiritual headquarters, wheedling in and out of the tiny cells occupied by the Cardinals, working skillfully among the caucuses which preceded the main voting.

On the thirty-sixth day of the conclave a puff of white smoke went up from the building. It signified that a new Pope had been chosen, the first American Pope in history, the brother of the Emperor of the American Republic—Sylvester, Cardinal Appleton, who chose the name Sereno I for his reign.

While he was pressing Sylvester's case, while he was doing his best to conform to the demands of Eddie Grogan's psychiatrists to absorb the principle of the divine right of kings, he lost Hedda Blitzen forever to a connection so unexpected, so utterly absurd in Chay's eyes that it very nearly broke his heart. It came as a twofold blow. Even though, in his anguish, he acknowledged the two or three hundred other women who had been strewn across the landscape of his life, as well as the women he had truly loved— Ulyssa, Liz Wantonberg, Sheila Plantenbower and what's-her-name—they had all been as the many military campaigns had been to him, a part of his daily life, little punctuations of no consequence when compared to his Hedda.

There was only Hedda Blitzen. Somewhere, deep within his soul, he knew that all the striving and reaching would cease, that he would find himself again sauntering along Third Avenue in New York's Yorkville, to enter a certain delicatessen and find happiness with his darling once more, never to be parted from her again.

In a way, he had always felt that he had never really lost her because she had always, one way or another, kept in touch. When she lost her little dog she did not call the ASPCA, she telephoned frantically to her Emperor. She sent him dress patterns for his approval; upholstery fabrics; recipes; asked for his help in filling out income tax forms. Such things were an enormous pain-in-the-ass for Chay even if they were easily handled because they took him away from his endless search for a solution to the Reagan deficits and the terrifying national debt the old outlaw had left behind.

When Hedda's father died there was contention among her brothers over who would be in charge at the store. She appealed to Chay, as Emperor of the American people, to settle the matter. This move may have intimidated her brothers but the matter was far from settled.

Chay was into government well over his head. The psychotropic drug-enforced biofeedback to induce his belief in his divine right had changed him greatly. Almost overnight his mind was transformed from ferroconcrete military to the swamp-brain of an absolute monarch. The totalitarian demand, together with Hedda's predicament, took its toll.

Problems were coming at him from all sides. The House of Lords was behaving as if the Commons did not exist. Sir William Richert, leader of the Tory Party, was making impossible demands. Chay had to have Grogan's people eliminate three of Richert's Party whips with extreme prejudice to make a clear point with Sir William.

Dudley had been arrested for indecent exposure outside a rather good girls' school. Chay had Grogan's people quiet the thing down with bribes and threats. He wanted to banish Dudley to the refractory chromite mines in the Philippines, but Dudley's loyal wife stoutly claimed that Dudley had done the shameful things because he had been brooding so heavily about wetting the bed because he felt he never got enough recognition. Serena made such a scene about the lack of recognition business that Chay was forced to make Dudley, and his wife, Frieda, King and Queen of Mexico. Even that complicated life for Chay because Mexico had to be annexed first.

The new and "greatly simplified" Congressional Pay Raise Bill was still in contention and there were dozens of other administrative, military, legislative, and political matters which needed Chay's attention while all of the infinite details of the post-coronation period needed to be worked out and decided upon. Forty-eight dukes in fifty states were awaiting investiture. There were 100 marquises to be invoked, 200 earls, 400 viscounts, 800 barons, and 2,500 knights to be created in the first wave.

Heaven knows he wanted to help darling Hedda with her delicatessen problems, but each time Chay would make a plan to slip into New York incognito, Keifetz and Grogan would increase the mood-altering drugs which led to more hypnosis, which led to more biofeedback, which led to making him feel more and more and more that he was actually Ronald Reagan, until he began to reach the point where he ran the country's foreign affairs and Defense Department purchasing by astrology. At times he would be so taken up with his divinity and his utter Reaganness, saying something so outlandish and so utterly cockeyed about what was going on in the Pink House, that he did not dare to appear in public but could only wave at the nonexistent crowds, as he and Ulyssa and the little dog flew back and forth to the Camp David II in the Texas Hill country.

Darling Hedda's letters became so pleading, so broken in their need for help, that he instructed his brother, Prince Jonathan, as to how he wanted matters to proceed in setting Hedda's problems straight and sent him to New York as the only man he could trust. At the time, he happened to need Jonathan out of the way because Jon's fiancée, Elizabeth, had moved him even beyond his own belief in any conceivable extent that a woman had ever moved any man. He needed time with her, alone, to measure how deeply he had fallen in love with her.

Prince Jonathan had been forewarned not to overdo his presence with Hedda: no bodyguards, no stretched Rolls, no princely uniforms with gold-fringed epaulets. He was to appear just as a guy who had come to New York from Dallas to help however he could.

Jonathan was resigned to losing his fiancée to the Emperor. He knew Elizabeth was turned on by power and that she did not have a romantic bone in her heart. He knew he had made an avalanche of a mistake by becoming engaged to her, and as much as he didn't like to stick the Emperor with her, he was comforted by the thought that he wouldn't be sticking Chay with her for long.

Prince Jonathan, for all the millions he had made out of real estate in Washington West, yearned for romance, and something about this helpless youngster Hedda in New York reached him before he ever met her.

Jon took the same ambling walk down Third Avenue from Eighty-sixth Street that his brother had taken a few years before. He was taller than his brother; well turned out in a breathtakingly tailored, three-piece Lincoln-green suit, a light pink shirt, and the broad-striped pink and green silk necktie of the Royal Academy of Hair Stylists. He wore a six-piece tweed cap to obscure his identity.

He turned off the pavement directly at Schwalhaber's and entered the delicatessen. His life changed.

47

HEDDA WAS ALONE behind the great glass meat sarcophagus, shave-slicing bologna, wearing what surely might have been the same slightly spotted apron she had worn the day Chay had found her. She had shampooed her honey-colored hair that morning and it looked lovely. She wore her bosom, thrusting out under the apron, like a tray of forbidden fruit. She stared directly into his eyes.

"*Ja?*" she said with the stage German accent.

"I am Jonathan Appleton," he told her simply.

"*Ja?*" The realization struck her. "*Brince* Jonathan?" she gasped.

"My brother, the Emperor, send me. I mean, sent me."

"Chay send you?"

"I wonder if we could make an appointment for this evening so that we may talk."

"Talk?"

"About your—uh—business problems."

"Not here!"

"No, no."

"Can you meet me at Nedick's on the corner of Eighty-sixth Street at six o'clock?"

He looked at his watch. It was 4:20. "Why not the Casino Latino room at the United Nations?"

"*Ja. Gut.* You better maybe buy something in case they are watching."

"What do you suggest?"

"The Emperor always liked the *feinbratwurst.*"

"Give me one of those, please."

"One?"

"Well—make it three."

He watched her go to the meat mausoleum and remove three of the sausages. "May I see those close up, please?"

She extended the blind, white thrillers upon her open palms.

"I'm not sure I like the looks of those," Jonathan said.

"You don't like the look? They are fresh at two o'clock!"

"Oh, indeed. I'm sure of that. It's just that—well—they make me think of a part of a very large man who has drowned. Does the store make sandwiches?"

"Oh, yes."

"Perhaps you would let me come back Saturday to buy some sandwiches and we could go on a picnic together."

"Couldn't we talk about that at the United Nations?"

"I have to report to the Emperor."

"Where would we go for a picnic?"

Jonathan knew that with one call to his brother the Emperor they could have Central Park shut off from the public for Saturday afternoon or that an aircraft carrier could pick them up to steam along the Hudson River to Bear Mountain and back while they picnicked on the flight deck. Ronald Reagan had vacationed for a few days on Barbados, visiting Claudette Colbert, and what with the U.S. Navy standing offshore, the Secret Service, military protection, Air Force One, and dozens of gofers and understrappers, the little holiday had cost the taxpayers about $690,000 a day. Being alone together in Central Park had enormous appeal. He thought of the schoolboy couplet:

> *Hurray! Hurray! The first of May!*
> *Outdoor (kissing) begins today.*

But because it was indicative of his real character he decided that would (a) be selfish, (b) perhaps overthrow the government if they preempted Central Park, so he said, "We could rent a car and drive out to Montauk."

"Better yet," Hedda said, "we could have the picnic on the roof of my apartment building, then the refrigerator would be right there because I, myself, live on the top floor."

Between the time he left Schwalhaber's and saw Hedda in the Casino Latino room, Jonathan went back to his hotel and called the Secretary of Holidays and Fiestas, a former impresario named Benn Reyes who held the new Cabinet post which had become necessary because there were now forty-three national holidays each year. The Secretary was on the line instantly.

"Your Royal Highness! What an honor!" He had been angling for a knighthood since the Imperial government had been announced.

"Please take down this address in New York, Mr. Secretary, and have your people design and build a picnic setting on its roof in time for noon on Saturday, day after tomorrow."

"Yes—yes, of course, Your Highness."

"Something bucolic but gay. Rural but environmentally sound." Jon dictated Hedda's street address. "It's for an intimate little *fête champêtre*, nothing permanent."

He had been installed at a table in the Casino Latino when Hedda arrived promptly at six o'clock that evening. When they had ordered two Baby Chams, Hedda asked if the Emperor, in his compassion, had had the time to think of a solution to her problem. Jonathan smiled and nodded. "I would say that he has provided quite a Solomonic solution. We will quietly arrest all three of your brothers. They will be sent to work in the refractory chromite mines on the island of Masinloc in the Philippines. You will have complete control of the delicatessen and the brinery."

"No, no!"

"No?"

"That is impossible. They are my brothers. I love them. I just thought that if Chay would make them members of the Order of the American Empire for their work in pickling, then whenever they saw their names with OAE added they would immediately see that I had arranged it for them, and because I had, they would treat me as an equal in the store."

"I suppose we could do that. After all, he made a Hollywood agent a duke."

"You know something, Prince Jonathan? You are very understanding. I like you very much." She looked upward into his eyes and the bridge was crossed.

The government conversion of the roof of Hedda's apartment building was nothing short of miraculous. With the knighthood in mind, Reyes had outdone himself.

The Prince arrived at Hedda's door at 12:17 P.M. on Saturday, bringing a sturdy split-oak picnic basket which was empty except for a magnum of Romanee-Conti '71 and a really splendid bottle of chilled Montrachet '74. The basket had bright brass hinges on its double-opening maple lids which Hedda immediately lifted to fill both sides with liverwurst sandwiches, a few pinkelwursts, covered dishes filled with hot potato salad; eagle's nests of cole slaw and many other indigestible delights including a chocolate wind torte. There was table silver, napkins, a tablecloth—everything but the ants.

When they climbed the short flight of steps from Hedda's apartment to the roof level and opened the door to the housetop, a faithful reproduction of the forest of Arden awaited them. The greenest of green sod had been imported by a supersonic fighter-bomber from Kilmoganny in Ireland—where the grass is so green that even the natives need to wear modulating eyeglasses—and it covered the entire surface of the roof. A genuine, full-grown weeping willow tree stood, unable to conceal its femininity, sighing in the breeze beside a babbling brook. Over all of it, some government scenic artist whose life's dream had been to put Mother Nature nude upon the model's stand had, with her, conceived a glass-domed sky, perfectly blue, stuffed with the same fluffy, immaculate white clouds as must have set off Olympus. An air-conditioned canopy had been erected facing the willow tree under which a picnic table, two chairs, and a full-length sofa had been arranged. A large state-of-the-art refrigerator was concealed by a painted screen on which Martin Battersby, master of *trompe l'oeil*, had created the perfection of a virgin meadowland which stretched away toward total bliss. There was muted but compellingly erotic music coming from somewhere near. The effect of the whole panorama was so lifelike that it was as if the dream of paradise had come true, and yet it had only cost the American taxpayers $1,297,849.12.

"Jonathan!" Hedda cried out, forsaking his title. "How beautiful! Oh, you shouldn't have! You really shouldn't have." He took her hand and led her toward the sofa.

The wine was no headier than their youth. The liverwurst sandwiches no heavier than their desire. The air-conditioning worked. The tent concealed. Wonderful things happened in that tent, and the spell Chay seemed to have spun around Hedda was cast off.

When Prince Jonathan returned to Dallas with his news of two young people in love, the Emperor sent Elizabeth, his brother's fiancée, back to California. She had been over-pushy, and after the first few times, had shown little creativity in the sheets. Chay filled her little Chanel handbag with a pint of Burmese rubies, gave her an autographed photograph of himself across which he had written, "I will always remember," and sent her away with an officer whose rank was in keeping with the morganatic fiancée of a royal Prince—a rather gaspingly handsome light-colonel of Imperial Horse to accompany her to her door in Holmby Hills.

In the aulic private chapel at the Pink House, as High Pontiff of the Church of the Upwardly Mobile, Chay dissolved his brother's engagement to Miss Danworthy even though the emotional cost to him was perilously high as, threatened with an aeonian sense of loss and grief, he personally married his own brother, the Prince, to the woman he, himself, loved more than life or power itself—a commoner, Miss Hedda Blitzen—and granted them an appanage which was most of South America by naming

the happy couple as King and Queen of Parabrazargiguay, com-
bining into one kingdom what had formerly been Paraguay, Brazil,
Argentina, and Uruguay, upon which his Grand Huntsman, Wambly Keifetz, had asked him to foreclose for nonpayment on mort-
gages which were held by Keifetz-owned banks. Keifetz
incorporated all four countries as a kingdom and personally un-
derwrote a bond issue for $2.8 trillion as well as floating
821,097,984 shares of common stock and 602,881,949 shares of
preferred. He made $2.2 billion on the deal. Chay had 3 percent
of the issue. The shares were sold out in Tokyo on the first day
of issuance at a price of 101 1/2 over a par value of 48.

Serena didn't stop there with her demands for recognition for
her children. When she had finished, she had changed the history
of the Western Hemisphere. She pointed out to the Emperor that
in order to permit Mexicans to enter the United States freely and
to permit Americans to enter Mexico without the wait for tourist
cards to get the better climate and the lower prices, Chay should
annex Mexico, a natural geographic kind of a thing, she said, when
you come right down to it.

In the Zocalo of Mexico City, before the television cameras of
the world, Chay crowned his brother Dudley and his brother's
wife Frieda as King and Queen of Mexico in a ceremony which
had resonances of ancient Aztec rites.

The change of government had not come about easily. Some
2.8 million rebellious Mexican civilians had to be imprisoned in
labor camps in Alaska and 190,000 troops on both sides of the
conflict were killed or wounded. The Emperor had the element of
surprise and state-of-the-art military equipment such as The Bomb,
although he fought the war, as always, fairly and squarely.

As soon as Dudley and Frieda were installed in Mexico, Serena
began to harangue Chay to take care of his other siblings. Within
the (relatively) short period of fourteen months, Brilliana was
crowned Queen of the Caribbola, a new nation formed by Chay
which extended from Staten Island in the north (a convenient
shipping point to the large cocaine market in New York) to Trin-
idad in the south, and including the Bahamas, Cuba, Jamaica,
Hispaniola, Puerto Rico, the Leeward and Windward Islands, all
of Central America (excepting Nicaragua), and Colombia.

The new nation Caribbola was achieved almost entirely by naval and Marine forces, with the minimal threat of The Bomb, as well as by considerable advance bribery by Eddie Grogan's people. The new thalassocracy would provide widespead bases for the Keifetz cocaine and marijuana operations which would be packaged by Queen Brilliana's island factories and merchandised by television commercials produced by Caribbola advertising agencies, with the proceeds to be banked in Caribbola banks and Federal taxes deducted at the source. Gambling casinos and brothels which would appeal to every pocketbook were installed throughout the island economy. Printing plants and mini-film studios for a heavy export trade in state-of-the-art pornography were moved into operation for an assured mainland market. Rather than disappoint any of her subjects by seeming to prefer one island over another, Queen Brilliana ruled Caribbola from Dallas.

The Emperor's younger sister, Berry, was crowned Queen of the Incas five months after Brilliana ascended to her throne, after a short, swift military campaign which had cost 852,761 (mostly native Indian) lives to consolidate countries which were prime cocaine producers and which had once been called Ecuador, Peru, Bolivia, and Chile. Queen Berengaria reigned with her reclusive consort, a willowy, blond young woman named Edwina who wore enormous earrings, with whom Berry had roomed since their college days.

John DeWitt Kullers was named as Viceroy of Canada. He was the American personification of the treaty signed in 1995 which had guaranteed Canada against Nicaraguan invasion. The Canadians had acted churlishly in reaction to this at first, giving up 231,769 Canadian lives in battle before they saw the value of the treaty. Kullers was an active viceroy. He ran the government as a tough top sergeant would run any unit under his command.

The Western Hemisphere had been secured forever for the American Dream. The Monroe Doctrine and television commercials had been extended to the outer natural boundaries of the United States. From the North Pole to deep Antarctica, every inch of it was paved with a freedom called The American Hemispheric Plan (AHP)—excepting Nicaragua, the canker which never stopped gnawing at the Emperor's vitals.

48

T HE EMPRESS ULYSSA had a secret. Eleven years before she met Chay, she had encountered a woman at a cocktail party who had raved about the occult powers of an alphabet soup reader who lived in Juneau, Alaska. Ulyssa had written to the woman who had replied by return mail, giving Ulyssa the recipe for making and shipping the soup. That part had been simple enough: "Cook two ounces of alphabet macaroni in boiling water for eight minutes. Strain but do not drain. Add alphabets to one (1) can of Swanson's Beef Broth. Stir well. Pour entire contents into mason jar. Seal jar. Wrap carefully and ship to me by Federal Express."

The results had been amazing. The woman, a total clairvoyant named Dame Maria Van Slyke, had been able to foretell Ulyssa's work "with a mysterious organization" which within two weeks turned out to be the CIA. She had predicted that Chay Appleton would come into her life with the foretelling, "You will meet a short man." In the past two months Dame Maria had been predicting that Chay was going to grow eleven inches and this utterly thrilled Ulyssa who had longed to wear high heels again since her marriage.

Chay loved Ulyssa deeply: in the backs of royal limousines, in the pagoda and on the snooker table at Rossenarra, in bathtubs. Although she could have had anything her heart desired and certainly didn't need money, she was still on Eddie Grogan's payroll for the simple reason that once on that payroll no one had ever gotten off it except by dying.

The Appleton family had moved into power with the determination to right the wrong which had not made them powerful until much later in life than they would have preferred. Dudley, Prince of Dallas, first in line to the throne, had schemed his way into the domination of the Ministry of Fiestas and Holidays and by his constant staging of corridas, World Series, Ping-Pong tournaments, and NFL point spreads; Mothers' Days, Foster Mothers' Days, and Step-Mothers' Days, all officially nationalized and heavily televised; by creating more and newer national holidays, he soon became the idol of bank employees, postal workers, and school teachers, and this was before he ascended to the throne of Montezuma in Mexico.

His brother, Pope Sereno I, had instituted mass absolutions for Americans every Monday morning at 11:15. All the shriven-to-be had to do was to stand at attention wherever they were in the country, observing fifteen seconds of silence, and to send two dollars in cash or money orders to the Pope at the Vatican. The burden of sin had become a luxury item for registered masochists.

Ulyssa and her alphabet soup reader in Juneau was one more way for Keifetz to manipulate the Emperor. More and more the soup readings showed that it was Chay's destiny, now that he controlled both North and South America, to rule Europe and the rest of the world so that the Appleton family might never again have to fear relative poverty and so that Keifetz could merchandise packaged cocaine to a wider market. But, in actual fact, Chay was no longer an altogether fit man. He had passed the middle-age center point. He no longer lived the spartan life of a commander in the field. His features were coarsening. His hair was thinning. He now wore the homburg indoors and out most of the time as if to remind himself of past glories. Since the CIA psychiatric treatment had taken over his personality, he expressed low opinions of everyone he met excepting John DeWitt Kullers. He believed everyone to be self-serving and incapable of understanding the larger concepts which sustained him. He withdrew.

Abner Stein, the Emperor's definitive biographer, wrote: "If ever a ruler deserved the popular title conferred by his people, The Great Waver, it was Caesare Appleton. Truly, he was an extraordinarily gifted waver who was said by the cognoscenti to be in a class with Ronald Reagan, as sacrilegious as that seems. He had mastered more complex and movingly emotional waves than any other great leader in world history excepting Reagan. His development of the rotary wave, the behind-the-head wave, and the two-handed upsurge wave were what secured his place as a leader in the hearts of his people."

As the biofeedback built in intensity, as the dosage of the psychotropic drugs doubled then tripled, the Emperor told Grogan, "My destiny is not yet accomplished. The picture exists only in outline. There must be one set of laws, one court of appeal, one coinage for all, and a single line veto for all. The states of the world must be melted into one nation and Dallas will be its capital."

Grogan gave the psychiatrists a 20 percent raise. "The blessings of television have prepared the world for the realization of your dream," Keifetz told the Emperor.

"What dream? I don't have dreams," Chay said. He was wearing a summer toga and sandals, his short, hairy legs holding up the medicine ball of his body. He had been drugged to the hairline.

"We are ready to make our move to take over Europe and Asia."

"How do we do that?"

"First, we will make a lasting peace with Managua."

"Peace with those madmen? Never! I will fight them in the fields, I will fight them in the towns—"

"No, no, Chay. We must think of world opinion. No one wants war but you."

"You think you can make peace with those demons? How? Just tell me how?"

"By easy stages. First you must divorce Ulyssa and marry one of El Supremo's two sisters."

"Wamb! Divorce Ulyssa? I couldn't. I—I just couldn't."

"In politics there is no heart—only head."

"Ulyssa has given me both, but I cannot do it, Wamb."

"Don't worry about Ulyssa. Grogan will handle that."

"What do the sisters look like?"

"I'm told they are quite attractive women, for Indians. Really good bodies."

"How old?"

"The older one—yours—is twenty-two. The younger one is fourteen."

"I'm not going to marry any fourteen-year-old Indian."

"I think we should send an ambassador to begin negotiations."

"Jesus, Wamb. I don't know. I'd like to see pictures first."

"That's not as easy as it sounds."

"But what if they turn me down? That would have to mean war."

"Good heavens, Chay, they'll leap at the chance."

"Who will negotiate?"

"The Duke of Westport. Gordon Godber Manning. The Great Trouble-Shooter."

"Well—" Chay was thinking of, and believing in, an inexpressibly lovely Indian maiden standing nude before him, her eyes downcast but smiling with lust. "When am I supposed to break the news to Ulyssa?"

"You won't have to, Chay. Grogan has a plant in Juneau, Alaska, who does readings for Ulyssa. She'll set the whole thing up."

"The alphabet soup woman?"

Keifetz nodded. "The friend is going to tell Ulyssa that she has to divorce you. You won't even have to use that line—'in politics there is no heart, only head.' "

49

GORDON GODBER MANNING, the Duke of Westport, was an accomplished diplomat, a former Secretary of State, and one-time presidential nominee of his Party. He was a seasoned spectator of the world scene and had developed as the outstanding American scholar of Sandinistaism. In the brief periods of peace between his country and Nicaragua, he had been sent to Managua as Chay's envoy starting when Chay had entered the Pink House as Chairman/CEO. He had become an intimate of El Supremo, admired him greatly and pressed him to see to it that Nicaragua maintained both the deed and spirit of the Queensland agreement which had ended the Australian war. The Duke was a man of high intelligence who never hesitated to speak his mind. Chay responded as the great have always done to their gofers whose honesty was greater than their fear. The Duke disdained flattery. He touched up nothing and disguised nothing in his notes to posterity (*Advice to an Emperor*, Haldemann-Julius Press, 4 vols., $93.95). He wrote that he had told the Emperor, "I am proud to be against war and will do all I can to prevent it."

Westport flew to Managua in Air Force Nine. He made the Emperor's proposal for the hand of El Supremo's older sister, Catalina. El Supremo stared at the Duke with Indian stolidity and said he would take the proposal under family advisement. When the Duke returned to the dictator's office the following afternoon, he was greeted with courtesy but was told that, unfortunately, El Supremo's sister had just been married to one of his generals that morning and, therefore, of course, could not be available to marry the Emperor. Immediately, Westport put forward his ruler's bid for the hand of El Supremo's younger sister, Inez.

"But she is a child, Excellency. She became fourteen years old only ten days ago."

"The Emperor will see that she attends good schools."

"Ah, if that were all. My mother, matriarch of our family, has sworn to Saint Eulalia that Inez will not marry until she is twenty."

"A long engagement, then."

"Impossible, I'm afraid. My mother—"

Westport returned to Dallas. The Emperor took the news as a direct insult. He threw a small page boy at the wall in his rage.

"I was insane to allow myself to be persuaded that that treacherous son of a bitch wanted peace," he yelled.

"He wants peace, Your Highness."

"After this mockery?"

"Well—really! You do have troop concentrations in Honduras, Salvador, and Costa Rica. And in Colombia, Venezuela, Guyana, Suriname, and French Guiana."

"I am only following the Reagan Doctrine!"

"But perhaps—being reasonable people—they may prefer an open state of war to such a shaky peace."

"They cannot dictate to me."

"No, Sire."

"The American people will not tolerate this humiliation. My God, if the Sandinistas want war, I'll give them war."

Keifetz requested and was granted another audience with the Emperor. He had a new plan for peace. "If you forge a really strong bond with the Soviets—and a consanguineous alliance is what I have in mind—Nicaragua wouldn't dare to continue its endless wars against us."

"Consanguineous?"

"Marry the daughter of the General Secretary of the Communist Party of the Union of Socialist Soviet Republics and we will have peace in our time."

"Peace? After the insult to American manhood we just got from Managua?"

"Your people want peace, Chay. A lasting peace. You must divorce Ulyssa and marry the Russian woman."

50

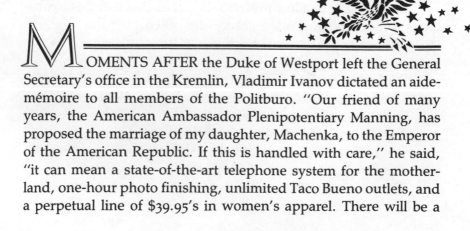

MOMENTS AFTER the Duke of Westport left the General Secretary's office in the Kremlin, Vladimir Ivanov dictated an aide-mémoire to all members of the Politburo. "Our friend of many years, the American Ambassador Plenipotentiary Manning, has proposed the marriage of my daughter, Machenka, to the Emperor of the American Republic. If this is handled with care," he said, "it can mean a state-of-the-art telephone system for the motherland, one-hour photo finishing, unlimited Taco Bueno outlets, and a perpetual line of $39.95's in women's apparel. There will be a meeting in my office at 7:15 tomorrow morning. Bring pads and pencils."

Westport sent a message via back channels to Keifetz in Dallas which said that the General Secretary had received the proposal without comment.

Eddie Grogan's man in the Kremlin transmitted a copy of Vovo Ivanov's memo through a member of the crew of the Soviet "Books On Wheels" cultural exchange with the German Federal Republic, leaving the message in a copy of a Polish translation of a Philip Wylie novel. The novel was bought in the East German city of Parchim three weeks later by an American tourist who said she wanted something to read on the way home. She got the coded message as far as Givet in Luxembourg where it was concealed in a Laundromat awaiting the arrival of one of Grogan's drops who was in traffic court for three days. When the drop retrieved the novel, he passed it along to an instrumentalist who was appearing with the traveling Dallas Symphony. The flautist, a Pole, made the mistake of starting to read the novel between rehearsals, was unable to put it down between traveling and appearances with the orchestra, and did not succeed in finishing it until two and a half weeks later. When he had finished the book, the orchestra had reached Rome where the novel was passed along by a secular member of Pope Sereno's staff and taken directly to the Pope, who ordered it wrapped securely in plain brown paper and mailed to his brother in Texas. Within nine weeks, the CIA had analyzed the message which was: "Stand by for report on Politburo meeting."

Eight weeks before that, the Duke of Westport had had in hand the Soviet's conditional acceptance of the proposal of marriage.

The conditions fell into two parts: (1) "open" conditions which would evolve into a formal marriage contract, and (2) "secret" conditions which were those which had been hammered out in the Politburo meeting.

The "open" conditions proposed that a Joint Soviet-U.S. Commission for the Exploration of Marriage Proposals be formed and that meetings begin within sixty days in Geneva to undertake solutions. This suggestion called for intensive meetings in the Pink House because the Emperor was still legally married.

The meeting with the General Secretary and the Politburo had not gone entirely smoothly.

"What kind crazy thing is this?" asked Marshal Zilkov to open the meeting.

"Please!" the General Secretary said. "The first thing is, after we give in after four months in Geneva, they'll come up with a new foolproof telephone system so that all of our people, if they feel like it, can reach out and touch someone."

"There's a second thing, Vovushka?" the Marshal asked.

Ivanov nodded benignly. "Oh yes," he said. "If the Emperor has a son then their law says that son must one day become emperor."

"So?"

"So he'll get his son and, through the son, we'll rule America. I admit it's a long-range idea but what the hell?"

"How are we going to control the son when the son will be born and bred American?" a contentious Armenian said.

"That's the whole gizmo," the General Secretary said. "The son will be born here and raised here."

"How?" four men yelled.

"My daughter will go there. They will do it like crazy—you saw his file—he can't stop doing it. My daughter will get pregnant—then we will announce that I am dying. Machenka will rush to my bedside, and by the time I get better, she will have the baby."

"So?"

"So—what?"

"Then she goes back with the baby."

Ivanov grinned broadly. "Only if she can get an exit visa," he said.

"A-HA!" the entire meeting shouted.

Even though the deal to provide the Soviets with a block-to-block, border-to-border telephone system would be worth thirty billion dollars, even though the credit card market alone in the USSR was limitlessly profitable, even though the computer industry and the Big Five of Detroit would drop everything to tool up to sell to the Russians, and the garment district would go bananas trying to count the number of $39.95's they would sell,

Chay could only think that Ulyssa's heart would be broken if the Soviet deal came about.

Then the word came through which for the fifth time in a row repeated Dame Maria's interpretation of the alphabet soup Ulyssa had sent her, telling Ulyssa that if she wished to spare Chay's life and her own, she had to demand a divorce from the Emperor. Grogan brought Chay the news. Tears welled up in Chay's eyes. "She wasn't very bright," he said, "but she was some woman."

Horror-struck, Ulyssa stared at the fifth message from Juneau. "You must divorce your husband or there will be terrible consequences for both of you." It was the most devastating thing that had ever happened to Ulyssa, but in spite of the grief and terror it brought, it made the clarion promise that when she did divorce, she would come into great fortune and have more shoes than she could ever wear. Dame Maria went further: "All of this forecast checks out with sand readings of your future and is consistent with your phrenology chart."

Staring at Chay's portrait by James Richard Blake which hung three times life-size on the wall of her boudoir, she did not doubt the truth of the prediction for a moment but asked herself over and over again, "How am I going to tell Chay?" She feared that Chay might try to kill himself.

She sat gripping the sides of her head as Chay came in.

"Just seven and a half months until our wedding anniversary, sweetheart," he said. "What would you like as a surprise this year?"

Ulyssa stared at him as if it would be the last time in her life that she would see him, and burst into tears.

"Darling!" Chay cried out. "Dearest! What is it? What have I said?"

Ulyssa took his hands and pressed them to her lips. "Oh, Chay!" she sobbed.

"Little dukke, please—tell me what has happened!"

"I—Oh, Chay. Dearest Chay, I have to divorce you."

"Divorce me? Di*vorce????*"

"It was written in the soup, Chay. Then Dame Maria checked it against sand readings and my phrenology chart. Terrible things will happen to both of us if I don't divorce you, but—as soon as I do—we will all be drenched in good fortune."

"But—but—"

She put a soft finger to his lips. "It isn't as though we won't be together whenever we want to be."

"But that wouldn't be legal!"

"We shall overcome," Ulyssa breathed and unzipped his trousers.

51

THE HELICOPTER having Air Force One markings, carrying Georgie Jumel, the Emperor's double, was put down in the forecourt of the Chartres Cathedral which had been placed to stand through time at the top of a hill in the capital city of Eure-et-Loire in France. Although the public had been well screened away from the actual arrival pad, there were over 2,700 journalists working outside the great church on nine-story-high tiered platforms. In addition, 1,787 world dignitaries had been jammed inside the church.

Jumel, a professional fatalist, was 1.2391 inches taller, two years younger, but not as pretty as his Emperor. Before Grogan's people had found him for the job he had been a car park valet at a jai alai fronton in Coral Gables, Florida. His resemblance to Caesare Appleton, viewed from any angle, was uncanny. For nine and a half months he had been drilled sixteen hours a day by teachers of the Method, an actor's curriculum, in getting "inside the character" of the Emperor. There was not a moue, a gesture, a carriage, a bodily- or facially-expressed prejudice of Chay's that Grogan's people had not secretly caught on videotape and which Jumel's teachers had not ruthlessly insisted that Georgie Jumel absorb. They had hammered Chay's external image into Jumel's physical memory because the memory of the world was draped with the black crepe of mourning for its great leaders who had been brutally assassinated. Despite the psychotropic drugs and the biofeedback, Chay said he wasn't going to lay himself open to being shot down by some mindless civilian, so Keifetz and Grogan had come up with Plan VI which utilized Georgie Jumel.

As Jumel stepped down from Air Force One wearing the Emperor's wedding suit, the blue dress uniform of the CINCAFUS-CIAFBIANSA with its twenty-seven rows of ribbons and decorations paving the left side of his chest and with his two Medals of Honor suspended around his neck, he *was* Caesare Appleton because he had to be. Five million people, sitting in semidarkness for years, knew every nuance of Caesare Appleton's personal statement, and although they spent their lives being fooled and knew they had been fooled from the beginning, they would be almost elemental in their fury if it were made sloppily clear that they *were* being fooled.

Standing in the open air, seen by 86.3125 percent of the television viewers of the world, Jumel was decorated with the Order of Lenin from the hands of the stand-in/double for his father-in-law-to-be, Vladimir Ivanov, General Secretary of the Communist Party of the Union of Socialist Soviet Republics.

Except for the 27 Secret Service and KGB bodyguards, and the 2,700-odd journalists, many of whom were operating the 172 television cameras which surrounded the small forecourt, the doppelgängers for the two world leaders stood alone. Below, in the town and in the surrounding fields, more than 1.6 million tourists from nearly every country in the world had bought their visas from the French government and had congregated for this event of the century. There were workers and capitalists, zealots and curiosity seekers, outstanding pickpockets, women in black *chadors*, grown men in soiled sneakers and jeans, publicity seekers, and tens of thousands who believed that their angle on the event was the only money-making angle. For two days many of them had slept where they stood, sustained only by the endless noise of wandering rock musicians. They had arrived in tour buses, limousines, private jets; on bikes and afoot from as far away as Bel Air, California, Athens, Dublin, Cordoba, Beijing, and Dallas;

streaming in from the airports of Paris; causing burgeoning employment (and problems) for plumbers, caterers, inn keepers, and police who had been working on the development of facilities for seven months.

Into utter silence—excepting for the noise of the departing Air Force One helicopter—crashed the sounds of the U.S. Marine Corps band playing a medley of "Yellow Rose of Texas" and Irving Berlin's "O Chichornya" as, in the distance, the Soviet chopper carrying the double of the bride could be seen as a speck in the sky. As it flew nearer, doubles for the Emperor of the American Republic and the General Secretary of the Communist Party withdrew to join the best men who were standing in a semicircle in the periphery of the forecourt: Princes Philip and Charles of England; King Juan Carlos of Spain; Dudley, King of Mexico; the Kings of Scandinavia; Jonathan, King of Parabrazargiguay; the President of France; the Prime Ministers of England, Italy, and Japan; the Chancellor of Germany; a massive delegation from the People's Republic of China; and Wambly Keifetz. The groom's party disappeared into the cathedral to take their places at the altar.

Chay watched the three screens in Dallas, with Eddie Grogan and the three CIA psychiatrists at his side, in his library at Rossenarra.

"I don't think Georgie Jumel bears the slightest resemblance to me," he said.

"He's your spittin' image," Grogan said.

"He could be your twin, Sire," the senior psychiatrist said.

"The whole thing is a fake piece of staging. Who does Keifetz think he's kidding?" He groused at every turn of the ceremonies until Machenka Ivanov stepped down from the helicopter. Then he said, "Holy shit!"

The bride's chopper touched down in the forecourt on the mark which was precisely equidistant from all cameras. The plane's door opened. An Honor Guard of Marshals of the Soviet Union stepped down, then the double of the bride emerged. A rehearsed gasp went up from the 2,700 journalists and photographers, not that she didn't rate a gasp—she was a stunning woman—but because there had already been four camera rehearsals during the two previous days which had forced the committee of network and cable producers to decide that a spontaneous gasp would give the arrival more drama, therefore more TV audience incentive.

Chay looked from Grogan to the psychiatrists then back to Grogan to see if they were seeing what he was seeing.

"Fine-looking woman," Grogan said.

"She's—she's breath-taking!" Chay said. His beatific expression changed. "But it's the double."

"Just as you are handsomer than Georgie Jumel," the senior psychiatrist said, "so is Machenka Ivanov more beautiful than her stand-in."

"No kidding?"

"She's the most gorgeous thing since Pocahontas," Grogan said. "And the beauty part is—our people passed the word back that, just from pictures of you, she is outta her skull about you."

"No kidding?"

Until the double's startling likeness to the bride was discovered, she had been a secretary in the Ukrainian Bureau of Fisheries. Like her counterpart, Jumel, Devushka Jupski understood the ever-present dangers of her assignment. Just as Georgie Jumel had reason to fear assassination by the terrible L-word people of his country, Devushka Jupski stood in the bride's place in fear of the right-wing reactionary hardcore Communists in her country.

"When does she get here?" Chay asked, controlling his heavy breathing.

"In about thirty-six hours," Grogan said.

Chartres was a town of about 40,000 people who, being French, were all violently opposed to the historic wedding of two foreigners being held there. The place had been named after a Celtic tribe, the Carnutes, who had made it a Druidic center which was ultimately burned down by the Normans in 858 A.D. The city was sold to the King of France in 1286. During the Hundred Years War the English had occupied it for fifteen years. Henry IV was crowned there in 1594. It stood in the region of Beauce, the breadbasket of France, prospering so well that, in the mid-thirteenth century, its citizens built the main part of its great cathedral, Notre Dame de Chartres, in less than thirty years. As thrillingly memorable as the inspiring dignity of its timeless exterior seemed, the stained glass of its interior conveyed the immortality of great art.

．　．　．

The doubles for the bride and her father walked slowly up the aisle of the church, seeming to float upon the great chords of music which lay as thickly in the air as folds of organdy, while the mighty organ gave forth great hopes. The surrogate father and daughter moved under shafted piers, quadripartite vaulting, and almost total elimination of walls and flying buttresses, flanked by chairs which were packed with great statesmen, scientists, film producers, industrialists, investment bankers, Liz Wantonberg, high and yet higher clergy, sports champions, and a few artists. Four queens were carrying the bride's train: Queen Frieda of Mexico; Queen Hedda of Parabrazargiguay, tears streaming down her face; the Queen of the Incas, Berengaria; and Queen Brilliana of Caribbola; all advancing with the great rose window behind them, passing the medallion windows which had been installed in the first quarter of the thirteenth century on the south side of the nave, as well as the north rose window, dedicated to the Virgin, with five lancets showing Melchizedek; David; Saint Anne, holding the baby Mary; Solomon and Aaron; all created in 1240, colored with molten metallic oxides—copper for ruby, cobalt for blue, manganese for purple, antimony for yellow, iron for green—upon sheets of medieval glass which had been blown, manipulated, and cut into cylinders which were split lengthwise and flattened into sheets while the glass was still red-hot and in a pliable state, stained with one basic color throughout then formed into great translucent mosaic paintings.

The massed choirs, singing on either side of the widened naves behind the smaller altars of the chapel, caroled *Te Deums*. The purity of the voices, the timelessness of the architecture, the passionate messages of the stained glass all combined to create a rich composite of every man's conception of an ecumenical heaven. Wambly Keifetz was having a videocassette made of all of it to show to Chay and his bride in Dallas or wherever they would be connubially joined.

The groom and his forty-three best men waited at the head of the aisle facing the inspiring presence of Pope Sereno I who was wearing the triple-crown miter of the ecumenical Papacy and an alb which was so chic that the three reporters from *W* magazine, seated in the fourth row, were sketching it for instant adaptation and copying by Seventh Avenue via FAX.

Before the exalted witnesses, Vladimir Ivanov gave his daughter in marriage to the Emperor of the American Republic while the mighty of the earth looked on and their wives wept with chagrin or joy, depending on whether they had marriageable daughters.

Pope Sereno pronounced the betrothed couple man and wife, and a new era for integrated international harmony began.

Almost at once the bride and groom were in the Air Force One helicopter to be flown to the Charles de Gaulle Airport in Paris where they transferred to an Aeroflot flight to Moscow which was equally manned by a Soviet and American crew and secretly observed and protected by flight attendants who were Grogan's people.

There was a somber, if any Russian party could possibly be described as somber, reception given in the Kremlin, during which the faux bride and groom slipped off at 4 A.M. Moscow time and were flown directly to Dallas where, after a ninety-minute photo opportunity, they were taken from the airport by Grogan's people to the Pink House behind high walls in University Park.

The KGB took the false bride, dressed in traveling clothes, inside the entrance to Rossenarra then out through a service entrance and loaded her into the back of a panel truck marked DANIELS' DRY CLEANING. She was flown by private plane to the Moisant Airport at New Orleans then transshipped to Moscow, via Rome and Belgrade, where she was sealed in a convent to spend the rest of her life in prayer.

Georgie Jumel was drugged and brainwashed by Grogan's people and flown to the Philippine island of Masinloc to work for the rest of his life in the refractory chromite mines.

The true bride, Maria "Machenka" Ivanov, who had flown aboard British Airways from London to Dallas, and had arrived by CIA taxi at the Pink House the previous afternoon, had already been made gravid by the Emperor who, not aware (nor she) that he had already done what was required of him, kept trying again and again. On the morning following their first night together, Machenka received word through her husband, via the hot line, that her father was dying. She left that morning for Moscow to be at his side.

52

URING THE SIXTEEN MONTHS since the Emperor, as
secular head of The Church of the Upwardly Mobile, had divorced
himself from Ulyssa, he had flung himself into the task of the
continuance of the American Hemispheric Plan. The plan was the
political cement which held together the tens of millions of people
from the North Slope of Alaska to the Straits of Magellan. There
were problems. The throne of his brother Don Dudley Primero
had been in dire peril of collapsing from its first day. Almost to a
man the Mexican people were determined to make full-time war
upon every manifestation of his reign.

Dudley was no soldier. He was a king because his brother
had told him he was king after Keifetz's reports had given the
insane impression that the Mexicans were cowed and docile. Keifetz had needed to change Mexico into an absolute monarchy to
streamline procurement, distribution, and marketing of the narcotics industry from all of Latin America northward.

Dudley was unable to establish himself in Mexico City until
an army of 70,000 Mexican irregulars had been beaten back by the
Emperor's troops. When he did enter the capital the streets were
empty and the buildings shuttered. All of the moneyed class had
left for St. Moritz, the shops and restaurants were closed, and
Dudley found himself reigning over what seemed to be a ghost
country.

There was a tiny, token pro-American Party called the Dud-
linos, which had been formed by Grogan's people, made up of
the offscourings of the prisons, but they were regarded as traitors
and collaborators by the Mexicans.

Dudley fell apart emotionally. In a FAX to Chay he demanded
the right to issue a decree which would, in effect, be his resig-
nation. It was too late. Sandinistas had picked up the thread of
rebellion and had woven it into a thick hawser. Nicaragua poured
arms and money into the Mexican resistance. Dudley had to flee

Mexico City supposedly protected by troops who were so drunk and mutinous that they looted his personal baggage train and strewed his horseshoe pitching equipment all over the landscape. Dudley walled himself in at Monterey, reasonably near and yet so far from the U.S. border. The Sandinistas occupied Mexico City with their armies. The unhappy Dudley held only two northern provinces whose economy was dependent upon trade with over-the-border American tourists.

Infuriated by Dudley's ineptitude, the Emperor had to invade Mexico to save him. His troops drove the Sandinista army out of the country. The Fifth Army, under General Bennett, himself born in Mexico of American parents, chased the Nicaraguans as far south as El Salvador, but as soon as the American forces withdrew from Mexico, pitiless guerrilla warfare began with hideous atrocities on both sides.

Dudley complained directly to Serena. Chay then permitted him to add the title "His Most Ecumenical Majesty" to his state and personal notepaper which allowed Dudley to say that he sought only "to sustain the unity of our holy religion." This new understanding was supported, in spirit and by a series of satellite television broadcasts, by his other brother, the Pope. Dudley was able to return to Mexico City where he boasted to Chay via FAX: "Give me five million men and three billion dollars and I will return peace to this country." One month later he asked to be allowed to abdicate—an offer which was to be repeated many times—if he were not allowed to govern the Mexican people in his own way.

Dudley was an irrelevance whose only justification was that he was an Appleton. He consoled himself with Clarinda "Tuti" Castillo, an eccentric dancer and extremely clever contortionist. His wife Frieda despaired. The Emperor referred to him in private as "my Mexican ulcer."

Dudley wrote to his mistress in Dallas, an oils applicator at an artificial suntanning salon, "I find myself as king of a people who reject me," adding with no small helping of self-pity, "I have been swept along by the guilty force of my brother's circumstances." The woman sold all of Dudley's letters to the *National Enquirer*, but by a stroke of luck, Grogan's people found out about it and were able to suspend publication before the damaging issue could appear in every supermarket in America.

Throughout the troubles in Mexico, the Emperor's other impossible brother, Pope Sereno I, spurred on by daily telephone calls from his mother, continued to be an embarrassment which further took Chay's attentions away from the projected strike on Nicaragua. Sereno had formed a company in Zurich called Sylvester Enterprises through which he ran a series of rather shaky business deals. He had become proud of his reputation as a glutton, gaining seventy-seven pounds in two years, which had swollen his thin frame all out of proportion and required an entirely new wardrobe. Worse, he proclaimed himself as the agent of the Emperor's ecclesiastical policy and weakened the Emperor's credibility throughout Latin America by imposing an extraordinary new catechism which contained such bloopers as:

Q: What must one think of those who fail in the duty to the Emperor?
A: According to the Apostle Paul, they are resisting the established order of God himself and thus render themselves worthy of eternal damnation.

Thinking he was currying favor, he introduced the Feast of the nonexistent Saint Caesare. Chay appealed desperately to his mother to intercede with Sylvester. Her flat answer was: "If you had signed with the Morris Office when I had it all set up, you wouldn't be in this fix today."

53

A HORRIFYING FLASH RUMOR spread across the United States that the Sandinistas had kidnapped Lieutenant Colonel North, the presidentially certified national hero, and were preparing to torture him in Managua. Within hours it was established by the State Department that not only were North's lawyers with him but so were his lecture agents. The nation breathed sighs of relief knowing that the gallant young man was safe, and public sympathy swung to the other side.

Thwarted in their plans to invade through Nantucket Island, then having been driven out of Mexico, Nicaragua launched a deadly response. It issued a proclamation which urged all Latin-American countries to withdraw from the American Hemispheric Plan. Only Panama complied—but Queen Brilliana's government stifled it with sanctions, had the chief of its military staff indicted in Oregon, closed all Panamanian banks, and put the country under martial law.

But a gauntlet had been flung down. The Emperor could no longer postpone the invasion which would be the last of the great holy wars.

The Duke of Westport warned the Emperor sternly about trying to wage a war on two fronts. "Even you can't fight the Mexicans on your right flank with the Sandinistas on your left."

"I have no choice," Chay said.

"Don Dudley must abdicate. Mexico must be neutralized."

"Try telling that to my mother."

"If the Mexicans cannot close the pincer on you, then you can take Nicaragua. Let me negotiate. Let me tell Mexico that Dudley goes if they will sign a peace treaty with us."

"Never. Let me show one weakness and the doubts will set in which will prevent me from ruling the world." The psychotropic drugs were really working that morning, and Chay had just come from a protracted session of hypnosis and biofeedback which had had to be administered because pressures were bearing down on him from all sides. He had to maintain his belief in the divine right of kings or utterly let the oligarchy down. A phenomenon happened. The psychiatrists had been administering their mercies to convince Chay that the Sandinistas really wanted peace. Chay still wanted war. The treatments which had been intended to make him agree with Keifetz in all things had somehow failed. Instead he violently opposed Keifetz on the war/peace issue, and insanely, he was trying to interfere with Keifetz's business plan to insert a rider in the Soviet-American treaty which concerned telecommunications/automobiles/computers/beer/infrastructure construction, but which also contained a mild little rider which would give his company "privileged medical merchandising rights," the exclusive agency for the sale of cocaine in the Soviet Union as a solution for the economic problems. It had reached the point where Chay was threatening Keifetz with imprisonment if he didn't have the House of Lords withdraw the proposed treaty.

Keifetz and Grogan fought back savagely through the three staff psychiatrists, but the more they drugged and manipulated Chay, the more opposed to Keifetz he became. The threats that Keifetz/Grogan represented would bring serious handicaps to Chay's conduct of the upcoming Nicaraguan invasion.

At the start of the bitterness Keifetz requested a private interview. The two men met seated on chairs at the center of an outdoor tennis court on the Pink House grounds with the PA system blaring rock music to stifle any attempt at electronic eavesdropping.

Keifetz said, "I have never steered you wrong, Chay. When we met you were a humble major general on old man Winikus's staff with no place to go but where you were. Am I right?"

"Approximately."

"You now have two or three hundred million dollars in number accounts in Switzerland, Hong Kong, and London. I got that for you. Right?"

"Partly."

"Even your mother became a multimillionaire out of all this."

"*Even* my mother?"

"Your brothers and sisters are all kings and queens, right? You are the Emperor. So your family did pretty well out of my advice. Do you hear what I'm telling you, Chay?"

"What do you want, Wamb?"

"Call off this invasion. Invite El Supremo to join you and your father-in-law in a tripartite commission to insure the peace of the world. Then we can all make a buck."

"Wamb, there is something I have been waiting to tell you since the day we met."

"What's that, Chay?"

"Get stuffed."

Diaries of Queen Hedda of Parabrazargiguay, published so many years later, state quite clearly that the Emperor, secretly and publicly, was deeply committed to achieving a lasting peace with the Sandinistas and not, as the Keifetz propaganda machine put it, determined to destroy Nicaragua forever by force of arms. Queen Hedda became aware of the Keifetz conspiracies against Chay sixteen years after his death; two years after Wambly Keifetz had passed on. She came upon the secret correspondence of the Emperor's sister, Queen Brilliana, in a walk-in secret cache at Rossenarra.

Queen Hedda's beautiful, if florid, handwriting, Germanic in cast, is on display at the Biblioteca Nacional in Buenos Aires where a section of the library is devoted to her diaries. There are twenty-nine morocco-bound volumes of these fragments of world history which are really a love story. The volume devoted to the final Nicaraguan conflict is so emotional it cries out to posterity to happen sooner so that Chay could be saved from despair. The diaries are referred to by scholars in universities all over the world as *The Kalbsbratwurst Papers.*

Their essence is found in the following paragraphs: "Both Wambly Keifetz and the Emperor wanted Nicaragua as a friend but for drastically opposing reasons. Keifetz wanted to pave the great land gap between Bolivia and Mexico with waterproof cement so that his gigantic construction company, Bahama Beaver Bonnet, could have the contract to build the longest, widest airfield-highway in world history so that the distribution costs of his wholly controlled cocaine cartel could be reduced drastically. His accounting staff had estimated that he could save 31.6 percent on deliveries to the North American market if those two economies could be effected. An annual net profit of some $9,342,570,131.22 was involved.

"The Emperor, on the other hand, wanted to convince the Nicaraguans in the only way he felt they could be convinced. They had been adversaries in battle throughout the world for twenty-three years, so the Emperor knew they would be conditioned not to listen to any peaceful overtures he would make. Worse, his brother, Pope Sereno I, had poisoned the Sandinista mind against him. Therefore, closely reasoned, Chay wanted to conquer the Nicaraguans, then talk to them in language they would understand and accept, to tell them that if they fought the drug traffic with him, shoulder to shoulder (and they were the most powerful country in Central America), that his country and theirs would not only henceforth live as equals but that he would invite them to join him, with his father-in-law and the USSR, in a Tripartite Commission which would stamp out the narcotics trade throughout the world by threatening to execute the users after the public execution of Wambly Keifetz. Keifetz could not possibly allow Chay to set up such a plan."

The diaries unfortunately were written in German, inasmuch as the native languages of Queen Hedda's subjects were Portuguese and Spanish, and because so much of what she had written in those twenty-nine volumes involved subtleties of emotion and degrees of passion which were entirely personal, and because, in the diaries, she had tried to provide sketches of some of the extraordinary positions she and the Emperor had achieved during coitus hardly without interruptus. Nonetheless, for those who were willing to take the few years necessary to master the German language, the whole story of a battle of titans and of an idyllic love affair is there to be read, giving a new understanding to the Emperor's life which it so richly deserves.

54

THE CRUELEST TWIST of fate's knife was Machenka Appleton's disappearance, which was part of a total blackout of any news concerning the birth of her child. Her father had definitely recovered his good health, according to the American ambassador, Grogan's people, and the world press. There had been no word, no phone call, no acknowledgment of any kind that she and her infant child existed. Chay's entreaties to his father-in-law, through channels and via the hot line, brought the blandest assurances that Machenka was "all right"; that she was "resting nicely." Wholly frustrated, Chay ordered Grogan to plant one of his people as a nanny for the royal issue and this was done. The birth of Chay's son was confirmed, announced by the American news media, then acknowledged in the Soviet press. Nanny Jupp, Grogan's agent, reported through drops that the baby was "amazingly healthy" and "very, very pretty," that his nickname throughout the Kremlin was Medvezhonok, for "Little Bear," and that she would try to have some Polaroid snapshots of the infant smuggled out, but these were lost in the cloak-and-dagger chain of drops, causing the deaths of twenty-three people.

Chay was too absorbed in plans for the invasion to be able to give true attention to the problems of separation from his son. And he had his mother to annoy him, Dudley and Sylvester to worry him, and constant threats from Keifetz. As a former monarch, Dudley had opened a popular Mexican restaurant in Laredo, Texas, a border town, called Olé Mole and was doing a booming business. Sylvester had excommunicated the entire Mexican nation because they had failed his brother.

All Chay wanted was to bring the Sandinistas to their knees so that he could help them to their feet again and unite the world in smashing Keifetz's cocaine cartel. All Keifetz and Brill wanted was to stop Chay. All Serena wanted was money and total power over her children, in that order.

In late April 1997, the Emperor showed his terrible strength by massing 1.4 million troops on Nicaragua's Honduran border, having sent his former vice president and batman, Mallard Tompkins, to lay down the bribes which would open the gates of Honduras to American troops. He concentrated the power of an enormous armada of fighting ships—carriers, dreadnoughts, submarines, divisions of Marines, and the Naval Air Arm—off Managua in the Pacific and along all the Costa de Mosquitos in the Caribbean.

Simultaneously, Eddie Grogan's people and CIA money circulated throughout the Nicaraguan cities, spreading fear, promising terror and starvation if the villages supported the Emperor's troops. From Queen Brilliana's realm wholly surrounding Nicaragua, more heinous threats were spread by Keifetz's people; influence was bought, and in the course of things, the conduits for increased narcotics movement north to the retail outlets were greatly strengthened.

There was extraordinary cause for Chay to worry: 690,000 of the Emperor's best troops were tied down in Mexico. The main body of his Order of Battle was not North Americans but 200,000 Argentinians, 291,000 Brazilians, and 603,000 from Uruguay and Paraguay. A large percentage of these were Indians who could not be said to be drilled in modern warfare.

His strike forces assembled, the Emperor called an Inter-Hemispheric Conference at Tegucigalpa, Honduras, to confer with his clients—kings and queens—in an attempt to overawe El Supremo while American food and gasoline depots were established by Grogan's people along the line of march to Managua. El Supremo mocked him by announcing to the world that King Dudley had had to leave the management of his Mexican restaurant in Queen Frieda's hands so he could attend the conference.

Little cruelties notwithstanding, the Emperor put on a magnificent show in Tegucigalpa for the assembled international television cameras: formal receptions, balls featuring the minuet in a cross with the rhumba, three great banquets, ecumenical state masses, operas, and a boar hunt—all of it done before a worldwide television audience rated at 68.3—almost 70 million viewers—with a resultant short-time billing of advertising revenue for cable and the networks just in excess of $156 million.

Throughout the pageantry, the Emperor conducted himself with courtly amiability, as if he hadn't a care in the world. He rode slowly through the streets of Tegucigalpa in an open car as thousands cheered, not in truth or reality but only on the sound-tracks of the broadcast tapes. The crowds themselves, under the rifles of the Emperor's troops, stood by sullenly as he passed. For all the bread and circuses, he was no longer popular with the crowds; and not only in Honduras. At home, Chay's projected invasion had become a fearsomely unpopular thing due to the growing effectiveness of a $31 million public relations campaign which Keifetz had underwritten and a (temporary) drop in the supermarket prices for cocaine, which brought out gigantic antiwar rallies, widely covered by television. No one was able to shut out the endless chant by stockbrokers, investment bankers, and com-modity dealers of "Hey, hey! Little Chay! How many kids will you kill today?"

55

T HE GREAT AMERICAN REFORMER, Hilary Hazelwood Jackson, then nine years old and living with her mother who was attached to the Permanent Governing Party which represented Queen Brilliana in Honduras, recalled in her autobiography, writ-ten forty years later, that she had run to her mother to tell her that if she came quickly to the window she could see the Emperor who was about to pass. She wrote that her mother replied, "I shall withdraw to the kitchen, for I have no interest in seeing a man who intends to crush a poor nation."

This passage revealed the effectiveness of Keifetz's extraor-dinary public relations campaign against the Emperor. For eight years, Ronald Reagan and little Colonel North had drummed into the souls of the American people that Nicaragua was America's blood enemy of all time, far more threatening than Hitler had been, easily replacing The Evil Empire, and yet, with a mere $31 million budget, Wambly Keifetz had been able to turn the public emotions around, proving how truly awesome the power of television had become.

Negative comment found its way into the world press. The Duke of Westport was quoted in *Foreign Affairs*, then re-quoted in *People* magazine, as saying: "There are painfully uneasy expressions on the faces of the courtiers and the generals alike who have assembled here in Tegucigalpa at the Emperor's bidding. The overall feeling, as I read it, is: Oliver North never declared war on Nicaragua and he had far greater resources and perhaps even better reasons than those of the Emperor."

Jaime Arias Hombria y Acebal, El Supremo of Nicaragua, made a simple announcement to the television cameras. Unrolling a large map of his country, he said, "I am convinced that Caesare Appleton is a great general and that his armies are the best trained in the world." He tapped the map. "But the mountains and jungles are our comfort. If my people withdraw, taking all food and fuel with them; if the mountains, the jungle and the terrible heat and the unrest in the United States work for me, then these will defend Nicaragua. These will have the last word."

Chay remained at Tegucigalpa until the 29th of May, expecting El Supremo to plead for peace. On May 30 he issued another of his stirring orders to the television cameras, saying, "Let us march!"

For the first time a member of his own family (actively) betrayed him. His sister, Queen Berengaria of the Incas, refused to march. Wambly Keifetz had sent two of Grogan's people to talk to her, promising her a 1.2 percent increase in her share of the cocaine street price (a share which amounted to $1,137,697.53 a week, on average) if she would do what the people of the United States hoped she would do—refuse to fight this unjust war. Had her armies come up the west coast of South America, into Costa Rica then forward into Nicaragua, it could have made a great difference. The war would have ended quite differently. Chay later claimed that the Sandinistas' southern flank would have been at the mercy of "a small Incan patrol."

Keifetz had Grogan's people offer a similar deal to King Jonathan and Queen Hedda, not as good, but one which would have made them about $3,723,871.35 a month, on average. Jonathan understood better than anyone in the Appleton family that one couldn't have too much money so he was inclined to go along with the Keifetz offer and withhold Parabrazargiguayan troops from the Nicaraguan conflict, but his wife, Queen Hedda, refused to let him be swayed. She presented a somewhat shaky argument but she carried the day. "Suppose Chay is wrong," she said, "and he probably is wrong. He is entitled to the luxury of his mistakes like the rest of us." Indirectly that caused her husband's death, but kings must die and Jonathan had had a good run of it.

There was no question of buying Dudley off. Neither Keifetz nor Chay wanted him, but Chay got him because Serena was so insistent.

Brilliana betrayed him, but Chay never knew it. She declared neutrality, then as a full partner with her husband in the cocaine entitlement, she worked covertly throughout Central America barring and blocking Chay's path wherever his armies turned.

By bailing Sylvester out of his mistakes in Zurich, Keifetz persuaded the Pope to condemn the Emperor's war. Ten thousand (ecumenical) clergymen cried out in horror from the pulpits of the world, urging all people to withdraw their support—moral, financial, or political, if they had ever given it—and asking them to send money to the Sandinistas to defend their homes from tyranny. Pope Sereno bestowed his blessing upon the efforts of El Supremo's troops by satellite from Rome, including plenary indulgences for all the Nicaraguan troops without fee or charges (directly).

56

ON JUNE 10, 1997, the Emperor invaded Nicaragua. General of the Armies Benito Juarez Bennett held the left flank. Prince Jonathan held the right. King Dudley was named Corps Commander of the greatest array of tanks ever to attempt to penetrate a dense tropical jungle. The Emperor took The Point.

Dudley had equipped himself elaborately. His wardrobe included 11 kinds of colorful uniforms, trunks with civilian clothes (for the occasional incognito rendezvous with a gay senorita) and hunting uniforms; 73 shirts (he was rather a perspirer); 34 pairs of shoes; and all of it kept up to the mark by 2 valets and requiring 6 caterpillar half-track supply wagons to be moved along with him. One of these contained his tents, dinner services, rugs and carpets, bedding, personal communications equipment such as his FAX machine to keep in touch with the grosses of the restaurant in Laredo, and hundreds of cases of Spanish champagne to be used as gifts for the natives.

The Viceroy of Canada, Sir John DeWitt Kullers, insisting upon retaining his military rank as sergeant, commanded combined zambos of a Sumo, Carib, Ramaquie, and Mosquito Indian division which had been formed from scratch and which Kullers now had up to fittest fighting form.

The Emperor rode in the cockpit of a scout vehicle, fully visible, at the head of the Army's Central Group. He was dressed in the battle fatigues of a sergeant of ¼ Infantry, wearing his famous black homburg crossways upon his head.

In the American popular imagination, over the thirteen years since Ronald Reagan had invented it and Colonel North had made it famous throughout Iran, Nicaragua had become a gigantic country, about the size of China, having a population of nearly 22 million people, all bloodthirsty fighters and dangerous Communists.

Actually, it was about the size of the State of Wisconsin, and before the dramatic development of new breeding techniques which had raised the population, it was the least populated of all Central American countries with a density of less than forty people per square mile, most of them registered Democrats. Nine-tenths of its people were crowded together in one relatively small section of the country, in the hot lowlands, despite the fact that most of the rest of it was covered with mountains and had a temperate, refreshing climate. More than half was covered with jungles and forests, and this trackless region was the area through which the Emperor's main attack would have to pass to reach Managua.

It was a pity that naval bombardments made for such monotonous television because Managua, the capital city, seat of government, was directly off the Pacific coast of the country. The naval guns and missiles could have wiped it out in no time, but that would have been pretty dull stuff to wedge in between television commercials, so as Reagan's Contras had done before them, Chay's troops came in from the north to sustain the best-running day-to-day television pictures.

The strongest characteristic of Nicaragua has been its geography. The Pacific zone of the country is occupied by a triangular region of mountains. One side of the triangle extends from northeast to southwest along the Honduran border, the second runs from Honduras to Costa Rica, and the third side extends from north to south through the center of the country. The rainy season, May to November, lasts for months and there is no well-defined dry season. This makes for heavy slogging with heavy equipment, through jungles and up and down mountains, in an area inhabited by various sorts of reptiles including crocodiles, snakes, lizards, and turtles.

The country's National Guard served as both army and police force and was composed of about 53,000 men, swelling from a force of 9,200 before Ronald Reagan discovered what a threat the country was to his people.

When the Imperial forces had crossed the Cordellera Entre Rios and had passed over the Cordellera Isabella, approaching the town of Matagalpa—which was in the Darien mountain range from which the bold Balboa had gazed upon the Pacific Ocean— Wambly Keifetz summoned Eddie Grogan to a power breakfast meeting in a suite at the Mansion on Turtle Creek in Dallas.

He didn't waste any time. "Chay is moving toward the center of Nicaragua now, Ed," he said. "It's time you got your people moving."

"They're in position, Mr. Keifetz."

"I've got a checklist somewhere." Keifetz fumbled in his pockets and pulled out a long white sheet. "Got yours?"

"Check, Chief." Grogan lifted a clipboard.

"You have the locations of his gasoline depots between Matagalpa and Honduras?"

"Two million gallons of gas, nine locations, so he can fill his armor and the supply vehicles on the way in and on the way out."

"And that goes for food and water storage as well, right?"

"Check, Chief."

"Now—let me be sure—your people will ignite or dynamite or otherwise destroy those depots behind him as he goes in, so when they're looking for food, and fuel, and water on the way out, it won't be there."

"Check. And we pour three tons of refined sugar into the gas lines of all supply and personnel trucks and into the ambulances."

"So by the time he gets to Managua, if he ever gets near there, nothing he has will be able to move because everything he has except the men is mechanized."

"Check, Chief."

"No matter how far he gets, he'll have to walk across those Marrabios mountains with Sandinista bullets nipping at his drawers." Keifetz sighed. "Jesus, all those fine young boys."

"Yeah."

"The list again. The naval task force magazines on both coasts are carrying nothing but blank shells?"

"Just like you ordered, Mr. Keifetz. They'll make a big noise but that's all."

"And the mess sergeants will dope those Marines before they can land at Managua?"

"Check, Chief."

"Little Colonel North himself couldn't have faked it better. Now, just one more thing. I'd like you to have two good riflemen to take out Brother Dudley and Brother Jonathan."

"Why not?"

"I offered Jonny a grand opportunity and he saw fit to turn it down. It could cost us respect if he isn't paid off for disloyalty."

"Consider it handled, Mr. Keifetz."

"You should hear my mother-in-law on Dudley. You'd think he'd invented money. Not that he'll be easy because he'll stay inside that tank."

"We have ways, Mr. Keifetz."

"Chay is going to have a lot to account for when he meets his Maker. Did you talk to your chemical warfare people about the tanked drinking water for Chay's troops?"

"It's all set, Chief. Malaria virus and amoebic dysentery. Cheaper than bullets."

"But—remember. The tricky part of the drill is to make sure that the media people don't drink the wrong water. They've got to be up and at 'em to cover Chay's retreat so the folks back home will know who stepped in the cowshit." He leaned forward and gripped Grogan's arm. "And keep that stuff away from Chay's water. He's got to get back here to face trial."

57

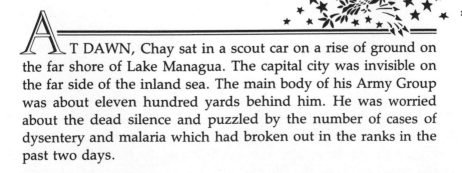

AT DAWN, Chay sat in a scout car on a rise of ground on the far shore of Lake Managua. The capital city was invisible on the far side of the inland sea. The main body of his Army Group was about eleven hundred yards behind him. He was worried about the dead silence and puzzled by the number of cases of dysentery and malaria which had broken out in the ranks in the past two days.

A rider on a white horse came galloping from the rear. "Sire!" he shouted.

Chay stared at him. "What are you doing on that horse, Lieutenant?"

"The advance has broken down, Sire. No gasoline. We haven't seen a fuel reserve caisson for over a hundred miles, sir."

"Broken down?" The Emperor turned in his seat and looked behind him.

"Everything is halted for about eighteen miles back, Sire," the lieutenant said. "About halfway along the road to León."

"What the hell is this?"

"More than half the men are down, sir. They dropped where they were standing or they couldn't get up at all. Dysentery and malaria, sir."

"*Half* the men?"

"About four hundred thousand men, Sire."

"That many men are down and you tell me about gasoline? Where are the Army Group commanders?"

"That's the bad news, sir."

"The *bad* news?"

"King Jonathan and King Dudley are dead, Sire."

"*Whaaaaaat?*" He thought of Serena. What was he going to tell Serena?

"King Jonathan was shot in his sleep, sir."

"In his sleep? In his tent? In the middle of an Army?"

"King Dudley caught it in the latrine, Sire. If it hadn't been for him having to go to the latrine, he would have been safe in his tank."

"Get going," Chay told his driver. "Get me back there."

The driver turned the ignition key but the motor wouldn't turn over. He tried it four times. "We're out of gas," he said. "I figured we'd be filling up before we ever got here."

"Get down," the Emperor said to the lieutenant. He was numbed by the news of his brothers but he got up on the horse, his short legs coming to about the halfway mark on the mare's belly. He pulled at the reins and kicked his heels into the horse's sides. They took off with Chay holding on to his crossways homburg with one hand while he tried to slow the horse down with the other, knowing that he had lost the game but not sure how it had happened—but knowing it had to be Keifetz. Keifetz and that filthy Grogan. Murdering an army was nothing to a man who had blown up the entire city of Washington.

Nine hundred and eleven thousand American troops died of dysentery or malaria or were left for dead. The remnants of the Imperial Army limped and dragged itself for almost three hundred miles to the Honduran border, through fetid jungles and over mountain ranges. The Emperor rode the white horse in the vanguard, his homburg low on his head, his right hand stuffed into the fly of his tunic, his shoulders hunched far forward in fatigue and despair. No effort had been made to bury the dead. The two kings were wrapped in canvas and thrown over the backs of a pack horse, but after the third day, they had to be buried in unmarked graves.

Three guerrilla armies blocked the advance and harassed the rear of Chay's ever-decreasing force, picking off stragglers and slaughtering the sick while CIA television crews shot thousands of feet of tape of the first absolute defeat American forces had suffered in the forty-odd years of fighting the Sandinista foe all over the world.

By the time the deadly retreat from Managua had reached the town of San Rafael del Norte, they had fought three major defensive battles, had lost 204,000 men, while 563,000 dropped with disease and died where they had dropped.

Only 26,212 men out of an Expeditionary Force of 1,400,000 reached Honduras to be transported by plane back to Army hospitals in San Antonio. Of these, 8,204 died in Texas hospitals.

Sergeant John DeWitt Kullers, Viceroy of Canada, sat holding his Indian troops in tight discipline along the Mosquito Coast, waiting for orders. Their culture wouldn't let them drink the Army's water.

58

THE HOUSE OF LORDS, which stood at the corner of Commerce and Akard Streets in Dallas, was a modern functional legislative edifice. It had a swimming pool, a gymnasium, a billiards hall, a splendid genealogical library, high-speed elevators, and a deliberating chamber which was a replica of the best features of the British Upper House, the Spanish Cortes, and the Japanese Diet.

The Woolsack, David, Lord Davis, sat at the far end in front of the throne which was, on this day of extraordinary session, ominously unoccupied. Benches for members ran on either side of the large room. They were cailed benches but were individual, upholstered, red leather swivel chairs, each with a built-in microphone and an air-conditioned back. The richness of spirit of the great room was upheld by an extraordinary tapestry hung under three semicircular windows which showed the Duke of Brooklyn, Beniamiamo Camardi, signing the great trade concordat with Outer Mongolia.

On this special morning a series of temporary galleries had been suspended ingeniously above the benches for the accommodation of television gofers, and print pools which would record the proceedings for history and spread the truth of justice throughout the world.

On the north side of the building were the offices of the Black Rod and other offices of both legislative bodies as allowed by the Constitution of the Imperial American Republic. Dormitories for the seventy-one witnesses who would be called had been built at the Fairgrounds, but these witnesses would be transported, by Dallas Area Rapid Transit buses, as required, to the Upper House at the beginning of each day of the trial. Taco Loco had been awarded the national advertising rights on all special printed material which would be circulated throughout the chamber, items which would assume great value to collectors in the decades to come. With Häagen-Dazs and Budweiser, Taco Loco would supply all food for the witnesses.

At a very early hour on October 13, 1998, workmen had fenced the two-block area around the House of Lords and built high-rise bleachers in the Sponsors' Zone within the courtyard to seat Gold Card members of both the Republican and Democratic Parties. High-cost celebrity boxes had been built facing both the courtyard and the interior chamber of the House of Lords, which held their own wet bars, bidets, and kitchenettes, as well as their own piped-in television systems, which had cost the companies entertaining clients therein $750,000 for the duration of the trial. It would be from these celebrity boxes that Miss Liz Wantonberg, Arnold Schwarzenegger, Oprah Winfrey, Sylvester Stallone, the ex-Empress Ulyssa, the Gabor sisters, the Mosbachers, the Emperor's mother, Donald Trump, the Pope, Morton Downey, Jr., and Wambly Keifetz (to name the most prominent out of dozens more) would watch the proceedings.

A strong body of Foot Guards was posted at all passages leading to the juncture of Akard and Commerce Streets which were closed off from the rest of the city by heavy steel and timber partitions. At nine o'clock, a troop of Life Guards rode into the courtyard and formed a mounted square around its perimeter.

Dense crowds lined the approaches to the House all along the way from the downtown area to the Pink House in University Park, 4.3 miles to the north, taking up positions to watch His Imperial Majesty pass. At half past nine the entire line of the procession was occupied by 1,730,000 people (police count) who had traveled to Dallas from thirty-one states of the Union and from seventeen foreign countries to witness history. Windows and rooftops all along the way were filled. Hundreds of buses were parked in side streets. By 9:20 the line of march was one long, solid human line, six deep.

At 8:35 A.M. Chay was in the final meeting with his counsel, Gordon Manning, the Duke of Westport, who assured him that what was about to happen in the House of Lords would be entirely ceremonial. "It is being staged to give people a high sense of justice and to pay off the television industry for their cooperation throughout this wretched affair."

"I hadn't noticed that they'd been cooperative," Chay said. "Unless they were cooperating with Keifetz."

"They wouldn't dare, Sire."

"Leave me, Your Grace," he said to Manning. "I must think."

Chay made his plan. He would consent to go through the motions of this ceremonial in the House of Lords to win the television people back to his side. To refuse to go through with it would alienate them forever because it would mean hundreds of millions of dollars of commercial time left unsold. But when the wretched business was all over, he would send for Grogan who would be made to understand that he worked for Chay and no one else, and Keifetz would be picked up in the dark of night and sent off to the refractory chromite mines in the Philippines. It would be hard cheese for Brill but it had to be done.

He picked up the hot line on impulse and when Moscow answered he asked to be put through to the Empress Machenka. To his astonishment, the call went right through.

"Machenka?"

"Yes?"

"Chay."

"Of course it's Chay. Is this the cold line?"

"How is the baby?"

"Perfect. Absolutely perfect. He looks just like Daddy."

Chay's heart soared. "Like me?"

"No, no. Like my father. How have you been, Chay? We were so sorry to read about your troubles."

"Are you and the baby coming back to Dallas?"

"That's still up in the air, I'm afraid. There's been some trouble with our exit visas."

"Oh. Can't your father do anything?"

"I don't know. I mean it's too soon to say."

"Oh. Well. It really is a mess, isn't it?"

"I'll say. Oh, damn, Chay. It's feeding time. I've got to go. Bye, now."

At 9:03 A.M. His Imperial Majesty, the Emperor of the American Republic, the only reigning monarch to be enthroned by a legislative rider within a Pay Raise Enabling Act, descended the great staircase at the Pink House on the arm of his brother, the Pope, because that was what their mother had wanted the television viewers of the world to see—fraternal harmony between two great men.

Each of the brothers wore a gold-starred mourning band on his left arm, signifying the deaths of their siblings who had died in combat on a foreign shore while fighting for freedom. The Emperor and His Holiness were joined at the foot of the stairs by their two sisters, the Queens Brilliana and Berengaria, and by the widows of the two fallen heros, Queen Hedda of Parabrazargiguay and Queen Frieda of the Olé Mole restaurant in Laredo. Off to one side, under a heavy veil but making notes steadily for a series on the trial which she had already sold to the *National Enquirer* was the bereaved Empress Mum. In a scrawling longhand she wrote: "The Emperor looks absolutely awful as if the terrible guilt he carries wherever he goes has taken from him any possibility of ever being able to sleep again." The photo opportunity lasted until 9:47 A.M.

The Emperor left the main portal of the Pink House and stepped alone into the gold latticework tumbril whose wires rode just high enough to protect him from any assassin's bullet and whose lacy roof was designed to see through but which would protect him from snipers overhead. The ingenious enclosure almost but not quite protected him from the cameras, but through its fine bulletproof mesh the Emperor could be seen sitting on a turkey-red silk moiré wing chair, staring backward at where he had come from, wearing a neutral uniform of a very senior Postal Service officer. He rapped on the floor of the tumbril with the heavy scabbard of his sword to signify that he was ready to go.

The tumbril was drawn by six caparisoned bay Clydesdale horses. Its coachmen, postilions, and footmen were habited in rich costumes of scarlet and gold with purple velvet facings, and black velvet caps of state, all of it embroidered with the golden bees of the House of Appleton.

As the tumbril was pulled through the high main gate of the palace grounds, the cry of "Hats off!" rang out through the square. A long line of stretched Rolls-Royce Phantom VI limousines, three to a city block, bearing royal crests, followed the tumbril in procession down Turtle Creek Lane, along University Boulevard, down Hillcrest into Cole then McKinney, along the historic run to West Akard.

The mob seemed drunk with admiration for their sovereign or perhaps just plain drunk. As the tumbril approached Commerce Street they were shouting hoarsely, demanding that the line of soldiers present arms as the Emperor passed. When the troops acknowledged him smartly the uproar of approval was almost hysterical.

At 10:30 A.M. the tumbril passed into the courtyard of the House of Lords and the great gates clanged closed behind it. The barriers broke. Gold Card members, every one of them a registered aristocrat, rushed in to surround the tumbril. Two women clutched the forelegs of the horses so tightly that they could not be disengaged. Men and women, distinguished citizens each of whose annual (declared) income exceeded four million dollars a year, attempted to squeeze their fingers through the latticework of the golden cage to touch Chay, if only to be able to say over the decades to come that they had touched him. Policemen and soldiers were swept away by the force of celebrities on all sides who were shouting, "The Emperor! The Emperor!"

The Life Guards moved in, riding their heavy horses. Foot Guards formed a square around His Imperial Majesty who sat calmly inside the golden mesh. A lane was formed through which the horses, servitors, and Emperor could pass.

The Emperor stepped down from the shining mobile cell and entered the House of Lords with the Black Rod, Sir Richard Gallagher, taking his right hand, and Gordon Manning, Duke of Westport, the Emperor's defense counsel, taking his left. The Duke wore a black silk gown and a white wig. He was solemn with a dignity which exceeded all understanding.

The Emperor was led into the chamber during the call-over of the roll of peers. All peers stood as the Emperor entered. He was asked to be seated at the table for the defense which faced the Woolsack. Lord Manning was at his right.

The Prime Minister, Sir William Richert, introduced a Bill of Pains and Penalties, an act for punishing a person of exalted rank without resort to an ordinary trial. As with any other bill, it had to be passed by Lords and Commons but, in this case, would

avoid the judgmental considerations of the Sovereign. The justification for a Bill of Pains and Penalties was that it could be used
where proofs of wrongdoing were unlikely to secure a conviction
due to the universal acceptance of the divine right of kings by the
television-struck American people.

The Bill enacted that the Emperor "shall be deprived of his
title, shall be punished for the crime of mass murder of 900,000
of his subjects through his determinations to carry out a reckless
adventure in a manner and at a time which counseled certain
failure, and did recklessly and heedlessly plunge his nation into
a war of attrition for which he and his armies were ill-prepared.
As due punishment, if found guilty of this murderous treason,
this Emperor, Caesare Appleton, shall be exiled to a place far, far
from his home to perish, in due time, of loneliness."

Chay looked blankly at Gordon Manning. "You call this entirely ceremonial?" he asked.

Lord Manning sprang to his feet crying outrage. "The deg-
radation this procedure brings," he said in part, "not merely at
home, but abroad, completes the picture of the Peers of the United
States, the noble families and the descendants of heroic ances-
tors—pillars of the state—who are allowing themselves to become
the tools of one loathsome group of the hateful enemies of our
great nation, who would bring to disaster the greatest hero of our
time. Is such the legitimate duty of a peer of Parliament? Is this
the mode by which the lawgivers of the greatest country in the
world should be employed?"

Manning was shouted down.

The second part of the Bill abrogated Imperial rule in the
United States and established the machinery for the repudiation
of the constitutional amendment which had created Imperial rule,
in its nationhood, territories, mandates, and possessions. This was
highly controversial. It presupposed that, because their Emperor,
Caesare I, had been found wanting, an entire system of government by divine right should be abolished. Moreover it took that
supposition as if the nobles and the American people wanted to
abandon the royalty which had exalted their history and had given
their lives real meaning.

At the end of the reading the reaction from the Peers was so
shocked, so outraged, that before proceeding further with meeting

due process for His Imperial Majesty, the House had to be calmed in a tumultuous, even violent, attempt which took forty-two minutes until Wambly Keifetz—a leading public servant who, although he had once served as Director, and even though his wife was a Queen, had steadfastly refused to accept any title other than that of Grand Huntsman—was summoned from his Celebrity Box to address the House from its floor under the relentless eyes of the assembled television cameras.

He spoke in humble spirit. "As God is my witness," he said, his eyes welling over with tears, "I have admired, nay loved, Caesare Appleton, as a man, as my Emperor, and as a military commander, from the day I met him—which was soon after the terrible incident which wiped out our nation's capital almost ten years ago. With the snap of a finger, the pop of an outlawed bomb, our hallowed democracy—as we had known it—was made extinct. We tried to revive it, God knows. We gave heart and soul to a government of the people, by the people, and for the people. We outlawed abortion and brought prayer and the Pledge of Allegiance to our schoolrooms in a struggle to bring order to wherever chaos had been triumphant. We had the holding action of the directorate. Then the people called out for Caesare Appleton to serve as their Chairman and CEO and—after his great victory over the forces of darkness in Australia—after he fought his way home through the adulation of the peoples of Asia and this country— he was exalted by his fellow Americans by an Act of Congress which provided for a ratified constitutional amendment—and the citizens of the United States of America elevated Caesare Appleton to the supreme, the total authority of Emperor of the American Republic—a station too high—in an atmosphere too rarified for any human being to sustain—as we should have known well before we allowed it to happen. Alas, he went mad with the power of all of it and caused the deaths not only of his two brothers but of over 900,000 of our finest and best boys and girls who had served us in battle.

"But it taught us something! It taught us America was not meant to have emperors or kings—as it was not meant to have dictators. We are the cradle of democracy, milords and ladies. We put our trust in God who put His trust in our people, all of the people. As our television cameras feed truth to the screens at every hearth in the land, recording every fact of our lives and holding this mirror of immortality up before us, they tell us what we have always known, which is: Here you are, people of America, in the glory of your history. Therefore, you must govern yourselves as you have from the beginning. Do not let others do this for you. Look into the mirror of television. Think. Govern yourselves and prosper." He sank back emotionally (and intellectually) spent.

The entire House stood to applaud him. The Emperor left the chamber with Lord Manning and twelve members of the Seventy-fifth Rangers who were his Life Guards. On the sixth day, in the withdrawing room, when oligarch after oligarch had risen to denounce him before his peers, the Emperor said to Lord Manning, "When will we have our turn at bat, Your Grace?"

"With your gracious permission, Sire, you will be sworn in as the principal witness for the defense, then we will bring up a battery of witnesses to support your accusation of conspiracy."

"How long will the trial last?"

"Eight or nine weeks. But, in the end, we shall have Wambly Keifetz at the point of our sword and we shall skewer him."

59

AT THE BEGINNING of the third week of the trial, the chief prosecutor rose to his feet, bowed slightly to the Emperor, then began to speak to the House. He was Lord Mayers, Earl of Manhattan, who had, only eight days before, sent Wilfred "Giggles" Bowner to the electric chair. His record of convictions stood at the bone-chilling score of thirty-one executed, three life sentences. He had a hostile manner which bore down relentlessly upon his victims.

"Your Imperial Highness," he drawled insolently, creating dipthongs where none had existed, attenuating each sound so that all of them came to the ears as a sneer, "with respect, I have a few questions." He snorted indignantly.

"Sire," he continued, "as the world knows, you have fought the Sandinistas all over the world but never on their home grounds, as it were. Never inside Nicaragua. Why is that?"

Manning was on his feet. "To have fought in Nicaragua would have violated the Reagan Doctrine! Worse, it would have left the gallant Contra leaders penniless in Miami!"

"Your Imperial Highness," Mayers said smoothly. "Your learned counsel has answered my question succinctly. Why was it then that at this later date, you chose to violate this sacred doctrine?"

"To bring peace," the Emperor said simply.

"Are you saying that after eighteen years of protecting Reagan from scandal, his own incompetence, his indifference, or worse, by taking the public's mind off his failures by invoking the threat of Sandinista hordes overrunning this country—that you deliberately threw away that political advantage in a vain attempt to secure peace for the world?"

The Emperor stared at him scornfully then spat directly on the floor of the House of Lords, at the prosecutor's feet, while forty-seven taping cameras recorded each sight and sound from the gallery.

Lord Mayers ignored the imperial rudeness. "I put it to you," he said, "that you gave no thought to any permanent peace when you planned the invasion of Nicaragua, but that the operation was designed for your personal monetary gain."

The House shuddered. A camera operator said loudly over the silence that ensued, "Holy shit!"

Mayers fired the next question rapidly. "Do you deny plotting with your brothers Dudley and Jonathan Appleton to sell 910,000 tons of gasoline and almost all of the entire supply of the drinking water intended for your troops, forcing those troops to drink contaminated water?"

There was a collective cry of horror.

The prosecutor stared at the Emperor coldly. "I say almost all because an ample supply of pure, safe, distilled drinking water was always on hand for use by you and your brothers. Do you dare to deny that charge, sir?"

"I deny it most emphatically," the Emperor said.

"Do you also deny that—following a falling out with your brothers, Dudley and Jonathan Appleton, over the split—as the criminals say—from the sale of the gasoline and the water to the Central American black market that you, in your raging greed, ordered the murders of your brothers, Dudley and Jonathan Appleton?"

Lord Manning climbed wearily to his feet. "I ask," he said wearily, "that these cheap tricks—these preposterous allegations—be stricken from the record."

"My lords," the Earl of Manhattan thundered, "those questions represent the basis of the government's case, and the most substantial credibility of each of them will be upheld by the testimony of unassailable witnesses."

The Woolsack, Lord Davis, ordered that the Emperor answer the Lord Prosecutor's questions.

Not until eight days later was the defense called to present its case. Lord Manning called the Emperor to testify. An imposing array of military and civilian experts backed his claims, and although hostile witnesses had testified that 910,000 tons of gasoline had suddenly appeared on the Guatemalan black market immediately following the fuel breakdown of the tanks and supply vehicles, to be sold for the benefit of Nicaraguan guerrillas, Chay said flatly that neither he nor his brothers had any knowledge of those transactions; that each of his brother's commands had depended upon a sure supply of gasoline.

He testified that he had had tests made of the drinking water which had infected his troops and that all of it was found to contain active bacterially induced viruses in an amount which was hundreds of times the amount which could be found in any naturally contaminated water. He produced samples of the water. He produced affidavits from the Department of Public Health as to the incredible bacteria count in the water. He said the water had been tampered with by saboteurs.

Lord Manning called epidemiologists and military historians to testify. When their qualifications had been admitted, they told the House that never before in the history of armies, wars, and plagues had so many men been so mortally affected simultaneously as to cause such a number of deaths.

Officers and men who had served on the military staffs of the kings, Dudley and Jonathan, could conceive of no motive or person who would murder either monarch, least of all the Emperor. But the cross-examination by the State of each of those arguments was so conclusive as to be devastating.

The State, represented by Edward Mulhaus Grogan, Attorney General and operating head of the Central Intelligence Agency, produced written records of heavy trafficking in Guatemalan and Central American black markets in the form of receipts signed by Dudley and Jonathan Appleton; merchants testified that they had done business directly with Dudley and Jonathan Appleton who had represented themselves as being agents of the Emperor in the sale of the gasoline and the drinking water.

Heavily accented Iranian moderates and Libyan scientists who had strings of degrees after their names and who had been granted immunity by the government in exchange for their testimony told the House, under oath, how both Dudley and Jonathan Appleton, acting, they had said, on behalf of the Emperor, had purchased enormous quantities of both malaria and amoebic dysentery viruses from the international terrorist supplies. Although no mention was made by either Appleton as to the uses to which the viruses would be put, all testifying scientists stated that the brothers had bought enough bacteria "to kill an army."

Bank officers of the Uptown & Oriental Savings and Loan Association of Hong Kong testified and submitted photocopies of bank records to the account of Caesare Appleton in the amount of $2,674,591 in the form of bank checks drawn against the accounts of the very Guatemalan black marketeers who had testified to their puchase of gasoline stocks from Dudley and Jonathan Appleton.

Chay stared at Eddie Grogan across the House. Chay's expression was blank, his face was drained of blood. He could not believe that he had heard what he was hearing. He had listened to Grogan make charge after charge against him and had seen him produce perjurer after perjurer. He had made Grogan. He had given him the power. He had even invested Grogan with the title and estates of the Earl of Canarsie, and all the while Grogan had been smiling that awful shit-eater's smile because he had been Keifetz's man. No compassionate crap like the refractory chromite mines for Grogan. He had to be blown away.

Chay struggled to his feet, swaying. He held tightly to the edge of the polished mahogany table. "What we have heard here today, my lords, are terrible lies," he said, wondering where the key cameras were positioned. "Enemies of the people are determined to railroad me. Guard! Guard!" he cried out feebly, falling backward into his chair. He had to be assisted out of the chamber.

In the withdrawing room, he ordered everyone out, holding Lord Manning by the wrist. "Get John Kullers in here," he said, "then get out of my sight."

"We were betrayed, Sire."

"Betrayed?" the Emperor said. "I suppose so. But, as you said that first morning, it was only ceremonial."

Chay had to wait for almost ten minutes before Lord Kullers was produced. "Sergeant Kullers reporting for duty. Sah!"

Chay motioned him closer. Kullers bent over him. "Do Grogan," Chay whispered in his ear.

60

TWO NIGHTS LATER, at an elaborate affair for the entire diplomatic corps at the Pink House, which senior members of the government had decided not to cancel in order to convey the impression that Chay's trial was not the catastrophe it seemed to be, as Lord Grogan was standing at the top of the marble main staircase chatting with Herbert Mitgang, the Swiss Ambassador, and Dame Graciela Winkelreid, a young officer of a Guards battalion stooped over behind Lord Grogan to retrieve Dame Graciela's dropped handkerchief just as Lord Kullers passed the group. Lord Kullers bumped into Mitgang, lost his balance, lurched sideways and crashed into Lord Grogan. Grogan was toppled sideways and backwards over the stooped form of the young subaltern. A scream went up.

Grogan was a frail and somewhat elderly man so his careening, eccentric course down the marble stairway, head over heels, together with his shocking outcries, produced a rather awful noise until the terrible sound was made worse as he slammed into the statue of Spiro T. Agnew which guarded the foot of the stairway forty-six feet below. The statue, a large, rose-quartz, fig-leafed nude, stood about nine feet tall. As Grogan came pitching into it with the accumulated velocity of a headlong roll down the fifty-six steps, his grotesquely folding and unfolding body pin-wheeling outlandishly, it slammed into the statue, which had feet of clay, toppling it over to fall precisely on top of the broken, even pulped form of the man who had been such a part of the destiny of the American Hemispheric Plan. The instant realization of who he was and what he had meant added an appalling perspective to the dozens of distinguished witnesses, to whom all thought of any possibility of culpability by the Emperor had never occurred.

Lord Grogan lay where he had landed, as crumpled as a used Kleenex under the 1,400 pounds of rose-quartz. He lay there as if he had never had any bones, as if he had always existed as the spatter which now sprawled in such disorderly disarray. His eyes were wide open in horror, but when the Surgeon General of the United States reached his side (it was that gala a reception), he was quite dead.

In the ninth week of the trial, after due deliberation by the Lords, Caesare Appleton was stripped of his sovereign rights, his mood and mind-altering drugs, and all of his military ranks but one, and sentenced to spend the rest of his life in perpetual exile at a barren military installation on Cape Disappointment in Graham Land, Antarctica, one degree of latitude within the Antarctic Circle. Out of compassion, after a heated plea by his mother to protect his pension and publication rights, the Lords voted that he be allowed to retain the rank of Marshal of the American Union which, with his Social Security entitlements and his civil service and military pensions, and the royalties from his autobiographies and honoraria from video-recorded lectures, would bring Chay a comfortable annual income of $1,721,963.22 a year. With his savings of $304,593,023.61, he would be comfortable possibly for the rest of his life.

He retained the privilege of designing his own hats and uniforms and was allowed to name his own staff to accompany him into exile (at highest civil service-ranking and hardship-pay benefits), and would be provided with a rotating benefice of replaceable young ladies having a CS-16 rating in their chosen profession.

The sum of $114 million was appropriated for the design, construction, and maintenance of the exile facility. The arrangements were approved by the House of Lords and by the Soviet Union and Nicaragua, as members of the new Tripartite Commission, with the Mossad organization of Israel as (invisible) consultants.

Although government by royalty was abandoned, an amendment to the Constitution of the United States retained the ennobling process of Peers, Knights, and Commoners, returning, then and forever, to the republican legislative concept of a Senate and a House of Representatives (excepting that these were termed the House of Lords and the House of Commons); a Supreme Court; and a Chief Executive who would be called the President of the United States of America. Gazing into the mirrors of television, the American people returned joyously to what the pundits and the Sunday morning gurus, the editorialists, and the think-piece writers assured them was self-government.

In due course (i.e., seven weeks later), a great ground swell of American need elected Wambly Keifetz, a nationally known leader and social conscience if a simple citizen, as the 43rd President of the United States; a patriot, at last, was at the helm of the Ship of State again.

In due course, as if to affirm the verdict of the investigation which had followed Edward Mulhaus Grogan's death, and over the baffled but weak protests from the President, Lord Kullers, a great Viceroy and one of the few heroes of the Nic-

araguan invasion, was named Attorney General of the United
States and Director, Central Intelligence Agency.

61

LISTS ARE ONEROUS but nonetheless necessary for historians. What follows is the list of the key staff members who accompanied Caesare Appleton into exile at Cape Disappointment:

   Arias, Jaime, Nicaraguan Commissioner

   Chauncey, Edgar, Majordomo at the New Rossenarra

   Gallagher, Richard, former Black Rod and NYPD (ret) Chief
      of Police

   Heller, Franklin Marx, United States Commissioner

   Axelrod, General George, historian

   Jupp, Jemma, spa leader, aerobics executive, Russian language
      translator

   Kemsley, Forrest, Dr., personal psychiatrist to the Marshal
      of the American Union

   Marxuach, James D., Military Governor of Cape Disappointment
      and representative of the Central Intelligence Agency

   Ueli Munger, chef de cuisine at the New Rossenarra

   Singer, Mark, Fleet Admiral, commander of escort to Cape
      Disappointment

   Smolenov, Igor, USSR Commissioner

   Tompkins, Mallard, former Vice Chairman of the United
      States and the Marshal's chief valet

   Dr. Abe Weiler, surgeon, free-radical pathologist and chelation
      specialist

Zendt, Peter, Commodore, commanding the Cape Disappoint-
    ment Small Boats squadron

Assorted Young Ladies; 3,000 troops; 2,000 seamen; 1,500
    Marines, all of

the Combined Tripartite Defense Force (CTDF); meteorologists;

engineers; geologic study teams; musicians; photographers;
    librarians;

volleyball professionals; videocassette maintenance personnel.

The naval escort which accompanied the Marshal of the American Union (MAU) to the Cape sailed from New Orleans on December 2, 1998. Chay would be forty-nine years old in eight months' time. That he had not been stripped of his American citizenship, as almost the entire House of Commons had demanded, was because of the intervention of his great and good friend President Keifetz, who had made a compassionate plea that the Marshal be allowed to remain an American, reminding the nation of Chay's place in the nation's history. He had, as Keifetz pointed out, been Emperor of the American Republic for two years and eleven months, and Chairman/CEO of the United States for well over five years more, so tradition must be served, the saddened President said.

This was Queen Brilliana's doing. She knew better than anyone, excepting Serena, what his pension rights meant to Chay, and these would have been taken away had he lost his citizenship.

It had been a whirlwind consequence. The television industry had grossed more than $227 million in sales of television time as a direct result of Chay's trial and the events following his dethronement; 1998 marked the biggest television commercial grosses year by three times since the Appletons had dominated world events. An editorial in *Variety*, the industry's barometer for television advertising sales, said in part: "The industry will mourn his passing, excepting that he isn't going. The TV coverage at Cape Disappointment, for the first year at least, will be bigger than it ever was in Dallas. Three prime time maxiseries are planned. The Morton Downey, Jr., and Oprah Winfrey shows will spend six months a year at the Cape Disappointment studios, and Bill Moyers is planning a six-year series on 'Flawed Concepts of Imperial

Government.' New record sales figures for commercials are expected by the industry for the next three (at least) years."

The upward profit cycle was endless. Not since Ronald Reagan's swap of arms for money to pay off the Contra leaders, and his 209 "explanations" for the sleaze and corruption in his government, had an American leader meant so much to the overcommunications industry. Chay's arrest on his return from Nicaragua had demanded that new increased rate cards be issued; a ruling had to be made by the Federal Communications Commission which would allow the lengthening of the broadcasting of commercials to thirty-nine minutes in each given broadcast hour, which had a dramatic effect on network and cable grosses.

The world stopped functioning for the duration of its attention span, three days, while it watched and suffered the agonies of the departure forever of the man who had—so many times—saved them from defeat and military occupation by a barbarian foe. They could not believe that Chay and his famous homburg were going out of their lives or, at the least, would not entertain them from a new location. Six-packs of beer had to be redesigned as twelve-packs. There was a very scary run on potato chips as the country watched history form before their eyes. It was tragic but it was also keenly pleasurable because they were watching a great man go down.

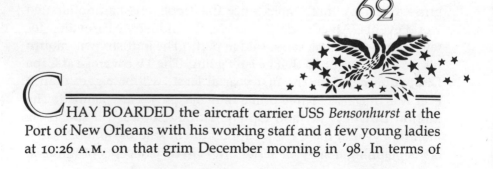

62

CHAY BOARDED the aircraft carrier USS *Bensonhurst* at the Port of New Orleans with his working staff and a few young ladies at 10:26 A.M. on that grim December morning in '98. In terms of the greenhouse effect made possible by the Reagan tolerance of fossil fuels, it was a fine fall day at 109 degrees Fahrenheit. No one had reminded Chay that it was well into spring in Antarctica, which was suffering the icehouse effect because the warm air of the Southern Hemisphere had been drawn into the northern zone.

A crowd of 96,000 people (police estimate) had gathered outside the embarkation area which was a congeries of piers and dry docks. The crowd was in an ugly mood, organized by Keifetz's people to punctuate the virulence of the public relations campaign which he had been running against Chay. If anyone in the enormous crowd cheered Chay, he or she would be set upon. Two of the Emperor's wildest supporters were lynched. The crowd had a plentiful supply of rotten eggs which they threw at every car which approached the dock's entrance, all of the scene covered comprehensively by the cameras which, now and then, would cut to one of the hundreds of professionally printed signs which said, GO AWAY CHAY or GOOD RIDDANCE TO A KILLER.

Chay was flown by B-1 bomber from Dallas in the charge of eight armed U.S. Marshals, each of whom was a foot and a half taller and wider than he was. The tight little group was lifted by helicopter from the New Orleans airport to the deck of the *Bensonhurst* where he was piped aboard by Admiral Singer and the commanders of the naval escort vessels.

An aircraft carrier had been chosen to take Chay into exile because its flight decks could accommodate the extraordinary numbers of television cameras and crews and satellite transmission equipment. The farewell itself was an elaborate enough ceremony. Serena had arrived in New Orleans by Greyhound bus the day before. She was on deck aboard the carrier to remind him where he had taken the wrong turning. "You coulda been nerving yourself up to accept like your third Oscar right now," she said, "instead of being led off like a convict to absolutely nowhere."

His brother, the Pope, was represented by a nuncio, but he sent Chay a blessed scapular on which hung a four-color portrait of St. John the Martyr with the papal message of *"Absit omen!"* — the ecclesiastical equivalent of touching wood to avert misfortune. The Incan and the Caribbola Ambassadors represented Chay's two sisters.

His Imperial bodyguard, the Seventy-fifth Rangers, had been

transferred to duty guarding shipments of basketballs to the troops at the weather stations on Greenland.

The Director of the CIA, Lord Kullers, came aboard for a tour of inspection to make certain that all possible precautions against the prisoner's escape had been observed. As part of the drill he spent a few moments alone with the MAU, but their time together was so brief that none of the 932 journalists who had gathered to report on the departure felt it was necessary to ask the Director for one of the Marshal's quotes. What had transpired in the forty-seven-second meeting was:

"Contact my man Marxuach when you're ready to go. Buenos Aires is set. I'll have the necessary troops to take Dallas on arrival."

"Thanks, Sergeant," Chay said, and Kullers got out of the stateroom.

The Empress Ulyssa, since remarried, now Mrs. Carraway, wife of a great bookmaker friend of her family's, was the last person to leave the Marshal's stateroom, although she stayed considerably longer than the forty-seven seconds which Kullers had required. She seemed greatly mussed and flushed when she left, and she was uncharacteristically euphoric, uncharacteristic because she had been with her Emperor for the last time. She came near to babbling at the cameras as she came down the gangway. "He's just wonderful! Absolutely fine. Just like the old days! He entered straight into it, if you follow. I can't remember when his spirits have been so high. He really is looking forward to the cruise."

There was no communication whatever, the State Department said, from the MAU's present wife, but as the nonstop commentators said, there was such a pile of greeting cards in the Communications Room of the carrier that the Empress could have sent him a "bon voyage" card from Moscow.

There was a raising of the flag then an immediate lowering of it to half-mast where it flapped mournfully until the escort—a light cruiser and four destroyers—moved the convoy out into the delta and into the Gulf of Mexico.

Off Jamaica, the TV commentators reported that the escort was reviewed from a royal barge by Queen Brilliana of Caribbola. She waved to her brother's ships prettily as the escort came quite close, within 1,200 yards, then the *Bensonhurst* steamed on; in any event, Chay had been in the john all through the encounter.

Chay remained in his quarters until the convoy was well out to sea, refusing to accommodate the cameras even with filler shots of pacing the quarterdeck in his famous hat. He was deeply depressed. "Am I blue?" he asked the two nubile young ladies at his side on the large bed in his stateroom. "Ain't these tears in my eyes tellin' you?" In a show of bravado, he did his Eddie Fisher imitation, and when it was over the young ladies applauded wildly.

"Oh, Chay!" the little blonde said. "You are so talented!"

But the deep sadness stayed with him. His people seemed to have deserted him, but that was a false impression. That was not the way it was. The public, so dazed by the charges brought against him in the House of Lords, so grief-stricken that he had been found guilty and sentenced to exile, had remained numbly silent, huddled around their television sets, until they saw that final, terrible symbol of farewell on their screens: the figure of their idol's sister waving her little silk handkerchief so gallantly as the greatest hero of their times sailed away forever into the endlessness of immortality. As one they burst into the streets to demonstrate wildly but it was too late; he was gone.

The AG-D/CIA, John Kullers, sent a full report of the public's feeling via a videocassette to his operative, James D. Marxuach, who was a part of the MAU's permanent party. Marxuach, who was Kullers's Deputy Director/CIA, had had his future laid out for him by Kullers. When Marxuach had successfully assisted Kullers in extricating the Emperor from Antarctica, the order of succession would be: Kullers to take over as Secretary of Defense and Treasury; Marxuach to become Director of the Central Intelligence Agency and Attorney General. The implicit message of the cassette Kullers had sent was that the American people would be ready to receive the Emperor with open hearts when he returned at the head of his troops after landing at the Dallas-Fort Worth Airport.

Chay was confident of his triumphal return, but what really stuck in his craw was that his wife, his wife's father, and his wife's father's government had not made one whimper of protest over the denial of an exit visa from the Soviet Union for his family.

Before he left mainland America he had even told Machenka on the hot line that he had arranged through his sister, Queen Brilliana, to have their son made the Duke of Cuba. What kind of people were the Ivanovs that they could just ignore the tragedy which had happened to him? He had never met his father-in-law, but he certainly felt like punching him in the nose.

The *only* people who had stood by him, sharing his exile, were his batman, Molly Tompkins, and Tompkins's fiancé, Chester Haselgrove; his breakfast cook, Evelyn Rose; his uniforms tailor, Jerry Pincus; and his majordomo, Edgar Chauncey. The rest of the official exile party were getting doubletime for the work and terrific exposure on the networks, although he was grateful for the nice gesture on someone's part of providing the pleasant young ladies on a rotatable basis.

He viewed his predicament as objectively as a trained military man can: "Here I am," he thought, "the greatest strategist in military history, even if I am a weak chess player. I can outthink all of them. The plan is flawless. Six months on Cape Disappointment to let the whole hullabaloo die down, then—OUT! Straight to Dallas to be met by my loyal troops! We will march on the Pink House, sweeping the country before us." God! He could hear the American people cheering his return with one voice! Perhaps even Ron and Nancy would come down from the mountain in Bel Air to meet him and greet him! He felt goosebumps cover his skin.

The armies would flock to rally round him again. Hundreds of thousands would break out their old uniforms. Then he would sit, smoking a Havana cigar, in the billiards room of the Pink House and have them drag Keifetz in to him, throwing him on his knees to plead before him, begging for his life.

"I don't want your miserable life, Wamb," he would say. "I just want your total attention." And he would send Keifetz to Masinloc to work that gross, obscenely overweight body into a sliver in the steaming refractory chromite mines of the Philippines. He felt much better. He rolled over on top of the brunette.

It was an uneventful voyage. The young women proposed all sorts of new ideas for "novelty" positions to cheer him up, but the ideas were neither new nor quaint. The younger generation just didn't know what it was all about, he thought. He went through the motions apathetically, remembering Ulyssa for whom really new positions were as many and as varied as there were patents in the patent office. The whole exercise made him realize that he would have to see that Liz Wantonberg was invited to Antarctica by the USO to entertain the Permanent Party.

63

ON THE LONG VOYAGE into the South Atlantic, Chay's routine was quite different from his sixteen-hour workdays at the Pink House in Dallas. He occupied the Commander's cabin on the starboard side just aft of amidships. It was a good-sized cabin with ample room to dance the hornpipe and store the Emperor's uniforms and the videocassettes by which he could remember happier days, when he had never missed a "Wheel of Fortune" nor a "Guiding Light." His personal physician, dentist, psychiatrist, podiatrist, and four jolly nurses occupied partitioned cubicles in the corresponding cabin across the companionway on the port side of the ship. The remainder of the Permanent Party slept in hammocks in tiny air-conditioned cabins which were hosed down and mopped by the swabbies at dawn every morning.

Molly Tompkins had replaced the Emperor's bed with his campaign cot. That is, he still used the king-size bed for workouts with the young ladies, but he slept on the same simple soldier's iron cot that had gone with him on every campaign since Portugal. Chay slept on the cot while Molly lay on a mattress which had been stretched out on the floor, alert for any command the Emperor might make during the night.

Each dawn to the sound of the swabbies singing their colorful chanties, Molly brought the Emperor a pot of strong Irish tea, a small individual box of Frosted Flakies over macadamia nuts, two sliced bananas, and a stack of buttered toast. At nine o'clock, Molly brought in a more formal breakfast of grilled meat, *rösti* potatoes, three kaiser rolls, and a half-bottle of Australian claret from the Coonawarra district. Chay had fallen into the habit of drinking Australian wine in a vain effort to keep the memory of Sheila Plantenbower alive, but after a few weeks of it, he discovered that although he enjoyed the wine exceedingly he could not recall what Plantenbower had looked like.

After breakfast, he would send for James D. Marxuach and his taping machine and for three hours until lunchtime, he would dictate a third, still-more-contrasting set of memoirs (*World in My Hand*, Prolix Press, 715 pp., $24.85) so that the cool, keen gaze of history would remain forever level and so that the watchdogs aboard would grow accustomed to his long, daily meetings with Marxuach. This final version of Chay's life in literary memoirs was so blameless, yet so revealing in his comments on the intimate lives of others, such as Wambly Keifetz, that it was to become a great best-seller from which three feature-length films and many miniseries would be made, the first two starring Liz Wantonberg as Queen Brilliana. Of the memoir, Abner Stein, Chay's most relentless biographer, wrote: "*World in My Hand* was a crafty work of effortless apologia which showed his life as a noble hardship in the cause of bringing freedom to humanity. Those turnings which his enemies had tried to expose as mistakes were explained away. All the wars he had fought had been just, waged to protect his beloved America from a barbarian force and out of them had come the great union of the nations into one glorious evolution of ultimate central government.

"There was no mention that Chay had been the architect of the first North American totalitarian state geared for war and only for war, or that the size of a state was the measure of its glory. By measuring the proportions of his Hemispheric Plan, the state which Chay had created exceeded the size of any conquered by Alexander or the Romans. For all that, *World in My Hand* is a masterpiece of self-justification."

Chay told his literary agent and his publisher that he was writing this third autobiography only to rally support for his son and for the continuation of the Appleton line. One or the other, he had reasoned silently, would accomplish the Appleton restoration if in the one chance in one thousand he should not be able to find a way to escape.

Marxuach pretended to the others in the little community that he had no idea how he had gotten the job as Chay's amanuensis and tape machine operator. He told them the AG-D/CIA had taken an instant dislike to him because (he said) Kullers had said he was too damned liberal. Marxuach told the others that he not only knew less than the MAU about recording machines, but that he had opposed the MAU's politics throughout his reign.

During the hours Marxuach was not with Chay, he met continuously with the Army, Navy, and Air Force commanders assigned to protect the world from Chay, going over—again and again—intricate plans for the placement of troops and ships and planes, day and night, creating a wall of men and armaments around the captive who was to be locked within rooms which would be locked within gates behind high electrified walls of Chay's Antarctic prison. Marxuach had been well-chosen by Kullers for his job because he was the master dissimulator, the most cunning exponent of covert action to mask covert action that the CIA had ever known. He had been briefed to the eyebrows by John Kullers and he knew exactly what he was there to do.

Every evening the dictation was typed. Every morning the pages were corrected. Every afternoon via satellite telephone and FAX the draft pages were sent to a firm of literary agents on lower Fifth Avenue in New York. Also, from time to time, he and Marxuach had certain conversations which Marxuach, through covert means at his disposal, passed along to Lord Kullers in Dallas.

Late each afternoon, Molly would dress the MAU in the uniform of a second lieutenant on the Toxic Waste Disposal Corps, sky blue tunic over lovely ashes-of-roses jodphurs, and Chay would stroll into the officers' lounge where he played Chinese checkers lackadaisically but democratically. Dinner was at eight in the officers' mess on the same deck, to which Chay wore the dress uniform of a Brigadier of Military Audits, always being careful in his choice of dress not to violate the chain of command. He sat at the head of the table with Smolenov, the USSR Commissioner on his left, F. M. Heller, U.S. High Commissioner at his right. Jaime

Arias, Nicaraguan Commissioner, was at Smolenov's left; James D. Marxuach was at Heller's right. The seating descended in rigidly correct order until the whole thing righted itself again with Admiral Singer, nominal host, at the other end of the table.

Jemma Jupp (the Russian-speaking aerobics instructor) and the jolly nurses dined at a separate table with the volleyball pros, the musicians, et al. The two (rotatable) young ladies ate all their meals in bed in their own stateroom after they had brushed and oiled their parts.

After dinner, Chay went above and paced the deck in the company of some one member of his party. One evening, long after the flotilla had crossed the equator, as he paced under his famous homburg, wearing thermal underwear and a great goose down padded coat which widened and foreshortened his roly-poly figure enormously, he chatted with Smolenov. He asked casually if the Russian had had any news about his wife and son.

"Nothing, my Marshal," Smolenov said. "About that they tell me nothing."

"Did you know that, around the Kremlin, they call him Little Bear?"

"Medvezhonok?"

"Yes."

"So appropriate."

"Do you think you could ask your government for a photograph of the boy? I would like very much to see one."

"I don't see why not. But it will take time."

"Why?"

"Red tape."

"Red tape?"

"It is no joke, my Marshal. It could take easily two or three years—maybe ten—to get such a picture out of Moscow. You would worry that the boy was so small for his age when actually in the photos he would be five or six years younger than he is."

Each evening after the walk on deck, Chay went back to the officers' lounge and played casino or pinochle. He played mechanically, just to show that he was one of the boys. Such a small disparate group, forced into each other's company, might have become bored but for the fact that Chay formed them into a platoon and drilled them from ten to eleven each morning and from four to five in the afternoon. They became familiars of the Manual of Arms. The chief meteorologist, Harry Taft, fell in love with Miss Trenchard, the small blond (rotatable) young lady whom the government had provided for Chay's use. They were married by the ship's chaplain. Until a replacement could be flown in, Chay would be down to the one therapy partner, but he soldiered on, and on the twenty-sixth day there was a shout of "Land, ho!" as Cape Disappointment was sighted.

64

THE FLOTILLA dropped anchors off South City, the only port not only on the Cape itself but within a six-thousand-square-mile area. The town had a population of 38 long-term residents and 786 Seabees. It would soon swell to over 5,000 when the troops were put ashore. Those 5,000 men guarding one man made it certain that he could never escape.

South City existed as an emergency fueling station for the United States Navy and for shipping in distress. It was "owned" by the U.S. Navy and operated under the command of CINCUS-NAVPAC, having headquarters on Attu, in the Aleutians, flashing its orders to the Tokyo naval base who signaled them to Norfolk, Virginia, who dropped them on Admiral Singer in Antarctica. Before the arrival of the Permanent Party, Cape Disappointment had lived on the sale of water, on bookmaking for bets on South African and Australian racetracks, and on its bar business generated among nautical passersby.

Everything to sustain life had to be imported. The National Rifle Association had demanded that the House of Commons extend the right to carry firearms to South City, so the murder rate was inordinately high until the military took over. Over the course of a year a few tramp merchant vessels, half-laden with cargoes, would put in to give their crews a change. There was a saloon/ dance hall where the men, if they wanted to dance, were forced to dance with each other, or with one of the two fifty-seven-year-old hostesses, each with a heart of gold and a crotch of steel, or with the occasional penguin who wandered in. There was a barbershop in the (ecumenical) church and a satellite antenna/VCR repair shop. That was all. That was South City until the exile's Permanent Party got there.

Whatever pitiable bravery the settlement pretended came from its position at the top of a 381-foot-high barren plateau of basalt which was covered with ice and snow for most of the year and across which constant forty-three-mile-an-hour winds, on the mild days and nights, never stopped. Upon this wide/long six-and-a-half-mile mesa which balanced the saloon, the church-barbershop and the few shored-up dwellings which had been dropped there, prefabricated, willy-nilly, there arose steel and concrete structures built by the Seabees to house the defenses of the Emperor against himself. That was what Chay was called by everyone in the community, the Emperor. Forget the Congress.

It was all laid out like a model town: barracks, an officers' club, enlisted men's clubs, brothels, bowling alleys, movie houses, two PXs, and public showers. Each man's tour of duty, except the Emperor and his batman, was limited to nine months. All food for all personnel, because the use of brothels was frowned upon by the Joint Chiefs and the National Ecumenical Council, was required by an Act of Parliament to be laced with anaphrodisiacs which had the effect of inflaming the men sexually; hence the need for brothels. There were eleven of these, one for each corresponding rank of all the services: private, corporal, sergeant, lieutenant, captain, major, colonel, brigadier, major general, with the lieutenant generals and air marshals flying their own stuff in from Capetown or Buenos Aires, bringing the population of working prostitutes in the settlement to 410 women for 7,000 men.

Standing on the bridge of the *Bensonhurst*, Chay was appalled by what he saw. On a rise of ground, beyond South City, rose the concrete blockhouse of the New Rossenarra, modeled on Canon City prison in Colorado but painted a lovely pink like the original, with white painted window frames and shutters.

As Chay stared at what his captors were sure would be his home for the rest of his life, he swore that he would have to escape from it, not only because he had to survive with his sanity but because it was his destiny to return to American soil and lead a victorious army in triumph while his people sang with joy and showered him with flowers. Then Wambly Keifetz would wish he was dead. Then the scores would be settled. Then he would conquer the world to bring peace to the world. Then he would prove that his mother had been insanely wrong when she had pressured him, again and again, to sign with the Morris Office.

65

THE FOLLOWING MORNING, the military governor, James D. Marxuach, went ashore with his staff to inspect the installation. The inspection lasted from 6:00 A.M. until 5:17 P.M. and resulted in Marxuach's order that mine fields be laid completely surrounding the building the Emperor would occupy, just behind the rows upon rows of electrified eighteen-foot-high barbed wire barricades which he had ordered to be installed that day. After divesting himself of the fur underwear and eider feather-packed middle clothing, Marxuach went to call on the Emperor in the wardroom of the *Bensonhurst*. In the presence of nine other officers, he told the Emperor that he would be sealed away more tightly than Churchill's "riddle wrapped in a mystery inside an enigma."

Admiral Singer broke the tension by announcing that the convoy had been ordered to sail in two days' time and that everything would be done to facilitate the MAU's transfer to shore.

"Is my prison ready to receive me, then?" Chay asked.

"But such a prison, sir," Singer said. "The outside of the place is forbidding, I agree, but the inside is a replica of most of the main rooms of your own house in Dallas."

The one remaining young lady was ready to be rotated out to Capetown the next morning, so the Emperor decided to accompany her ashore and inspect his new home all in one go. He spent the forenoon in sentimental farewells with the girl then occupied himself throughout the rest of the morning with dictating his tiered memories of things which (mostly) had never happened in days of yore and in ages and times long gone before.

Once he had been transferred ashore, the rhythms of his life changed again. He rose at dawn, as always, not to plunge into his work as he had done for all of his life in the past, but to escape his sleepless bed, in the great bedroom which was decorated precisely as he had slept in it with Ulyssa, down to the last Warhol, Motherwell, and Jasper Johns. He didn't sleep as he had slept in the great days because there was nothing to do with his life except to romp upon the rotatable young ladies and dictate fables about his life to the little machine; nothing at all which would have tired him; so he grew rounder. The plumper he became the shorter he seemed. The rounder and shorter he became the sillier and more ineffective he looked, but he was entirely unaware of all that because there was no one to see him. When John Kullers gave the signal, he would be ready, he told himself. But Capetown was 2,750 miles to the east. Buenos Aires was 2,800 miles to the west. South City was 6,000 miles from Dallas. When the armies were massed, he would fly home to lead them. He wasted time thinking about the titles which must be conferred upon his son because if he thought about more serious things he would consume himself with bitterness over the indifference of his sisters and the deaths of his brothers.

He wrote in his diary: "Kings have need of me against upheavals of their people. All people have need of me against the cruelty of their kings. In the immense battle of the present against the past, I am the solution and the victory."

Over the next five months he evolved into a fiction of himself, but somehow he got through the terrible winter. He was chelated daily to sluice plaque off the walls of his arteries. As the time to move out came closer he went on crash diets which left him aged, weak, and wrinkled; fifty-four pounds lost in two months. He was too weak and unfocused to exercise. Jerry Pincus, his uniforms tailor, worked day and night trying to keep up with the alterations on his seventy-three uniforms and costumes.

Two days before the first day of spring, September 19, 1999, a month after Chay's forty-ninth birthday, James D. Marxuach brought the secret word from the DCI that the foolproof escape plan was ready to be executed.

Marxuach had been recalled to Dallas and had been briefed by Kullers personally. It was a sweet plan, utterly military (in a Command Sergeant Major's if not the unified command sense).

In itself, all was simplicity. Marxuach had returned to Dallas whenever Lord Kullers had ordered him there, for debriefing at two-week intervals. After the ultimate meeting, one hour with the DCI, and using fake paper and pocket litter, an ingenious false nose and mustache, he flew by commercial airliner from Omaha to Manila. The Outfit's Chief of Station had been advised to have him admitted to the access room at the refractory chromite mines on Masinloc where the miner, Georgie Jumel, was released into his custody.

Kullers had told Marxuach, "When you see Jumel, you must not be shocked. He has been working hard. But no matter. The job at hand will be to fatten him up until, once again, he looks just like our Emperor. You will fly him from Masinloc to the island of Terafoa, where we maintain a rest camp in the South Pacific. To bring Jumel back to standard, the specialists tell me, will take about two months. During that time you will be flown back to Cape Disappointment to wait until our people have Jumel ready."

Georgie Jumel plumped up nicely. He would never recover his sanity, but other than the permanent daze, he was a sweet and amiable man always ready to do as he was told and was easily trained to respond when addressed by the call-names of Emperor or Sire or Marshal. When he was ready to leave Terafoa he looked exactly as the Emperor had looked when Chay had left the Port of New Orleans, at a time when Chay had been only twenty-six pounds overweight. Jumel's figure necessitated that Chay gain thirty-four pounds if they were to seem to be clones of each other, but in gaining the weight, the deep lines on his face and the wattles in his skin did not go away. This aged Chay into an elderly-seeming cartoon of what he had been before his arrest.

Marxuach ran Jumel into Cape Disappointment in the total darkness and silence of a late-May morning and installed him in the Emperor's bed with Molly Tompkins as his keeper, while Marxuach took the Emperor off in a dinghy to a Parabrazargiguayan tramp steamer which had put in that afternoon to lay on some water. Chay was installed in the captain's quarters. The ship sailed for Buenos Aires at fifteen minutes before dawn that day. On the afternoon of the second day the ship rendezvoused with a Parabrazargiguayan warship to which Chay was transferred by helicopter. The warship proceeded at once to Buenos Aires.

When the ship docked, a Foreign Office man came aboard with proper documents, including a British passport which carried Chay's photograph and the name Geoffrey Bocca, which passed the unshaven Chay through Immigration without questioning. Chay was driven to the Royal Palace in an enclosed van.

He was assigned a suite of rooms in the Palace where he shaved himself and put on the first suit of civilian clothing he had worn since the few short, happy days when he had met and courted Hedda Blitzen. A note on royally crested paper informed him that he would dine with Queen Hedda at eight o'clock that evening, in her boudoir, which was two doors down the corridor to the right.

66

T HEY SAT TOGETHER until almost one o'clock in the morning. He held her hands in both of his as he stared into her lovely eyes, mourning that she wasn't the beauty she had once been. He felt, also, that a feeling of merriment and carelessness had left her forever. He regretted the loss (for her sake). They talked about him because they didn't have other recent experiences in common, and it would have been too painful for both of them had he chosen to talk about Jonathan. Not that he felt responsible for Jonathan's death, but he certainly didn't want to think about that at a time like this. He concentrated on adoring this little immigrant whom he had found, long ago, in a delicatessen, faking a vaudeville German accent and selling those ridiculous sausages. He couldn't even measure how long it had been since he had had a *kalbsbrat-wurst*. But even out of such stuff as that, he thought, I made her a queen, and the people of four countries combined into one, by him, had accepted her, perhaps even loved her.

"Kullers is rallying the old campaigners," he said. "When I land in Dallas tomorrow night, 97,000 troops will be waiting for me, and as we march into Dallas we will pick up 50,000 more. No one will oppose me. The people will weep with joy that I have returned to protect them from the Sandinistas and to bring their television entertainment up to the standard which they have every right to expect. Television will be my recruiter from the moment my plane touches down on Texas soil, and I am able to look into the No. 1 and the No. 3 cameras and make the plea for my fellow Americans to rally to the flag. By the time we reach Dallas—who knows?—there will be 500,000 under my banners."

"Oh, Chay," the Queen said, "how perfectly thrilling for you."

"Then I'll handle Keifetz."

"Will you ever come back to me?"

"Hedda, lissena me—I hardly know the woman to whom I am chained in marriage. I spent one night with her—one night!—

almost entirely in darkness. She got up sometime in the night to go to the john and that is the only clear picture I have of her—as the bathroom light fell on her just before she closed the door."

"Oh, Chay! I never dreamed—"

"I will have to get my son away from her, of course. That will probably mean a nuclear war with the Soviet Union. But I am the pontiff of our national religion, and before the network and cable cameras, I will divorce her. Then—in the next breath—I shall tell the world that I am going to marry Queen Hedda of Parabrazar-giguay."

"Still," she said sadly, "it will be some time before we will be together."

"Perhaps less than a year. Surely not more than two, depending on how the war goes."

"Well, at any rate, it is certainly something we should think about."

"Darling Hedda. You haven't understood me, have you? I am going to *marry* you. We will be together for the rest of our lives— we will be together, sweetheart."

She stared sadly at the wattled lump of a prematurely old man and racked her brain to remember what he had been like on that first day in her father's delicatessen—under that wonderful hat, worn properly as a homburg should be worn and not with the comic grotesqueness with which he was wearing it now, in her own palace, with a roof over his head.

"But we don't have to decide all that now, do we, Chay? There is so much to do—your return to power, your son, the divorce, possibly a nuclear war and all the vexations that can bring. And my people. I have to think of the happiness of my people. Hold me, Chay."

Despite the fact that he had difficulty catching his breath, and the crass humiliation of almost not being able to summon an erection, he managed somehow to work up one very nearly faithful copy of a realistic copulation on the huge chaise longue at the center of the carved V'Soske rug in her boudoir. He was glad to be able to do it and not only for reasons of etiquette and old-times. He knew how happy it had made her even if it had damned near killed him.

When it was over he excused himself as gently as he could because he was ready to drop, and he had to be on that fighter-bomber which would be ready to fly out to Dallas at 4 A.M. the next day. More than anything else, he needed a good hot bath and some sleep. He knew he would sleep. At last the bad times were over, he thought, as she helped him to his feet. She pointed him down the corridor to the second door on the left. He patted her on the cheek and left her.

Chay had to undress himself and draw his own bath because they could not risk having servants identify him, which would set off alarms in Dallas and Cape Disappointment. He got out of his clothes awkwardly and unsteadily. The tub was almost filled. He turned off the taps and climbed stiffly into the comforting hot water which almost filled the eight-foot-long imported English bathtub.

Standing in the hot water which covered his stubby legs to a place well above his mid-thigh, he reached across for a washcloth before he settled in the bath. His right foot, about as big and as pink as a pork chop, came down on a cake of soap on the floor of the tub. He fell as if pulled by dolphins. His legs were flung high into the air. The back of his head came down with a terrible noise upon the edge of the marble tub and then his blood stained the water. He sank underneath it.

He seemed to be somewhere on the grounds of the old White House in Washington. How did he get there? he wondered. He was standing in the garden at the back of the lovely old building. A helicopter landed close by at his left. A tall man and a pretty woman got out of it. They had the dear little rented dog. The little dog darted from right to left, almost tripping the two people who were like great acrobats as they executed a complex series of intricate waves to him. The man was grinning like a happy child on Christmas morning.

It was Ron and Nancy!

Chay almost freaked out with the ecstasy of recognition. It *was* Ron, but how did he get here? The Reagans were writing their fifth autobiographies in Bel Air, California. Washington was gone. Had the city been rebuilt behind his back? Had Ron been able to put through a fourth and fifth term for presidents? Chay started forward to take his rightful place with them, but Nancy muttered some order and Ronnie reached over somewhere and turned out all the lights in the world just as Chay was about to shake his hand.

Everything went black. Chay floated within nothingness. He was lost in the oblivion of eternity.

ABOUT THE AUTHOR

RICHARD CONDON is the author of twenty-three novels, which have been translated into twenty-two languages; one fractional memoir; one Mexican cookbook (with his daughter, Wendy); several dozen magazine articles; a Broadway play which, had it opened on a Monday night, would have doubled its run; and a screenplay which was nominated for an Oscar and which won a British Academy Award. He lives in Dallas, Texas.